Mark Dapin is a freelance writer who lives in Sydney with his partner and two children. He has degrees in Social Policy, Art History and Journalism. This is his first novel.

Also by Mark Dapin

Strange Country

KING OF THE CROSS

MARK DAPIN

PAN
Pan Macmillan Australia

This is a work of fiction. Whilst inspiration for this story is taken in part from historical events over a period of many years in the Kings Cross area of Sydney, there is no connection at all between any real individuals or businesses and the fictional ones in this book.

First published 2009 in Macmillan by Pan Macmillan Australia Pty Limited
This Pan edition published in 2010 by Pan Macmillan Australia Pty Limited
1 Market Street, Sydney

National Library of Australia
Cataloguing-in-Publication data:

Dapin, Mark.

King of the cross / Mark Dapin.

9780330426121 (pbk.)

Criminals – New South Wales – Sydney – Fiction.

823.4

Typeset in 12.5/16 Adobe Garamond by Post Pre-press Group
Printed in Australia by McPherson's Printing Group

Papers used by Pan Macmillan Australia Pty Ltd are natural, recyclable products made from wood grown in sustainable forests. The manufacturing processes conform to the environmental regulations of the country of origin.

To Mr Sutton
RIP

Inspired by an untrue story

ONE

[Seaview House, Greenknowe Avenue, Potts Point. 03-12-01. 2:05 pm.]

Mr Mendoza, I'm Anthony Klein, from the *Australian Jewish Times.*

Nice to meet you, Anthony. Would you like a coffee? Lazarus here can bring us a coffee.

A flat white?

Why not, Anthony. Live dangerously. I always look forward to reading your excellent newspaper on a *Shabbos*, with a slice of challah and a cappuccino from Vitto's. I particularly enjoy the weddings pages – although, of course, I'm more likely to know somebody in the obituaries these days. Do you go to all those weddings yourself, Anthony?

No, actually, I'm the features writer. People send in their own wedding photographs.

Is that so? Do you do the bar mitzvahs, then?

The bar mitzvah reports come from the readers, too. I don't have much to do with them.

So, if I want my daughter's wedding to appear in the *Australian Jewish Times*, I contact you?

No, that's not . . . You just send in the pictures.

It doesn't matter, Anthony. That one's not going to get married any time soon. She is a journalist, too. Perhaps you know her.

I don't think so.

She calls herself Sharon Stevens. My name's not good enough for her.

Why is that?

You'll have to ask her.

Obviously, we're here to talk about the five million dollars you have pledged to the renovation of the Great Synagogue.

Obviously.

But, on the subject of names, could I ask how you became a Mendoza?

How did you become a Klein?

My father was a Klein.

Was he? Or was he perhaps a Kleinmann or a Kleinberg? They were weak bludgers at immigration in those days. They didn't want to waste their time writing difficult foreign words while they were busy waving through Nazi war criminals. And the Jews hoped to assimilate, to be like everybody else. So they let the immigration officers shorten their names, and Grinowitz became 'Green', and Kapovsky became 'Capp', and so on.

But your father's name wasn't Mendozawitz, was it?

What is your father's name, Anthony? Do I know him?

Gerard.

No. More likely, I knew your mother.

Your name wasn't changed at immigration, was it?

I don't remember where it was changed. It was a long time ago.

You were twenty.

And now I am eighty-one.

You were about to go into the army.

Yes, and fight fascism, but there was also fascism here at home, Anthony. There was anti-Semitism in the Australian army. They had games they played with Jews in the barracks: Jewball was one. They kicked the Jew as if he was a football.

But you changed your name to a Jewish name.

A proud Jewish name, yes.

So how did that help you in the army?

They thought I was Spanish, perhaps. I don't know.

Can I ask what was your original name?

It's not important for your story. It will only confuse the readers. A boy of twenty didn't give five million dollars to the synagogue. That was the gift of a man of eighty-one.

Of course, in the 1950s, 60s and 70s, most people didn't know you as Jacob Mendoza.

No, they knew me as Mickey Mouse.

[Laughs.] A lot of people still call you 'Mr Big'? Why is that?

Because I have a shlong like a roll of *vorsht*. Why did they call you 'Mr Little'?

I'm sorry . . .

You don't know your own name? 'Klein': in German, it means 'small'. In Yiddish, too.

Who was it that first called you 'Mr Big'?

Some anti-Semite.

Was it the Royal Commission into Organised Crime?

You are asking about things that were over when you were still at school. What did they call you at school, Anthony?

I'm not . . .

Would you expect to be asked about it when you are eighty-one years old and have just given five million dollars to the synagogue? You seem obsessed with names, Anthony. Should we talk about my gift?

Of course. Obviously, it's a huge sum of money. You were born in Balmain, you left school at fifteen. How did you become so wealthy?

I'm a businessman.

What kind of businessman?
A successful businessman.
I mean, what is your line of business?
I'm involved in the hospitality industry, the construction industry, investments, property development . . .
You're a landlord?
I am a landlord, yes. I have properties in Perth, Adelaide, Geelong, Melbourne, the Gold Coast, Goulburn and Sydney.
Do you still own property in Kings Cross?
What is the relevance of this question? I am giving the *shul* five million dollars, not a strip club.
Do you still have an interest in strip clubs?
I'm eighty-one. Do you have an interest in strip clubs, Mr Little?
They say you once controlled Kings Cross.
They say the Jews control the weather.
Did you?
If I did, I would make it rain on the Bulldogs, but never on my beloved Tigers. What kind of interview is this, Anthony? A police interview?
No, it's just that I need some background.
Aren't we from the same 'background', Anthony? Isn't that why we are here? Ask me about the *shul.*
Okay, what motivated you to give such a large amount of money to the synagogue?
I wouldn't say I am a religious man, but I am a man who understands the importance of tradition. We must never forget our roots. At high holy days, I put on the tallith and pray like my father and his father before him.
Was your father a member of the Great Synagogue?
The Great Synagogue? No.
Where did your father pray?
This happened before you were born. What can you say, with any certainty, about the time before you were born, Anthony?

But was your father a religious man?
Religion, to him, was a private matter.
How well do you know the treasurer of the Great Synagogue, Henry Aaron?
Henry is a great friend and a business associate. Everybody knows Henry. Do you know him?
No, I don't.
His grandson has his bar mitzvah in October. Perhaps you will be there to record the event.
[Laughs.] I don't write the bar mitzvah page, Mr Mendoza.
Today, you don't. Tomorrow, who knows? Your editor is my great friend Bob Stein, isn't it? We used to play golf together. He had impeccable enthusiasm but poor technique.
He's gone now.
None of us keeps our jobs forever, Anthony. What else would you like to know for your story?
Do you give a lot of money away?
What else is it for? I have donated to the Jewish Communal Appeal since 1967. I have provided money for the Jewish National Fund ever since they distributed those blue and white collection tins. Do you remember those tins, Anthony? I don't suppose you do. I am also a regular and enthusiastic contributor to police charities, or so they tell me.
What do you mean by that?
It's a joke, Anthony.
Of course, you have had problems with the police in the past.
Of course. In the past.
Beginning in 1948?
I had no problems with the police in 1948. I got married in 1948, in the Great Synagogue, to which I have recently donated five million dollars. Is that against the law? I stayed married to one beautiful, devout Jewish woman for forty-nine years. Is that a crime?

Before the war, you were convicted in the Central Court of Petty Sessions for handling stolen goods.

Was I? You would know, I suppose. How old are you? Twenty-one?

Thirty-one.

You've never been in a war, have you, Anthony? You've never held your mates in your arms and watched them die.

With respect, Mr Mendoza, you served out the Second World War in Liverpool, New South Wales.

Anthony thinks I'm talking about the Second World War, Lazarus.

[Laughter.]

You have been accused of profiting from the black market during the war years.

I've been accused of everything, Anthony. Let me ask you something: why have I never seen you around?

I only arrived in Australia a few months ago.

And you already have a job in the media? *Mazel tov*. You must be a very talented young man. You are from London?

Yes.

Ah, I thought I could hear the sound of Bow Bells.

Do you remember what was said by the Great Bell of Bow, Anthony? 'I do not know.'

And you do not know, either, do you? You don't know the whole story. How could you? You've obviously read Laurie Block's book about me, and – perfectly understandably – come away with the wrong impression. So I'm pleased to have the opportunity to set you straight about every single tiny detail of my life before you were born – even though we are supposed to be talking about my five-million-dollar donation to the Great Synagogue – but, through inexperience rather than malice, you seem unable to ask the right questions. I'll make it easier for you, shall I? I'll tell you everything you need to know, then you can write it down.

I was born in Bondi in 1920. My father was a draper. We were poor but we never went without. At school, I excelled at both academic and sporting pursuits, but I chose to leave at the age of fifteen to help my *tate* in business. In 1940, at the first chance I got, I enrolled in the Citizens Military Force to fight against Hitler. I served until 1944, by which time the tide had turned against the Germans, and the Allies had liberated Paris. I was discharged with the rank of corporal, and proudly wear my Returned Servicemen's League badge to this day.

After the war, I entered the hospitality industry and became a pioneer of Parisienne-style entertainment in this city. I brought Sydney the cancan and Frank Sinatra. I entertained a generation of servicemen like myself, taking rest and relaxation from the war in Vietnam. I bought first one nightclub, then two, then five, then finally . . . who knows, Anthony? I may have overstretched myself, but when you are in the business of making people happy, you don't count the cost. A smile is payment enough.

Yes, I have attracted criticism. Why? Because I am 'colourful' – and you know what that means: 'Jewish'. Because I am 'well connected' – and you know what that means: 'Jewish'. If my name were MacDonald rather than Mendoza, you would never have heard of me.

What my critics often forget is my long-time, proven commitment to socially progressive causes, such as liberalisation of the laws regarding the service of alcohol, the emancipation of homosexuals and other minorities, and the social integration of negroes and midgets. It was my actions that brought about the end of the six o'clock swill, and the horrific orgy of domestic violence that was a predictable consequence of that short-sighted policy. My clubs in Kings Cross were the first to offer a safe meeting place to the homosexual community. Many of the liberties now taken for granted by the fetishist community were secured by my pioneering actions in the 1950s. There was no segregation in any of Jake Mendoza's establishments during the 1960s. Negro soldiers enjoyed the same freedoms as their Caucasian officers.

As you point out, Anthony, I have, from time to time, attracted the attentions of the New South Wales police, known colloquially as 'the best police force money can buy'. There have been attempts to prosecute me as a 'sly grogger', which is no longer an offence; as a bingo caller, which is no longer an offence; as the proprietor of adult-entertainment establishments, which is no longer an offence; as the keeper of a disorderly house, which is no longer an offence; and outraging public decency, which is no longer an offence.

All my life I have given generously to good causes: Catholic, non-denominational and Jewish. I am the originator of charity bingo in Australia, a founding member of the Hakoah Club in Bondi, and a life governor of the Benevolent Society of New South Wales. Today, as a retired businessman approaching the end of my life, I have resolved to crown my career of philanthropy with one final honour: five million dollars towards the renovation of the Great Synagogue, the loveliest in New South Wales and one of the finest in the world, and the *shul* where I, a returned serviceman, married my one, beautiful, devout Jewish wife, Deborah, in 1948.

Now, that should be enough for you to write your story, Anthony, shouldn't it?

That's very helpful, Mr Mendoza, but I do still have a few questions.

No doubt it's your inquisitive nature that makes you such a fine journalist. Myself, I prefer to accept people as they are.

There is some disquiet in the community about the source of your five million dollars. People point to your conviction for handling stolen goods; your jail time for tax evasion; the dismal reputations of certain of your nightclubs; the fact that

your name has come up in no less the six royal commissions; the fact that premises you own and insure seem unusually susceptible to arson; and your alleged connections to the deaths of Maurice 'the Little Fish' Bass, Big Stan Callahan and Gozo Joe Stone, the punishment beatings of Mad Dog McCoy and Izzy Berger, and the disappearance of the retail heiress, Anita King, as reasons why it might be inappropriate to accept a donation for a house of prayer from a man identified by lawyers, police, politicians and criminals alike as 'King Sin', 'Mr Big' or 'the King of the Cross'.

Are you speaking from notes, Anthony? Or do you have a partner standing on the window ledge, holding up cue cards for you?

I've done my research, that's all.

The money is from brothels, blackmail and bashings, Anthony. There, now you have the answer you want. Are you going to use it in your newspaper?

I regret the passing of Big Stan Callahan – although I had nothing to do with it – just as I'm sorry that Mad Dog McCoy had his legs broken. On the other hand, Maurice 'the Little Fish' Bass and Izzy Berger got what was coming to them, and, generally speaking, I've spared more low dogs who deserved to die than I've had blokes knocked who should've lived. I am thinking here of bent coppers such as Fred Carol and Dynamite Danny Dawson, and that weak-gutted mongrel Frankie Latimer. As for the bullshit about Gozo Joe Stone, I'm not going to put my hand up for that. I'm not good for the fire at Aphrodite's, either, or the one that started the blue with the fucking Maltese in the first place, and I never even met Anita King – although, of course, I knew who she was.

If it rains on Melbourne Cup Day, you maggots blame Jake Mendoza. If lightning strikes the SCG, the jacks try to fit me for it. I've got fuck all to do with what goes on in the Cross these days. I'm just a kindly old tenant-manager with blind eyes, deaf ears and tight lips. If there were more like me, the world would be a better place.

But no imbecile in Sydney wants to believe that, so they send shitmen like you to ask me about 'events' (and I use the term loosely) that occurred (if they happened at all) when the children of Israel were still wandering through the fucking desert.

Do you know who controls the Cross today, Anthony? Fucking camelcock-sucking, schoolgirl-raping, towel-head-terrorist Lebbo cunts. Do you think when they sub their quid to Hezbollah, their imams ask, 'Where did this come from, Abdul? Did you sell a bottle of Reschs Dinner Ale after hours in 1955? Oh, well, I'm sorry then, we can't use it to buy our Jew-killing rockets. We'll have to raise the money with a car-boot sale.'

Grow up, Mr Little. I would find this kind of interview funny, Anthony, if cunts like you didn't cause such monumental fucking problems for me. Because every time some can't-read, bomb-building carpet pilot hears that a Jew is still 'the King of the Cross', he loads up his fucking stolen-from-the-army Steyr assault rifle and comes looking for me, and I have to deal with him like I dealt with Maurice 'the Little Fish' Bass, and didn't fucking deal with Anita fucking King, no matter what you dogs like to fucking think.

So you're putting my fucking life in danger, shitman, with your 'research' and your 'with respect' and your 'just a few questions'.

Okay, now you've got your story: 'JAKE MENDOZA TELLS ALL TO THE FUCKING *AUSTRALIAN JEWISH TIMES*'. What do you think?

Well, I . . .

Take the tape out of his machine, Lazarus. Smash it, unwind it, and make him eat it.

He can wash it down with Vitto's fucking dishwater coffee, which cost me three dollars fifty and he hasn't even touched a fucking drop.

[Ends.]

TWO

It took me ten minutes to walk from Mendoza's Potts Point apartment, through Kings Cross, to the *Times* office in Darlinghurst. By the time I arrived, Spiegeleier had already taken Mendoza's call. He was sitting at his desk, rubbing his head with his stubby fingers. He didn't look up when I entered, but started to speak anyway, as if he were talking to his tie.

'I was always concerned that you might be overqualified for this job, Tony,' he said. 'Now I have an additional worry,' he paused to tap his pen, 'that you are a fucking idiot.'

He took off his spectacles and laid them on his desk. They stared at me through empty eyes.

'This isn't the *Sunday* fucking *Times*,' said Spiegeleier. 'It isn't even the *Belfast Telegraph*. We practise a different kind of journalism here.'

On the walls around the office hung mounted copies of *Jewish Times* front pages, with headlines such as YESHIVA BOYS VISIT ISRAEL and IT'S OFFICIAL! MELBOURNE HAS BEST BAGELS. Spiegeleier picked a page proof from his desk and wiped his weeping nose across a photograph of the Women's International Zionist Organisation.

'We wanted to sell him some *advertising*, Tony.'

I said I was sorry, but Spiegeleier kept doing things with his nose and his glasses and his head.

'What did you get anyway?' he asked me.

'Nothing,' I admitted. 'He made me eat the tape.'

'You'd better watch you don't get tapeworm,' said Spiegeleier. He frowned at his joke. 'Jesus Christ, Tony, Mendoza's an influential voice in the community. He could get *Shabbos* moved to Wednesday.'

'He's a gangster,' I said.

'So who are you?' asked Spiegeleier. 'Eliot Ness?'

His desk phone chirped. He answered brusquely, and listened without comment.

'That was the publisher,' he said as he put down the receiver.

I turned up my palms.

'Tell me,' said Spiegeleier, 'did you eat the protective plastic shell, or just the magnetically coated tape?'

I guessed it wasn't a real question.

'Let me take you for a drink,' he said.

Spiegeleier initialled a pile of proofs and transferred them from his in-tray to his out-tray. He squeezed his feet into his soft shoes and stood up with a splutter and a sigh. I checked my email while I waited for him to arrange his glasses on his nose. He led the way down the corridor, past a map of Jerusalem and a poster advertising holidays in Eilat, dragging his left leg behind him.

Spiegeleier limped downstairs and past the Jewish War Memorial room, where twin marble slabs remembered the names of servicemen from two world wars. An arch above the tablets carried the words *Your youngest and strongest shall die by the sword* and among the Goldbergs, Berkovitzes and Steins was a cluster of Kleins.

We signed out with the security guard as we left the building. He was fat, young and unsmiling, and Spiegeleier believed he was an anti-Semite because he wore a uniform and carried a gun.

'It must've been hard,' said Spiegeleier, 'being the only Jewish boy on the *Belfast Telegraph*.'

'Nobody in Belfast was interested in killing Jews,' I said.

'Makes a nice change,' said Spiegeleier.

On the steps outside, he lit a Winfield Blue and noisily sucked the reassurance out of it as he shambled down Darlinghurst Road towards the Coca-Cola sign, with his shirt front poking out of his fly.

'You think you know Kings Cross,' he said to me, 'because you think you live here. But you don't. Home is where your head is.' He flapped a hand towards a pavement-surfing junkie. '*She* lives in Kings Cross. You still live in London.

'Do you know why she's swaying? It's because she's in tune with the undercurrents. She can sense the ground moving beneath her.'

'You mean the trains?'

'No, Tony,' said Spiegeleier. 'I mean the metaphors. She is being metaphorically unbalanced by metaphorically invisible forces. So are you. It's just that you can't feel them.'

I followed him down William Street, the highway to the city. He stopped at the corner of Lower Bourke. 'This is where you'll find the girls who fuck in car parks and cars,' he said. 'Across the road, at Upper Bourke, it's all Asian ladyboys. If you're looking for a white transsexual – although I don't suppose you are – they hold the corner of Lower Forbes, with the Islanders.

'Other girls work in Liverpool Street, on Oxford Street and Victoria Street, all the way down to Yurong Street. At the end of Talbot Lane, there's safe houses for girls who need somewhere dry and quiet to take a mug. Ten years ago, rent boys stood like parking meters along the wall, just south of our offices, one boy to every car. But the drivers were bashing them and one team was standing over the rest, and now you might see half-a-dozen at the weekend, come in from the bush to earn a bit of drug money.

'The rent boys might have addresses in Bathurst or Parkes or Mount Druitt,' said Spiegeleier, 'but they live,' he tapped his temples, 'in the Cross.'

'What's your point?' I asked him.

'My point, Tony, is this is the Darlinghurst that Mendoza made. All these miserable men with tits and dicks, who sell their arses for heroin, sleep in the house that Jake built. People in the Jewish community don't realise that. They don't come around here, they don't see the devastation. To them, Mendoza's just the man who can get Johnny Farnham for their son's bar mitzvah. That old crook's the most popular uncle in Woollahra. You know why? Because chartered accountants like to introduce him as their kid's *godfather*. It makes me sick.'

He headed back up the hill towards the Cross. It was late afternoon, light and bright, and the smackheads were wearing sunglasses.

'Do you know the Southern Star Bar?' asked Spiegeleier. 'It's one of Mendoza's hotels.'

I had seen the pub, lodged between a gift shop and a bondage boutique, but never thought to have a drink there. With platinum fittings and laser lights, it looked like it was meant for younger people, or maybe astronauts.

'I didn't find it under Mendoza's name on the land-title search,' I said.

'He did a land-title search for a story about a synagogue donation,' said Spiegeleier to his god.

Spiegeleier tugged on his earlobe, and stepped in a puddle of kebab meat and salad.

'The Southern Star Bar is owned by Southern Magen

Holdings,' he told me, 'which is a subsidiary of Patton Hospitality which leases the building from Rosenblatt & Grandson, which is owned by Patton Hospitality which is managed by Amy Monk, who is a proxy for Mendoza. He rents out the building to himself. Patton Hospitality is the semi-legitimate arm of Mendoza's empire.' Spiegeleier talked quickly, as he veered around the pavement, looking at everything but me.

'There're nine strip joints on Darlinghurst Road between the El Alamein Fountain and the Coca-Cola sign,' said Spiegeleier. 'Mendoza owns six. He leases them to brothel keepers, who sublet one level to a lap-dancing bar and another to a porn shop, and run girls from the upper storeys. A lap dancer might pick up a mug in the bar and take him to a room, but that's a transaction between two businesses – three, if she stops to pick up condoms and lube from the shop – and nothing to do with Jake Mendoza.

'It never used to be like that,' said Spiegeleier, wiping sweat from his forehead with his shirt cuff. 'Up until the eighties, Mendoza ran the clubs directly, but he got tired of all the royal commissions and paying off the crooked cops, so he franchised out his operation.'

Spiegeleier's bald head looked like a ball of sweating cheese by the time we reached the Southern Star. His spectacles wobbled excitedly on the bridge of his nose. A Maori doorman with a head like a boulder stood aside to let us into the bar. Spiegeleier panted and pushed his way through a loose, yielding crowd.

'Look, Tony,' he said, 'I admire you. You remind me a lot of myself when I was younger, although I was better looking. We all start out wanting to be Woodward and Bernstein, but we all end up as Spiegeleier and Klein.

'I admire your integrity, your ambition and your talent. I even admire your misguided support for the Palestinian cause.'

Spiegeleier rested an elbow on the bar and asked what I'd like to drink.

'Pint of lager,' I said automatically.

'You won't get a pint in here, Dick Whittington,' said Spiegeleier.

'A schooner, then,' I said, although I hated the word.

'Me,' said Spiegeleier, 'I never drink.'

He ordered himself an orange juice, carefully studied the arc of the barmaid's breasts, squelched an eyelid with his fist, patted down an imaginary hair on his head, tapped his foot, scratched his nose and took a big gulp from his glass.

'Cheers,' he said, smearing a bright stain across his lip. 'You're fired.'

Spiegeleier waited in the bar while I drank a couple of beers, and I was grateful for that, then he shook my hand and said he hoped we would meet again under different circumstances; ie, with him not firing me.

The beer was swishing around my stomach like water in a washing machine, because I hadn't eaten anything since breakfast, except for a micro-cassette tape. I got talking to a South African sitting alone at the bar. I couldn't tell if he was a good South African who had left because of apartheid, or a bad South African who had left because of Mandela. He could see where my questions were leading and tried to change the subject to rugby, which is a sport played by cunts.

Finally, I came out and asked him.

'Are you a cunt?' I said.

He picked up his brandy and Coke and moved to a table at the far end of the room, leaving me mumbling the things I wanted to say to death's-head Mendoza and that idiot Lazarus. Silly old bastards, playing at being gangsters when they ought to be playing bingo. The Aussie Mafia? I've shit 'em.

Back on Darlinghurst Road, the sun was still shining. I was

sick of the sun always shining, as if there was no such thing as weather. I had lost my job. It should be raining. It would be raining at home. I missed England in the soft light at dusk, with its chills and drizzles and evenings when you could watch your breath rise like cigarette smoke in the cold air. I was tired of Kings Cross, whether I 'lived' in it or not. You call *this* Kings Cross? I'll show you a real Kings Cross, where you can get stabbed just for staring, or kicked into hospital for knocking over a drink. I'd had enough of Australia, where you can't buy a pint or a balti and the chocolate tastes like paste. I'd been here nine months and nothing had gone right. I thought I could start again, but maybe there are no second chances, maybe shit sticks no matter how hard you scrub and you might just as well try to rinse off a tattoo.

The spruikers had started work outside the strip clubs, fat-fisted men in tuxedos, trying to scoop up the football teams and stag parties and bowl them into the lap-dancing bars. A junkie outside McDonald's asked me for two dollars for a cup of coffee. Across the road, a couple of big bearded men from the Cannibals MC were guarding their choppers outside the Ink tattoo studio. I nearly crashed shoulders with a lovely European girl with a caramel tan and glossy pink lips. A Japanese tourist asked me to take her picture, and I wondered what it must be like to be Japanese, travelling all around the world dressed for a game of golf.

I reached my apartment block but couldn't find my keys. I buzzed Helen on the intercom. She said my keys were in my pocket, and she was right. A junkie tried to walk in behind me, but I elbowed him away. The lift was out of order, so I climbed two flights of stairs. I spent so long trying to line up my key with the lock that Helen came to open the door for me.

'I've been sacked,' I told her.

I fell onto the couch and stared at her. She looked shop-soiled and shameless, still in her pink dressing-gown at 7 pm.

'Haven't you even got up yet?' I asked her.

'Of course I've got up,' she said. 'I'm up now, aren't I?'

'Have we got any beer in the fridge?'

'We've got half a carton of semi-skimmed milk that you bought when I asked you to get skimmed,' said Helen, 'and a piece of cheese that's gone dry because you didn't wrap it up properly. There's half a jar of strawberry jam that's gone mouldy because you never put the lid back on, and a takeaway tub of Thai sweet chilli sauce with two tiny bits of chicken floating inside, like bacteria. There's also a box of chardonnay, because you put it back in there when it was empty.'

Her breasts trembled angrily inside her dressing-gown.

'Spiegeleier said he'd pay me until the end of the week,' I said.

'Jesus,' said Helen.

'I've only been there a fortnight. I haven't written a single story. He didn't have to give me anything.'

Helen shook her head and went to open the cupboard over the stove top. She had to stand on tiptoes to reach it, and the fringe of her robe rode up to her hips. She pushed aside a box of pasta and a bag of rice and scrabbled around among the loose onions until she found what she was looking for.

She emptied out her handbag on the kitchen bench, pulled out her compact, opened it, racked up two fat white lines, rolled a plastic five-dollar bill into a funnel and passed the whole kit across to me.

'Get that up your Jewish nose,' she said, and – just for a moment – I was in love with her again.

THREE

Two weeks later it was another pointlessly sunny morning and I'd had enough of everything. I left Helen snoring lightly and went out to get a paper. I was trying to decide whether to buy it or steal it from the library, when I saw Mendoza sunning his charcoal Armani suit, drinking coffee at a table outside La Fontaine, the cafe that overlooked the El Alamein Fountain.

'Anthony!' he called.

I waved vaguely, and walked on. He beckoned Lazarus from the table behind and sent him lurching after me.

Lazarus was tall and wide with long, thick arms. His nose had been pounded back into his head and his brows beaten over his eye sockets, almost closing his eyes. He must have been at least sixty-five years old. I let him catch up with me alongside a white Telstra transit van.

'The old man wants to buy you a coffee,' he said.

'Forget it,' I said.

Lazarus blinked, and blocked my path with a raised hand. I sidestepped and he followed, as if we were line-dancing. He grabbed my shirt and I pitched myself forward, smashing my shoulder against the side of the transit van. From Mendoza's distance, it would have looked as though Lazarus had pushed me. I dropped my head and hit the van for a second time, butting it so hard I made a dent in the bodywork.

'There's no need to kill him!' shouted Mendoza, and Lazarus, puzzled, let me go.

'You're a big man,' I told him, 'but you're out of shape.'

We walked back to Mendoza's table, where the old man handed me a napkin to dab the cut on my forehead.

'Sit down,' he told me. 'It's no use trying to fight Lazarus. He's the best there is.'

Mendoza filled his suit like a skeleton. A gold Rolex hung loosely from his left wrist, and a Star of David signet ring weighed on his right hand. He was polished and shaved, massaged and trimmed, manicured, perfumed and tanned, and almost dead.

'So, Anthony,' said Mendoza, 'what are you doing with yourself these days?'

'Get fucked,' I said.

Mendoza arched an eyebrow.

'I didn't tell your employer to fire you,' said Mendoza.

'Well, they did fire me,' I said.

An oval-faced waitress came over, with soft white down on her thin brown arms. Mendoza asked her for a flat white and a cappuccino. She silently spelled out the words as she jotted them on her pad. He smiled slyly, as if he'd passed her a message in code.

A moist and panting flabby man, with sagging arms and cheeks like rump steaks, noticed me from the pavement and shuffle-jogged over to our table.

'Hey!' he cried. 'What happened to my story? You said it would be in the paper this week.'

'I'm not sure what you mean,' I said carefully.

'You're from the *Catholic Herald*,' he said.

'Sorry, mate,' I said, 'you've got me mixed up.'

'Anthony worked on the *Jewish Times*,' said Mendoza, like a proud mother.

'I wouldn't be talking about my business to the Jew *Times*,' said the flabby man.

Mendoza cocked his head.

'I make christening wear,' said the flabby man.

'Good business?' asked Mendoza.

The flabby man shrugged. 'Everyone born's got to have a name,' he said. 'When's my story going in?'

'You'll have a struggle getting it into the *Jewish Times*,' said Mendoza.

'I don't get the Jewboy jokes,' said the flabby man. 'What am I missing?'

'Manners,' said Mendoza.

The flabby man stared at him. Lazarus stared back.

'You can leave now,' said Mendoza.

The flabby man experimented with looking insulted and angry but settled for puzzled and misunderstood. He waddled off down Darlinghurst Road, glancing in the windows of the kebab shops and cafes. When he thought we couldn't see him, he crossed the road and doubled back to a sex shop.

Mendoza held out his hand and Lazarus passed him his phone. He rang a number on speed dial, and said, 'Hello, Dennis? You've got a sweaty white maggot coming down in about five seconds. Blue shorts, red nose . . . Yeah, that's him. Whatever he tries to buy, switch the disc with *My Girlfriend's Got A Cock*, eh?'

Mendoza passed the phone back to Lazarus, who laid it on the tabletop and smirked.

'Mr Fathead moves from one unusual misunderstanding to the next,' he said.

The waitress brought over my flat white. This time I

remembered to look at her face. She had auburn eyes and ochre hair, dark pink lips and creamy tanned skin. She smiled when she put down my cup, and her sandalwood perfume blended with the scent of coffee. It smelled like breakfast after sex.

Another man came to our table, wearing a linen jacket and a pork-pie hat. Mendoza rose to shake his hand, and they spoke quietly in a foreign language, before the visitor scuttled away.

Mendoza's mobile phone buzzed. Lazarus picked it up and passed it to Mendoza. The old man pressed it hard against his ear and turned his head away from me.

'No,' he said, sadly. 'I didn't know. How many men do you need?' He shook his head. 'I've only got Lazarus, and he's no good for that.'

He covered his phone with a liver-spotted hand. 'Anthony,' he said, 'I'm going to need you for the morning.'

'No,' I said.

'He's in,' said Mendoza. 'We'll be over there in twenty minutes.'

I stood to leave. Lazarus stood to stop me. Mendoza grabbed my wrist.

'You'll want to see this, Anthony,' he said. 'I promise.'

I guess I still thought I might get the story. I didn't want to talk to Helen, and I had nothing else to do, so when Mendoza sent Lazarus to fetch his car, I swept my wallet and keys into my pocket and followed the old man to the kerb.

Lazarus pulled up at the fountain in a black Rolls Royce Corniche with the numberplate *Big 1*, and held open the door until Mendoza and I climbed into the back seat.

'Botany,' said Mendoza to Lazarus.

We cruised through the Cross with the roof down and the sun shining. Hookers and waiters whistled and waved. Mendoza acknowledged them with a brief, tight smile.

'You like the waitress,' he said to me as we turned into William

Street, past shabby car dealers and a tired gym-equipment showroom. 'I can get her for you. It's what I do. I find out what people want, then I find somebody who has it, then I bring the two of them together.'

'I don't need your help,' I told him.

'Of course not,' he said. 'You have a girlfriend, after all.'

Lazarus closed the roof as we went into the tunnel.

'What language were you speaking to the bloke in the hat?' I asked Mendoza.

'Yiddish,' said Mendoza. 'Just Yiddish.'

Mendoza imagined dust on his lapels, and brushed it away with his fingers. 'That was Eddie Finkel,' he told me. '"Slow Eddie", we used to call him. Not that he was slow – although he has lost a bit of speed since he put on weight – but there used to be a lot of "Fast Eddies" around, and it just didn't seem right for him. It worked out okay. People always thought he must be a bit retarded, so they underestimated him. He learned how to make use of that, and turned an obstacle into an asset. Did you ever have a nickname, Anthony?'

'"Slick",' I told him.

'That's an unusual nickname for an "Anthony",' he said. 'Normally, it's "Slick Nick" or "Slick Rick".'

'I used to wear a lot of hair gel,' I explained.

'There are worse names to live with than "Mr Big",' said Mendoza, 'Slick.'

Lazarus crossed himself as we drove past the walls and towers of Long Bay Jail, then followed the road to Botany Cemetery. He parked the Corniche in a space marked *Ministers only* outside the funeral chapel complex. The buildings looked like the bone house at Verdun, bleached to cream in the Pacific sun.

'I don't suppose you have a *kippa* on you, Anthony,' said Mendoza. 'At my age, you learn to carry one always.'

He took an embroidered skullcap from his pocket, and Lazarus gave me a plain *kippa* from the glove compartment. We arranged them on our heads – Mendoza to cover his bald patch – and stepped out of the car. Lazarus lent me his black sports coat, which sat sternly on my pink polo shirt like a police officer wrestling down a drunk. When I fastened the buttons, something small and hard, like a hipflask, dug into my chest.

Seven men and one woman were waiting below the stained-glass windows of the west chapel. With them stood the rabbi, a young man with an old man's beard.

'Ah,' said the rabbi, 'a *minyan*. Plus one.'

'Lazarus is a goy,' said Mendoza. 'Only Anthony here is a *haimisher* Yid.'

We needed a quorum of ten Jewish men to pray at the funeral. The rabbi shook my hand as Mendoza exchanged quiet greetings with claw-fingered turtles in well-worn suits.

'They're from the *chevra kadisha* burial society,' Mendoza told me. 'This is their idea of a day out.'

'Whose funeral is it?' I asked.

'They called him "Mad Dog",' said Mendoza. 'Or, rather, I called him that.'

'Mad Dog McCoy was Jewish?'

'You disappoint me,' said Mendoza. 'I thought research was supposed to be your thing – lifting the veil, looking beyond the obvious and so on.'

We filed into the chapel and filled only the first two pews.

'That's the thing about nicknames, Slick,' said Mendoza. 'They're largely alliterative or rhyming or traditional. A McCoy who showed signs of violent insanity might reasonably expect to be known as "Mad Dog", whereas a Klein who began foaming at the mouth would more likely be called "Crazy", or even "Killer".

I knew a "Killer Klein" once. He wouldn't hurt a fly. That brings us to our fourth category of nickname: ironic.

'There is also a fifth kind, which I would describe as "redundant". For example, I have patronised the same tailor ever since the war: Solomon Solomons, known as "Solly the Yid". The problem here is that the nickname adds no new information.'

'You've studied this,' I said.

'Nicknames and aliases are an important part of life,' said Mendoza. 'A man may have one name to his wife, another to his girlfriend and yet another to the jacks.'

Mendoza was interrupted by a short man, built like a giant, who tapped him on the shoulder from the seat behind. They bumped fists like rappers, and their signet rings rang as they clashed.

'Beware of men who have no nickname,' Mendoza told me. 'This is Dror – just "Dror" – my head of security.'

'G'day, mate,' said Dror, like a Queenslander. When he pushed his Ray Bans onto his head, I saw he even had the sunshine squint. His lime-green eyes reminded me of the boys in Aldershot who used to play chicken with trains and grew up to have their faces slashed with Stanley knives and their noses broken by bricks.

'Anthony's a journalist,' Mendoza explained, 'but he's here today to do his duty as a Jew.'

The rabbi paced slowly to the podium, took his place in front of the draped curtains, and looked out into the large empty room. He wore a black skullcap like a hanging judge, a banded prayer shawl and a shirt buttoned up to his throat. He named the dead man as Moshe Maizel.

'Moshe will be remembered as a memorable character by everyone who met him,' said the rabbi. 'I myself only came to know him in the last days of his life, but I do know he had a lot of friends,' the rabbi looked around the silent hall, 'not all of whom could be here today.

'He was the first to admit that he wasn't an educated man. He told me he was schooled at "the bluestone college", by which he meant the university of life.'

Mendoza shook his head.

'He was not religious in the usual sense,' said the rabbi, 'but he told me he had lived by a code, and he'd never once violated that code. How many of us can say that? That we stayed true to our beliefs, without wavering or flinching, until the end of our days?

'Moshe is survived by a wife and a daughter, and he will live on in their hearts forever. They tell me he was a wonderful husband and a model father.'

Mendoza sniggered. He was the oldest person I have ever heard snigger.

'After Moshe was discharged from the military in 1946,' said the rabbi, 'he had a long and varied career in many different businesses. He was always modest about his professional achievements, but he was a success at everything to which he turned his hand, and he will be deeply missed, both here in Australia and in his second home in Central Luzon.'

The rabbi hung his head. Mendoza hissed an instruction to Lazarus, who murmured to the rabbi, who beckoned to Mendoza to take his place. Mendoza gripped the lectern with both hands, and spoke with sadness.

'I didn't know Moshe had passed until thirty minutes ago,' said Mendoza, 'so I haven't had time to write a speech, but Moshe was one of my best friends. I've known him since high school. In that time, we have, of course, had our disagreements, but he never once lost my respect or my love. In a blue, he was worth ten blokes. I have so many great memories of Moshe, and I'd like to share just one of them with Moshe's friends . . .'

he looked around him, '. . . and, of course, his beautiful wife, Cecilia Preciosa Bong Bong McCoy.'

Cecilia looked to be in her mid-twenties, but her face was obscured by a giant pair of sunglasses.

'It's difficult to tell true stories about Moshe because, often, the other participants are still alive.' Mendoza thought for a moment. 'Although, often, they're not. Even if, at the start of the story, they were.'

Dror nodded and tapped his foot.

'Anyway, this happened in 1959, when Izzy Berger and I brought Frank Sinatra to Australia – although what Izzy had to do with it, other than get his name in the paper, I'll never understand – and Frank was having a party after the show in the old Patton Lounge in Kings Cross. Technically, I think, the address today would be Potts Point.

'So Moshe is working the door for me, and every moll in Sydney is trying to squeeze in through the gaps, when up walks a *shiksa* who's stacked like a cruise ship. I mean, she's got balconies on her. She's the sweetest thing Moshe's ever seen – except, he later told me, his lovely wife, Cecilia Preciosa Bong Bong – and she's rubbing herself against him, whispering into his cauliflower ear, "If you'll introduce me to Frank, I'll do anything you want for a shilling." "Are you any good on your knees?" asks Moshe. "I've never had any complaints," says the *shiksa*. "Okay," says Moshe, "I've got three very short words for you: pave my yard." '

Dror, Cecilia and I laughed. The men from the burial society set their faces like tombstones, and Mendoza stepped down from the podium.

'The widow is Jewish by association only,' Mendoza whispered. 'He met her in the Philippines.' He coughed into his fist.

The pallbearers carried the coffin into the graveyard, where the Jewish section was hemmed in on three sides by Greek icons and angels. The flatbed graves were crowded together and there was barely room to stand between the rows of headstones. Most were engraved in English and Hebrew, but there were those inscribed in Russian, cut from black marble and shining like dark stars, etched with pictures of young men in their Red Army uniforms. They died at eighty years old in Sydney but were remembered as twenty year olds in Moscow, proud and frightened, ready to go to war. Lazarus walked among the Russians, pausing to look into each set of bullet-hole eyes.

On the rise of the hill, looking out at the container ships moored off Port Botany, we swayed and prayed as Moshe Maizel aka Mad Dog McCoy was lowered into a fresh hole, and we took our turns to shower the casket with a shovel load of dirt.

Mendoza drew a deep, trembling breath, and wiped his eyes with his silk handkerchief.

'He was the last one,' the old man told me, 'and now there's no one left but me.'

FOUR

A mourner with a nose that hung like a hound's ear touched Mendoza lightly on the shoulder and asked, 'Will there be sandwiches, Jake?'

'Salt beef like they serve in heaven,' he promised.

The old men split off into two small circles, comparing Moshe's funeral with other recent events, such as Fritzy Lieberman's stone-laying ceremony and the Jewish ex-servicemen's Anzac Day march.

'In this world of maggots and dogs,' Mendoza said to me, 'a bloke who's staunch is more valuable than pearls. And Moshe was solid as a rock. He wouldn't let his mother into his house without a warrant.'

Cecilia danced between the knots of men, accepting their condolences and inviting them back to her home. As she reached Mendoza he wrapped an arm around her waist and drew her towards him. He rested his hand below her ribcage, like a tango partner.

'I wasn't there for Moshe at the end,' Mendoza told her, 'and for that I will never forgive myself.'

'He spoke about you often,' said Cecilia, smiling sadly, 'and all the things you used to do when you were young. They were golden days for Moshe. He never forgot them.'

'I know he was never happier than when he met you,' said Mendoza. 'You were the light at the end of his path.'

Cecilia let a tear drip out from under her sunglasses.

'He was a lovely man,' she said. 'I'll miss him so much.'

'We'll all miss him,' said Mendoza, 'even those like Anthony here, who never actually met him. But what makes me fucking sick – and please pardon my use of language that was alien to you during your employment in Angeles City – is all the low dogs who didn't turn up today. Moshe was a true mensch. He'd help anybody – pollie or punter, junkie or judge – and now they're all too busy to see off a man with a heart as big as WA and, I've heard it said, a shlong to match.

'Where, for instance, is Hymie the Bookie?' Mendoza demanded of everyone at the funeral.

'Dead,' said a mourner. 'Five hundred turned up for that one.'

'Such sandwiches,' remembered another.

'All right, so why can't Freddy Freed be here? Or Plastic Sam? Or the Human Dartboard?'

'Freddy's buried over there,' said a mourner, pointing.

A man with short legs and a large head stepped out of his circle. 'There were two men known as "the Human Dartboard",' he said. 'The goy overdosed on heroin in 1986; the Yid was run over by a cement truck. Plastic Sam passed away in August.'

Mendoza examined him intensely, as if surprised that small people could speak. 'It's a talking book,' he said. '*The Yiddisher Book of the Dead.*'

We drifted back to the car park. Mendoza offered the rabbi a ride.

'It would be an honour,' said the rabbi. 'Tell me: this woman who laid the paving in Moshe's yard – did she do a good job?'

Most of the old men drove Volvos. Cecilia had a Volkswagen Beetle which, in her sunglasses, she slightly resembled. Parked two spaces behind the Corniche was a white gravediggers' transit van.

Mad Dog McCoy lived the last years of his life in a two-bedroom unit in Maroubra, where nobody knew him as either Moshe or Mad Dog. The neighbours called him 'Muscles' because he kept a dumbbell and bench on the balcony and lifted weights every morning until his eightieth birthday. He gave up, he told them, to leave him more energy to make love to Cecilia.

We were met at the door by Cecilia's mother, Gloria, who had flown over from Luzon when Moshe fell ill, and Moshe's three-year-old daughter, Maria Graciela Rivka.

Mendoza looked over at the table of sandwiches and cakes that Gloria had prepared, and sent Lazarus to Bondi to pick up pastrami and a dozen bagels.

'It's the custom to serve round food,' Mendoza explained to Gloria.

I sat with Dror on Moshe's bench on the balcony. In the distance, over red rooftops, we could see the ocean.

'I used to want to be a journo,' said Dror, 'but I couldn't spell. So I joined the military instead.'

'The Australian army?' I asked.

'The Australian army, the Israeli army, the Russian army,' he said. 'It's all the same.'

'And now you're in Mendoza's army,' I said.

'And you're a journalist,' he said.

We both looked out to sea.

Lazarus called us inside for a glass of Johnny Walker. The old men from the *chevra kadisha* each ate one salt-beef bagel and drank a cup of tea, then continued their journeys back to Dover

Heights and Vaucluse. Mendoza played peek-a-boo with Maria Graciela Rivka, but he was watching Cecilia all the time.

'I would like to do something for you,' he said to Cecilia, and wrote her a cheque for the funeral. 'Please accept this gift from a friend who considered himself a brother to Moshe,' he said, 'and, by extension, a brother-in-law to you.'

Cecilia kissed him on the cheek.

The rabbi said it was a pity there were not more men like Mendoza, who were prepared to share the fruits of their labour with the rest of the community. He told me Mendoza was highly regarded, and I should be proud to call him my boss, then he asked for a lift back to Maroubra Synagogue. He had another funeral in the afternoon, but the whisky had made him woozy and he hoped to take a nap before lunch. Mendoza hurried to leave. He hugged Cecilia and had Lazarus give her his card.

On the drive down Anzac Parade, Mendoza said, 'Does the Philippines have one of those cultures where the brother-in-law inherits the widow, I wonder.'

We dropped the rabbi off, leaving Mendoza as the holiest person in the car.

'Now,' he said to me, 'you have seen the real Jake Mendoza: a valued and valuable member of the community; a busy man who is willing to drop everything to attend to his religious obligations; a tough man, who is not above shedding a tear at the memory of an old friend and is, in fact, happy to pay for the funeral and a reasonable quantity of refreshments; a confidant of widows and rabbis; a comfort to children . . . Why don't you write a story about that?'

'Because I don't work for a newspaper any more,' I told him. 'You lost me my job.'

'I could get it back for you,' said Mendoza. 'It would only take one phone call.'

I ignored him.

'I've been talking to Spiegeleier,' he said. 'He tells me you've got a reputation, you're a great writer, you worked in Northern Ireland. Surely it can't be difficult for you to find another position.'

'My first job here lasted twelve days,' I said. 'How do I explain that?'

'Blame Jake Mendoza,' he said. 'Everybody else does.'

We arrived back at the La Fontaine. Lazarus stopped to let me out.

'I'm sorry for what happened,' said Mendoza. 'Let me see what I can do for you, Anthony. I'm having lunch with the premier, but I'll be free again at around four o'clock. Why don't you join me here, and we can go for a drink.'

Helen was awake and dressed, sitting at the table, running her fingers through brochures. She didn't ask where I had been, because we didn't do that any more. I looked into her eyes and saw everything I wanted to leave behind, then she smiled at me, showing pink lipstick smeared across cream teeth.

She poured me a mug of tea from the pot. She had even bought some milk.

'You've been out,' I said.

'Out and about,' she replied, which didn't add anything to the conversation.

I sat next to her, dropped one hand on her soft thigh, and she opened a catalogue of tours to Alice Springs and the red centre.

'I was thinking maybe we could get away,' said Helen, 'Go off into the desert and ride kangaroos.'

She leaned into me. I breathed vanilla perfume.

'We could sleep in a tent,' she said.

'I've slept in enough tents,' I said.

'But not with me.'

Our forearms crossed as she stroked my leg. She kissed me, like I had hoped she would. I lifted her loose white T-shirt over her head and noticed, for the thousandth time, that one of her breasts was bigger than the other. I wondered if she examined me this way, weighing and measuring, judging me against the promise.

I took one of her big brown nipples in my hand and squeezed it softly.

'Let's get a pet koala,' she said, 'and teach it to chase boomerangs.'

'There's no point,' I said. 'They always come back.'

'That's okay. Koalas don't move. He'll be there to catch it on the rebound.'

She tickled my belly.

'Like me, you mean?' I asked.

My phone rang. She told me to leave it. Her phone rang. She tried to roll me onto my back and pin me down. My phone beeped with a message. Hers did the same. Then mine rang again.

'It's the Jedi,' said the caller, and I could hear him munching on his lunchtime pizza. 'What're you doing with Jake Mendoza, Slick? Are you working for him now?'

'I'm not working for anyone,' I told him.

'We need you back on the team,' he said.

'There is no team,' I said. 'There is no "we". There's just you and your pizza-eating head and your tiny, withered, other-people's-girlfriends-shagging cock. Get fucked. By a trannie. With AIDS.'

I cut off the call, but Jed rang me back.

'Look,' he said, 'whatever you're doing might clash with what I'm doing.'

'That would be ironic, then, wouldn't it?' I said.

'Tony,' said Jed, 'this isn't the *Aldershot News and Weekend Advertiser*. You don't know your way around. There's some serious people involved.'

I turned off my phone.

Helen tried to get me back into a submission hold. I pushed her away.

'That coke you had the other day,' I said. 'Where was it from?'

'I don't know,' she said. 'Columbia?'

'Where did you *buy* it from?'

'That bloke in Newtown,' she said. 'The one who used to be in that band.'

'Yeah, sure,' I said, buttoning up my jeans, and I stood up, stormed out of the apartment and slammed the door.

Mendoza wanted to have a drink at the Hamilton Private Hotel on Bayswater Road. He said he liked it there because he had no business interest in the place, so he didn't need to worry that the staff were stealing. He walked down Darlinghurst Road, with Lazarus by his side, like a prince among his subjects. He told a spruiker to button up his collar and asked a prostitute not to smoke in the street. The bouncer fiddled with his shirt and the girl stubbed out her cigarette. Mendoza laughed.

'I've got nothing to do with that whorehouse,' he told me. 'But the workers on the strip respect me. If it wasn't for Jake Mendoza and the Coca-Cola sign, there wouldn't be a Kings Cross.'

Lazarus left us at the hotel steps and crossed the road. Every afternoon, said Mendoza, Lazarus liked to visit the New York restaurant on Kellet Street and sit in silence with men his own age. Mendoza waved me into the Hamilton. The hotel's receptionist was asleep in his chair. Mendoza rang the desk bell, just to wake him up, then walked past him and into the public bar. A butter-blonde barmaid served me a beer and Mendoza a glass of shiraz. At the pool table a man with an angry moko played silent eight-ball against another Maori, whose colossal fists were mottled and ridged like seashells.

Moko stepped in front of Mendoza to line up his shot. The old man raised his hand and swatted the cue away.

'Watch it, snake face,' said Mendoza.

'Sorry, Mr Mendoza,' said Moko.

Mendoza caught me looking at the barmaid. 'Do you like young girls?' he asked.

I pretended not to hear him.

'How was the premier?' I asked.

'How are any of us?' said Mendoza. 'He is my age. His cock died before he did. He's not going to be climbing on top of Cecilia Preciosa Bong Bong McCoy any time soon.'

'I thought the premier was in his fifties,' I said.

'Not that maggot,' said Mendoza. 'He doesn't deserve to be called premier. He doesn't run fuck all in this city. The bloke I'm talking about left office in 1975, but I still call him "the premier" and I always will. But that's the problem with me, isn't it, Anthony? I live in the past.'

He lit a small cigar.

'I live in the past,' he repeated, 'but I can't tell the truth about it. And when I do, I make some poor young bloke eat the tape. What do you think about that, Anthony?'

'I think you're a complicated character,' I told him.

He laughed.

'I've lived for money and cunt,' he said. 'It's not fucking rocket science.'

He smoked distractedly.

'I always knew that I would be the one to grow old,' he said.

'My lieutenants turned on me, my enemies became my allies, but everyone who goes into this business is in it to die – except me. I wanted to live, so I knew I would survive them, but I never thought that when I grew old I would have nobody to talk with about the past, because I'd killed them all. No one can share my war stories, Anthony, because I won the war.'

He swirled sediment around his glass.

'I have become lonely in the company of women,' he said. 'All my life I've been able to lose myself inside them, now I am a thing apart. I've lost my solace, Anthony. And I have too many secrets. I used to cherish them, but now I want to set them free. They are cords that bind me to this life and I need to cut them. Do you understand?'

I said I did.

'I want to write a book,' he said, 'an autobiography, not an excuse. But I can't do it alone. I need a writer. I had hoped to dictate my life story to my daughter, Sharon, but she is only interested in propagating lies about her father. She has not been trained to recognise the facts, like a British journalist from Fleet Street, where the news stories are every bit as true as the comics, and even the horoscopes are unfailingly correct. I'm thinking of asking you to help me – you have the qualifications, you have the experience, and you have the spinelessness that might make it possible for me to trust you – but I don't know yet if you're right for the job.'

FIVE

Like Spiegeleier, Mendoza left me in the pub alone. Everybody had places to go but me. The barmaid was prettier than I first noticed, although a bit plump. She leaned across me to take my empty glass, and the stiff cup of her bra brushed against my shirt. She said sorry. I think I blushed.

She asked where my accent was from.

'The same place as the rest of me,' I said, like a twat.

She went to talk to the Maoris but came back to my table for her break. She said her name was Leah, and she came from the country. She said it was hard to meet nice people in Sydney. She was used to pubs where the drinkers were friendlier. She had pixie eyes and a fairy nose, and the more I drank the more I liked her. She said she had dumped her boyfriend when she found out he was seeing another of the barmaids behind her back. He was the drummer in a band, and she had only got talking to him because she fancied the singer, but it turned out that the singer was gay. Leah thought most single men in Sydney were gay.

Leah had only been in love twice, and neither of them had

deserved her. She liked strong men who reminded her of her father. She planned to go to England one day, probably with her mate Caitlin. It would be part of a ten-year round-the-world trip, and she would also visit friends in America, Spain and China, although she didn't have any friends in China yet. People told her she talked too much, but that was just the way she was. She wasn't always going to work in bars. One day she would be a singer, or an actress, or a housemate on *Big Brother*. She felt like she was full of potential, at the edge of her future, and anything could happen.

She asked me if I was happy. I told her I had lost my job. It was stolen from me, I explained, by a notorious criminal.

'You're funny,' she said, playing with loose curls in her hair.

She taught me how to put songs on the video jukebox without paying, and I watched her as she walked back to the bar. I was thinking of all the things I would like to do to her, on the counter, on the pool table, in the cellar.

She brought me another beer and, when I tried to pay, waved my money away.

One by one the afternoon drinkers slipped out of the pub. For a few minutes we were the only people in the bar. She ignored me and concentrated on wiping the tabletops and emptying the ashtrays. I found it hard to breathe when I looked at her. I felt like I was being dragged towards her on the end of a rope.

A rugby team on a bucks-night crawl scrummed up around bar. They ordered their drinks, then the captain blew a whistle and they each shotgunned a rum and coke.

A scrum-half shaped like a photo booth beckoned Leah over. When she smiled at him he leaned across the bar, grabbed one of her breasts and twisted it. The captain pulled him back, and they all drank a beer. In London he would have got a slap for that.

I got up to use the toilet and I was standing in the urinal when the tit-grabber came in behind me. He stood a step back from the trough, reading a newspaper framed on the wall. You know, really, it had nothing to do with me.

I wondered if he could fight.

'What are you staring at?' he asked. 'Are you queer or something?'

'Yeah,' I said.

He flushed.

My heartbeat, my breathing and the tension in my head and my hands told me I should go. Leave. Go.

He jabbed me in the chest with his index finger – once, twice, three times. He said 'Get-the-fuck-ou-'. Then I grabbed the finger and twisted it back on itself, and held him while I punched him twice in the face. His head bounced off the tiled wall, so I hit him again. He tried to twist out of my grip, but I swept his legs from under him, and he had to throw out his hands to try to stop himself from falling into the piss. He turned around and I caught him with a right hook just under the ear. I grabbed him around the neck, pulled down his head and kneed him in the face – one, two, three times. His nose exploded, and showered us both in blood. I changed knees and struck him again.

Oh no. Oh no. Oh no.

There were two doors out of the toilets. One led to the poker-machine lounge, the other to his mates in the bar. I opened the first and told him to fuck off home.

He started to cry. He was only about twenty years old.

Oh Jesus Christ. I've done it again.

'We'll back up and fucking kill you,' he said, struggling with his sobs.

Don't say that. Don't make me.

'You're fucking dead,' he said.

Sometimes, no matter how hard you try to be somebody better, you end up acting like the person you've become, and it seems like there's nothing you can do but give in to the voices in your head and hope that hell is a story told to frighten little children. So I pulled out the little American Derringer sub-compact pistol that Lazarus had left in his coat pocket and pointed it at the kid's teeth.

'No, you won't,' I said.

He shook his head and sobbed with fear. I picked him up and marched him through the pokies, behind fat people blinded by hope, and delivered him to a cab outside.

I saw the kid into a taxi and told the driver he'd been fixing up the stage for the DJ when an amplifier had fallen on his head. I was left standing under the Coke sign in a polo shirt soaked in blood, but I felt like an airman in Trafalgar Square on VE Day.

I stripped off my top and stuffed it into a bin, and walked bare-chested down Darlinghurst Road, behind another half-naked man who scrambled screaming into an alley when we reached the tattoo studio. Outside Ink, two restless bikers from Cannibals MC were scowling around their Harleys: the bearded guy who guarded the place every night, and a younger, clean-shaven man, who wore a sergeant-at-arms patch below a thin strip with the word *Devil*.

The bearded guy modelled the usual jumble of biker crap: swastikas and smoking skulls, iron crosses and runes, and a patch that said he was called Rabbit. 'Rabbit' didn't seem like much of a name for a biker, but I would back him over Devil if it ever kicked off, from the dagger in his belt loop to the shottie in his saddlebag. But the bikers didn't know what they were doing. There were enough of them to make a target but too few to defend the shop. I wondered if they had somebody guarding the back entrance. I guessed they were expecting a drive-by. The attacker would have to be another biker, because a car would get stuck in the traffic on Darlinghurst Road. I wouldn't have staged the assault that way myself, but then I had no reason to do it, or to think about it at all.

Rabbit looked past me to a future threat. Devil stopped me at the tattooist's door.

'What's your problem, mate?' he asked.

'No shirt,' I told him.

Devil ducked into the shop and came out carrying a black T-shirt with a picture of a screaming white skull and the word *Tattoo!*

'We've only got extra large,' he said, almost apologetically. 'Twenty bucks.'

It was one size too big and ballooned out around the belly, and I wished I hadn't hit that boy, or at least that I had only hit him once.

I went back to the Hamilton, where a bouncer pulled me up because I was wearing trainers. It was the brother with the mottled fists, and when he remembered I had been with Mendoza, he let me through.

'New shirt,' he said. 'Nice.'

Leah said the footie team had passed around the hat and raised fifty bucks for her to get her tits out. She said the tips were better than the wages in this job.

'Do you know who you look like?' she asked me. 'Rob Lowe – the movie star who made that horrible video.'

'*St Elmo's Fire*?'

'The sex tape,' she said, 'with the underage girl.'

'It's not me,' I said.

'But you look like him,' she said. 'You've got the same eyes.'

I bought another drink and asked if she wanted one for herself. The bouncer was watching, so she took a dollar from my change and dropped it into a glass of grenadine beside the till.

'Have you seen that video?' she asked. 'It's very grainy. You can't make out much, except for his cock.'

In the casino room, a machine sang a song of celebration for a small win.

'He has a big cock,' said Leah, 'and he looks like you.'

Leah was working the lunchtime to evening shift and it was almost over. I asked if she wanted to go out after she finished.

'No,' she said. 'I'm too tired.'

Another heavy-hipped blonde with a pouty mouth and dimples came to relieve her. Leah picked up her clutch bag and painted on some lipstick, and took me by the hand.

'There's a room upstairs,' she said, 'that we sometimes use on our breaks. It's got a bed and chair, and there's a shower down the hallway.'

We were kissing on the second step. Halfway up I slipped my hands inside her blouse. She stopped and pressed against me. I buried myself into her jeans. She broke into a trot and I chased her to the top of the stairs, along a dingy corridor and into a windowless room that smelled of bleach and tobacco. The bed was a single bunk. I pulled her onto the soft mattress, she undid my belt. I kissed her and kissed her and held her tightly, because I hadn't realised how much I needed to be with her, how completely alone I had felt since I found out about Helen.

'Condom, condom,' she said.

'I haven't got one,' I admitted.

'In my bag,' she told me. 'Take one.'

She wrapped her legs around my hips and said, 'Oh, Tony. Oh, Tony.'

I was grateful and gentle and slow, but she squirmed and she scratched and she cried, 'Go faster! Slap me! Pull my hair!'

'I don't want to hurt you,' I said.

'Fuck me up the arse,' she said. 'Hard. Like you hate me.'

*

I wasn't looking forward to going home. I didn't know how I would explain to Helen where I had been, or what had happened to the polo shirt she had bought me. I was drunk, but all the lies I could think of seemed ridiculous, even to me.

The first thing I noticed when I opened the door of my apartment was that there was no TV on the coffee table. Then I noticed there was no coffee table. Our books had gone too. What kind of burglar takes a Lonely Planet guide? The fridge was empty, but the fridge was always empty. I opened the wardrobe, and all of Helen's clothes were missing.

'She's going to be so pissed off,' I thought, then I flopped onto the bed and fell asleep.

I woke up to go for a piss. I would have cleaned my teeth but I couldn't find the toothpaste. When I came back to bed, I put my arm around Helen, but the ridge I thought was her body was just a lump in the quilt. I went to the kitchen to get a glass of water, but there were no glasses.

I noticed a note on the kitchen benchtop, written on pink paper.

Dear Slick,
I'm sorry but I don't feel we can pretend that we're together any more. It's not fair to you or me. We have made mistakes and now I feel we should go our separate ways. I will always cherish the time we had together. You are a good man and I'm sorry if I hurt you but you should know that you hurt me too in other ways. Whatever happened to forgiveness, Slick?
Love, Helen
PS If you look for me, you'll find me easily enough. But I'd ask you not to come running after me, at least for a while.

I was not going to look for her. I was glad she had gone. I just wished I had left first.

I was going to celebrate with a cup of tea. She had left me the kettle. She had even left the tea bags. Unfortunately, she had taken all the cups. Then I saw two chubby trails of powder, laid diagonally across the mirror like a goodbye kiss.

I snorted her gift with gratitude – even though she had probably sold my TV to buy it – and went out to get coffee and croissants, but I found I didn't feel hungry or thirsty, and I walked around the cute little police station to the fountain, then I walked around the fountain a couple of times, and I realised it was the best fountain I had ever seen. It roared like a storm in the shower, like a flood racing through a drain. Its bronze pipes, clustered like rifles, perfectly symbolised the Western Desert Campaign. I wished the fountain were bigger, so I could spend longer walking around it, and thinking my thought, which was the best thought I had had since I came to Australia, although I couldn't fully remember it. Several times on my way around the fountain, I passed the cafe where I had met Mendoza yesterday. Mendoza was a nice old fella, a good bloke really, maybe a bit dodgy in his youth, but who wasn't? He was a straight-backed military man, who wore his RSL pin on his Armani suit, even though it might spoil the cloth. He could have been in the Western Desert himself, if he hadn't been in Liverpool. I wondered if there was a Liverpool Fountain somewhere, to commemorate the sacrifices made by the flat-footed, the asthmatic, the short-sighted, the deaf and the gun-shy gangsters without whom the necessary paperwork would never have been completed. I wondered how much kit Mendoza had plundered from the stores, how many soldiers' lives he'd put at risk, out there in El Alamein.

I marched towards William Street, convinced this was the best morning of my life. I was glad to be rid of Helen, but that was only a small part of it. Why had I never seen the true loveliness of Kings Cross, when there was no one around apart from beautiful single women and a tourist vomiting into a waste bin?

At the Coca-Cola sign – *Enjoy Coke* – I turned right into William Street and found a huddle of tall men dressed as tall women, and two Aboriginal guys who would have knifed me if I hadn't looked confident and tough and able to take on any bandy-legged petrol-sniffers with my bare hands and, of course, my snub-nosed derringer. I turned off into Crown, which was quiet until it met Oxford Street, where the road was crowded with cars. Where was everybody going? They were already in paradise.

It seemed as if I had only been tramping for a couple of minutes before I reached Hyde Park, where I stood under a tree and watched for possums, and followed an avenue of giant figs to another fountain, where I started to whistle. I couldn't remember when I had last whistled.

I was soon in the city, looking up at the statue's breasts on the roof of the QVB, trying to think if I had ever met a woman with tits like those. The closest I could think of was a hairdresser on the Shankill Road. I never got near her nipples, but Jed told me he nearly chewed them off. I had shared some good times with Jed over the years. He was not a bad bloke. He just couldn't keep his cock to himself. I would have liked to have a drink with Jed then and there, to tell him I forgave him and that we would always be brothers, but I suddenly felt tired, as if I had been walking for a week.

I decided to take a train from Town Hall back to the Cross, but the gates to the station were closed. I had never seen that before.

A bored security guard watched me push against a lock, then walked over to say, 'It's closed, mate.'

'Why's that?' I asked.

'Because it's four o'clock in the fucking morning,' he said.

SIX

[The West End Hotel, Balmain. 20-12-01. 2:07 pm.]
There were five Jewish children at Balmain Boys School in 1930. Now that Mad Dog McCoy is dead, I am the last of them. The others were Maurice 'the Little Fish' Bass, Big Stan Callahan and Ernie Katz. Only Katz was known by the name he was born with, and I wouldn't swear that was his family name, any more than I am convinced that your great-grandfather was a Klein.

In those days Australian children knew their own religion and the religion of all those around them. The Catholics and Protestants had few areas of agreement beyond that the Jews had murdered Jesus. I used to say that the Australians tried to get me to put my hand up for killing Christ, but I had four mates to swear I was somewhere else at the time, and it was the first in a series of goyisher verbals that have dogged me all my life. This was not much of a joke in the 1930s, when the crucifixion was seen as a recent local homicide that still needed to be cleared up. I myself was crucified once, the day before the Easter break. They bound my wrists and ankles to a fence, and splayed me like Christ on the cross, then jabbed a broomstick into my side to help me die more quickly. I remember all of them – the centurions, the legionnaires, the cackling faces in the crowd – with a hatred that burns just as strongly today, and a thirst for revenge that, I fear, has sometimes been channelled in less deserving directions – but, sadly, you can't kill maggots who are already dead.

The school was divided into gangs based on streets and lanes. The Jews were only loosely regarded as part of the neighbourhood. Although Moshe, Maurice and I lived around the south end of Mullens Street, we would only be called upon to stand alongside the other boys in the event of an invasion from, for example, Rozelle. Otherwise, we were fair game for everyone. As a result, we banded together. It was a measure of our status that each of the gangs had a headquarters in a milk bar, a bandstand or, at worst, an old shed. We Jews met in a stormwater drain. We called it 'our cave'.

The Australians ran all the rackets at school. They stood over the younger boys and sold shoplifted lollies and cigarettes. The leaders inherited their positions from their elder brothers, so felt no real drive to innovate. The Catholics, in particular, had organisation but no imagination.

I was not a natural leader. All that came later. Maurice was the toughest of us all, an amateur boxer with a love of the gouge and the stamp, the butt and the bite. Big Stan, a short, puny boy – here is an example of the ironic-style nickname we discussed earlier – was the comedian. Moshe was the brains, although he could be vicious when he had to be. Katz was the dreamer, the artist, the holy fool but, without Katz, we would never have had our racket. It started out as a thing between the five of us. We would ask Katz to draw a naked woman, and we'd take the picture into our cave to study. We called this 'art appreciation', because Katz often copied famous nudes from the Art Gallery of New South Wales, with the addition of dripping vaginas. We discovered by chance that there was a market for his work when Katz's schoolbag was upended by Frankie Latimer, a boy who called himself 'the Hammer of the Jews'. Latimer stole a reclining Venus along with Katz's pencils, lunch and the bag itself, and passed it around under the desks in the back row of geometry class. At the end of the day he sold it to Peter Curtis for a halfpenny. Maurice was able to repossess the drawing for Katz, but I realised we had a product that we could sell.

Katz spent the next weekend knocking out fifty loose sketches in the 'Dripping Vagina' series, and he numbered each one in the corner, which was a touch of class. I took them to school in a folio and sold them at four for a penny. My commission was a halfpenny, or fifty per cent, because I was taking the risk. Maurice was my muscle, with Moshe as back-up, and I paid them out of my share. Big Stan occasionally added humorous captions to the drawings, but I am not sure if he got a cut.

The pictures were popular, although the market was soon saturated and most boys' appetites sated. At this point, demand arose for more explicit material. The boys wanted to see Venus in flagrante. At first, it was difficult for Katz to get this right, since he was working from imagination. He made simple mistakes, such as portraying her in the missionary position, from which no genitals were visible. We had to consult older boys – Maurice had a cousin in the army – who suggested Katz concentrate instead on the doggy position and what now seems to be known as the 'cowgirl'. It was also Maurice's cousin who came up with the idea for our most successful line, the 'Fellatio Series', and eventually supplied Katz with a copy of an Indian sex manual for inspiration.

Katz's father ran a greengrocer's on Darling Street, and Katz's men had *putzes* like cucumbers, the women breasts like watermelons. Buttocks were a dimpled peach. His drawings swept the school. If you didn't own one, you were either a poofter or you had been robbed by Frankie Latimer.

But money – even lunch money – is power. We soon had several pounds in the kitty and were able to pay a young pro from Maurice's gym to break Frankie Latimer's jaw in two places. Thus ended the standover career of the Hammer of the Jews, at least until after the war, when he became a detective on the consorting squad.

In order to stay at the top of the market – and by this time we had attracted a small number of inferior competitors – we had to continually innovate. Although we persevered with the generic sketches for the younger boys, a boutique market opened up at the older end of our client base. They wanted the drawings to show women they knew – local identities such as Frida the fishmonger, and famous actresses such as Fay Wray from *King Kong* – on their knees in front of schoolboys in Balmain uniform. Because these were made to order, we were able to charge a premium price, and we soon captured the aspirational consumer as well as the broader demographic. Then Katz left for Fort Street selective school and we had nothing to sell.

So what did you do?

When I was fourteen, I met a black-haired girl called Rachel. She had a body like one of Katz's sketches – all grapefruit and melons – but a head like a carthorse. Rachel and I led similar lives. Her family was Russian, her father was a small player in the rag trade, she went to a school where most of the other students were Australian, and she suffered for it every day. We quickly became good friends. We both liked Duke Ellington, Louis Armstrong and Bessie Smith – all the great niggers. At first, of course, she would only let me kiss her, which was difficult enough because of the substantial obstacle presented by her nose. I, too, have a strong and prominent bridge, and we would often clash like fencers in moments of passion.

Our relationship progressed in the traditional way. I paid off her chaperone, and Rachel was soon rubbing my cock outside my trousers, then inside. It was not until I took her to see Jimmy Cagney in *The Mayor of Hell* at the Amusu Theatre that she finally played the masterstroke. I was shamefully grateful to Rachel and announced her officially as my girlfriend, so as to ensure regular – if overvigorous – hand relief. I look her home to meet my mother, who embraced her like a daughter, and my father, who eyed her like a whore.

Today I can admit without embarrassment that I found it arduous to coax Rachel to move beyond her pile-driver grip, but that difficult experience honed certain skills that would often come into play later on in my life. It was three months before she would offer me her mouth, and a further fortnight before she could overcome her gag reflex. This is social history, Anthony, do you realise that? This is the unwritten story of the sex life of my generation. Yes, many of the women were technically virgins when they married – although many were not – but every prissy little princess, gentile or Jew, had sucked more sperm than you have drunk warm, flat beer in your cold, hilly homeland. Your own grandmother, Anthony, would have swallowed the seed of soldiers and schoolboys with indiscriminate relish.

While Rachel and your grandmother were sucking, squeezing and blowing like four-stroke engines, I was trying to figure out how to bang them. I had my eye on the gold medal which, in those days, Anthony, was the *pirge* rather than the *tokhes*. To my generation – often known as 'the greatest generation' or 'the ANZAC generation' – entering by the back door was nothing more than a way to keep the hymen intact. To yours – often known as 'Generation X' or 'the slackers' – it seems like a natural ending to the evening, like brandy and cigars in more well-mannered times.

I met with Rachel's parents, who invited me to their home for the *Shabbos* meal. Her father was a dark-eyed, beaked, suspicious man. He questioned me like a cop about my plans for the future. I told him my mother hoped I would become a doctor or a lawyer, but I was thinking about entering my father's drapery business. I thought that would please him, since he was a draper too, but instead he dismissed me as a person of low ambition.

My father didn't like me to be away from the house on a Friday night, so he asked Rachel's parents to our home. Soon I had two angry, overbearing fathers and two fearful, credulous mothers, and a girlfriend who was more like a sister.

Occasionally I was able to entice Rachel into the bedroom I shared with Abie, but Abie would refuse to leave, and I made no further progress towards my goal. Finally I consulted Maurice's cousin, who advised me to tell Rachel that I loved her, or offer her some money, or both.

I opted for the cheaper option, but Rachel told me that I didn't love her and I was only trying to compromise her virtue. I said I didn't want to see her again, because she had questioned my integrity and shown me I was nothing more to her than a source of free cinema tickets and broken my heart.

I didn't hear from her for a week, then received a note via her erstwhile chaperone suggesting we meet at 'our cave'. So it was that Rachel and I exchanged our virginities in a stormwater drain, among newspapers, lollypop sticks and a large felt hat with a hole torn through the crown.

I had become a man – and before most of my friends, and even my brother Abie. As the only adult, I became the undisputed leader of our gang and began to feel it inappropriate that I should make my headquarters in a waste pipe, so I rented a shed in a builder's yard. We drew a curtain over the window and laid a mattress on the floor, and Rachel and I met there after school, while Moshe and the others waited outside, their ears pressed to the door. This satisfied them for a while, but – and this is always the case, Anthony – they soon wanted more. They asked me to leave the curtain open, just a couple of inches, so they could see inside. They took turns in watching Rachel and I together, and also sold time at the window to a few trusted classmates.

Big Stan's father had bought a camera, with which he was trying to start a business selling photographs of sailors and their sweethearts dressed as stars of stage and screen. The only costume he owned was a gorilla suit, and his idea was that young couples would play the roles of King Kong and Fay Wray, then take away a set of prints to keep alive the golden memory of that day. Unfortunately it's impossible to gauge the identity of a person in a gorilla suit, unless they take off the head, which, in turn, destroys the illusion of a giant ape. So the pictures tended to look as though the girl was being menaced by an ungainly and anonymous monkey, which was not an image many midshipmen wanted to carry across the oceans.

Since Big Stan's father's camera often lay idle in its case, he was able to borrow it one afternoon, press the lens against the window, and – without my knowledge – take a series of photographs of Rachel and I in performance. He developed these in his father's darkroom and brought them to show us all the next day. They were badly composed and unclear, but I could see the potential for a new product range.

The next time I enticed Rachel to the shed, I made sure we were correctly oriented in relation to the camera and hung a thinner curtain to give Big Stan a better light. Initially we repeated Katz's early sketching errors, and Big Stan photographed us lying on top of each other like two slices of bread. In the weeks that followed, Rachel and I had to learn a repertoire of positions before we had any marketable images.

As you might imagine, since my boys were virgins who spent their spare time watching me work my way through Katz's *Kama Sutra*, a certain amount of sexual tension developed among us. Moshe, in particular, believed himself to be in love with Rachel, and she with him. He came to think I was using his beloved badly and, rather than discuss the matter with me, the dog rolled over to the girl herself and told her what we had been doing.

It was the first time I was betrayed by a lieutenant, but far from the last. Wise men advise you to keep your friends close and your enemies closer, Anthony, but there is often no need to observe the second tenet as long as you stay true to the first. Your enemies and your friends are the same people on different days. You can't be deceived by somebody you don't trust.

Of course, Rachel was far from happy with me – in fact, she tried to kill me with a kitchen knife – and it became clear our relationship had run its course. She demanded the return of her pictures – although they had never belonged to her – or else, she said, her father would shoot me. I knew, however, that her father would shoot *her* first, so I felt safe enough to offer her a deal. She could have them 'back' if she first agreed to do with Moshe, Maurice and Big Stan what she had already done with me. If she refused, I would sell the photographs in our school playground and at her school gates, at three for a shilling. This may have been a hollow threat, since I was not certain I could achieve that price for an untested product, but I was, at last, able to sit as a spectator to Rachel's contortions while Maurice and Big Stan clumsily lightened their loads. At first, Moshe refused to take part, but when Rachel screamed and cried and swore at him, and said she hated us all, he realised it was the only chance he would ever get.

I saw the episode as a team-building exercise, and it cemented a new loyalty in the gang. Previously, you see, our only bond was in being sinned against – tortured and tormented by the Australian boys – now we had a link forged through sinning. It might surprise you to know, Anthony, that a union of the second kind is very much stronger than the first. If you want to own a man – or a woman – for life, all you need do is first corrupt them.

What happened to the photographs?
What do you think, Anthony? I sold them in our school playground and at her school gates. I made five guineas in a week. I became a rich man.
And Rachel?
She left the school, obviously. And the family left town. They came originally from Bathurst, and I think they may have gone back there. Although, of course, her father may have put her on a ship to England, where she met your grandfather in a wharfies' hotel in Wapping.
How do you think Rachel felt about what you did?
How would I know? Perhaps it taught her not to trust the wrong people. Perhaps it made her realise her true vocation was as a prostitute. I am responsible only for the deed itself, not for the way she chose to react to it.

And what does it matter in the long run? We all end up the same way, in a coffin covered in earth like Mad Dog McCoy, who loved her forever but fucked her only once, in a shed in a builder's yard, in front of his three closest friends.
[Ends.]

I didn't know what had persuaded Mendoza he could trust me with his autobiography, but I was desperate for the money. With Helen gone, I couldn't keep up the rent on our unit. I was thinking about moving to the backpackers' next door when the old man called.

He offered a fee of $60,000, which would be paid over one year in twelve $5000 instalments. Copyright would stay in his hands, and it would be up to him to decide if and when it would be published, but it would not go to the printers until after his death.

'It's not that I regret what I have done,' he said, 'but I'm not going to spend the last of my years back in the fucking Bay, either. As for my family, they will have to bear the shame of knowing where their money came from. My wife of forty-nine years has passed away, my daughter will not even take my name. My son is a clown. For a large part, I blame his mother. She never showed him how to be a man. You might argue this was my fault, because I was an absent father, but perhaps I was away so much because Deborah didn't know how to keep a man at home – although some would say I am too much man for any one woman.

'That,' said Mendoza, 'is for the reader to judge.'

Mendoza would allow me to record our interviews, but at the end of each sitting he would take away the tape and have it transcribed. I didn't know who produced the typescripts, but they did a beautiful job. On the afternoon when he told me about his schooldays at Balmain Boys, he gave me word-perfect minutes of our interview for the *Jewish Times*, right up to the point where I ate the tape. Mendoza had taped it himself, through a microphone under his desk, just as he recorded all his meetings, just as he photographed everything.

A couple of days after each sitting, Lazarus would come to my apartment with a computer disk containing the text, and a print-out of everything that had been said. Mendoza checked the pages before they went to me but, as far as I could tell, he changed nothing beyond a few spellings, and occasionally deleting the word 'cunt' when he'd used it to describe, for example, a crim, a pimp and a judge in the same sentence. He usually replaced it with 'dog'.

He liked to give the interviews in the places he talked about on the tape. We held the first in a private room in a Balmain pub that Mendoza had taken over in 1946, although he'd transferred the licence to one of his brothers when he'd begun buying up hotels all around Sydney. When it was over, Lazarus drove us back to the Cross. I walked up to the Hamilton Private Hotel, to see if I could catch Leah before the end of her shift.

The bar was empty. I asked the barman if Leah was working tonight. He laughed. 'You won't see her in here again, mate,' he said. 'Turns out she was only fifteen.'

SEVEN

[The West End Hotel, Balmain. 10-01-02. 1:55 pm.]
I know it's fashionable to blame your parents for everything that has happened to you, but I had a good upbringing and I can't complain about anything. My father was born in Tetiev, which is now a part of the Ukraine. He came to Australia with my mother in 1919, after the pogrom in which the Jews of Tetiev were robbed, tortured, raped and murdered by drunken Russian mobs. You know something? I piss on their Ukraine. I shit in their Black Sea. They hunted Jews for sport. While the Russians burned my father's house, stripped him naked and beat him in the street – all the time chanting, 'Death to the Yids!' – he didn't raise a hand against the dogs for fear that they would kill him. The next morning, with the smoke still rising from the ashes of their home, he and my mother gathered my brothers Saul and Abie in their arms and fled that dog-shit country for England. Upon their arrival in Liverpool, they boarded a boat bound for Australia, which they believed to be one of the forty-eight states of the USA. In Tetiev my father was a poor pedlar. In Sydney he became a draper and mercer. You don't hear those words often

now. They live on in the surnames of old rag-trade families, but not among the *Yidden*. He bought and sold cloth to make clothes. It earned him a living – in the war, it earned him a good living – but never a fortune. He was greedy but not ambitious. He wanted everything but he wouldn't do what had to be done to get it.

I remember my father as a tall man, but stooped, as if he were afraid to pull himself up to his full height in case it brought him undue attention. He had a small amount of hair. His hands were wide and thickly veined. His eyes, to a child, always looked surprised.

My mother haunts my memory as a short, broad woman who stood like a gum tree. In her youth, I am told, she was a beauty, and my father charmed her with his prowess as a wrestler, but my mother's good looks and my father's fighting spirit both fled them after the Tetiev pogrom. Like most Jewish boys, I loved my mother deeply, but she could be a cold and distant woman, in the way of her generation. My parents spoke Yiddish in the home, and I grew up understanding the language, but I never had much need to use it until I was banged up in a police cell with Mad Dog McCoy and Big Stan Callahan. All the imbecile goys thought they could fool the jacks with their boys'-home backslang, but we three Yids had a code nobody but our shyster lawyers could break. My father learned English quickly, but always spoke with the accent of Kiev. My mother never embraced new words and new ways and, in her mind, she stayed in Tetiev until she died.

Our family lived in three rooms above my father's shop in Mullens Street. My two sisters, Dora and Hannah, slept together, and I shared a bed with my older brothers, Saul – until he left – and Abraham. I remember little about those days, except for rolling in the night into puddles of Abie's cold piss, and waking in the darkness to see my father pacing the yard, cracking his knuckles, kicking at dirt, waiting for the Cossacks to come.

My brother Saul was like my father, in both appearance and temperament. He was big but a coward, and his hair was already thinning in his teens. Australian boys loved to flog Saul because, despite his size, he didn't fight back. When Saul asked for help, my father told him to stop whatever he was doing to aggravate the bullies. There was no point in retaliation, he said. Saul was the only Jew in his year, and what could one Jew do against black hundreds? One afternoon, Saul was hit in the face with a brick, and finally my father took him into the yard with a kit bag filled with rags and trained him to box and wrestle. He taught Abie too. Abie was smaller than Saul – only a little taller than me – but he was born knowing how to look after himself.

My father never hit Abie or Saul, except when he was showing them how to fight, but he beat me with his hands, with a stick, with a strap and with a poker. He hit me around the legs and the shoulders, and later in the face and head. He said I was wild and rude to my mother and I would surely end up in jail. I'll never forget the stupid smirk on his face when the beak suggested he might send me to Long Bay. It was my father's dream come true, the only accurate prediction he'd ever made.

My mother often stepped in to save me from my father's anger, although she would also sometimes stoke his rage. It took me a long time to understand this, Anthony. It was the conundrum of my childhood.

Since I was flogged at home by adults, it was not particularly onerous to be flogged at school by children. I could hold my own in a one on one, and I could even take on two boys my own size, but they came at the Jews in gangs. I was not easily scared, but it's a frightening thing to fall to the ground in the centre of a scrum of boys who are trying to kick you in the teeth or the eyes or the balls.

The day the Australians crucified me, the legionnaires cracked two of my ribs with their broom handle. I told my father what had happened, and he agreed to teach me his secrets.

We trained together three afternoons a week. My father showed me chokes and holds and locks and throws; left hooks, uppercuts and overhand rights. Although he could box, he preferred to wrestle. It suited his build and his temperament. He knew he could use his weight to bully most men to the ground. We grappled on the grass. He smothered me with his smell: sweat and garlic and scraps of cooked meat trapped between his teeth. Time and again he overpowered me. He crushed me when he pinned me, held me so tightly I almost feared he would force himself inside me. Twice, he choked me unconscious, and he laughed when I came back twitching and throwing my arms into the air. My father took delight in hurting and humiliating me, but those afternoons in the yard were among the happiest of my childhood. He was paying me attention.

When my father had taught me as much as he could, he sent me to the Police Boys Club where Maurice boxed. I practised for three months, then the trainer put me in the ring with a much smaller boy, and the fucking midget knocked out my front tooth. By the time I was fourteen I didn't fear a blue, but I didn't look for them either. My friends were the same. Only Maurice swaggered like a goy.

My father often quoted the Torah, although he only attended synagogue for bar mitzvahs and weddings. As you may be aware, Anthony, the Lord handed down ten commandments, and my father abided by several of these, at least in part. For example, God mandated that a man should not covet his neighbour's wife, nor his donkey. My father kept strictly to the latter stipulation, and any man's mule was safe in his company. Nor did my father ever make idols and bow down to them, or take God's name in vain. But his preferred commandment was 'remember the Sabbath and keep it holy', because it's among the easiest of the laws to keep, and because he was lazy. Every Friday night we ate together as a family. The first person to be excluded from our *Shabbos* dinners was Saul, who went against my father's will and married a Catholic, a daughter of the Inquisition. Ironically, she was to prove Saul's thumbscrew and torment, an iron maiden who spiked his heart, but she was the first girl who would let him into her pants, so his cock said 'I do' on behalf of his blue balls. My father prayed the Kaddish for his firstborn son and behaved as if he were dead. My mother kept in touch with Saul in secret, and visited the grandchildren my father denied.

My mother hoped I would become a doctor or a dentist or, at the very least, a veterinary surgeon. My father was not interested in my progress at school. He said I hadn't inherited his brains, and that was that. He was satisfied when I left school at fifteen to join him and Abie in the family business that Saul had abandoned.

What was the name of your father's shop?

Rosenblatt's. My family's name was Rosenblatt.

Why did you change it?

Yiddisher boxers often fought under ring names so as not to shame their families.

But you never fought.

In the ring? No. But nonetheless I brought shame to my family. Moshe, Maurice and Big Stan all left school when I did. The gang stayed together and we found different ways to make money. We chose our new names one night at the Police Boys Club. Maurice, of course, already had a nom de guerre. His father's was Baser, so he called himself Bass, after Benny Bass, the great Yiddisher fighter who won the world featherweight championship in 1927. For some reason Maurice, who fought as a middleweight, also adopted Bass's nickname, 'the Little Fish', which I always thought insufficiently intimidating for a fighter.

Following Maurice's lead, Moshe, who was born Maizel, named himself McCoy, after Al McCoy, who served as world middleweight champion from 1914 to 1917. 'Mad Dog' came later and was, I think, my own addition.

This raises two points worth mentioning: Al McCoy himself was born Alexander Rudolph, and was Jewish. Maizel is the German word for 'mule' and was among the many pejorative surnames names forced on Jewish people by the Austrian Empire. Others included Rindskopf, which means 'cow's head'; Nachtkafter, which means 'night beetle'; and Lumpe, which means 'crook', and also Spiegeleier. My intention here is to illustrate the fact that Jewish surnames are fluid and non-traditional. We can choose to name ourselves after beasts and beetles, or heroes and kings. Big Stan opted for Callahan, after Mushy Callahan, the first champion in the light-welterweight division, who was born Vincent Morris Scheer. I borrowed the name of the greatest Jewish fighter of them all, Daniel Mendoza, the bare-knuckle champion of England and the father of scientific boxing.

At first we only used our ring names among ourselves but, in time, other people began to call us Mendoza, McCoy, Callahan and Bass. We sounded like a law firm, which, in a way, we were.

You asked me why I changed my name, Anthony. I ask you why you keep yours.

You said you brought shame on your family.

In their eyes, yes. Although the disgrace was nothing compared with Saul's marrying out. In 1940, when I was still working for my father, Mad Dog began trading in car radios, which were then a new product that sold for about twenty pounds. He acquired the radios from rich Jews with big houses and unlocked motor cars. It's a source of fascination and sadness to me that people only rob their own kind. Look at the Italians: the Mafia's a protection racket run against other Sicilians. Look at the wogs:

whenever there's a shooting war in south-west Sydney, the Lebs neck the Lebs, the Assyrians knock other Assyrians. Even squareheads keep it in the family. If the wife has her skull caved in, the husband did it. If the kids are drowned, it was the father. If I am betrayed, it's by my fucking lieutenant. Do you see what I mean?

Unfortunately, many of the wealthier members of the Jewish community were connected with the legal profession and able to make enquiries that led them back to a humble draper's in Balmain, from which I was retailing secondhand car radios at ten pounds a pop. Mad Dog was arrested, claimed never to have seen a car, a radio or his own dear mother, and ended up doing three months in Pentridge – he was sent there because he lied to the jacks that his family, the fictitious Yiddisher McCoys, lived in Melbourne. I copped it sweet, and before sentencing, the beak suggested that I might better myself by enlisting in the Citizens' Military Force. I told him I had already been called up and was ready to report to Victoria Barracks. He gave me six months, all suspended – much to my father's disappointment – and put me on a two-year bond, since it was my first offence.

Truth be told, however, it was only my first offence as Jake Mendoza. As Jacob Rosenblatt, I had already been fined once for handling stolen goods.

I earned a prison sentence as Mendoza and I joined the army as Mendoza. As a man, I have always been Mendoza.

I had other reasons for wanting to shed my name. I haven't said much about my mother. You don't seem particularly interested in women, Anthony. Nor they in you, from what I observe. I, of course, have had the opposite experience. I think perhaps I love women so much because they remind me of my mother, who was both giving and forgiving. My father, on the other hand, was a taker and a curser. He was never faithful. I knew that even as a child, when I watched him flirt with wharfies' daughters over cotton sheets. He didn't come into his own until the war, when he was able to take advantage of the black market and trade rare silks and stockings for God knows what, but he practised his skills in the depression years.

I remember one day when I was a child, an angry husband came into the shop and tried to hit my father, and I was excited because I knew my father could fight, and I looked forward to seeing the wharfie laid out on the pavement. But my father *let* him punch him. He just stood there and took it: once, twice, three times, while the man yelled and swore and called my *bobe* a whore. Unable to raise a reaction, he kicked in the shop window and left. My father said he hoped I had learned a lesson. If he had fought back, he said, the man would have returned with his mates and burned down the shop, abused my mother, speared me on a bayonet, and taken everything.

In all my life, through all the indignities my father suffered, and they were many, I never knew him hit anyone but me. In summary, he was a bully, a coward, a bludger, a weasel, a black marketeer and a thief. This was the example I had when I was growing up, the father held up to me by my mother as a 'good man'. Children, like chimps, learn by imitation. I like to think of myself as a self-made man, but the raw materials came from elsewhere. Every low thing I have done, I saw my father do first. So, when you think about it, I certainly wouldn't have turned out the way I did if he hadn't been such a low, lying dog.

[Ends.]

EIGHT

[The Bellisimo Restaurant, 32 Orwell Street, Potts Point. 01-02-02. 2:12 pm.]

What was wrong with that guy? It looked like somebody'd tried to chew his nose off.

There's a lesson for you, Anthony. He shouldn't poke it where it doesn't belong.

There's blood all over this table.

Observation is your strong suit, only analysis lets you down. Natural Science, please wipe the table clean. Your leftovers are offending our colleague.

What's *he* doing here?

He's a temp from the agency. I've given Lazarus the day off.

Agency?

I'm joking, Anthony. Actually, you and Natural Science have a lot in common: you've got no sense of humour and you'll eat whatever I tell you. You can leave now, Natural. Go and sit outside the door and bark at everything that moves.

Now, where was I?

You were going to set the record straight about the war.

I don't want to say a lot about my service. Much of what we did in Liverpool is still classified.

I thought you were a clerk in the medical corps.

That is what the records show.

Are you saying you weren't?

I am saying records – especially old records – are not always an accurate reflection of events. Take it from me, Anthony: I invented double bookkeeping. I am saying the war in the Pacific was not fought only on the Kokoda Track.

How close did Japanese forces come to Liverpool?

Don't fuck with me, Anthony. Don't bait a baiter, or you'll end up as shark bait.

How long were you in the army?

Officially? I was called up in 1940, but I feared my father would be unable to operate his drapery business without me, particularly after Saul ran off with the *shiksa*. My initial application for an exemption from service has, from time to time, been used against me by my enemies, but you must remember that an army needs drapers as much as it needs armourers. You can't send soldiers off to battle in bowling shirts, Anthony. War is not a game of fucking skittles.

As far as I am concerned, I was an active part of the war from the day I was summoned to Victoria Barracks in 1940 until I was discharged in 1944, there being 'no suitable vacancy' in which my services could be employed.

But how long did you actually serve?

Are you listening to me, Anthony? I served the entire length of the war, from 1940 to 1944 – first as a draper, then as a citizen soldier and then, when the army freed me from my patriotic obligations, I enlisted, entirely of my own free will, for six months in the merchant navy.

So how much of the war did you spend as a soldier?

You now seem obsessed with soldiers and armies, Anthony.

I wonder why that is. Perhaps it's because you have never heard the bugle call yourself and proudly marched to war wearing a uniform of cloth supplied by drapers, and kissed the tears from the eyes of your sweetheart as she watched you board the train.

The train to Liverpool?

Yes, Anthony. The train to fucking Liverpool. I was called up in 1942 and made a corporal in 1943. Unfortunately my fitness was downgraded from 'A' to 'B', possibly as a result of anti-Semitism, so I was prevented from serving my country overseas, and discharged in 1944. I returned to Sydney a changed man.

In what ways had you changed?

The army gave me discipline. I can always tell if a man has been in uniform, Anthony. It lends him a dignity that stays with him throughout his life. The army instilled in me the value of regular physical exercise. It taught me how to use a gun. I have kept my old service revolver to this day, both for sentimental and other reasons.

When I left the army I could not mix with men who hadn't served. They didn't understand the mindset of a soldier. I missed the camaraderie and the danger, so in 1944 I signed on with the merchant navy, ferrying troops to Milne Bay, where a famous battle had been fought against the Japanese only two years previously.

It was difficult, hazardous work. The Coral Sea was rife with Japanese subs, and shipping was regularly straffed by the Imperial Air Force. Although I worked mainly on the clerical side, I risked my life on countless occasions, simply by stepping on deck of the unpromisingly named SS *Charon*, which had already played an important part in Australian history, having been the probable source of a famous outbreak of cattle plague in 1923.

Imagine my surprise when who should I meet on board ship but my old friend Mad Dog McCoy, who I hadn't seen since one week earlier in Woolloomooloo and who had recently got over his loss of Rachel, only ten fucking years previously. McCoy had served in the merchant navy throughout the war and survived countless encounters with dangerous women in the great ports of South-East Asia. By 1944 he ran all the rackets on the *Charon*, including spirits, stockings and cigarettes, and also took a cut out of introducing new sailors to allegedly clean girls in dockside cat houses where they performed every unlikely trick you'll ever see in Patpong, and a good many more besides. The beauty of McCoy's scheme was he earned kickbacks from both sides – the brothel keepers as well as the sailors. In fact, he operated in much the same manner as the financial-planning industry today.

For a brief and slightly humiliating period I worked as McCoy's lieutenant, but that finished when the war ended in July 1944.

The war ended in 1945.

Some say that, yes. Some say it never ended, that we are still feeling its reverberations today, in our society, in our economy and in the psychology of veterans. But my war ended in July 1944, as did McCoy's. We signed off the *Charon* and returned to civvy street or, more accurately, Victoria Street. We took two rooms in a private hotel in the Cross and chased recently widowed skirt while we planned our next move.

It was during this time that I was lucky enough to bump into Phil Jeffs, on one of his infrequent visits to Sydney to set up a baccarat school with the entrepreneur Dick Reilly. Before Jake Mendoza, in the days of the razor gangs, Phil Jeffs ruled East Sydney, but by wartime he was semiretired and living in Ettalong, with a library full of philosophy books and a bed full of whores. Jeffs was a nightclub owner and man about town who invented many of the business ideas I later perfected, including the provision of unsolicited souvenir photography of a hostess and her customer.

Jeffs was a generous man with everything but money. Before he left the Cross he gave me some sound advice: get out of Darlinghurst Road until the troops come home, then come back shooting.

As a digression, Anthony, one pertinent point about Jeffs was his nickname: 'Phil the Jew'. Bearing in mind that we occupied similar positions in different generations, it might be thought that I would become known as 'Jacob the Jew', especially since Jeffs's contemporaries, such as the drug dealer Harry 'Jewey' Newman, and the Riley Street Gang leader Samuel 'Jewey' Freeman, were recognised largely by their religion. I like to think that I was instead described as the 'King of the Cross' because my success transcended ethnicity and, as such, could be held as an inspiration to second-generation migrants of every race, colour and creed (apart from Malts, wops and the fucking Lebanese). There is also, I suppose, the fact that 'King of the Jews' was a title already claimed by a certain fictitious Goy.

So what did you do?

McCoy and I heeded Jeffs's advice and caught the country train to Goulburn, where McCoy's mother, a deafening woman but an unlikely landlady, had inherited a pub from her brother, Sam Moses, who had died fighting at Tobruk.

It may surprise you, Anthony, to learn that the New South Wales city of Goulburn, home to the locally famous Big Merino, was once the site of a large and prosperous Jewish community, but that is because you are ignorant in matters of history, as in so much else. In Goulburn in the mid-nineteenth century, six of the eight hotels were run by Jews, including the Moses family's Railway Inn. A century later, the *shul* lay in ruins and McCoy's mother was the last of the Yiddisher hoteliers.

She needed a man to run the pub, and her own husband barely fitted that description, even when he was alive, so she asked McCoy if he would take over the licence.

McCoy was willing but not able, because of the small matter of sixty bottles of black-market whisky with which he was busted on the *Charon* in 1943, leading to a three-month suspension from the merchant navy and a lifetime ban from holding a liquor licence.

Luckily I was able to step in and offer my services, with McCoy as a silent partner. And what a fucking eye-opener that pub was for me, Anthony. If you scoff at the idea that servicemen faced dangers in Liverpool, you should have been in fucking Goulburn in 1945. Every bar was a dead-set, bare-knuckles-and-boots bloodhouse. McCoy and I got in more blues in the Railway Inn than in the rest of our fucking lives.

When the war officially ended there were imbeciles out in the streets singing 'Pack Up Your Troubles' and 'Roll Out the Barrel'. They should have been singing 'Pack Up Your Barrel' and 'Roll Out the Trouble', because these were the days of the six o'clock swill, when a man only had a couple of hours' drinking to fortify himself for an evening of country cooking and marital sex. Most working squareheads chose to cram a whole night on the piss into the time it took to watch a movie, and tended to get toey when they were chucked out. This was not necessarily the freedom they had fought for in El Alamein and Tobruk.

When Bass was finally demobbed – he'd been all over the world with the AIF in the Silent Seventh – we called him up to Goulburn to help out. The Little Fish didn't stand for any shit, I can tell you. Fuck me, he was a danger to that town. He cleaned up the pub in a couple of months, put two shearers and three jacks in hospital, and we had to smuggle him back to Sydney in the middle of the night before the locals lynched him like a nigger.

After that I ruled the pub by diplomacy and charm. The first of my diplomatic initiatives was to cease to recognise six o'clock closing, a largely legalistic notion that Mrs Maizel had taken too literally. In deference to the wishes of the remaining members of the local constabulary, I closed the front bar, but kept the back bar open all night to anybody – cockies and jacks alike – who tapped on the window and gave the password.

What was the password?

Whatever they said when they tapped on the window.

Did you have the cops on side?

Obviously a businessman can't just flout the law and expect to get away scot-free. I paid a weekly consideration to the sergeant and let his men drink on the house. This was a custom I continued throughout my long career in the hospitality industry, and one which has always served me well, along with the practice of only hiring barmaids with big tits.

At the Railway Inn I also learned the importance of an alternative supply chain. The beer we got from the brewery was enough to last until six o'clock on a good night. After six I sold long necks I bought from the pub in Bengonia, which had more beer than drinkers. The Bengonia beer cost a few cents extra and, since I was a secondary customer, sales were recorded in a second set of books.

I liked running a pub. It suited me. I'm a convivial man. I enjoy the company of good, honest country folk. But I was never going to stay in a retarded mong-pen of six-fingered sister-fucking imbeciles like Goulburn for long. I left McCoy in charge and came back to Sydney, where I bought the licence to the West End, just across the road from my father's old shop – although by this time my father's business had moved to the city, and his home to Bondi.

In the 1940s it was illegal to own more than one liquor licence. Don't ask me why. I don't make the laws, I just break them. That was a joke, Anthony. Smile. As St Augustine said, 'An unjust law is no law at all.' As a strict follower of the Augustinian school, I refused to recognise both the draconian regulation that denied a working man a beer after 6 pm, and the unreasonable prohibition that prevented a businessman from expanding his operations. I came to control several more hotels, the management of which I entrusted to Abie, my sister Dora, Big Stan, and certain people of whom nobody can speak ill, including one who was dead at the time he took over the Victoria Hotel in North Sydney.

In 1947 I bought the Patton in Kings Cross, with McCoy and Big Stan's father as my partners. This was the best decision I ever made, in business or in life. Without the Patton, Jake Mendoza would never have been made King of the Cross. Have you ever loved a place, Anthony? Not a woman or a girl, but a building or a room? I loved the Patton. It was founded by a draper and mercer, Bernie Roth, at the start of the war, and it quickly became the spot the American officers went to meet a good standard of local woman (who, nevertheless, could be bought with a box of chocolates and a pair of nylons). The local boys, in their Dedman victory suits, had no chance against flash rats with sleeve buttons, trouser cuffs and exotic venereal diseases. As a club that catered to Yanks, the Patton needed to show Hollywood class. Even the waiters cleaned their fingernails. Australia had never seen anywhere like the Patton. Until then, the only nightclubs in Sydney were places like Romano's in Castlereagh where, on a good night, Azzalin the fucking Dazzalin might turn up and sing in Italian. That was never going to cut it with the Yanks, whose brothers and cousins – led by the great General Patton himself – were dying in Sicily to save the whole of Europe from turning into some ridiculous fucking opera set and in whose own country the resident wops were locked up in internment camps. So the GIs made a forward base in the Patton instead.

Unfortunately once the war ended and the Yanks went home – leaving the good standard of women with fraudulent forwarding addresses and bawling, big-mouthed babies – the Patton went to shit. By the time I took it over, the place was rotten with Malts.

Have you ever heard of Malta, Anthony? Imagine the Mediterranean is the belly of Europe, and the Gulf of Gibraltar is its sphincter: Malta is two turds waiting to be passed through the bowel and into the bowl. It's a great historical irony that the Knights of Malta once fought for control of Jerusalem, but if they went to war against Israel today, Valetta would be wiped off the map in the time it takes to eat a fucking pastizz. And, as it would've been in the Mediterranean, so it was in the Cross.

The first thing I did was get the Little Fish to belt the daylights out of a couple of Maltese hoons who had made the club their base, and this started a monumental fucking blue that ended up dragging on for ten years. He flogged a bloke who turned out to be the cousin of someone's grandfather in Gozo, and the hoon lost an eye. Have you ever come across Gozo, Anthony? It's an island shaped like a cunt.

The war took something away from the Little Fish, but it gave him something too. After the war, the Little Fish was ready to die, he was just looking for somebody to kill him. So nothing could scare him. He was more afraid of living with what he'd seen than getting his throat cut by the family of some Maltese Moshe Dayan, so he became unstoppable, like a boulder rolling down a mountain, gathering pace until it crashed. If you'd given me four Jews like the Little Fish, I wouldn't just have been the King of the Cross, Anthony, I would've been the King of the Southern Cross. I would've run this fucking country, and we wouldn't have half the problems we have today with the wogs, because we would have massacred their fucking grandfathers.

Despite the fact that we had the most dangerous maniac in Darlinghurst on our side, I heard around the traps that the Malts and the Mafia were laughing at us. 'The Jews have a hard man called "the Little Fish",' they said, and made it sound like he'd named himself after the clitoris. I took Bass aside to see if he would alter his nickname to something more daunting, but still in the spirit of his original idea. I tried to interest him in 'the Shark', for instance, or even 'the Fighting Fish', because they are tough little buggers, but Bass was determined to stay true to the memory of his hero.

That was the Little Fish for you, and if the biggest problem I'd ever had with an associate was their name, I'd be a happy old man. This business attracts the wrong types, Anthony. It's a magnet for the disloyal, the erratic and the unreliable. In those days, the Little Fish would never let you down. He wouldn't know how to let you down. He was a mensch.

But I know what you're thinking now, Anthony: where was Mendoza greasing his shlong in those days? Surely he had a feast of opportunities as a pioneering nightclub owner and close friend and confidant to the rising stars of cabaret? And, for once in your life, you would be right (I am reminded of the old joke about the stopped clock). These were great days, but also wonderful nights. I was a beneficiary both of my finely honed hiring practices, and what were commonly described as my 'movie-star good looks'. If you look at a picture of me in the 1940s you will see a fit man –

But classed 'B' by the army.

Who can account for the quirks of the anti-Semitic mind, Anthony?

As I was saying, you would see a fit man, with broad shoulders and a square jaw, and eyes that a woman could drown in. That face would not have looked out of place on a billboard outside a cinema, or a promotional still for a romantic drama. I had many admirers, Anthony. A gentleman says no more than that. Although I will add that if I had a dollar for every time I had my cock sucked by a showgirl in the immediate postwar years,

I would be able to buy the Patton again, three times over. I tell you this purely for the sake of historical accuracy.

As well as my looks and my profession, I had other factors on my side. Many men of my generation had fallen in the war, leaving many women lonely and unfulfilled. I saw it as my duty to my dead comrades to look after the girls they left behind, which is why I was so famously generous to my mistresses. They deserved to be the brides of heroes, Anthony. The least I could give them was a rented unit in Potts Point and a reasonable weekly allowance for perfume and clothes.

Of course, among all my women there was one who stood out from the rest, because: (a) she wouldn't blow me; and (b) she had a brain for business. This woman was Divora Cohen, soon to become Deborah Mendoza, a Dutch beautician I had first met, ludicrously enough, in Goulburn.

I was in love with her, and she with me. 'What is love?' you may ask, Anthony – and I, of all men, should be able to tell you. But I find I can't put into the words the feelings I had for Deborah. She was never a stranger to me. From the moment we started talking it was as if I had known her all my life. I even knew she wouldn't blow me. She was well groomed – as you might expect from a woman in her profession – and glamorous, with a kiss curl and an inviting smile. She loved to come with me to the Patton, to mingle with the social set and have her picture in the magazines.

At the Patton, we were multicultural before the word even existed. I had all the races in there, even niggers. We had girls dancing the cancan. We had the stars of tomorrow performing songs and dances from the hit musicals of the day. I made it my policy to hire ex-servicemen wherever possible. I had Katz, who spent much of the war in a Japanese POW camp, doing our sign-writing and stage design. Carpentry was coordinated by Jimmy Reubens, a cabinet maker who had worked with Katz on the Burma Railway. Many of the waiters were former merchant seamen.

My choreographer at the Patton was Ira Brodsky, a true professional and an original thinker in an industry dominated by imitators. We were sitting up in bed one evening, discussing the finer points of cabaret, when she asked me, 'Jacob, why do men enjoy watching our shows?'

'My interest is purely professional,' I assured her, 'but some of the paying customers may be trying to imagine the dancing girls' breasts jiggling around in their bras.'

'So why don't they take off their bras?' she said.

That is when I knew I loved Ira too.

At the time it was illegal for women to appear topless on stage, unless they were standing still. (Lord knows what St Augustine would have made of that, although I doubt if the bishop was ever seen near a topless dancing establishment – at least not in his home town.) Even if the performers remained motionless, they had to wear tassels over their nipples, which no doubt further contributed to the disappointment and confusion of young men when they discovered that their bride – or, in your mother's case, their recent acquaintance – couldn't be made to double as a windmill or a fan.

I remembered something McCoy had told me about a bordello in the mysterious East where one of the girls was known as 'the Filipina Picasso' because of her ability to paint pictures with her nipples – which, I have to say, is how Picasso's paintings always looked to me anyway. Who can even guess how the Filipina came to discover her talent? I asked her once how she did it – in that same bed in the same room above the Patton – but she was unable to give a coherent reply. She appeared to have unnaturally close control of the various smaller muscles that underpin the pectorals.

I sent McCoy back to the East to track her down. For one

year I had a handful of topless and tasselled models standing like statues on the stage, while fully dressed chorus girls danced around them. Then McCoy arrived with Miss Paintbrush Breasts, and she changed the face of entertainment in the Cross. She also changed McCoy, who'd had to marry her to get her out of the country, and convert to Catholicism to marry her. I remember him at the dockside, full of pride, in his double-breasted suit and hula-girl tie, with his bride of Christ on his arm, beaming like a fucking imbecile. He really believed the whore was his wife, a delusion I was forced to dispel by paying her to fuck me, Big Stan and the Little Fish all on the same night. McCoy, understandably, regarded this as grounds for divorce. He re-embraced the faith of his fathers, but nonetheless established the habit of taking brides from the Philippines, which stayed with him all his life.

Where was I? Ah yes, the Patton. We rechristened the Filipina Picasso's act 'Tina's Talking Tits', and the crowd rushed our doors like we were giving away money, rather than the reverse. Filipina Tina used to take to the stage, and her hands and feet would comply strictly with the letter of the law, while her breasts and nipples would take off on fanciful flights of their own.

Her act was particularly popular with the local jacks, whose task it was to monitor the degree of toplessness practised by dancers. Augustinians to a man, the jacks privately railed against the unjust laws regulating stripping and liquor sales, although truth be told, they made more fucking money out of them than even I did.

The Patton didn't serve last drinks at six o'clock – it was a nightclub, for Christ's sake – but I had to pay every jack from Liverpool Street to Cowper Wharf Road to turn a blind eye. I got my late-night liquor allowance from an alternative supply chain made up of our city pubs and a bottle shop on Crown Street that was registered to McCoy's mother.

If customers ordered their drinks before six, the waiters were legally permitted to serve them all night, and 'all night' meant all night at the Patton. People from every level of Sydney society came to eat, drink and be entertained there. I had police chiefs and politicians, actors and boxers, cocksmen and queers. It was where I first got to know men of influence, and came to understand that even the richest and most powerful want the same thing as the lowliest unwashed garbo: half an hour with a girl – or a boy – who moans and squirms and swallows. At first, I let the big jacks and judges fuck the showgirls, but the dancers arced up, so I brought the professionals in.

[Ends.]

NINE

The man sitting next to me smelled of horse piss and dog sweat. As he turned the pages of the *Sydney Morning Herald* he made a sad hissing noise, as if everything that happened in the city made him despair. A red-haired librarian brought me a pile of books from the local studies shelves, including a biography of Jake Mendoza, written by Laurie Block, a crime writer on the *Daily Telegraph*. I had read it before I interviewed Mendoza for the *Jewish Times*, but I hadn't paid much attention to the earliest chapters. I went through them again, to see if there was anything Mendoza had told me that I could check against the record.

Block confirmed his father had been a draper and mercer, based on an interview he had given to *People* magazine in the 1950s, but his story didn't properly begin until the war years, when Block confused two details and had Mendoza serving in the army in New Guinea.

McCoy and the Little Fish were mentioned, but only by their assumed names. Block had Mendoza meeting McCoy (described as 'of Celtic descent') in the merchant navy, and the

Little Fish ('a former boxer with an undistinguished record') at the war's end.

I couldn't tell if Mendoza was giving me an untold true story or inventing a new and complicated lie. I could confirm only small facts. There was a pogrom in Tetiev in 1919. Rosenblatt was a Tetiev name. There was a steamer called the SS *Charon*, she did go to Milne Bay in 1944 and she had transported infected livestock in 1923. A man named Solomon Moses had owned a pub in Goulburn in 1841.

It was exciting to be on the edge of a story like this. It made my knees jump around under the table. I smiled and hummed and kissed my teeth as I checked off facts and cross-referenced dates. The whistling man moved away from me, thinking I might be a lunatic. Coming to Australia had been a good idea after all. No, it had been a fantastic idea. Fuck Helen. Fuck Jed too, and fuck the *Australian Jewish Times* – and the *Catholic Weekly*, for that matter.

Outside the sun was gleaming, the buskers were singing, the junkies were screaming. I knew it was going to be a great day. I smiled at the tall white waitress at La Fontaine and a huge black customer smiled back: Mendoza's substitute bodyguard, Natural Science, who was drinking an orange juice with a tower of ice. He waved me over and shook my hand.

'Make sure Mendoza pays you upfront,' he said. 'He's tighter than a twelve-year-old.'

Natural Science's voice was deep and warm, and his accent reminded me of home. He wore gold signet rings, a good tooth and a gold chain. He said why didn't I sit down. Mendoza's boys could drink on the boss's tab at La Fontaine, and their custom protected the cafe from all the mysterious things that might otherwise happen to a tourist restaurant, such as a spate of camera thefts, a flood or a fire.

'But the old man ain't got nothing like the power he used to have,' said Natural Science.

'Back in the day, you could warn people off just by using his name. Now people are scared even to say the names of the Lebs who run the place.'

He called for another orange juice, and a coffee for me.

Natural Science was a freelance and he assumed I was hired muscle like him. He worked for Mendoza or the Lebs, depending on who needed him.

'They call it "crossing the Golan Heights",' he said, 'but I ain't interested in politics.' He rubbed his black knuckles. 'I'm just fists and feet.'

'And teeth,' I said.

'I don't want you to get the wrong impression,' he said. 'I ain't a biter. I mean, I will bite, obviously, but I ain't Mike Tyson. You don't have to count your ears when you leave the ring with me. I don't take souvenirs.' The way he said the word, it sounded like 'southern ears', and made me worry about mine.

He drank his second orange juice in a single gulp. His Adam's apple bobbed like a cue ball.

Natural Science said he grew up in Fleet, a few miles from Aldershot. He used to come into town on Saturday afternoons for the football, back when the Shots were still in the fourth division, before we got kicked into the minor leagues for being shit and broke.

'Jesus,' I said, 'I know who you are.'

For a second I had a memory of him at the football, the Black Prince of the East Bank, storming the Cardiff City Soul Crew, waving a builder's shovel over his head like a kung-fu monk.

'How the fuck did you get out here?' I asked him.

He smiled and his gold tooth winked at me.

'They've got special visas for nutters,' he said.

Two backpacker girls walked by, wearing cut-off jeans that buried into their buttocks, and crop tops that crept to the curve of their breasts.

'We've come a long way, ain't we?' said Natural Science.

He pronounced long as 'lang', like the Yardie boys do.

Natural Science used to kickbox out of a club in Fleet and practise on the terraces of the East Bank. He worked on building sites and on the door at Fleet Country Club. He had met an Australian girl in a bar in Basingstoke and fallen in love with her voice and her smile and her passport, and when she ran out of money he followed her home to Sydney. They got married in the Botanical Gardens, and Natural Science planned to become the heavyweight boxing champion of Australia. He was amazed to learn that Joe Bugner held the title. He said it was like turning on the TV and finding that Tom Baker was Dr Who. There weren't many black men in Sydney in the 1990s, and Natural Science tried to make up for the shortfall on his own. He started lying to his wife that he was going training, when he was meeting strippers in the back rooms of Mendoza's clubs. In the end, he found there was no time to do both, so he gave up his professional career – he had been worried, anyway, that he might kill Joe Bugner – and took a job working club doors, so he could combine fighting with looking after the girls.

His wife put up with it for about a year, then divorced him and tried to have him deported. Mendoza had contacts in the immigration department and managed to get him a visa as a security specialist. It was the same time the old man first hired Dror, and the two of them were supposed to be Mendoza's personal security, but Mendoza didn't seem to be in any danger, apart from the threat of Lazarus shooting him by mistake. Natural Science used to think Lazarus was punchy, then he realised he was a retard. Dror was sharp, though, and a nice guy. He could fight if it came to that, but he tried everything else first.

'I'm like that myself now,' he said. 'I got my nutterness cured. That's why I don't want you to think I'm a biter.'

He flashed his teeth unnervingly.

He said he used to fight the pikeys when the fair came to Aldershot. 'The pikeys are biters,' said Natural Science. 'It's the way they get their protein. They didn't want a brother living in Fleet. Nobody did. Times was different then.'

He looked up sharply. 'Why's that bloke staring at you?'

I followed his eyes. There was nobody there.

'Young geezer,' said Natural Science. 'Legged it.'

He rubbed his teeth. 'There's no future in biting,' he said, 'when every poof and junkie's got AIDS.'

I asked him what had happened that afternoon with Mendoza.

'They were arguing in Jew,' said Natural Science, 'and when the old man'd had enough, he told me to shoot him. I ain't a killer, not for nobody's money, so I took the end off his nose. I ain't saying it was an act of mercy, but it released the tension.'

He rubbed his own flat nostrils experimentally. 'The geezer had a big nose anyway.'

A block down the road a prostitute was screaming about her pay. From the back she looked a bit like Helen.

'I wonder what he'll do now,' said Natural Science, 'without his nose.'

Natural Science was working the door of the Magic Circle Club, which was run by a fringe Lebanese operator. He said I should come down to the club one night and we could take a couple of girls onto the roof.

I started remembering Jed and the things we used to get up to at the *Aldershot News and Weekend Advertiser* when we were nineteen years old and didn't have a clue. We shagged the secretary, the copy taker and the mail-room girl. Jed even had the tea lady. Afterwards, he said, she had fed him a biscuit.

In those days it didn't matter that we were after the same girls because there weren't many women in Aldershot – just mad Paras and quiet Gurkhas and one or two lesbians in the WRAC.

I'd never met anyone like Jed. He lived on speedy Es, coke and complicated pizzas. It's hard to lose your best friend. Every day something would happen and I'd think, *I can't wait to tell Jed about this.* Then I remembered he was a cunt, and if I ever saw him again I'd have to hang him upside down and beat the shit out of him.

Natural Science was on his way to the gym. He invited me to come with him. Mendoza's boys didn't have to pay for their workouts either, he said, because they were the gym's only guarantee that all the treadmills wouldn't run off by themselves one night and the dumbbells wouldn't leap into the air and fly through the windows.

I said I needed a bit of time to think – and besides, Natural Science would drill me into the ground. I sat alone with another free coffee and tried to work out what I really felt about everything. It was a relief not to be around Helen any more, but I wondered how I was going to tell my mum that we had split up, when I knew she was hoping Helen would come home pregnant.

I couldn't feel bad about Leah. You don't expect to meet a schoolgirl working in a pub, and it's the bar staff who're supposed to check your ID, not the other way around. Besides, I liked her. Maybe I should go to the country to find her, although 'the country' sounded like a big place.

I'd done the wrong thing to the poor kid in the toilets, though. He hadn't asked for that. I could've sorted him out a bit more gently, but once I'd started on him I couldn't finish until I'd taken him apart. I was in touch with the undercurrent, dancing to the rhythm of the Cross. As for the metaphor I'd jammed into his mouth, I'd learned in Belfast that guns have their own agenda. They lie in wait to terrify a lairy drunk, or blow the face off a British soldier. That's the kind of thing guns live for. I knew I should give the derringer back to Lazarus, or drop it into a drain, but I'd already planned to go home and clean it, then buy some ammo.

TEN

[The Bellisimo Restaurant, 32 Orwell Street, Potts Point. 15-02-02. 2:08 pm.]

All women are whores, Anthony: your grandmother, your mother, your sister, the whole lot of them. It may be a pair of silk stockings in a shipping container in 1944, or a diamond ring in the Great Synagogue in 1948, but every moll has her price. I learned this in the merchant navy, prompted by certain experiences recounted by McCoy, but confirmed it beyond question in the years after the war. I first brought whores into the Patton when Ira started complaining she was losing the best of the showgirls to my insistence that they blow the jacks. She said they had no problem fucking me or McCoy, but if I wanted molls who would service any fat-pig copper who stumbled through the door, I needed to pay the going rate. Ira called some friends from Melbourne and we picked them up from Central Station the next day. There were three of them, but two were twins, named Sylvia and Goldie. Their friend, who told me she was Russian, called herself Daryna, which I had to change to 'Darling', so the punters could pronounce it.

I interviewed them up the Patton in my office and felt confident to offer them all positions. The Malts heard about it and figured I had set myself up in competition with the whorehouses they ran on Palmer Street. The first thing they did was send around this greasy-quiffed imbecile bodgie, Gozo Joe Stone. He could hardly speak English, and I thought English was the fucking language on Malta. His business proposition – as far as I could understand it – was that I should cut them in on a piece of my takings from the club and the girls, and they wouldn't burn me out. I offered him half an hour with Sylvia – out of goodwill, and the fact that she had just come down with a dose – but he was more interested in threatening to kill me.

Let me tell you about Malta, Anthony: in the days before the Ice Age it used to be the land bridge linking Sicily and North Africa, ie, between the Mafia and the Lebs. And the trolls that lived under this bridge were exactly the kind of treacherous low-lifes you'd expect to be born from a marriage of goat-fuckers and camel-humpers. But the Malts in Sydney had a jack in their box, a Sergeant Fred Carol. Rumour had it that he was part Malt, but he was all cunt. He raided the Patton that night, with six boys from the licensing squad and two from the consorting squad, to make sure nobody was consorting with anyone else. They were tough blokes when they were in a mob, and they knocked over a couple of my customers, smashed a few tables just to make a mess.

I was expecting a blue, so I had the Little Fish working the door. It took four jacks to get him on the floor, and they had to almost cave in his skull to keep him still, but once they had knocked him out, they dragged him into the van and took him back to the station, along with all the liquor in the club. The jacks held a party until four o'clock in the morning, according to the Little Fish. He wasn't wearing a watch, but he thought it was four because the jacks told him they would come down and bash him on the hour every hour.

When I came to bail him out in the morning, every part of his face was bruised, and both his eyes were swollen closed, but he was joking with the jacks as if they had all just come off the footie oval. He was charged with all the usual stuff: assaulting a police officer, resisting arrest, carrying a concealed weapon, attempted murder, consorting . . . It all got no-billed in the end.

That weekend the Little Fish brought his new mate Fred Carol in for a drink. I suggested to Carol that the Malts might be a bit unreliable and pointed to a number of shooting murders that could have been avoided if any sober person with half a brain had been involved. Carol said he would take Malts over Yids any day, because he knew where he stood with the Gozo boys. Jews were always conspiring, in his opinion. I said I could make more money for him and make less noise about it. He said he was not interested in any fucking jewbaggery.

While all this garbage with the Malts was going on, I was trying to get married to Deborah, partly to please my own mother, who was very fond of her, and partly to get rid of hers, who had come to hate every hair on my head and considered me one step away from a goy because of my line of business. Ira, who had sophisticated tastes, helped me choose a ring from Alfie Diamond's jewellery shop, and I presented it to Deborah over dinner at the Patton. She said she had always loved me and always would, and I promised to look after her for the rest of her life. However, I explained that, due to the nature of the entertainment industry, I would have to be away from home a lot – rehearsing with actresses, singers, choreographers, et cetera – and she said she was willing to do whatever was needed to make our marriage and our business a success.

The next night the Malts broke into the Patton, blew the downstairs safe, stole the takings and tried to set the place on fire. I called in the armed robbery squad and had a word with their sergeant, Dynamite Danny Dawson, the fattest man I had ever seen. He used to sit on suspects and break their backs.

Dawson had no love for Malts or Jews, but I gave him Darling – who was clean at the time – and a brown paper bag full of immoral earnings, and asked him to broker a truce with Carol and the Malts. All of us met – jacks, crims and imbeciles – to discuss terms at Vitto's, which was a small place for a big man like Dynamite – he must have touched everyone there with some part of his body. I gave a speech about the long-standing friendship between Jews and Maltese, for which I relied heavily on historical fabrication, but pointed out that both people had their strengths and their weaknesses. The Malts had the muscle, we had the brains. If we combined, we would be unstoppable. Gozo Joe said something I didn't understand, and Fred Carol said there was no reason for debate because he could force an agreement then and there. He suggested I might want to relocate my business interests to Palestine and leave the holy land of Darlinghurst to its traditional stewards, the Knights of Malta.

I thought I had hired Dawson to be on my side, but he seemed to think I had paid him as an advisor. He pointed out the many business opportunities open to a man such as myself in North Africa, where he happened to have served during the war. This led to a happy discussion between him and the Little Fish about the whores of the Maghreb.

In the course of these good-natured reminiscences, the Little Fish mentioned that the most accurate word to describe the prostitutes of the Orient might be 'Maltese'. Gozo Joe, sensing insult, jumped up and slashed at the air in front of the Little Fish's nose with a razor. The Little Fish grabbed Dawson's piece out of its holster and shot Gozo Joe in the face.

It cost me every penny of my savings to pay off the jacks, the Malts and Vitto, but it turned out to be money well spent. Gozo Joe retired. The armed robbery squad, the consorting squad and the liquor police all reached an arrangement with the Patton, by which nobody would have to explain what we were all doing in Vitto's, how Dawson had lost his revolver, why Carol was consorting with Bass – who was supposed to have assaulted him – or how a criminal could get shot in the company of two senior police officers.

In return for regular payments to three sergeants, I secured a number of variations on NSW licensing laws and a new source of security for the club. In essence I hired half the police force. It was the partial privatisation of an inert state-owned monopoly, whose functions were taken over by free enterprise on a user-pays basis. The jacks now had a stake in my success, and even my expansion.

When Deborah and I got married, Dynamite Dawson took up two seats at the Great Synagogue. I don't remember a lot about the day because I was still drunk from the night before. I don't, as a rule, drink so much that I forget, but I was a club owner in his prime, holding his own bucks' night on his own premises, and if I didn't fuck the entire chorus line, it was only because I accidentally did a couple of the same girls twice.

My bride and I stood under the *chuppah* and signed the *ketubah*, I drank sweet red wine and crushed the glass under my shoe, then we danced. My mother cried and my father attempted to insert his ring finger in one of the bridesmaids. Deborah and I spent that first night at our new home, an apartment I had purchased near Centennial Park, then embarked on a honeymoon cruise to the South Sea Islands. During our time on the ocean Deborah put forward two suggestions to help me run my business. She believed I should get rid of Sylvia, Goldie and Darling, and also Tina's Talking Tits. She felt they were lowering the tone of an otherwise classy establishment. In their place, she imagined, we could stage jazz acts and – this was her genius – female impersonators.

I told her I would look into it, and also tried to negotiate some rules for our married life that were not covered by the *ketubah*. Although I was prepared to spend every Friday night at home, I couldn't make a similar commitment on Saturday, or Thursday, and I would generally be away on business on Wednesdays also. Deborah pointed out that the distance between Potts Point and Centennial Park was not so great that most people would choose to spend a night in a hotel rather than, for example, take a taxi home, but I explained that the owner of a club never sleeps, particularly the owner of a club that was now open twenty-four hours, seven days a week. She agreed, in principle, for the time being, but I could sense there would be trouble ahead.

When our ship sailed back into Circular Quay, Deborah was already pregnant with my son. I gave him the name of Daniel Mendoza, because I thought he would have the heart of a lion, but he proved a source of great disappointment to me, as well as tremendous pride. You might think the fact that I had impregnated my bride on the first week of our honeymoon would have scotched forever any rumours that I was impotent but, paradoxically, questions about my cock-power continued to be asked by the same imbeciles who maliciously claim that I am the father of my own grandson.

Business was good for a while. I had a baccarat game going in an upstairs room at the Patton, and that kept Deborah and Ira in furs but meant I had to add the racing and gaming squad to my payroll. I'm not boring you, am I, Anthony? You seem a little distracted.

Personal problems, Mr Mendoza.

Anything I can help you with? I am something of an expert in affairs of the cock.

I don't think so.

Well, feel free to come to me for advice if you change your mind.

In the meantime, if you will do me the courtesy of trying to look just the *tiniest bit fucking interested*, I will tell you a story you can take home to your bachelor flat and wank on until your balls shrivel, okay?

It started like this: Fred Carol, who seemed to have partially conquered his aversion to Jews, asked if I could throw a smoko for some of his big jack mates. I think one bloke was leaving and another was turning forty. Apart from the jacks, the only guests he wanted were whores – of which there were now about a dozen working the Patton – and showgirls. I arranged for a hall behind the Palmerstone Hotel to be made available and a few of my men to go along as minders for the girls. The evening opened with the showing of a program of movies that I had picked up from a bondhouse in Suva during a quiet moment in my honeymoon. They had been supplied – and, I believe, manufactured – by Vicky Raisins, a Maltese pornographer who still operates off the Old Kent Road. I lent the cops Big Stan as the projectionist and sent him along with two movie cameras in case one of them broke down. The films featured kidnapped molls hanging from trees, if my memory serves me correctly.

The jacks loved them, so Big Stan continued to project them on the screen while the live performers took to the stage. Sylvia and Goldie did a double act with a dildo, then asked if any officers had brought along the tools of their trade and completed an imaginative cabaret routine with truncheons, handcuffs and an unloaded shooter.

Goldie then offered the jacks the chance to go where their truncheons had just been. It surprised me they were not bashful about performing in front of each other, but I suppose some of them were queers with a point to prove, and others hadn't had a fuck since the night they came back from the war.

To save time, Big Stan suggested they play two-up. Sylvia and Goldie each took one in the back and one in the front, until all jacks had had enough, at which point the showgirls came on and danced the cancan with no pants.

Every jack in the room agreed it was the best smoko since Dynamite Dawson got shot in the arse with his own piece, and nobody noticed that both cameras had been running all afternoon. While one was projecting, the other was filming. I got footage of Fred Carol riding Sylvia's haunches with a smile on his face and a horsewhip in his hand, while his deputy filled her throat with jack juice.

I showed the movie to my senior staff at the Patton, and told them if they ever had trouble with any of these officers – should they happen to recognise them with their clothes on – they should come directly to me. Fred Carol heard a rumour that the film existed and came storming into the club demanding this and that and generally signalling a return to his previously held position on the treachery of the Jews, but I assured him there was no movie, a position I maintained until the day he tried to betray me.

I became known as the man to see if you were organising a smoko, and I began to throw small parties of my own. I invited the cream of my club's patrons – for the most part, luminaries from the worlds of politics, journalism, the law, entertainment and armed robbery. I carefully sounded them out first, to ascertain their tastes and preferences, then tried to match them with others of the same frame of mind. There was no use inviting a screaming fairy to a party with Tina's Talking Tits – although everyone seemed to get something out of that show – or a true-blue pantsman to an evening with Donald and Dave, two waiters at the Patton who served up less than they swallowed.

As time went by, I came to cater for niche markets. I held parties for men who liked black girls, Asian girls, young girls and fat girls. Not all the sex was commercial. Some of it was simply the result of like-minded people converging for the first time.

I was a harbinger of the sexual revolution, Anthony. I brought the sixties to the fifties. I encouraged the leaders of our society to throw off the shackles of their inhibitions and find out who they really were through the medium of fucking the arse off strangers. And I always made sure somebody was there, behind a mirror, inside a wardrobe or peering through a hole in the wall, filming every moment of their journey of self-discovery.

What is that screaming outside, Anthony? It sounds like a nigger's raping a kitten.

[Ends.]

ELEVEN

I had never shopped for myself. I had never cooked a meal. I didn't know how to make an appointment with the doctor, and I was not sure how to pay the rent. I kept finding stuff Helen had left behind: a magazine, a lipstick, a packet of mints, and I felt that if I gathered up everything I could put it together and make a new Helen who wouldn't leave.

When my home phone rang I thought it must be her, but it was Spiegeleier.

'Are you offering me my job back?' I asked.

'No,' he said. 'I've got a woman who wants to meet you.'

'How old is she?' I asked.

'How old?' repeated Spiegeleier. 'Late twenties. Why?'

We met at La Fontaine. I sat down with a coffee, watching a Chinese tramp rinse his dreadlocks in the fountain, and Spiegeleier waddled up, arm in arm with an Irish elf with Guinness-black eyes.

'So you're Billy Cobbett,' she said.

I laughed.

'One of many,' I said. 'We changed the writer every couple of years, for security reasons.'

'I used to love that column,' said Siobhan. 'It was the only good thing in the *Belfast Telegraph*.'

'I was lucky,' I said. 'I had good sources.'

I spun a salt cellar and tried not to stare at the rise of her breasts.

'Siobhan's a friend of a friend,' said Spiegeleier. I had forgotten he was there. 'She worked on the *Irish Times* in Dublin.'

'Did you know Mike Gore at the *Telegraph*?' she asked. 'I used to go out with him.'

That meant she slept with journalists.

'How is Mike?' I asked.

'Still fucking half the news desk,' she said.

Siobhan was on a working holiday – 'more holiday than work,' she said; I imagined orgies by a pool – and stringing for papers in London and Dublin. Spiegeleier asked what I was doing, and I asked what he was doing. I lied to him, and he told me he was finishing a story – 'a nice story, Tony' – about all the new Russian restaurants in the eastern suburbs.

He seemed embarrassed to talk about his job in front of Siobhan. There was even more rubbing and tugging and panting and squelching than usual. He kept trying to change the subject from journalism to sport, or the weather, or Australia's many venomous snakes, but all she wanted to know was if he had broken any big stories.

'Tony's your man for that,' said Spiegeleier. 'He was my organised-crime writer.' Spiegeleier wrapped his fat arms around his belly and held his breath, as if he were trying to squeeze himself smaller. His bald head turned puce, and I had to jab him in the thigh to remind him to breathe. He expelled all the stored-up air in a shivering blast through his nostrils, whinnying like a carthorse.

'I've got to get back to the office now,' he said. 'I'll leave you two to reminisce about life in the cold countries.'

He shook my hand, kissed Siobhan on the cheek – a little bit further to the left and I would've chinned him – and bumbled off to attract abuse from homeless people.

Siobhan looked at me the way I was looking at her, like there was something she really wanted and only I could give it to her.

She said she was disillusioned, which was a pity for someone with such nice tits. She had become a reporter to give a voice to the voiceless but had ended up on the city desk, rewriting press releases from multinational corporations. She had hoped she might redeem herself in Australia by writing about the plight of Aboriginal people. So far the London papers hadn't shown much interest in her social justice journalism, but they had flown up her up to Darwin when a boy was eaten by a crocodile, so at least she was getting to see the country.

Mendoza and Lazarus sat down behind us, at their usual table. They saw me but didn't show it. Mendoza often ignored me in the street, like a one-night stand the morning after, embarrassed by the intimacies of the night before.

I would've liked to carry Siobhan to bed, and slip into the shower with her the next day, and take her out for breakfast to this cafe, and run my fingers lightly up her thighs. She fixed her eyes on mine, as if she were thinking the same.

'Dan said you used to come to work looking like you hadn't slept since Christmas,' she said.

I scratched the back of my neck.

'He thought you might know where to get hold of some coke,' she said.

Oh.

I told her I would see what I could do, and watched her leave with familiar disappointment. Mendoza was watching too, as he spoke on the phone. He finished the call as I approached his table.

'Cute,' said Mendoza, 'but you let her go.'

I shrugged.

'I thought your luck had changed,' said Mendoza. 'You haven't had much going on since blondie left, eh?'

I sat down.

'How did you know about that?' I asked.

'I saw her go,' he said. 'She got into a cab with your television. Just there.' He pointed.

'You were watching my flat?' I asked.

'I was sitting here, having a coffee,' he said, 'while you were getting shickered at the Hamilton.'

Mendoza was distracted by the sight of a dwarf on a skateboard, circling the rim of the fountain.

'I feel sorry for midgets these days,' he said. 'They used to have all kinds of opportunities: midget wrestling, Santa's elves, strippers' little helpers, dwarf bowling . . . These days, it's all banned. You can't even call them midgets any more. It's as if they don't exist. A lot of midgets tend to kill themselves. One day, I'll tell you about the real Mr Big. That fella had a shlong like a baby's arm, and arms like babies' arms too. Women loved him. Up to a point.'

The dwarf did a kickflip off the library steps, landed cleanly and cruised off.

'What was it that the colleen wanted, Anthony,' asked Mendoza, 'that you weren't man enough to give her?'

'A gram of coke,' I said.

'Why don't you help her out?' he asked. 'It's the quickest way into her pants.'

'I don't know where to get it.'

'Get it where you got it before.'

'I can't.'

'Lazarus,' said Mendoza, 'call Dror. Anthony needs to anesthetise a woman before he operates.'

As Mendoza cut into a slice of chocolate cake Lazarus folded away a Russian tabloid.

'Lazarus has a new wife,' said Mendoza. 'She's from St Petersburg. He bought her on the internet. It was the best fifty dollars – including postage and packing – he ever spent, wasn't it, Lazarus?'

Lazarus scowled.

'And, as a special present, today he has bought her a *newspaper*.'

Lazarus rang Dror and grunted and snarled.

'How's the book going, Anthony?' asked Mendoza.

'Great,' I said. 'It's going to be a classic.'

'You'll have to show me some pages soon,' he said.

Dror came out of a Thai restaurant on the other side of the road. He looked as crisp and cold as a winter's morning and wore a black skivvy that fitted his body like a sock, but when he smiled and spoke he was a country boy again.

'G'day, Tony,' he said, and passed me a menu. Inside was a clear plastic envelope the size of a tea bag, half filled with white powder.

Dror said he'd been interstate, checking up on certain individuals and organisations.

'And how is my security?' asked Mendoza.

'Secure,' Dror assured him.

'No threats from the Italians?'

'Not for twenty-five years,' said Dror.

I thanked Dror and went to the library, where the coke nestled unhappily in my pocket, like a pistol asking to be fired. I knew I could skim a line off the top without Siobhan noticing, but if I started it I would probably finish it, then there would have been no point in having got it in the first place. At a quiet table near the reference shelves, away from the skippers and bumpers, I searched bound newspapers and magazines for stories about the Patton Club. On yellowed paper pressed between leather covers I found the memories of a lost nightlife, when men wore hand-painted ties and women nestled in furs, and every spine and smile was stiffened for the camera. I could almost hear the piano and smell the smoke of corona cigars.

By the time I had finished at the library it was dark and I was hungry. I ended up at McDonald's on Darlinghurst Road, sitting by the window looking out on the Ink tattoo studio, where Rabbit and Devil were talking to a man who stood as tall as traffic lights, a storybook giant with knee-length boots, a leather jerkin and a white beard that hung from his chin like a plastic bag.

I picked the gherkin off my burger and stuck it to the window, where it looked like a patch on the giant's jacket, or a big green target.

Everybody who passed the Cannibals glanced up at the giant then looked away.

Siobhan called to see if I had scored. I suggested we could meet in a bar, but she said McDonald's would be fine. I bought myself a Coke that tasted like detergent. The shirtless shouter I had followed up the road a few weeks before was making his demented way past the bikers, who didn't look up when he yelled at them. But instead of turning off at the alley, he took a kick at Rabbit's chopper, sending the shotgun flying into the road. The bike went down, Siobhan walked into the McDonald's, and the Ink tattoo studio exploded, as two men dressed in black jumpsuits and ski masks blasted out the windows from the inside and walked calmly onto Darlinghurst Road, shooting bikers.

Siobhan stood in the doorway. I thought she was in shock so I tried to pull her down, but she just stared at the shooters. I managed to drag her behind a pillar, but that was as far as she would move. The gunmen levelled their M4 Carbines at Devil, who was trying to point a pistol, and Rabbit, who was scrambling for his saddlebags, and blew their insides out. Two metres is a horrible range to take a bullet, although I don't suppose there's any nice range.

Caught without a weapon, Giant tried to throw a haymaker at a gunman. It was one of the bravest, strangest acts of violence I have ever seen. It was as if he hoped he could swat away the bullets. The gunman shot him in the throat and left a hole as wide as a drainpipe.

'They dropped the door guard first,' said Siobhan, 'then the ugly one, then the big one. Their blood splattered over their own bikes. The ugly one reached for something and they blew off his hand. There are body parts in the street, as if there has been a bomb. People are screaming – the kind of people you wouldn't expect to scream: nightclub bouncers and hard-faced streetwalkers. Everybody is throwing themselves to the ground, as if the ground is a neutral area that bullets can't reach. Cars are screeching around and heading off against the traffic.'

I realised she was talking into a voice recorder.

My heart was thumping like old-school jungle. I was scared and thrilled, and alive in the moment. I wanted to throw myself in, to choose a side and take a weapon, and stand in the street blasting away at the enemy.

The gunmen were resting on the pavement with the confidence of killers, enjoying all the shouting, waiting for their pick-up, when the back doors of a white transit van burst open and half-a-dozen Cannibals leaped out, yelling and waving their weapons, angry and panicked, running into and away from the gunmen, pointing their four-tens at each other, at the street and at the sky.

The gunmen were onto them, rising without cover, laughing at the amateurs.

'The men in black are reloading their . . .'

'. . . M4 Carbines,' I said.

'The bikers have cheaper, simpler looking . . .'

'Shotties,' I said. 'Legal weapons. Farmers' guns.'

The Cannibals had the numbers but no tactics. A gunman stepped contemptuously close to a fat biker, who was struggling to drop another cartridge into his weapon, and just blew his arm off. The side of the van looked like a butcher's shop that had been hit by a storm.

'All these pieces of meat,' I said, under my breath. 'This is how people are made.'

'What? What's that?' asked Siobhan. 'What did you say?'

'The door guard was called Devil,' I told her. 'The ugly one was Rabbit. I didn't see the giant's patch.'

I was bouncing from toe to toe, breaking cover and taking cover, bobbing around the pillar like a buoy in the ocean. I was trying to pick the direction the gunmen's back-up would arrive from, when I saw they were already there. The shirtless shouter had picked up and hot-wired a chopper. A blind busker, who I had noticed earlier but never seen before, was kicking another of the bikes into gear. It was impossible to make out either of their faces because their cheeks were smeared with street dirt. Men who had looked filthy and starving now seemed camouflaged and stripped of fat.

'I think there are only three dead,' said Siobhan to her machine. 'Most of the bodies are still moving.'

The gunmen jumped on the back of bikes ridden by the beggars. As the first chopper revved past the transit van, the pillion passenger put a bullet through the driver's-side window.

'This is brilliant,' I said.

Everybody started screaming, except for a few spruikers crying or laughing, and one man doing both at once. The police, who only had to travel two hundred metres, took five minutes to arrive. All that was left were shattered bikes and bikers, and the smell of spilled petrol and spent ammunition.

'Are you going to file?' Siobhan asked me urgently.

'File what?' I asked.

'Copy. You know, a story.'

'I don't work for anybody,' I said.

'Well, help me then. Quickly. What else do you know?'

'The bikers've been expecting a battle,' I said. 'You can imagine them training at their clubhouse, running through the bush with their shotguns, a bunch of fat, panting grease-monkeys playing at commandoes in the long grass. Fuck.' I shook my head. 'They didn't know what hit them . . .

'The other team could've come in the back way,' I said, 'but I doubt it. I'd guess they abseiled through the skylight. The building's got an odd structure. What looks like the top floor is just a facade. The rooms behind it used to be a brothel, but they got burned out in the seventies. Mendoza wanted to turn the place into units, but the unions put a green ban on the deco frontage, so he trousered the insurance money and used it to buy a place on Victoria Street.'

'Do we think the killers were a rival biker gang?' Siobhan asked.

'We haven't got a fucking clue,' I said.

TWELVE

Siobhan sang 'The Croppy Boy' as she cooked eggs on the stove top in the kitchen of her one-bedroom flat. I looked around at her bare traveller's walls. She brought breakfast into bed and snuggled next to me, wearing my shirt.

I felt lucky and horny and trapped. Siobhan looked even prettier without make-up. I wanted to grab her, but I also wanted to go home.

'Do you do this a lot?' she asked.

I told her this was the first time. Siobhan quizzed me about Helen, what she looked like, what she tasted like, what she smelled like. I said Baby Spice, white wine and heather.

'Now answer those questions about me,' she said.

'Kate Moss, honey-butter and me,' I said.

She asked what kind of girls I usually went for. I told her it was pretty much a buyers' market.

We talked about the shooting. Siobhan had seen the bodies of murder victims in Dublin, but she had never watched anybody die. I said I had seen too many corpses in Belfast. She asked if I had covered any other wars, and I told her

I had been in Kosovo. I kissed her eyes.

She wanted to talk about what it was like to be Billy Cobbett and write the gore 'n' gossip column the paramilitaries had to read to find out what they'd been doing. I said the hardest part was having to spend so much time with people you hated, egg-white toe cutters with pig-pink eyes. They all hid behind Cobbett's anonymity to spread lies about their victims and try to get their rivals killed.

Siobhan had just come out of a year-long relationship with a political correspondent who was working for a PR firm while he tried to write his novel. He was a nice guy, but he didn't know what he wanted. He kept photographs of his ex-girlfriend under his bed. Before that, she had lived with Mike Gore, who used to keep his real-life ex-girlfriends under his bed.

She asked how I'd come to be on the *Belfast Telegraph*. I said I'd been following a woman, but she had shaken me off. Siobhan ran a finger over the tattoo on my biceps – two hands clasped above the words *Slick, Jedi* and *mates*. It looked to her like a Claddagh ring. The lines had thickened and the colours faded over ten years. I told her I was planning to have it lasered off.

The *Irish Times* rang to say they had used her copy, but they needed a local angle. Were any Irish backpackers injured? Were any of the bikers Irish? We decided to walk to the Cross and see what we could pick up. I fought Siobhan for my shirt. She rented a unit in a shabby Art Deco building near Taylor Square. Most of the other tenants were gay men, which meant she always felt safe. The lift was broken, so we walked out through the fire escape. She told me Mike Gore knew Spiegeleier in the 1970s, when Gore was a junior reporter and Spiegeleier was working in London. Gore had a lot of respect for Spiegeleier as a journalist and couldn't understand how he'd ended up on the *Jewish Times*.

Siobhan didn't know much about Jews. She'd never had a

religious experience – 'Catholics don't, generally,' she said – but she felt it would be like an orgasm, only darker.

I liked talking to her. She was clever and funny, and I was glad I had stayed. By the time we reached the Coke sign, we were holding hands.

The strip was closed from Bayswater Road to Llankelly Place, but the pavement on the west side was open and crowded with photographers, pushing against the police barriers and shouting questions. I asked a young guy which paper he was from. He answered me in Italian, another boy shouted in French: the crime scene was an outing for the backpackers' hostels. Siobhan found a gap-year couple from Dundalk and interviewed them, while suntanned Swedes took pictures of the forensic team at work, and Japanese office girls posed by the bloodstains. A man with a handlebar moustache rattled up in a mobile hotdog stand, and the morning felt like a street party, until the Cannibals arrived.

They came up from the railway-station escalators, wearing their colours like soft, battered armour. The first dozen or so men were from the Sydney chapter, but they were followed by Cannibals patched in Brisbane, Melbourne and Bathurst. The highways must have been crowded last night.

The Cannibals fanned out to the north and south, made two walls of black leather and marched at the tourists, who had nowhere to move but backwards. Siobhan and I were caught in the sudden retreat. She lost her footing and tripped into my arms.

I tried to turn around, so I would at least be walking forwards, when a voice called my name. A big hand reached out to me and Natural Science pulled me into the entrance of a street-level sex shop called 'The Lash'.

'Get inside, Slick,' he said.

I dragged Siobhan along behind me. When tourists tried to follow, National Science raised his wide, open palm like a stop sign and sent them crab-walking back into the crowd. All the shops and clubs had put extra men on the doors. Every organisation was muscling up. The Lash was run from one of Mendoza's premises, and the old man had supplied guards to protect the property.

'The Cannibals are holding a memorial service for their brothers,' said Natural Science. 'They've demanded all the sex businesses close for an hour.' He laughed. 'They were a lot scarier two days ago.'

Nobody knew what might happen, so Natural Science was running a security team that included lookouts on the rooftops and informers in both the cops and the bikers.

'I didn't know Mendoza could still mount that kind of operation,' I said.

'It ain't the old man,' said Natural Science, 'it's Dror. He loves this shit. We'd all be wearing uniforms if it was up to him.'

The Lash was brightly lit and overstocked with thousands of X-rated DVDs, classed from 'Anal' to 'Wrestling'. Among all the normal fetishes, Siobhan managed to find a film of Germans shitting on Asians. She held it up.

'Pornography?' she asked. 'Or art?'

'There's no need to buy that one, love,' said Natural Science. 'Slick's already got it at home.'

The Lash was operated by a fat woman with six rings in her lower lip and black polish on her nails. She had a nose like a pig and ears like a cat, but she smelled like a nurse.

'Slick, this is Greta,' said Natural Science. 'They call her "Lady Lash".'

'I nail men's balls to wooden boards,' she said. 'Would you like a cup of coffee?'

Lady Lash passed me a business card, advertising *bondage and erection* at the First Presbyterian Church in Cleveland Street.

'I rent out dungeons by the hour,' she said.

'I'll call you if I need one,' I said.

'Be sure to,' she replied, as if it might actually happen.

Siobhan picked out another DVD.

'*Diarrhea Bukake*,' she read. 'What the hell is that?'

'Don't look,' warned Natural Science, 'or it'll haunt your dreams.'

Natural Science talked to his men on a two-way radio, and I wanted a radio too. I love protocol and code words. I wanted to get up on the roof and look down and report back, to be a part of the drama.

The door rattled as Dror unfastened the locks, then jogged in from the street, wearing a tight black silk shirt, tailored trousers and toe-capped shoes.

'I've spoken to the Cannibals' president,' said Dror. 'They'll be finished in ten minutes.'

He noticed me and Siobhan.

'What're you two doing in here?' he asked. 'Spicing up your love life already?'

Siobhan needed to file her copy, but the internet cafes were all blockaded by Cannibals. Lady Lash said she could have used the shops inventory computer but it wasn't connected to the internet. It wasn't connected to the inventory, either, because the book-keeping was done by hand.

'We do have one terminal that's online,' she remembered.

'Anything with a keyboard's fine,' said Siobhan.

'It's coin operated,' said Lady Lash. She pointed to the cubicle next to the front desk and passed Siobhan a roll of paper towels.

'You might want to wipe the screen down first,' she said. 'And put something over the chair.'

Siobhan opened the door.

'And try to breathe through your mouth,' said Lady Lash.

Siobhan came out of the cubicle after ten minutes, which Lady Lash said was 'about average'.

Dror offered to buy us lunch at a Japanese restaurant, and invited Leila, the oval-faced waitress from La Fontaine, too. She had strong legs that lifted her taller than Dror, and I'm not sure if she knew she was on a date. I sucked grilled meat off a stick while the others chewed slivers of raw fish. Dror ordered sake and told a funny story about a bloke he knew who had got his cock stuck in a bottle. We moved from rice wine on to whisky, and washed it all down with Sapporo Dry. The owner wanted to close for the afternoon, but Dror racked up white slug lines on the table. The owner asked him not to do that in here, but Dror said it was okay, he was protected.

'Let's go to a club,' said Dror.

'The clubs are shut,' I said. 'It's only four o'clock.'

'No,' said Dror, 'a strip club.'

'Why would I want to go to a strip club?' asked Siobhan.

'Come on, it'll be fun,' said Leila.

'In what way "fun"?' asked Siobhan.

'You can look at naked women,' said Dror, 'and think about them afterwards.'

Siobhan wrinkled her nose.

'Have another line,' said Dror.

'Please leave now,' said the owner.

After the coke, everybody wanted to carry on drinking.

'We might as well go to a club,' said Dror.

I gave Siobhan my arm and we stumbled onto the strip. The police were still working behind their barriers, but the bikers had gone, and the spruikers were out, dressed in shabby dinner suits, their lapels embedded with razor blades.

A fat pimp and his thin, long-armed buddy stood under a pink neon sign saying *Baby Dolls*, as if they had been placed on the wrong shelf in a toyshop.

'Let's check out the competition,' whispered Dror. 'This place is run by Lebs.'

Dror and I walked in front of Siobhan and Leila, so the bigger spruiker could steer us towards the doorway.

'Come on, fellas,' he said. 'Fuck shows, suck shows.'

They started to walk into the club, as if their charisma would suck us in behind them. Dror stood his ground on the pavement. The fat pimp looked back and pretended to be surprised.

'How much is it?' asked Dror.

'Twenty-five bucks,' said the pimp.

'I'll give you twenty for the four of us,' said Dror.

The spruiker shook his head, then rubbed it.

'C'mon, mate,' he said. 'The girls need fifteen, and there's five for the girl on the door and five for the book.'

'What do you mean "the book"?' asked Dror. 'There's no such thing as "the book".'

'All right,' he said. 'Twenty dollars each, and we'll waive the book.'

'Five bucks each,' said Dror.

The thin pimp stepped in.

'Look,' he said. 'I'll do you a favour: fifteen bucks each, take it or leave it.'

'And what's the favour?' asked Dror.

'Let's just find a bar,' said Siobhan. 'I don't know why we were going there anyway.'

Leila agreed, and the girls started to walk away.

'C'mon,' said the spruikers in chorus.

'Okay, here's the deal,' said the thin man. 'You get a discount because it's early and business is quiet. You get a discount because there aren't many girls on yet. And you get a discount because you're bringing in ladies with you. So we can do youse for five dollars each, but it's now or never, boys. If you come back later tonight and ask to get in for five bucks, I'll laugh in your faces. I'll say, "Five bucks! You've got to be joking!"'

'He'll say, "This isn't Thailand, mate,"' his fat friend predicted.

'It's not Patpong,' said the thin man. 'Fuckee Suckee, two hundred baht.'

This time we followed the spruikers up the narrow glowing stairs to a perspex window where a girl with a lazy eye sat writing in a diary. The thin spruiker whispered how much we had paid and added loudly, 'Special discount.' The fat one stood in front of Dror with his hand out.

'C'mon,' he said. 'Tip for us, lads. That's how we earn our money.'

The small bar smelled of uncirculated air and rotten carpet. A silent video of a woman masturbating played on a wall-mounted TV, while a skinny girl wilted on a pole for two American sailors: a black man and a farm boy.

I tried to buy a drink from the bar, but the barmaid waved me away, then a tired blonde waitress with an empty stare asked if we would like beer or Jack Daniels. It was hard to adjust to artificial light. Siobhan stood with her eyes closed, as if she couldn't bear to look. Dror dropped twenty dollars into the stripper's pants, then turned away.

'What do you think of the old man?' he asked me. 'There's a lot of goodness in him, but he isn't proud of it. He'd rather you only saw his cruelty. He thinks that makes him strong.'

The Americans called for the stripper to turn around. Leila whispered in Dror's ear. He passed her a closed fist and the two women went to the bathroom together.

The black sailor asked the stripper how much she would charge to go upstairs.

She shook her head.

'Do you speak English?' he asked her.

'English?' she said. 'Fair dinkum. Jesus. I'm horny.'

'She's Russian,' said Dror.

'Thank you, sir,' said the sailor.

Dror said something in Russian to the girl. She looked

surprised that he'd spoken, but bored by what he'd said. She left the stage and came back with a slim brown-haired teenager in a glittering g-string, who grabbed the pole and shimmied for the sailors.

'Are you with the *Galaxy*?' Dror asked the black guy.

'Are you a Russian spy, sir?' the sailor asked Dror.

'There are no Russian spies any more,' Dror assured him. 'We're all on the same side.'

'I heard that,' said the sailor, as if he didn't trust the source.

'What's your rating, sailor?' asked Dror.

'GM,' he said. 'Mean anything to you?'

'I used to be a marine,' said Dror.

'A Russian marine, sir?'

'No, sailor. I was with the good guys.'

The music in the club swelled louder, as if the management were trying to direct our attention back to the stage, but there's something tragic about cheap strippers, an injury that makes me want to look away. I felt happier talking to the Yanks.

'Where've you boys been?' I shouted to the farm boy.

'We were in the Gulf last year,' he said. 'Enforcing the no-fly zones.'

'Did you see action?'

That was always the question.

'Hell, yeah,' said the black sailor.

'You're a gunner's mate, yeah?' I said. 'You working on the twenty mils? The Phalanxes? What's your rate of fire?' I asked.

'Three thousand rounds a minute, sir.'

The girls came back sniffling, Leila was smiling. The two strippers danced together, almost rubbing, nearly touching, kissing the air between their faces.

When the brown-haired girl handed Siobhan her g-string, Siobhan folded it neatly and left it on the stage like a parcel.

'This isn't fun at all,' she said to me. 'It's sleazy and I hate it. Let's go home.'

'You girls got any friends?' the black sailor asked.

Leila laughed but Siobhan scowled.

'I hate blokes like that,' she said to me outside.

'What, Yanks?'

She shook her head.

'Blacks?'

'Don't be so fucking stupid,' she said.

THIRTEEN

[The Bellisimo Restaurant, 32 Orwell Street, Potts Point. 01-03-02. 1:46 pm.]

In 1958, just when I had everything sweet as a nut, the Malts and the squareheads arced up again. The Malts shipped in some new blood from Rabat, and Gozo Joe Stone – who made more comebacks than Whispering fucking Jack – came out of retirement to lead them in the Cross. The problem with the Malts was they only had one idea. They broke into the Patton again – at 5 am, our quietest time – cracked the safe and tried to set the club on fire. I don't know why they wanted to burn the place down. They call arson 'Jewish lightning', but to me it has always been Maltese safe-breaking.

They didn't get much, but they coshed one of my boys and left him paralysed down one side. I told the cops that the Malts had gone off with the weekend's takings and I had no way to pay them. They sent Fred Carol to mediate. I hated that cunt. He came back with the Malts' story, which was that they were all eating rabbit in Valetta at the time. I tried to convince Dynamite that Carol had teamed up with the Malts to keep the payroll for himself, but Dynamite was not going to turn on another jack on the word of a Jew.

In the courts, Police Commissioner Amos, who turned a blind eye to Maltese crime, became obsessively concerned with who owned which pubs and where. This was a matter of great interest to the law-enforcement authorities in the 1950s, Anthony. Amos had already spent a great deal of salaried time and public money trying to get the Patton declared a 'place of ill repute' or some such rubbish. I mean, obviously a club is going to get a bad name if officials of his stature traduce its reputation in the fucking courts. According to Amos and his cronies – who I must have forgotten to pay off somehow – a number of hotels, which were apparently the property of various members of mine and McCoy's families, were actually run by a nefarious partnership consisting of the two of us. We denied everything, of course, but our case was weakened somewhat by the fact that two of the nominated licensees were now dead, and another had joined the Rechabites temperance movement.

In the end, I gave up my pubs but kept the club and went to war with the Maltese. We didn't know how many Malts there were, or what they were capable of, or even what they wanted, but I figured that if one idea worked for them, the same thing might do for us as well. I arranged a meet with Gozo Joe at Aphrodite's in Orwell Street – which, at the time, I didn't own – but, at the last minute, found myself unable to attend and had to send the Little Fish along instead.

Gozo Joe was sitting at a booth with Fred Carol when the Little Fish walked up to their table and ordered three whiskies. He drank his whisky, then Stone's, then Carol's, then shot Gozo Joe in the face. Again.

This time Fred Carol shot back at the Little Fish, which left Bass in a quandary, since you can't shoot a jack but you can't let a jack shoot you either. The Little Fish dived for Carol's legs, took him down and clouted him until he lost consciousness and – miraculously – all memory of the incident. A similar amnesia struck every other patron and employee of Aphrodite's, including Gozo Joe Stone, who believed he must have shot himself before he went out that night. It cost me more money than your grandmother could earn in a lifetime's whoring, Anthony, but it brought peace to the Cross through an unexpected alliance between the Little Fish and Carol. Now that each had bashed the other senseless, they felt the kinship of the violently insane and became like brothers. The Little Fish even ended up as godfather to Carol's youngest son.

Meanwhile, my own son, who was now six years old, was becoming something of a problem. His mother held that his presence in our apartment should be motive enough for me to come home every night, rather than the four out of seven to which we had agreed. She argued her point ferociously and, at times, hurtfully, until I realised there was only one way to rekindle our romance. I took her on another cruise, this time to Europe, and when we got there, we left Daniel in France with some family friends. I had intended to send for him after a month or so, but other matters got in the way and, unfortunately, I didn't see my son again for two years. Daniel has never forgiven me for this small oversight, even though I bought him a toy gun *and* a pedal car on his return. He argues to this day that he was too big for the pedal car.

With Daniel in France, I was able to devote all my energies to defending myself against charges of 'scandalous conduct and outraging public decency', which, like almost everything else I have ever been charged with, is no longer an offence. The details of this story are well known to everyone, but I will rehearse them once more for your book, Anthony.

Pay close attention – forget Helen, who left you; and Siobhan, who only wants you for drugs – because these are the pages your readers will turn to. McCoy, my no-good brother Abie and I were having a drink at the home of a prominent property developer when it was suggested that the afternoon might be enlivened by some female company. I thought immediately of Sylvia, Goldie and Darling, who were not working that day, and sent my driver to their Potts Point rooms to pick them up. I directed him also to bring along some of the props from their stage act – dildos, cat-o'-nine-tails, cuffs and the like – and some instructional literature that had recently arrived from Soho. This was a largely selfless gesture, since I was sick to death of fucking these three whores and watching them impale themselves on various extruded plastics. A girl in a club has a commercial life of about eight months. These women had been around for almost eight years. It was all new to Abie, though, and McCoy, as usual, had fallen in love with Darling, so it did him good to see her roughed up by other men. It reminded him what she really was.

The girls came in, dressed in plain frocks, which was something I rarely saw and found quite erotic. They did a slow strip down to their stockings and their Sunday-morning underwear, and started kissing each other on the tits. Abie loved that sort of thing, but when you have seen three tired molls dress up as dykes a dozen times, you feel there are other things you could be doing with your life.

The property developer leaped on Darling, pulled her out of the threesome and pushed her head between his legs, and it was decided that she should blow us all while Sylvia and Goldie worked the double-headed dildo. This upset McCoy but, in a funny, way I think he enjoyed the pain. Our host wheeled in a couple of buckets of champagne and we toasted the girls, who rubbed their nipples with ice cubes and performed tricks with the corks that involved a quite extraordinary degree of physical control. Goldie, in particular, was a gynaecological gymnast and had chosen the only profession that suited her talents. Abie jumped the queue and started fucking Darling while she was blowing McCoy, which I swear brought tears to my old mate's eyes, and I dipped the whip in water and practised a few cuts in the air.

As a result of this one incident I have a reputation as a whipper of women, which is a bit like you making a name for yourself as a cocksman by climbing upstairs with one slutty barmaid on a quiet night in the pub. I won't pretend I hadn't whipped women before – or that I haven't since – but the lash is only a side dish on the sexual smorgasbord, and my satisfactions come from more intimate contacts. On the other hand, I felt like giving McCoy's whore a beating she wouldn't forget in a hurry and, as soon as he and Abie were finished, I set to work with a professionalism that might easily be mistaken for enthusiasm. The girl didn't object, beyond the usual shrieks and moans that enlivened her circus act, and the party continued for several hours afterwards.

Back in the 1950s there were many crimes but few victims. Weeks later I was visited by the vice squad and informed that it was illegal to whip a consenting woman in a private home in the company of invited guests. I wonder which twisted soul sat up all night devising that particular statute, and what solitary gratification he drew from its careful wording. McCoy, Abie and I, and several other party guests who came and went during the course of the afternoon, all appeared in the Central Court to face the ludicrous charges.

At first I couldn't imagine who the jacks might call to testify against us, but it turned out to be Darling, who had gone to the police station of her own accord, only weeks after the alleged episode, to turn me in. Apparently McCoy had translated the words I used as I beat her. *Ukrayner zoyne*, he told her, meant Ukrainian whore in Yiddish. Russian, my arse. That cunt was from Kiev, and it seems I hurt her feelings more than her fat peasant's buttocks.

Since there were no other witnesses, I assumed Darling was the public and it was her decency that was supposed to have been outraged, which was a half-arsed fucking joke if ever I heard one.

As if that were not enough, Darling persuaded another moll to say I had banged her by the back entrance, in the Patton the week before. I was accused of 'an unnatural offence', which is now considered neither unnatural nor an offence, based on an event that gave birth to the briefly popular expression, 'taking it up the Patton'.

On my initiative certain police officers, among them both the armed-robbery squad's Dynamite Dawson and the licensing cop Fred Carol, took statements from Darling, even though there was no prima facie case that an armed robbery or a breach of liquor-licensing laws had taken place. During the course of their interviews Darling realised she had been mistaken in thinking she had been whipped and fucked, and could actually produce witnesses to say she had been shopping for a hat on the morning of the alleged outrage.

Also, the deluded moll who had complained of my 'unnatural' behaviour towards her realised that she had forgotten to move to Perth, an omission she remedied within days of the charges being laid. She started a new life in a suite at the Singapore Hotel, my pub in Canning Bridge, WA, where I would often take her up the Patton in later years.

In order to stay out of Long Bay I had to invite the vice squad to become associates of my organisation too. This put a considerable strain on my financial resources, since I was now paymaster to every cop outside of the lost-dog squad. I suffered only one other prosecution in the 1950s, for giving cash prizes at a game of housie. I need hardly remind you such actions are no longer illegal, and how I got lifted for that one I just couldn't fucking tell you.

Can I ask you something about more recent events, Mr Mendoza?

You can ask me anything, Anthony. Think of me as a father figure.

I was in the Cross when the bikers were attacked.

Is that so? What did you see?

A well-planned operation. A lot of shooting.

Indeed. Indeed.

What was going on?

If I knew, Anthony, your little selkie maiden would be the first to hear. I would bring the information to her myself, and reap the rewards of her gratitude by taking her up the Patton, a club I used to own on Orwell Street, which is now this romantic Italian restaurant.

I have never had much to do with the bikers. They strike me as neither kosher nor *treif*. What kind of crim wears a jacket linking himself with every one of his known associates? And why do they bother with the motorcycles? It's like the Mafia pretending they are united by a common interest in bocce. Also, for me, a beard belongs on a rabbi.

There have been biker wars on the strip before, but everything had been peaceful for years until last night. But that is the way it goes, Anthony – war and peace, armistice and ambush, partition and expulsion: in Kings Cross, as in the world outside.

Ask me about Frank Sinatra, Anthony.

Tell me about Frank Sinatra.

Ah, Frank. What a singer! What an actor! What a cunt! In the late 1950s I teamed up with a young fellow named Izzy 'the Ham' Berger, who made my acquaintance by pretending to have met me before. He wore a green blazer, a waxed moustache and a yellow trilby. He looked like a Jewish leprechaun. He came up to me at the Patton and shook my hand, and told me it had been years since our last discussion about Sinatra, but he felt things were finally coming to fruition.

Berger was a dreamer and a liar and an absolutely fearless conman, but he really did know somebody who knew Frank Sinatra. I had my contacts in the Sicilian community check out this third party, and within weeks I was on a plane with Berger, heading for Las Vegas, the Kings Cross of the desert. Ira travelled as my assistant, although it's possible I neglected to mention this to Deborah, since it was impractical to make my wife privy to all my various business arrangements.

When Deborah discovered I must have been away in Nevada when Ira fell pregnant with her daughter, Sharon, she was at first jubilant, because she calculated that I couldn't be the father. When she realised that Sharon had been conceived in Nevada, she had a mental breakdown and took to her bedroom for several months, emerging only to cook the *Shabbos* dinner and supervise other domestic chores.

Sinatra was an associate of Lucky Luciano, among others. Through Berger's surprisingly useful friend, and my own distant connection with Meyer Lansky, we were able to arrange a meeting, in which Sinatra agreed to play concerts in Australia provided we paid him a sum of money beyond which I had ever heard spoken of before, and guaranteed him three women a night, including – and he was specific about this – at least one full-blood native woman, and a pygmy from Borneo.

I knew that Jeremiah Cain's World Famous Boxing Troupe travelled with a sideshow that included the Wild Man of Borneo and his Pygmy Queen. I also knew that both showies were actually undersized Abos from Beagle Bay, with bones stuck through their noses. But I was confident I could arrange things to Sinatra's satisfaction, even if I had to take one or two liberties with anthropological fact.

The midget boong moll was sent down from Queensland

with a bodyguard, to make sure she didn't escape. Her minder was Lazarus Lakes, the middleweight champion of Mt Isa, who had been travelling with Jeremiah Cain since he lost his boxing licence due to a misunderstanding about the amount of lead a fighter is permitted to carry in his gloves. Lazarus had never been to Sydney before, but soon fell in love with the glamour of institutions such as the New York restaurant, the likes of which he had never seen in Winton, or even Cloncurry. I mistook his obtuseness for discretion and hired him as my personal assistant, and he has been joined to my side ever since, like an overgrown *goyishe* Siamese twin who cannot spell his own name.

But the Sinatra tour made *my* name, Anthony, and it made me a fucking motza. I learned everything I know about the entertainment industry from that crooning old cunt-hound and his arse-licking entourage. It wasn't until I had Sinatra singing after supper one night in the Patton – on the promise of a Tasmanian Aborigine, a kind of pussy that Frank had thought was extinct – that I could truly call myself 'the King of the Cross'.
[Ends.]

FOURTEEN

I came back from Vitto's with coffee and croissants, to find Siobhan still lying in bed, humming a tune I recognised but couldn't name, as she read through my raggedy cuts.

'This stuff you did for the *Belfast Telegraph* is shit hot,' she said.

We had breakfast and made love. Then we had lunch and made love.

Mendoza had called a meeting on William Street, in a low-rise motel that squatted in the afternoon shadow of a block of serviced apartments. I left Siobhan in bed, still reading Billy Cobbett. I walked along Darlinghurst Road, whistling Siobhan's ballad until I found the words. It took me back to Irish music nights at Republican clubs in the Falls, where the bands played on as Geordies and Scousers tore their bars apart, as if music were a weapon and soldiers could be beaten by rebel songs.

Outside the William Street apartments was a filthy white van, parked in by a limo and a decorator's ute. I stopped to write 'clean me' with my finger on the back door, then added 'you cunt'.

Mendoza and Lazarus were waiting for me in the motel room, standing by the window. They had propped up the bed against the back wall, below a painting of white horses galloping through surf. In the middle of the room was a line of three chairs. Two of them pointed towards the door, the third faced the bed frame. Lazarus took the rear chair, and I waited for Mendoza to take his place in the middle, but he shook his head.

'You're in the hot seat today, Anthony,' he said.

Lazarus passed Mendoza his briefcase. He showed us his back as he worked the combination.

'What did you use this place for?' I asked him.

'The motel?' he said. 'I've never been here before.'

When Mendoza faced me again, he had my manuscript rolled up like a truncheon in his fist.

'I read this last night,' he said, 'instead of making love to my girlfriend. Or Cecilia Preciosa Bang Bang McCoy. Or my hairy fucking hand.'

I smiled and nodded.

'Bearing in mind my age,' he said, 'and the number of fucks I'm likely to have left in me, do you think this was a useful way to spend my time?'

'I don't know,' I said.

'"I do not know,"' Mendoza chanted, 'said the Great Bell of Bow.'

I gave him another nod, as if he'd said something funny or interesting.

'Why do you think the Great Bell of Bow said, "I do not know", Anthony?'

I shrugged.

'Perhaps,' he suggested, 'it's because it was a mongrel dog maggot Pommy imbecile.'

He curled his fat lips over his teeth and slapped his palm with the paper roll.

'This,' he said, holding my manuscript close to my face, 'is the stupidest piece of half-arsed dog shit I have ever read.'

He pulled off the first page and began to recite: ' "Jack Mendoza was borne" – with a fucking "e", Anthony; where were you educated? Medieval England? – "in 1920 in a Jew-ish family" – what's that, Anthony? A family that shares certain characteristics with the Jews? – "in Balmain, where his dad was a draper and a Mercian" – do you know what a Mercian is, Anthony? It's a native of fucking Coventry – "and his mum was a simple housewife. He fell into a life a crime at any early age, through the inference" – I presume you mean fucking "influence" – "of a bad crowd. He lift school" – did I fucking really? – "at fifteen, and was further educated at the school of hard knocks" – hard fucking cocks, more like – "and the bluestone university" – the "bluestone college" was Pentridge, and I've never even visited that cunt-hole – "where he majored in standing up for himself and his fellow Hebrew brethren." '

He screwed up his face and screwed up my manuscript.

'Is this some sort of fucking joke, Anthony?' he shouted. 'I'm eighty-one years old and I've wasted six of my last precious days on God's earth telling my life story to a fucking retard.'

'It's only a first draft,' I said. 'We can cut out the bits you don't like.'

Mendoza hammered his fists on his thighs. 'You're not a fucking journalist at all, are you, Anthony?'

I shrugged.

'I trusted you, Anthony,' he said. 'Do you know why I trusted you? It wasn't because I liked your silly fucking head, with your bug eyes and your bulging neck and your short hair like some kind of bathhouse homo, and it damn well fucking wasn't because I thought you were a piece of Pommy fucking Grub Street pond scum. It was because I've got something on you, shitman.

'Remember little Leah? The fifteen year old who takes it up the tailpipe? Well, she's my girl, Anthony. She works for me. She's a porn star, and so are you. We got you on camera, filmed through the light fitting, Vegemite-mining an underage country runaway. Because the Hamilton Hotel *is* one of mine, as you would have discovered if you were a real muckraking journo and not some Munchausen's-by-proxy mental case who goes around pretending to be a writer to torment vulnerable war veterans.'

Suddenly I hated Mendoza. I promised myself to choke the life out of the feeble old fraud. He was a butchered chicken from that day, and would only seem alive because he was running around without a head.

'But one thing *really* surprises me,' he said. 'Lazarus and I finally got around to watching the video of you and Miss Anal Sex Queen 1986 – that was the year of her birth, if you remember – and I can tell a lot about you, Anthony, from your fifteen-minute, four-position performance. I can tell that you care if the little slut is enjoying herself, that you're counting to keep yourself from coming, and that you like it best with her on top. I can also tell that, as far as I can see, on close examination of the available evidence, by any reasonable measure, *to all intents and fucking purposes*, you're not even fucking Jewish.'

'No,' I admitted. 'I'm not.'

'So what the fuck are you then?'

At that moment an explosion of glass sent Mendoza flying to the floor, as a bullet, like an insect enraged by light, buzzed through the open window and slammed into the mirror behind his head. I leaped on Mendoza's back. His bony shoulders dug into my chest, and something cold and hard pressed against my pelvis. Another two gunshots tore plaster out of the back wall, showering my eyes with dust.

Lazarus stayed in his chair, pulled out his pistol, but didn't seem to know where to point it.

'Take cover and return fire, you fucking idiot!' I shouted.

His hands were trembling. A pair of bullets pierced the painting on the wall, ripping the hindquarters off a stallion. I figured there must be two shooters, firing in a V-formation from the apartment building's balconies. I shot back once with the derringer, but it was useless at this range.

I knew Lazarus carried another weapon.

'Give me your gun!' I shouted to him.

His eyes were dull and watery.

'Pass me the fucking gun!'

He handed it over slowly.

'Now get the fuck down!' I ordered.

He stood the fuck up, and lurched towards the bathroom door, drawing fire away from Mendoza and me. Then he stopped and turned back in our direction.

'Fuck off!' I shouted, waving him away with the pistol. 'Get fucked! Go!'

Lazarus's gun was the Webley .38 service pistol Mendoza had stolen from the army in 1944. It wasn't even loaded.

'Oh, you fucked fucking fuckhead,' I said to Lazarus, and rolled back onto the ground.

I crawled on my elbows to the front door, as if I were scrambling under barbed wire, then came to my feet when I was out of sight of the window. The door was about a metre from the axis of the V. The snipers were blasting the back teeth out of the window when I charged into the street and grabbed cover behind Mendoza's Corniche.

Either all the pizza he ate had turned Jed's brains to mozzarella, or he didn't realise I was in the room with Mendoza. I couldn't understand why he would be shooting at anyone, but I knew he would stop trying to kill me once he saw who I was. I threw the empty Webley high into the air, gave Jed a minute to call off his partner, then stood up, waving my arms.

Both men shot at me. One missed everything, the other hit a no-entry sign.

'Jed, it's me!' I called out. 'You stupid fucking cunt!'

I rolled under the car, and they shot out the tyres.

Mendoza himself pelted out of the door, shooting high and wide with a Heckler & Koch. He hadn't yet gauged where the gunmen were positioned, so he stood in the street and stared up at the sky, like a tourist under Centrepoint Tower. He looked heroic, stupid and dead. It took him a couple of seconds to pick out the guy on the motel balcony who was kneeling with his rifle butt hard against his shoulder. Mendoza let off two shots at the sniper, and he turned and ran. The other shooter had already retreated into the building.

Police cars screamed down William Street, running against the traffic. Cops sprinted into the lobby of the apartment building and towards Mendoza in the car park. He dropped his pistol and raised his hands. I decided to stay put under the Corniche, while they handcuffed Mendoza and pulled Lazarus out of the motel room. When the tarmac seemed clear of size-twelve shoes, I edged out from beneath the car.

A policewoman standing on a step watched me with zoological curiosity. She waited until I had dusted down my trousers, then marched me into the motel room with the others. Mendoza was showing a police sergeant his permit to carry a pistol.

'This,' said the sergeant, examining the licence, 'is for a revolver.'

Mendoza stared at it closely, as if he'd never read the small print before.

'This,' said the sergeant, showing Mendoza the bagged-up Heckler & Koch, 'is a semiautomatic pistol.'

'That's not my gun,' said Mendoza.

'So whose is it?' asked the sergeant.

'It's mine,' I said.

'And would you, sir, have a licence to carry a semiautomatic pistol?'

'Yes,' I said. 'Of course.'

Mendoza managed to look composed and unsurprised.

'Look, Sergeant,' said Mendoza, 'who's your boss at the station? It's Ray Robertson? Or Blackie Whitburn?'

'I don't know who you're talking about,' said the sergeant.

A detective was examining the bullet holes in the painting. 'Ray Robertson left the force in 1994, Jake,' he said. 'Blackie Whitburn passed away three years ago.'

'What about Len Forbes?' asked Mendoza.

'Retired with Robertson,' said the detective. 'Under the same cloud.'

'Stan Fuller?'

'Dead,' said the detective.

The policewoman looked through Mendoza's wallet.

'I know who you are,' she said, suddenly. 'Didn't they used to call you "Mr Vice"?'

'No,' said Mendoza.

'It was "Mister" something though, wasn't it?' she asked. ' "Mr Greedy"?'

'Mr Greedy's one of the Mr Men,' said the detective.

' "Mr Evil"?'

'You're thinking of Granny Evil,' said the detective. 'In Melbourne.'

'It's Mr Mendoza,' insisted Mendoza.

Dror barged in with a baseball cap on his head and a heavy sweat on his lip. He looked as though he'd just left the gym. He seemed to know a couple of the police, who let him inside the motel unit but stopped him before he could reach Mendoza. He shouted was everyone all right, and did anyone need a lawyer. He'd heard what was happening on the radio. I knew he meant the police scanner, and the cops must have realised too, as even the friendly officers bundled him out. I was still hyped up, waiting for another attack – wanting it, even. This time, I would know to go for Mendoza's Heckler & Koch. That was a nice weapon. The old man had used it well, but I could have done better. I could have taken out one of the gunnies and watched his body tumble off the balcony and break on the ground.

The policewoman searched me and found the derringer.

'I'm good for it,' I said.

Lazarus was back in his chair, staring at the wall. Even the police barely bothered to talk to him. Mendoza dropped a hand on his shoulder. The detective walked over, holding a notepad and pen. He was a rhino-faced bruiser in his mid-fifties, just old enough to have worked in the glory days.

'Are we looking at a new gang war, Jake?' he asked.

'I wouldn't know,' said Mendoza. 'I don't have a gang.'

'So what have you done to piss these people off?' he asked.

'I don't even know who they are,' he said.

'I find that hard to believe,' said the detective.

'And yet you've got no trouble with the idea that Lazarus and I, with a combined age of one hundred and forty-six years, are a criminal gang?'

'What about your young friend here?' asked the detective, pointing towards me.

'I've no fucking idea what he is,' said Mendoza. 'He's a man of fucking mystery, that's all I know.'

The policewoman checked my gun licence against my driver's licence.

'Nicholas Anthony?' she said.

'Yeah, that's me.'

FIFTEEN

[Seaview House, Greenknowe Avenue, Potts Point. 15-03-02. 2:07 pm.]

My name's Nick Anthony. Some of my mates call me 'Slick', others call me 'Tony'.

Where did Klein come from?

I read it off the war memorial, when I was doing recon for my interview with the *Jewish Times.*

What religion are you?

I don't know. Church of England. Something like that. I've never given it much thought. You don't, do you, unless it's something weird. I'm not Catholic.

Why did you pose as Jewish?

I never said I was Jewish.

And you're not a journalist either?

Not by training, no. I'm a soldier.

In which army?

The British Army. I was dishonourably discharged two years ago.

What for?

Dealing ecstasy.

So why aren't you inside?

They didn't want to prosecute me. It would've brought the whole unit down. Everyone was using. They caught me by accident. They weren't looking for drugs. Somebody in the unit was selling arms to the Kosovars. They searched the barracks but they didn't find any weapons, because the Kosovars had them all. But they lucked on my stash and that was that: ten years of service down the drain.

I said I had post-traumatic stress disorder and needed a hundred Es for my personal use, to help me cope with the nightmares. The docs signed off on that. I'd served in Northern Ireland, Kosovo. I'd been in the army since I was nineteen. I was obviously fucked in the head.

Did you come to Australia to infiltrate my operation?

No, I'd never heard of you.

So why did you come here?

I wanted to become a journalist.

Don't fuck with me, Slick.

Why would I? I'm telling the truth.

Start from the beginning.

I was born in a military hospital in Colchester, Essex. My old man was a sergeant in the army. He was a hard man, but he's nice enough now. I grew up wherever Dad was stationed – in Belize, in Gibraltar, in Winchester, but I ended up going to secondary school in Aldershot, the home of the British Army, as it says on the road signs. Moving schools is tough on a kid. As soon as you make friends you lose them. You're always having to fight for your place.

I liked to read, so Dad thought I might be a poof and decided to toughen me up. He used to take me out into the woods and show me how to draw maps and make hide-outs. He bought me an air rifle and we'd find places to shoot birds. He was a good bloke, you know. Old-fashioned but well meaning. I like him a lot. My mum too. I was the only child. Did I say that? I think that's important.

Not to me, it isn't, Slick. I'm not writing your fucking memoirs. Where is this story going?

Mate, I never rushed you.

Yeah, okay, okay, go on. But get on with it.

I wasn't a great pupil –

Oh, for fuck's sake . . .

Listen to me. It's all part of the story. I wasn't much use in class because we had moved about so much, and nobody in my family'd had an education, and Dad kept taking me to the woods when I should've been doing my homework. I was good at football, but my best subject was English. We had a great teacher – Mr Sutton – who encouraged me to write compositions. I always thought that when I wrote my first book I'd dedicate it to Mr Sutton.

I started to change when I was about fourteen. I got into a bit of trouble, fighting at the football. We used to defend the East Bank against the away fans. It started off with fists but ended up with knives and bottles. I got nicked and fined and that was it. I never went again. But they got worried about me at school because I never used to be a bad kid, and the teachers thought that maybe I needed a bit more direction. I obviously wasn't going to do well in my GCSEs, so the careers master suggested I should learn a trade. I told him I liked writing and wanted to be a journalist, but he said I should probably think about joining the army, which usually took the boys who got arrested at the football.

At home, of course, my old man was saying the same thing. But he knew a lot about the army that the teachers didn't. Everybody thinks it's all pig-thick Geordies and Scousers who just want to fight, but the army's full of blokes who are good at their trades – if you're a mechanic or an engineer, it's life or death – or crap at their professions. It's a rest home for useless dentists, lawyers and vets, people who'd never make it in civvy street because they're lazy or drunk or just stupid. But there's also another layer of blokes you wouldn't expect to find in uniform: chippies and physios and even photographers and journalists. Once you get into the army, you can move sideways from blowing people up to reporting on other people doing it. That's the theory anyway. My dad said I ought to join the infantry, learn a bit about the military, then get transferred to *Soldier* magazine in Aldershot. Then, when I got out of the army, I could be a defence correspondent for the *Sun,* which was the only newspaper Dad knew. It wasn't a bad idea, really, but I took no notice because he was my old man. Instead, I failed a load of exams and got a job selling advertising on the *Aldershot News and Weekend Advertiser.* I gave it up after a few months, but I had learned the words people used around papers – 'proofs' and 'type' and 'body copy' and all that. I'd had drinks with journalists – not many of them, because they tried to keep away from the ad staff – and got an idea of how their jobs worked. I taught myself to type on an old office Remington and learned shorthand from a book.

I had to leave the *News* when I got into a scrap with the production coordinator, a kid called Jeremy Knight. He was always going on about how he knew jujitsu, and grabbing people from behind and acting like he was going to choke them out and stuff. He did it to me in the South Western, just around the corner from the paper, and I threw him and punched him. I thought he was just bullshitting about the jujitsu, but it turned out he really was good at it, and we had a big rolling fight that ended up getting us banned from the pub. We accidentally broke a window and got picked up by the cops and it got into the paper – the fucking *Aldershot News,* would you believe it? – and we were both told to find another job.

Jeremy – Jed – became my best mate. We practised jujitsu

together, and I didn't even mind when he started calling himself 'the Jedi' or 'Jedi Knight'. We both got bored of jujitsu but we liked keeping fit – even though all he ever ate were pizzas the size of bike wheels – so we moved to Hackney and took jobs as cycle couriers. That was a fucked idea. I broke my ankle and my collarbone, and Jed split his head open. After about a year, we figured out we might be safer in the army. So we joined up together, and I'm sure my old man had his suspicions.

Basic training was nothing to me. We were older than most of the other recruits, and Dad had already taught me everything anyway. Jed found it a bit harder, but I helped him along, and we didn't take shit from anyone.

It was okay being in the army. It felt – how can I put it? – inevitable. Once we were in, more or less everything was taken out of our hands. We were told what to do and how to do it, where to go and how long to stay there. Doctor, dentist, food, drink, travel: everything was taken care of. All we had to find for ourselves was women.

There was always something to do: you could blow up something or crash something or shoot at something. I played a lot of football – me and Jed both got into the regimental second team – and boxed a bit. Jed fancied himself as a swimmer, but he wasn't all that good. Everything was pretty cruisy until we got sent to Belfast and the Paddies started trying to kill us.

We did two tours of Northern Ireland and I found out what it was like to have people want you dead. We got shot at and bombed, and we fucked the palest skinned, rattest-faced Proddie women you could imagine, and made it all better with pockets full of Es and trips.

At first we were buying pills retail, but that was a mug's game. Jed made a connection with a UVF guy, and we started pulling in bulk supplies at wholesale prices and selling them in the barracks, then at discos and dance parties. Everyone was taking pills anyway: us, the paramilitaries, the ratfaces, the RUC. It was turning into a smiley war, with no hard feelings when you blew some Paddy's arse back to the Vatican, and even ugly Belfast looked pretty in the light.

Jed was the best mate I ever had. He was always there for me, watching my back. He saved my life at least twice in Belfast, and I knocked out a bloke who tried to stab him in a pub. I took twenty-five stitches in my forearm to save his ugly fucking face. I loved Jed, you know. He could make me laugh about anything. And he had all these plans for our future.

But I still wanted to be a writer. I used to send these stories about a soldier's life to the *Belfast Telegraph*. They printed bits of them, but with most of the words changed. I never got paid and they never used my name. They were treating me as a source instead of a writer. Then this 'Billy Cobbett' got in touch and asked if I knew anything about the Unionist feuds. I did, as it happened, because whenever we lost a man we leaned on our moles to tell us who did it. Sometimes they knew, most of the time they didn't. Once we had names – usually the wrong ones – we went to the UDA, or the UFF, which was the same thing, to help us find them and fuck them up. It always felt like we got our revenge, but it usually turned out that we had killed a dissident UDA man or a fucking nuisance neighbour.

One time, Jed took off his uniform and went out with the UVF and shot a Catholic boy dead. They told him he was a terrorist, but he was just a kid who worked for Sinn Fein. Because of that, Jed can't admit we were wrong to fight. Otherwise he would be a murderer. Jed remembers that boy's face, and sometimes he sees it on other kids, who stare back as if they recognise him too. Once or twice he's seen the boy in an empty room.

You get hard in the army. You laugh at things that aren't funny, like the idea of some poor bastard getting shot in the head for waking up a UDA commander with 'Shaddap Your Face'.

Me and Jed were brothers, because we both knew what the other had done. It could've been either of us that shot the kid. The reason Jed went out hunting Catholics was the IRA had attacked our patrol and blown up the driver, Bob Edmonds. Jed had been sitting with him in the front seat, and afterwards he'd had to pull pieces of Bob's brain out of his hair . . .

[Inaudible.]

Let me pour you a whisky, Anthony. I understand. The horrors of war rest heavily on us all.

Thanks, Jake.

Call me that again, son, and you'll be pulling bits of your own brain out of your hair. Now, tell me about this Billy Cobbett. Was he another dead war hero whose name you stole?

There's a pub called the William Cobbett in Farnham. I don't know if he was related to the people there or what, but he wrote this column for the *Belfast Telegraph* that was supposed to look inside the paramilitaries. I told him what I knew about that lunatic Johnny Clarke, and gave him the squaddies' view of one or two other things that were going on. I saved all the cuttings that I helped with. It was good to see the papers get something right for once. I kept asking the journalist if there was some way I could get into working for the *Telegraph*, and he promised he'd do his best.

We got a great story about Clarke's lieutenant having an affair with another commander's wife, and the bloke who was doing Cobbett got me in for an interview with the general manager of the paper, who said that, bearing in mind my experience, he'd be happy to offer me a job selling display ads. I told him I'd rather be a British soldier in Northern Ireland: fewer people would hate me.

When we were rotated out of Belfast, I went to the boys on *Soldier* magazine and asked if there was a chance of getting a billet there, but they were all sitting on their postings until they retired or died, and it's been a long while since anyone was killed in the line of duty on *Soldier* magazine.

We spent a few weeks training in Aldershot, wasting most of the time tripping in these terrible nightclubs, until we suddenly got sent to Kosovo. We had no idea why we were there. Jed had never even heard of Albania; he thought it was a joke country where James Bond villains come from. It was hard to get drugs at first, which pissed everyone off, but as usual Jed met a bloke in a bar, and we started taking shipments from Italy.

Everything was great until the Italians upped their price and Jed started talking to the Kosovars. The thing was, the Kosovars didn't want to be paid in cash, they needed weapons, and – I didn't know this – Jed set up a deal where he'd disappear some quite heavy kit in exchange for ten thousand Es. It was another Great Fucked Idea of Jed's, because (a) they might've used the guns to shoot at us eventually, and (b) it would take us months to sell ten thousand Es in Kosovo. Now the army don't care if you're all loved up on a Saturday night, but they're not happy if you love your enemy and pass on your kit to him. It's against the spirit of the whole thing. So Jed got shopped by an outraged corporal, and I was caught up in the slipstream. The fact that we'd both seen combat went in our favour, and the army didn't want a scandal. In the end we were both dishonourably discharged, and we lost our entitlements but we were happy just to dodge ten years in Colchester.

We went back to Aldershot and got a flat together near the South Western, and in two fucking weeks we were barred again, this time because Jed nutted the landlord after a row about whether Priština was founded by the Romans. Jed wanted to do history at university, and we both thought about studying, but then Jed decided we should be private detectives instead, because somebody in the pub had told him the PI's course was easy to pass. Jed said it would be a way into journalism for me, because I'd be learning the skills I'd need as a reporter: observation, interviewing and writing reports. We mainly did surveillance for compensation claims, sitting outside people's houses in a white transit van, trying to catch blokes with broken backs landscaping their gardens, then we were hired to gather information on this pikey family who kept pretending to get run over by their own uncles and cousins. They figured out what we were doing and came at us with shotguns. I didn't realise it but Jed was armed too. We had a firefight in Ash. That's when I realised our lives were fucked. I'd had enough of being attacked by strangers, and chased through the streets by nutters, and always being hated by everyone.

I was going out with a girl called Helen from Trowbridge in Wiltshire; before we'd got together she'd been thinking of going to Australia for a working holiday. We were both going on twenty-nine and the cut-off date for applications was thirty, so this was our last chance. We decided we were going to leave our old lives behind, and start again. The funny thing is, I never thought of going without Jed.

So we came to Sydney as a threesome, although not literally – at least, not at fucking first. We stopped off in Thailand and Jed met an Aussie girl on Ko Samui. He moved in with her when we got to Sydney, and me and Helen rented the flat behind the police station in the Cross. Life was pretty good for a couple of months, until the money ran out. Helen got a part-time job as a sandwich hand. Jed subcontracted as a PI to a big local outfit, doing pretty much the same as we'd done in Aldershot, and I invented a CV and tried to get a job as a journalist.

Australia's like the army. You've got all these shit people in mid-level trades. We met loads of backpackers in Thailand who had blagged their way into good jobs, and the first week I came here I hit the jackpot. I applied for something I figured nobody else would go for – a reporter on the *Catholic Weekly*. I told them I used to work as a section editor on the *Sunday Times*. I said I knew I was overqualified for the job, but it had become important to me to work in a religious environment. I felt this was the next stage in both my spiritual and my career development. They hired me on the spot.

And then?

They fired me when I turned in my first story.

So what did you do then?

I worked with Jed, just to get a bit of money. He'd established himself as a PI pretty quickly, plus he had his usual thing going on with Es. He'd somehow got himself involved with these Russian coke dealers too, and we all hoovered up a gram or two at weekends. Then Jed started employing Helen. She was good at the surveillance, because it used her two main skills: sitting around and staring at things. We split our case load, so she sometimes did jobs with me and sometimes with him. Then work came in bodyguarding the Russians in Bondi. I had to take a firearms course – which was a joke – and Jed got me a permit. They don't normally give them to non-residents, but there's a loophole for overseas-born security staff working for foreign diplomats, and the Russians had bought some kind of accreditation from their embassy. They were supposed to be attached to a trade mission.

While I was looking after the coke dealers – who never once sold any coke – Jed was doing Helen in the back of the surveillance van. I never caught them at it, but it was obvious what was going on because Jed's Aussie girl kicked him out and he had to get a place of his own.

I kept on applying for small jobs in journalism and spent two days as a subeditor on *Supermarket News* before they realised I couldn't use their computer system. Then I saw an ad in the paper for a reporter on the *Jewish Times*. I thought if I could get the Catholic job I could probably get the Jewish one. Even less people'd want to do that. I copied my name from the war memorial, changed my references to fit and played Spiegeleier just like the Catholic guy.

I lasted longer at the *Times* because Spiegeleier gave me a week to settle in. All I had to do was edit wire copy. Then your story came up and I thought I'd go all out to impress him. You know, I might not be the greatest writer in the world, but I'll go in there and ask the tough questions, and I thought maybe I'd come back with something so good that he wouldn't sack me as soon as he read the lead.

I told Helen she had to leave her job or leave me, and I'd be bringing in enough from the *Jewish Times* to look after both of us. She quit, and we were sort of getting on all right, then you fucked everything up by making me eat the tape.

I told you that was a joke.

It was the sort of thing we did in Belfast. I met one guy in the UFF who could eat a motorbike.

And that's it? That's your whole story? You're a dishonourably discharged British soldier who came to Australia and pretended to be Jewish, pretended to be a journalist and just happened to find me? This is all a fucking accident? You expect me to believe that?

It's true.

Christ, Anthony, you are a fucking idiot.

SIXTEEN

It was a relief to have told Mendoza the truth, and the next thing I had to do was explain myself to Siobhan. I wasn't much of a liar – except to officers and cops – and it bothered me to be sleeping with somebody who thought I was somebody else. When Siobhan tossed back her hair and cried 'Tony', I kept thinking she was yelling out for an old boyfriend. And when she called me 'Anthony', it felt like I was in bed with one of my teachers from school (Mrs Clarkson – and that wasn't so bad).

The only problem was, I couldn't tell how much she liked me because she thought I was a journalist. I'd always done all right with girls – especially Irish girls – but my confidence had taken a headbutt when I'd found out Mendoza had paid Leah to take me upstairs. I'd never slept with a prostitute. I didn't like that sort of thing. Even the strippers at Baby Dolls made me uncomfortable.

I must've given Siobhan a set of keys, because she was in my flat when I came home, going through my cuts again.

'I've read everything now,' she said. 'It's all brilliant. I love the way you can move so easily between different styles. And some of your pen-names are hilarious.'

Siobhan was beautiful, and my throat went soft when I looked at her. I wanted to cuddle her under white sheets all weekend, and march around her with a rifle, protecting her from all the bad things in the world.

'I love people who can use words the way you do,' she said.

She asked if I ever read poetry, and I didn't know how to answer. 'Come to bed,' she said, and this obviously wasn't the time to bring up the fact that I had failed English in the end.

Siobhan wanted to go out to dinner – which was just as well, because I didn't have any plates – but she didn't feel like fancy food. Spiegeleier had already taken her to Darley Street Thai and Bistro Moncur, and I wondered what he hoped he would get out of that.

She said he was the perfect gentleman. I couldn't figure out how old he was – it's always hard to tell with bald guys – but Siobhan reckoned he must be in his early fifties, and she didn't know how he could be happy in such a small-time job.

'Not everyone's a good writer,' I said, since not even everyone in my bed was one.

Siobhan asked me to take her somewhere that had the real flavour of the Cross. I thought of piss and kebab meat, and speed cut with Ajax.

We held hands as we walked past the fountain. She circled my palm with her finger.

Early evening was the time the ruined people came out: cracked and blistered men with skin stretched like cling wrap across the bones of their faces, and toothless women whose lips had collapsed into their gums, all eyeballing a gang of pale British lads looking for a happy-hour drink to kick off their evening. The gap-year boys wore their hair shaved tight to their heads, with England football shirts or Ralph Lauren polos, like hooligans abroad. But they were exaggerating their accents, swaggering in a foreign country when they'd have been cowering at home. I could drop two of them with one punch and sort out the rest before they had time to run.

I had to stop thinking like that. What did I care if a law-school cricketer from High Wycombe acted hard on Darlinghurst Road? They weren't having a go at me. I switched from screwing out the boys to checking out their Home Counties girls, with their hair scraped back and tied up, and big looping earrings. I watched their fake-tanned breasts quiver under low-cut T-shirts, and I thought if I could have any woman in the world it would be Siobhan.

'Stop leching,' said Siobhan unfairly. 'Dan's sorry he sacked you, you know. He wishes he'd stood up to his publisher.'

'To tell the truth,' I said, 'he made the right decision.'

'No, Tony,' she said, 'someone like you could've transformed that paper. You might even've got Dan back on track, once he saw what you could do. That thing you have, it's a gift, Tony. It's precious.'

People were standing around on the corners, waiting for the night to begin. A bouncer wearing a number on a lanyard around his neck chatted with a shopkeeper while an Asian girl read the *Daily Telegraph* under an awning. Another woman came and stood beside her, and suddenly there were half-a-dozen people, all in the same spot, like a queue without a bus stop, or a gang of builders waiting for a white van. I could tell the bouncer wanted to order them to move along but couldn't point to anything they might be doing wrong.

I led Siobhan into Kellet Street, around the back of Darlinghurst Road, where the strip clubs, from their rear entrances, were more clearly brothels. They had all put out their bins on the kerb for collection, crammed with unimaginable waste. Through the window of the Continental Barbershop I could see an old man who looked a bit like Mendoza, draped in a smock, his cheeks lathered for a shave. A little way down the street I showed Siobhan the New York restaurant, huddled between two neon-lit doorways. She read from the menu on the window. The daily special, described in hesitant arthritic letters on a scrap of lined paper, was fillet steak with potatoes and two veg.

Two white vans were parked opposite, in the loading zone outside the Mansions Hotel's pokie-room casino. One was marked *Jim's Mowers*, the other was making a delivery to the hotel kitchen. There were a lot of white vans around. It was difficult to tell one from another.

We stood in the doorway of the New York, ignored by customers and unnoticed by staff, until Siobhan coughed, and they all looked at us at once. Each of the restaurant's formica tables was taken by a slate-haired, cancer-skinned man sitting on his own.

'One minute, darlings,' the waitress said to us.

She looked around the small room, sucking her teeth, until she found a tattooed pensioner who was staring at his plate as if he could read the future in the pattern in his gravy.

'Billy, love, could you go and sit with Derek, please?' the waitress asked.

'But Derek's a dog, Rita,' said Billy.

'I know he is,' said Rita, 'but these young lovers need a table to themselves.'

'Why don't you move Apache Frank?' he asked.

She glanced at a tall man with a ponytail that hung to the small of his back. 'Because Frank's asleep,' she said.

When Billy came to his table, Derek settled his bill, stood up and left. He paused at the doorway to say goodbye to everyone except Billy. Two old men lifted their forks and cocked their heads, including Apache Frank, who had only been pretending to be asleep.

We sat under a ceiling fan and looked at our reflection in cracked mirror tiles on the wall. Rita brought us the menu. Most dishes cost about eight dollars. It was only eighty cents extra for a bowl of soup, but Siobhan wasn't interested.

'Everybody else is having the soup,' I told her.

'That's because they've got no teeth,' she said.

The old man from the barbershop hobbled in, freshly shaved. A couple of the others looked up at him and nodded. He found his own table in a corner and, after a moment's wait, the waitress brought him soup.

Slow Eddie, still wearing his battered pork-pie hat, looked around for a free place. The waitress sat him next to the shaved man, and they ignored each other. Eddie knew he recognised me from somewhere, and winked a hooded eye.

'There'd be hundreds of stories in this room,' said Siobhan.

She asked what exactly I was doing for Mendoza, but I didn't exactly know. I said I was helping him with a book.

'Ghost-writing?' she asked.

'We're writing about his ghosts,' I said. 'But I'm not a ghost writer.'

'Of course not,' she said. 'You've got your own voice.'

She had the most beautifully even teeth.

She reached across the table. 'You've got real man's hands,' she said, playing with my fingers. 'They're not like writers' hands. They're like brickies' hands, all callused and scarred.'

'I worked as a brickie's mate once,' I said.

'Isn't it funny how writers always have these weird jobs,' said Siobhan. 'I spent a summer as a psychic's assistant. Were you at college when you were a brickie's mate?'

'No,' I said, 'I wasn't at college.'

'Do you talk to Mendoza about what's going on in the Cross?' she asked.

'About the troubles?' I said. 'Not really.'

'Don't call it "the troubles" if it's a war,' she said.

She smiled. She was beautiful. I wanted to lick her teeth.

'What's he like to interview?' she asked.

'He describes things that happened honestly, I think,' I said, 'but he can only see them in the way they affected him.'

'That's the same as any interviewee,' she said, 'isn't it?'

'I don't know,' I admitted.

'Are you ready to order?' asked the waitress, dropping onto the seat next to mine. 'I can recommend the fillet steak.'

She pronounced it 'filly'.

'I'll have that, please,' said Siobhan.

I chose the schnitzel.

'But what's Mendoza's justification?' Siobhan asked me.

'For what? His life? He doesn't think he's done anything wrong. I'm not sure he even believes in right and wrong.'

'What does he believe in?' she asked.

I loved the sound of her voice. She spoke as if she were singing.

'Taking what he wants,' I said.

'And what do you believe in?' she asked.

I touched my forehead and looked down at the table.

'I'm sorry,' she said. 'That's a typical interviewer's tactic, eh? Asking about someone else to get the subject to open up about himself.'

'Look,' I said, 'I'm happy to open up –'

'So what do you believe in?' she asked. 'I mean, you're obviously not orthodox.'

Uh?

'Religious,' she said. 'Orthodox Jewish.'

'No,' I admitted, 'I'm not even Jewish. I just said that to get the job.'

'Really!' said Siobhan. 'That's fantastic! I did wonder about your . . . you know.'

'Why is it fantastic?' I asked.

'That you could fool somebody like Dan – you know, a professional Jew. You must be great undercover, Tony.'

'I've lied about everything,' I admitted.

'Who hasn't?' said Siobhan. 'Tell me more about Helen. What was she really like?'

'Ah, she was –' I stopped. 'You don't honestly want to know, do you? You just want to hear the way I talk about her.'

'Of course,' she said. 'Why would I care about your skanky ex-girlfriend?'

'She was lovely,' I said. 'All my ex-girlfriends were lovely. I have the greatest respect for anyone who sleeps with me, and I send them cards and presents for the rest of their lives.'

'That's funny,' she said, 'because all my ex-boyfriends were bastards. I'd have them rounded up and shot if my uncle was still around.'

At this point, looking back, I should probably have asked who her uncle was, but I was still trying to explain who I was, so I let it drop.

'Was Helen a writer?' asked Siobhan.

I told her she wasn't.

'I don't think I could be with somebody who wasn't a writer,' she said.

'Well, you have,' I said, meaning me.

'Of course I have,' she said, 'but it's never worked out.'

Rita brought us each a side plate with two slices of white bread and a knob of butter.

'Was Helen pretty?' Siobhan asked me.

I told her she was.

'Do you want to get back with her?'

I told her I didn't.

'Am I better than her?'

I asked in what way.

'In every way.'

I told her she was.

'Good,' she said. 'Now you can eat your schnitzel.'

My schnitzel looked like emery cloth. Inside, it was grey and soft. Siobhan ate her fillet delicately but quickly, and mopped up the meat juices with a slice of her bread.

'The biker shootings've had a good run in Dublin,' she said. 'They've asked for more background. Do you think you could get me an interview with Mendoza?'

I promised I'd ask him.

The bill arrived on the back of a Post-It note, and we paid it at the mechanical till.

'Well,' said Siobhan, 'we won't have a meal like that again for a long time. I promise you.'

She said we should find somewhere quiet to have a drink, but to Siobhan a quiet place was a place with quiet music. We walked down William Street to O'Malley's, where she could hear a guitarist singing Christy Moore songs by the window. We drank pints of Guinness and listened to 'City of Chicago', and I remember thinking the world was a perfect place.

SEVENTEEN

[Ava's Backpackers, 6–8 Orwell Street, Points Point. 20-03-02. 1:59 pm.]

You are a shit writer, Anthony, and everything you write is shit. Despite all you have told me, I'm going to keep on calling you 'Anthony Klein', because it is not the name that is chosen for us that counts, but the name that we choose for ourselves. I selected a title that personifies power, courage and strength: Mendoza, the champion of the Jews. You pilfered a surname that means 'small', 'little', 'lower', 'runty', 'petty' or 'slight'.

You're probably wondering why I'm carrying on with this fucking farce, acting like you're Boswell to my Samuel Johnson, even though I know you can't write a fucking word, and you don't even know who Boswell was. Tell you the truth, I'm wondering that too. But I enjoy talking to you, Anthony. I've never been in therapy, but I imagine it's something like this, except with a real Jew instead of an uncircumcised impostor. I'm enjoying the experience of mulling over my life's successes, and the women I had forgotten I had ever fucked, such as McCoy's various wives. Then there's the fact that you might have saved my life. You might have got me killed too, but I could see you had the best of intentions when you ran outside and threw Lazarus's gun into the air, then hid under my Rolls, attracting gunfire that destroyed the tyres. I could see your British military training was coming into play, and you were saving me like your forefathers saved the Australian infantry at the Fall of Singapore.

You are a failure, Anthony. You have failed at school, with women, as a soldier and as drug dealer. You are thirty-one years old, and you haven't got a house, a car, a job or a girlfriend. I'm not going to let you fail again! My book is the thing that will make you a man, Anthony! You will start it at the beginning and finish it at the end, and you will not fuck it up! You will listen to what I say, and you will try to take it in, because there are many lessons to be learned from my life! You will find somebody to help you write the fucking thing, because you are a spastic!

Okay, okay.

No, it's not fucking 'okay', Anthony. I am giving you a gift. I am handing you a future. *I* am saving *your* life.

What do you want me to say?

I don't want you to say anything. I want you to shut up and listen. I have received intelligence – which is not something you could ever claim, Anthony – on who was behind the attack on the tattooists and the attempt on my life. It's taken more than thirty years, but I knew it would happen one day: the Malts are back.

Maltese?

No, the Maltesers. Of course, it's the Maltese, Anthony. It's always the Maltese. Have you heard of Charlie Adami, the president of the Mutineers MC? You might have seen him on television, whining on about how bikies are all misunderstood Father Christmases who cry into their hankies at romantic comedies? Adami is a second-generation Malt.

His Mutineers were once members of the GraveDiggers MC, which sought to control the amphetamine and ecstasy trade in Newtown and the inner west. Adami's faction split from the gang many years ago, after an esoteric dispute over who had second rights to a used woman. The GraveDiggers labelled them 'mutineers', and they adopted the name with the kind of fierce pride often displayed by imbeciles with nothing else in their life to feel satisfied about.

Adami took his men to Parramatta, to build themselves up on pastizzi and pasta, before storming back to the city to attack individual GraveDiggers on the doors and in the street, and finally firebomb their Petersham clubhouse. The GraveDiggers knew Adami was a psychopath, and none of them had the guts to knock him, so the club surrendered and Adami closed them down and transferred their membership to the Mutineers. By the arcane rules that supposedly regulate the behaviour of these fat fools, the Mutineers were entitled to inherit the GraveDiggers' territory – from King Street to Homebush – but, in the manner of the Maltese throughout history, they wanted the Cross too. It's in their blood.

The Maltese are not generally smart, Anthony, but Adami thought solidly for about a decade and realised that what was holding back his gang was the fact that whenever they committed a crime they did it with their name on a little patch on the front of their jacket and their address on a big patch on the back. It occurred to him that maybe if they didn't wear their colours *all* the time, they might get away with something once in a while. And imagine the havoc this would cause in the rest of the imbecile community, who would no more knock a bloke while wearing a T-shirt than drive around in a Hyundai Excel. Then Adami realised that if they didn't need the jackets to sell drugs, they might not need the bikes either. With this revelation foremost in his mind, Adami planned to take over the Cross, which had been the territory of the Cannibals MC ever since I made the uncharacteristic error of leaving the drugs trade to a self-promoting shower of unshaven imbeciles.

The Cannibals kept their pill press in the basement of the Ink tattoo studio. They knew the Mutineers would come for them, and that they would hit at the heart of their business, but they imagined they would arrive on bikes, en masse, wearing their silly fucking sew-on tough stickers and other clothing that was last fashionable – and last washed – in 1969, and therefore be visible from ten kilometres – or three decades – away.

Instead, Adami, a former serviceman like ourselves, used his contacts in the army to get hold of special forces weaponry and mounted the commando-style assault you were fortunate to witness from the confines of McDonald's, where you were staging what passes for a sophisticated, romantic rendezvous in the Hampshire town of Aldershot.

And Adami's pièce de résistance, his coup de grâce, his piss in their fucking petrol tanks, was the fact his men didn't even bring their own Harleys: they stole them from the Cannibals.

My sources tell me the Cannibals struck a deal with Adami to let his men into the Cross. And once they had dealt with their fellow imbeciles, the Mutineers turned their attention to more established powers. The Maltese have an unsettled feud with me, and Adami feels strong enough to even up the score. So they came after me, Anthony, after all these fucking years. The bastard sons of Gozo Joe Stone have returned to wreak their revenge.

And what are you going to do?

What do you think I'm going to do, you imbecile? I'm going to call the old crew back together – McCoy, Big Stan, the Little Fish, all of them – and we're going to face down these Maltese cunts once and for all. Lazarus, get them on the phone now – starting with the Little Fish. I need him the most of all.

But they're dead. They're all dead.

Don't talk to me about 'dead', Anthony. Gozo Joe Stone is fucking dead and he's reaching out to me from beyond the grave, trying to squeeze the life out of my throat with his fingers. Lazarus, get me the phone.

Lazarus isn't here.

Of course he isn't here. He's in St Vincent's hospital, the poor fella. Your adolescent gunplay nearly gave him a heart attack. He's a good man – as tough as they come – but you can't expect him to beat back the bikers with an unloaded gun.

Who's driving your car?

The Roller? Some fucking cheating Arab grease monkey. I told you, Anthony, it's in for repair.

How did you get here?

Natural Science is looking after me. He's standing guard at the door. I will share my memories in front of Lazarus but not a giant rent-a-*schvartzer* with a cudgel for a cock.

I didn't notice him outside.

I'm not surprised, Anthony. After all, Kings Cross is full of one hundred and forty kilo, six-foot-six niggers. He was probably hiding in a crowd of them.

I'm just saying –

Perhaps the New York Nicks are in town.

Maybe you should get on with your story. You might drop dead tomorrow.

I'll go at a moment of my own choosing, Anthony. I can assure you of that. Which is more than I can say for poor Mad Dog McCoy, who passed away when his commercially acquired wife still had a dozen good fucking-years left in her, and thus perhaps he did not get full value for his money.

I believe that time ironed out some of McCoy's worst character flaws, Anthony, but, in the past, his biggest problems were jealousy and greed. He found it hard to share a woman, a friend or even a boss. When I came back from Vegas, he was jealous of my relationship with Izzy Berger, which was a joke, since I couldn't stand the silly-hatted cunt. But we had made a truck-load out of Sinatra, and Deborah was keen to see me move into areas of business that she could discuss with her friends in the newly established Hakoah Club, so I called a meeting of the boys and announced my intention to dominate the fields of music management and concert promotion. Berger and I had identified a number of Australian singers and bands with the potential to become as big as Sinatra. Berger was going to manage most of the acts in the new business, which would employ our existing skills in nightclub administration, licensing variation, debt collection, crowd control and creative advertising. The idea was that the same heads that rechristened the Filipina Picasso 'Tina's Talking Tits' could be used to generate ideas to improve the fortunes of my wife's cousin Arnold Zwaybil, 'the Eastern Suburbs Frank Sinatra'.

We also had on our books Giuseppe Milano, 'the Western Suburbs Frank Sinatra'; Alf Cockburn, 'the Sinatra of Sydney's South'; Col Tanner, 'the Aussie Tony Bennett'; and Freddy Freed, 'the Dover Heights Dean Martin'. I gave Milano to Big Stan, Tanner to the Little Fish, and Freed to McCoy. This last decision was a terrible mistake, since Freddy Freed, like Dean Martin, had a limited vocal range, and was compelled to fill out his sound with two back-up singers who went by the stage names Ada and Ava.

Ava was not much of a vocalist either, but I auditioned the female vocalists with the same rigour I had brought to choosing hostesses for the Patton, and I realised immediately that Ava's throat would be better deployed in more traditional areas of our business. McCoy, of course, was in love with her. He took her out to dinner three times a week and kept her up all night talking about his childhood, but not the bit where he fucked

Rachel what's-her-name after three of us had already been up her, because he knew it was 'now or never', as Elvis sang that same year.

When McCoy was not boring Ava with stories from Balmain Boys, I was introducing her to various important jacks, who would take her for a tour of their beat and return an hour or so later a little lighter around the balls. Eventually McCoy found out and came crying to me that he and Ava were going to get married and how could I do this to him and all the usual shit I'd been hearing since he was fourteen years old. I said, 'Mad Dog, if you want a back-up singer, why don't you take the other one? She's a better singer, and she fucks like a statue, which means (a) she's no good to me and (b) she'll stay still while you tell her about the fucking kelpie your mother wouldn't let you keep in nineteen-thirty-fucking-three.'

I thought I was doing him a favour in letting him know that Ava had leaked his lame pillow talk. I hoped it would make him understand that she didn't care about him the way he cared about her. But McCoy didn't think, *I'm better off without that little slut.* He thought, *I'll knock my best friend, then I'll knock her, then I'll neck myself.* He was always looking for a woman to kill or to die for. He should have been born an Italian, or one of those psycho Yids that hang around the wops for so long they go wop themselves, like Bugsy Siegel and Meyer Lansky, or Jack Spot in your own unwashed and wintry homeland.

I don't know if you've ever killed anyone, Anthony, or if every time you come under fire you run towards the gunnies throwing your piece in the air, but let me tell you this: if you are going to knock a bloke, you don't go around telling his mates and the jacks because this will eliminate what we call 'the element of surprise'. Once you've made up your mind to do it, the next step is the planning, followed by the execution. McCoy added a redundant stage that we might call 'the skiting', in which he informed anyone and everyone that he was going to shoot me at my private table in the Patton. I heard about his plan from the drunken magician, Morrie the Magnificent, and asked the Little Fish to sort him out for me.

What do you mean by 'sort him out'?

I mean what I say, Anthony. I don't go around saying I'm Jewish, or I'm a journalist, when I'm not.

McCoy had been one of my best mates all my life, and my lieutenant since the war. I didn't want to hurt him – although, I must admit, he'd always grated on me a bit – but I needed to warn him off, and all the others too. They all knew he was coming after me – the wops, the Malts, the Paddies (Christ, they were useless) and the jacks – and they all had to see that he couldn't get away with it.

The problem was that McCoy was the Little Fish's mate too. Not a close mate, because the Little Fish didn't get close to people after the war, but the two of them went back a long way. So the Little Fish persuaded me to give McCoy a chance, and just warn him off.

I sent a pair of nobodies around to his apartment in Malabar. They delivered their message, and McCoy threw one man off the balcony – luckily, it was only a second-floor unit – and hit the other across the face with an iron, which was red hot and still plugged into the wall, as they had surprised him while he was ironing his best shirt for his regular date with Ava the Swallow (I chose that name because a swallow is a noted songbird).

When he saw what McCoy had done to the imbeciles, the Little Fish packed a cricket bat in his kitbag and got Big Stan to drive him to Malabar and wait outside while he did what needed to be done. He told me afterwards that McCoy had treated him as a friend, invited him in, sat him down and offered him a drink. When the Little Fish had agreed to a malt whisky, McCoy tried the clothes-iron trick again. I don't know what it is with people: something works for them once – when they have surprise on their side – and it becomes the thing that defines them. If I hadn't cut short his career then and there, McCoy would have been known as Moshe the Iron for the rest of his life.

As soon as the Little Fish saw the iron but no shirt, he figured out McCoy's plan, and was ready to duck and slip as the appliance came flying at his head. McCoy couldn't control his swing and ended up tangled up in the cord and toppling over the board, like a hammer thrower who had forgotten to let go.

He had knocked himself down and tied himself up, which made the Little Fish's job considerably easier. He took to his old friend with the cricket bat, careful not to damage the fine features that had attracted so many prostitutes in the past. He worked on McCoy's legs, breaking his femur, tibia and metatarsals, but leaving his patella intact. Before he left the unit, he called an ambulance.

This was the end of McCoy's underworld career. You may have seen a series of newspaper articles based on McCoy's 'revelations' about my 'organisation'. I let them pass, because he was saying nothing that was not already known, but it saddened me that a trusted friend could turn on me that way.

With McCoy gone, I had a vacancy for a lieutenant. I was wary of promoting the Little Fish, but he'd done a careful and controlled job on McCoy – one year later, he didn't even limp – and I thought perhaps he'd mellowed as the war had become a more distant memory.

'You've got to think about what you want to do in the future,' I said to the Little Fish. 'You can't keep on shooting Gozo Joe in the face. You need a career. Where do you see yourself in five years' time?'

The Little Fish said he wanted a club of his own, but he was prepared to work for me until he had enough money to buy one. I liked his ambition – and the fact that he had no fucking chance whatever of realising it – so I made him my right-hand man, although I didn't use him in an advisory capacity the way I might have consulted McCoy.

I realised we were heading in the wrong direction with the music. We weren't going to get anywhere copying international acts. The Eastern Suburbs Frank Sinatra might go down well at the Hakoah Club (although, as it happens, he didn't), but we were never going to be able to sell him overseas, or even in the western suburbs. It would be like the Yanks sending over the Connecticut Crash Craddock. What was the point?

We needed to develop Australian talent to an international level, or keep on bringing stars like Sinatra over here. I took a long look at Giuseppe Milano and Freddy Freed and the rest, and realised that Ava was the only one with star quality, and even she didn't have anything you could set to music.

I split the business into two divisions. I gave local to that imbecile Berger and kept international for myself, but with an agreement that if any of the local acts became big enough to tour overseas, they would revert to joint control, and Berger could keep a hand in organising the big stars' visits to Australia.

What happened to McCoy?

He died. In Maroubra. A couple of months ago. You were there, at the funeral, pretending to be Jewish, and robbing him of the *minyan* he needed to consecrate the ceremony. My guess is that he currently languishes in purgatory, unable to enter either heaven or hell, cursing your name – or, rather, the name of a hero you stole from the Jewish War Memorial for opaque and imbecilic purposes of your own.

I mean, what happened before that?

You were dishonourably discharged from the British Army, and your girlfriend started fucking your best mate behind your back.

To McCoy.

Oh, he made his way, as we all do. He employed the sympathy

gambit to prise Ava away from me and rob her of a lucrative and satisfying career. He attempted to use his nonexistent expertise to launch her as a solo artist, but I put the word out that she was never to play a gig at any club in the Cross, whether it was owned by me, the Malts or any other imbecile. After a couple of years doing weddings – but no bar mitzvahs; I saw to that – she went back to sucking cock, but her looks had faded and she had lost the enthusiasm that had made her famous in those circles where enthusiastic cocksuckers are evaluated and compared.

McCoy moped for several years, as was his custom, then took off for the Philippines with an imbecile junkie called the Human Dartboard. There was no bad blood between us. In the early 1970s I flew out twice to the Philippines with the US Mafia's man in Australia, Jack the Cat, to look at a business proposition put to us by McCoy and the Dartboard. It was just like the old days. We drank, we laughed, I fucked his wife. Not Cecilia Preciosa Bong Bong, but another bar monkey with similar tits.

When he came back to Australia in the 1980s, I lent him some money to get himself set up as a property developer with the late Hymie the Bookie and Plastic Sam, but I didn't see much of McCoy socially. He was a very jealous and suspicious man.

Was music promotions a legitimate business for you?

Yes, it was. Within reason. I'm not saying we always met our tax obligations, but it was no more crook than the average squarehead enterprise.

We didn't just do musicians either. We also handled athletic amusements, such as professional wrestling. And what a fucking crock of shit that is. Personally speaking, I would rather watch you fuck a fifteen year old up the arse than sit through two hours of fat imbeciles jump about pretending to blue. What a pathetic shambles. What a squalid excuse for entertainment. But the mugs loved it. And so did my silly-arse son.

The biggest promoter in Sydney was a poofter who went

around telling everyone he was a millionaire when he was just a crim robbing the wrestlers. He used to stage his cuddling matches at Sydney Stadium, on the nights when there were no real fights. He had a bunch of local actors, mainly Greeks, Italians and Turks, who jumped around the ring sticking their noses into each other's cracks and copping a feel of wog cock. Old people and kids used to scream, 'I'm gonna kiiiiiiill you!' like Mad Dog McCoy yelling at a friend who had fucked his wife. The Yank wrestlers were better, but not by much. They had more of the showie in them, and they were a bigger draw. So I did a deal with the poof to bring out the Yanks for a tour. You wouldn't've known it, but in some parts of Australia these cock-jockeys were bigger than Sinatra.

I took my son along to a couple of shows at the old tin shed, and the one thing I enjoyed was the midgets. They had these two little fellas – one of them could wrestle, the other couldn't – who got the biggest cheers out of everyone. It was funny to watch them run around on their little legs and wriggle about on the floor. I could see why people would pay for that.

After every show, the poof held a party and tried to get in the arse-sniffers' pants, but most of them were cunt-hounds and there were always a few girls who would grapple with them in the changing rooms. Sometimes they'd do tag team. I had a camera installed in the showers and I got some passable movies. They were no good for blackmailing the wrestlers, obviously – what sort of a reputation have you got to lose when you make your money pretending to be an athlete? – but I'd show them at smokos and they went down well.

The thing that surprised me, though, was the midgets got as much action as the big boys. You'd see them at the parties, scurrying around, ducking under some moll's skirts, and then they wouldn't come out for half an hour. I'm not saying they had universal appeal, but every woman loves a man whose cock is as long as his forearm. That was another thing about them: their hands were in proportion to their legs, but their cocks were in proportion to their heads. Maybe God didn't hate them, after all.

When I showed the midget movies to a bunch of jacks, they enjoyed it so much they threw money at the screen. It was like a miracle. I don't think I'd ever seen a jack open his wallet before. I didn't even know they carried them.

Years later, I borrowed a midget from Jeremiah Cain's World Famous Boxing Troupe, where he used to wrestle cowboys and other bush imbeciles, and I put him on with the strippers at Aphrodite's – but I'm getting ahead of myself. It seems, Anthony, I am doomed to forever be ahead of my time. Today I asked you here to talk about the Ligato Club, which I opened in Orwell Street, just a few buildings down from the Patton, when I got back from Vegas in 1959. That was the year I invented striptease.

Don't smirk, Anthony. The smirk is the province of the knowing fool and, although you are certainly a fool, you know fuck all about anything. I'm not claiming to have to been the first man ever to persuade a woman to get undressed, or even to get undressed in public, but I brought the art of striptease from the US to Australia and have never received the plaudits I deserve.

They say what happens in Vegas stays in Vegas, but that's only true if you don't have the imagination to bring it home with you. I saw shows that straddled the border between what I could do with the showgirls in the Patton and the whores at the smokos. I realised that society was moving on – I foresaw the sixties at the end of the fifties – and public tastes were changing.

They say striptease is all about the tease, but that's garbage, of course. It's all about the strip. According to the letter of the law, I still couldn't display woman in the way God intended, ie, with no pasties over her nipples and nothing between her smile and the sunshine. According to Sergeant Fred Carol, however, I could do whatever the fuck I wanted, so long as I paid him his cut. Carol had drifted away from the Malts when he saw they were a spent force, relying on the reputation of Gozo Joe – which only seemed to become enhanced every time I had him shot – rather than strength in terms of numbers and ideas.

At the Ligato we began with burlesque but quickly moved on to naked erotic dance shows, often incorporating elements of the vegetable kingdom. I knew this shift in focus was likely to antagonise Deborah, who affected to believe that I ran all my business for my own gratification (but that didn't stop her from spending all the fucking money that flowed out of them). She asked to visit the Ligato, to see for herself if there was any truth in the rumours that were circulating among the poisoned perms of the eastern suburbs chapter of the Women's International Zionist Organisation.

She was my wife, I had no secrets from her and, in addition, I was proud of my pioneering work. I was happy for Deborah to attend a night at the Ligato and witness everything that went on – albeit, of course, in modified form. Deborah hoped to take in dinner and a show but the listed chef was the Little Fish, who couldn't cook to save his life, although this was not generally an issue because the Ligato didn't actually have a kitchen. We only nominated a chef to fit in with licensing requirements. Luckily, I was able to prevail on Jimmy Bend, the proprietor of the floating restaurant in Rose Bay, to float his silly fucking boat to Woolloomooloo so I could use his chef – Deborah's favourite – for the evening. Bend protested that he would lose thousands of dollars' worth of business if he did so. I explained he would lose his entire fucking business if he didn't do so, as I would use skills learned in the navy to sink his ship.

The merchant navy?
Yes, Anthony, the merchant navy. How many times do I have to fucking tell you? I served my country both on land and at sea. My only regret is that I was not also able to join the air force and shoot down Hitler from the skies.

Bend reckoned he was a tough guy – which is a fucking laugh, since he made his living as a roller-skater – and he told me all the things he was going to do to me if I so much as touched a plank on the deck of his bathtub. The Little Fish pulled out his gun and Bend talked to that for a while until, between them, they settled the matter.

It was at this same time that I had the idea of becoming a patron of the Jewish community. At first, you see, I didn't have many friends at the synagogue. Many squarehead Jews resented my prominence, particularly when it came to royal commission time, when I was invariably named as 'Mr Big' or 'King Sin', and slurs were cast in the press as to the trustworthiness of my coreligionists. There were people who felt that I gave the community a bad name, although it is not as if it was a particularly popular group to start with. I tried to remedy this by performing acts of philanthropy, which displayed to the public the generosity of the Jews. This mainly took the form of donations to police charities, but I also gave from the start to the state of Israel, despite my misgivings about that particular enterprise. As Lenin said, the state is an armed body of jacks, and I couldn't see why the Jews needed a state when we already had the one we were living in. It seemed to me that, if you had two states, you'd have two lots of jacks to pay off. I had the idea that all Jews everywhere would be answerable to Israel and, if you did anything that wasn't one hundred per cent kosher, you'd be deported to face a court of rabbis or communists or some other such crap. But I got Israel upside down. It wasn't a trap, it was a hideout. You could do whatever you wanted in a *goyisher* country and, as long as you could demonstrate that your mother cooked chicken soup, they'd let you into Israel and never give you up. In fact, their beaks would protect you from your own fucking beaks!

I realised the idea wasn't watertight when the Israelis deported poor Meyer Lansky back to the States in the seventies, but in the fifties the holy land looked like a solid-gold insurance policy for a man in my business. So I gave to every appeal, planted trees in the desert, had my name etched on plaques. I even thought about visiting Jerusalem, but the place looked like a sandy shithole. Good for Arabs, but that's about it.

It wasn't until I began to bring joy to the older members of the Jewish community – Holocaust survivors and such – that I received a measure of respect from my peers, and this came about as a result of Deborah's dinner.

I didn't feel that my wife would mix well with the regular patrons of the Ligato, so I posted guards at the top of the road to keep the mugs away. Instead, in my first act of kindness towards the frail aged, I organised and funded a bus trip to Kings Cross for the residents of the Moses Montefiore Home for the elderly in Hunters Hill. That night forty-six retired Jewish ladies dined with my wife and I at the Ligato, while Arnold Zwaybil, the Eastern Suburbs Frank Sinatra, sang 'Some Enchanted Evening', 'South of the Border (Down Mexico Way)' and 'Three Coins in a Fountain'.

Deborah realised that the gossip she had heard about the Ligato at the hairdressers and the Hakoah was just a bunch of lousy lies, and I was awarded my conjugal rights twice that night. Which was a post-honeymoon record.

The Ligato didn't last. The best clubs never do. They are a blip in history, a moment in time, an explosion of joy that can never be recaptured. I sold the building just before the Vietnam War, to Morrie the Magnificent and his able assistant, Ava the Sword Swallower. They ran it as a cabaret restaurant, then a short-time hotel, until Morrie passed away in the 1980s. Ava's daughter still owns the place. You might have seen her as we came in, pushing her tits into that Scandinavian boy at the front desk. She put Ava in the Montefiore Home, where her talents, apparently augmented by the fortuitous loss of all her teeth and applied indiscriminately as a result of Alzheimer's disease, made her the most popular inmate among male residents, visitors and staff members alike.

Are we finished for the day?

Yes, Anthony. You can go home now and pretend you're a writer to the cockroaches in your kitchen and the silverfish in your shirts.

A friend of mine's asked for a favour. Do you remember Siobhan, who writes for the *Irish Times*?

Stripper's tits and eyes as brown as arseholes?

Whatever. She wants to know if she can have an interview with you.

An interview? Sure she can have an interview. I'll interview her for a job at Aphrodite's! I'll take her up the fucking Patton! Interview me? Who does she think I am? Chopper Read? Just because I give an interview to one so-called journalist – who turns out, by the way, to be as much of a reporter as I am a Christian Scientist – does she think I'm going to talk to a fat whore's hole full of them? Interview me? Yeah, we can do it on camera, in the room above the bar at the Hamilton Private Hotel. You tell her, Anthony, the only way she is going to get an interview with me is lying on her back and staring up at a blinking light on the ceiling. You got that?

You want me to say you're not doing interviews at the moment but you'll keep her request on file.

She can use my cock as a microphone and write notes with her tongue on my balls.

[End.]

EIGHTEEN

The smell of melting cheese and baking dough made me feel like I hadn't eaten for days as I kneeled beneath the low wall behind Pizza Gourmet in Rozelle, listening to scooters buzz into the car park and the delivery boys jog to the counter to pick up their orders.

I had been waiting for half an hour with my knees jammed into my chest when one of the riders finally left his engine running. I wrapped a scarf around my face and secured it with a silly helmet that made me look like a biplane pilot. I had found it in a junk shop and, when I tried it on, a kid looking at a train set had called, 'Where's Snoopy?', which was dumb since, as far as I can see, Snoopy and the Red Baron are the same dog. He should have asked, 'Where's Charlie Brown?' or just shut the fuck up.

I stepped over the wall and onto the bike, pushed it off its centre stand and took off. It was a bit of a thrill, being on a scooter again. It took me back to days I barely remembered, drinking Strongbow cider and smoking menthol cigarettes.

The scooter carried me back to the Cross in ten minutes. I wished I had longer to play around with it, but it had a design that would make it easy to track down, especially if you knew it was being driven by a bloke in a stupid hat.

I parked it in the street outside my unit block and draped it with a sheet of tarpaulin.

Upstairs in my flat I kicked off my shoes and lay on the bed, looking at the ceiling. I remembered the day Helen and I had moved into the place, and how we had made love on the bed, then the table, the chair. Helen was always keen to involve the furniture in our sex life, perhaps because it was the thing she loved the most. Ah, that's bullshit. To be fair, Helen had looked after me when I felt helpless. I wished she hadn't slept with Jed, but it was not as if I had never slept with Jed's girlfriends. I tried to reimagine the best time with Helen, the night she came home giggling after drinks at the sandwich shop. A delivery guy had muscled her into the storeroom, muttering all the things he wanted to do with her. He was good-looking, she said, tanned and strong, a man who spent all day lifting heavy boxes in the sun. She fancied him like fury, but she had come home to me instead and she wanted me to do everything he'd promised. We had four lines of coke and half an E each, and we stayed up all night, on the couch and the balcony and the kitchen benchtop. In the morning she admitted there had been no delivery guy.

Now I thought maybe there was a delivery guy after all, but that just made the story even better somehow.

At 6:45 pm, I went out to get the scooter. The limp tarpaulin lay in a puddle on the pavement, and my space had been taken by a Honda Goldwing. I kicked the tarps, got my foot caught in the fabric and nearly fell on my face. What was I supposed to do now? I dialled Mendoza.

'Somebody's stolen my scooter,' I told him.

'And what?' asked Mendoza. 'You think it was me? What did it look like?'

'It was bright purple,' I said, 'with a signboard with a picture of a pizza on it.'

Mendoza laughed. 'Were you trying to impress a girl?'

'I thought you'd know where the thief might try to sell it.'

'There is no secondhand market for bright purple scooters with pizza signboards,' said Mendoza. 'Children took your pussy magnet, Anthony, and crashed it into a wall.'

I kicked the tarpaulin again, even though it was already dead. I threw my stupid helmet on the pavement and it smashed into four pieces, which is what would have happened to my head, too, if I had worn it.

The next day I went back to Pizza Gourmet. They had put a security guard on the car park and a handwritten sign in the window that said *Delivery Drivers Wanted. Immediate Start.* A big red-haired guy in a short-sleeved purple shirt was boxing pizzas behind the counter.

I stood watching him, waiting for him to look up and speak.

'Can I help you, mate?' he asked.

'I've come about the job,' I said, imitating his sing-song Scouse accent.

He asked if I could ride a scooter and read a map, and whether I would work for two dollars a delivery. I said I could and I would.

'I'll need to see your driver's licence and your tax file number,' he said.

I opened my wallet and shuffled my credit cards.

'I didn't bring it with me,' I said.

'Where do you live?' he asked.

'Kings Cross,' I said.

'We've got plenty of customers up there,' he said. 'These are the best pizzas in the southern hemisphere. Where do you think's the furthest we've ever been asked to deliver a Pizza Gourmet Supremo?'

'New Zealand,' I said.

'That's right,' he said. He sealed the lid on a box. 'The driver only took it as far as the airport, of course.'

He sprinkled grated mozzarella onto a stodgy base smeared with tomato paste.

'You can start when we get our first delivery to the Cross. Drop off the pizza, pick up your licence, and we'll be right.'

I filled an application form with terrible lies, and he gave me a new-employees' pack including a purple shirt, a fluorescent vest, a purple crash helmet and a laminated menu. He told me I could expect about ten dollars a night in tips, more on a Saturday. He said most of the managers at Pizza Gourmet had started off as delivery boys, and if I looked after my customers Pizza Gourmet would look after me. The company saw its drivers not as employees but as family. If I liked, I could call him 'dad'. Then he told me that was a joke.

At half past five, the orders started to come in, but we didn't get one for the Cross until six forty-five.

'Yeah, I know it sounds weird,' said the manager. 'We don't do many like this, but he's a regular. He orders the same thing at the same time every day. He just parks in different places.'

The chef had already cooked the pizza: a Supremo with beef, mushrooms, capsicum, olives, pineapple and mozzarella.

The delivery address was opposite Sax's garden restaurant on Kellett Street. As I pulled up at the kerb I saw Mendoza slicing into a steak under the frangipani trees. Across the road was an electrician's white transit van. I tapped on the back doors and Jed opened up.

'Have I been looking forward to this!' he said, and I punched him in the face.

I was wearing my crash helmet with the visor down as I hit

him left-right, right-left, right-right. He fell back into the van, landing on the mattress, where Helen was lying in a silk slip and knickers. Even while I was hitting Jed I noticed that one of her breasts was bigger than the other.

Jed had a go back, but there is not much you can do against a man in a crash helmet and motorcycle gloves when you are lying in bed with your girlfriend – or his girlfriend – and he is headbutting you on the nose. He tried strangling me but I kept landing heavy punches and watching his stupid face come apart. I smashed him against the surveillance equipment, shattering his two TV screens. He got small fangs of glass stuck to his head; I rubbed them into his scalp.

Helen was screaming and swearing at me, but I was used to that. The fourth time I headbutted Jed, I knocked him out. I pushed his face into the mattress, pulled a gimp mask on backwards over his head and fastened his hands behind his back with cable ties, ignoring Helen as she grabbed her clothes and ran out onto the street.

I picked up the scooter and hauled it into the back of the van, almost crushing Jed under its weight, then slammed the doors, lifted the keys from Jed's pocket and scrambled over into the driver's seat.

I drove towards Surry Hills, where I parked in a side street and stripped off all the electromagnetic signs. Jed kept about a dozen different ones in the back; I thought of becoming the cable guy – that was his largest sign, so it made the biggest change to the appearance of the van – but if you parked in a residential street homeowners would usually tap on the window and ask how much it cost to install Foxtel on a one-year plan.

I steered the plain white van down the driveway of the First Presbyterian Church and around the back of the building, where the graves had been removed to make way for parking spaces marked by headstones. I pulled up in a spot *reserved for the undead.*

The back entrance to the church (marked *rear entry*) was a dark timber door. It was dragged open by Lady Lash, wearing a studded dog collar and rubber underwear, smoking a cigarette.

'I need somebody to help me with a slave,' I said.

'So bring out the gimp,' said Lady Lash.

'I think the gimp's asleep,' I told her.

She grabbed Jed's feet while I lifted him by the armpits, and we carried him from the van. The church smelled of lubricant, bleach and semen. Jed was beginning to wake up, so he was able to take some of his own weight as we walked him down the steps and into the vault.

'You can have the third chamber,' said Lady Lash, 'the Freezer, but I'll need it back in an hour.'

The Freezer was sandwiched between a medieval dungeon and a padded cell and was decorated like an abattoir with a rail of meat hooks along the roof.

We propped Jed's body against a wall.

'Will you need any lube?' asked Lady Lash.

Jed made a funny strangled noise under his mask.

'I think we'll be all right,' I said. 'Can you help me string him up?'

Lady Lash looped a chain around Jed's ankles and lowered the meat hook to the ground. We fastened it to the shackles, then I supported Jed's body while she cranked it up like a carcass, until he was suspended from the ceiling.

Lady Lash went back upstairs, and I took the mask off Jed.

'You've gone fucking mad,' he shouted, and I realised that in all the years I had known Jed I had never seen him upside down.

'Fucking let me down,' he demanded.

His face was badly cut. I punched him in the stomach.

'You're crazy,' he said. 'You're cuntstruck. I don't even want her, mate.'

It was hard to understand exactly what he was saying because of the position in which he was hanging, but I could tell he had the wrong idea.

'This isn't about Helen, Jed,' I said. 'It's about you shooting at me.'

'What? In Kosovo?'

'Don't be fucking stupid, Jed. Last week, in William Street. It was like fucking Belfast on a bad night.'

I punched him again and he puked blood.

'I've no fucking idea what this is about,' Jed shouted. 'You fucking delivered my pizza. Then you punched shit out of me and, when I woke up, you were talking to some woman about how you were gonna fuck me.'

'I'm not gonna fuck you, Jed,' I said, 'but you are fucked. Who are you working for?'

'The Russians again. The same Russians.'

'What's the job?'

'You figured that out three months ago when you started head-butting my van. I'm watching Mendoza.'

'Why?'

'Why? Why do you fucking think? Because the Russians want him watched.'

'And what did you see?'

'Absolutely fucking nothing. An old man who has dinner with strippers and lunch with you.'

'It was the Russians who shot at us, though, wasn't it?

Jed shook his head, which made his whole body wriggle.

'I don't know,' he said. 'I'm just their shitman. But I know they had a team come in from overseas to do a job. I had to pick them up from the airport.'

'How many?' I asked.

He coughed into his own nose.

'Four,' he spluttered. 'Let me down, Slick. All the blood's running to my head.'

'If you didn't shoot me,' I said, 'you set me up.'

'I don't know anything about any fucking set-up,' said Jed.

'Did you give them my position at the motel?'

'I didn't know you were there,' said Jed.

'There was a white van outside the flats across the road.'

'Have you any idea how many white vans there are in Sydney?' asked Jed. 'I can hardly find mine in a fucking car park. Anyway, I was nowhere near William Street.'

'So where were you?'

'Parked up an alley off Ward Avenue. I didn't think anything important was going to happen, so I was just, you know . . .'

'So where were you?'

'I didn't think anything important was going to happen, so I was just, you know . . .'

'Fucking Helen in the back of the van?'

'Well, yeah,' he said.

'You're a cunt, Jed,' I said.

'And you're a fucking idiot,' he said.

I could have hugged Jed, but that would have meant rubbing my face on his cock. I called in Lady Lash to help me get him down.

'Oh dear,' she said, 'you went a bit hard on the poor gimp.'

'I love it,' said Jed, rubbing his ankles

He looked at his face in the big gothic mirror – a purple hood over one eye, his lips slit and swollen, his nose knocked across his cheek – splashed himself with unholy water, made a sign of the cross and said, 'Drink, soldier?'

Jed drove his van up William Street to the Cross. As we passed the apartment block opposite the motel, I saw the white van was still outside, and relaxed my grip on the pistol in my pocket.

We started off drinking in the Goldfish Bowl, but ended up in the Southern Star. I was hugging Jed and ruffling his hair in the pokie room at midnight when an ex-con with roses tattooed on his throat asked Jed if he thought he was hard, coming into a pub like this with a face like that. Jed said he should have seen the other guy.

'I'm the other guy,' I said.

The next thing, Jed had him in a headlock and I was on the ground, wrestling with his mate. It was just like old times.

NINETEEN

[Aphrodite's, 2 Roslyn Street, Kings Cross. 27-03-02. 2:05 pm.]
Have you seen your black cunt [coughs]?
What are you talking about?
Have you seen your black countryman, the absurdly named 'Natural Science'?
Not since the Cannibals' memorial service. I thought you said he was working for you.
Work? His kind don't know the meaning of the word.
What've you got against blacks?
Who said anything about blacks? I'm talking about Poms.
So when did you last see him?
He was meant to be waiting outside Ava's while you and I did our last recording, but when I came out he'd disappeared like shit down a toilet. Dror can't raise his mobile, and nobody answers at his unit. Do you suppose he's gone back to his tribe?
If I bump into him I'll let you know.
Do that, Anthony. I've got Dror watching the door until he comes back, and that's no job for a Jewish boy. But I don't want you to concern yourself with the politics of race. After all, I am

not, by nature, a political person, although I have counted many politicians among my friends.

As a rule I don't take sides in a quarrel unless I'm affected by its outcome. I might have a position on the recent street-fighting among Assyrians in Fairfield, for example, but no opinion either way about the wars in the Balkans. All my life, however, I have made an exception when it comes to communism, the most pernicious and treacherous idea ever to lodge like a tumour in the brains of men. If God had meant us all to be equal, Anthony, he would have given slopes the cocks of niggers and Paddies the brains of Jews.

Look at what Castro did to poor Meyer Lansky. In a single stroke he obliterated every one of his business interests. He closed down Cuba's casinos and nationalised hotels that had been built by capitalists, not communists. He stole from Meyer to give to the niggers and, of course, they wrecked the place.

Despite what you might hear today, Anthony, from draft dodgers who have never – like you and I – put on a uniform and risked their lives for a cause, the Vietnam War was a justified conflict fought to protect the interests of legitimate businessmen. If we hadn't stopped the Vietcong at Saigon, communism would have spread through South-East Asia like crabs in a whorehouse, and today we would be struggling to rebuild this great state in the ruins of the People's Republic of New South Wales.

In fact, the opposite occurred. On May Day 1965, the people voted out the incompetent communist Labor Party state government and voted in the Businessman's Republic of Sydney and Beyond. At last our state had an Augustinian premier, who realised that the interests of the jacks and the informal business sector were not necessarily at odds. But our biggest stroke of luck was that we had a police commissioner of a similar mind. Crime fighting and criminality, Anthony, are two sides of the same coin – and the important word here is 'coin'. In every conceivable circumstance, if a crim can make a buck out of a racket, a cop can too.

The problem was that the system of bribes, kickbacks, sweeteners, cuts, jokes and pay-offs that every businessman paid to the police force and the Liberal Party had developed in a haphazard, piecemeal fashion, and there were now too many jacks biting crims for a slice of the same cake. Traditionally highly profitable enterprises, such as running a brothel, became barely sustainable in the face of taxes levelled by different branches of the police force, not to mention various standover men. Also, revenue didn't always find its way to the top of the tree, due to the fragmentary nature of the tributary system.

In addition, too many cops were seen with too many crims in too many clubs, creating the impression among the drinking public that the line between the hunter and the hunted had been obscured in some important way.

The premier and the commissioner identified the need both for a consolidated payment system and a centralised business model. They were both family men and didn't relish dealing with the dregs of society who habitually pollute the darker corners of what could broadly be defined as the 'gratification industry'. They wanted to work with a man who had accountants rather than accomplices. They were both Catholics, but even the Pope couldn't persuade them to sit down with that psychotic bunny-strangler McPherson when they could just as easily deal with me.

We arranged a dinner at my home in Vaucluse – Deborah cooked her roast beef, as I recall – and nutted out the details of our agreement over four bottles of burgundy and a decanter of tawny port. Basically the jacks consented to cut in the middle man. I would become the intermediary between the underworld and the state, the bagman for police and pollies, the ambassador for Kings Cross to the outside world.

Our most important task was to get rid of the last of the Malts. Gozo Joe was a dinosaur, and his kind were almost extinct. Most of his countrymen had moved on to legitimate business or, at least, employment, but Gozo Joe and a handful of irreconcilable imbeciles persisted in hooning girls, standing over market traders, running crooked card games and handling stolen goods. There was a nobility to their position that I couldn't acknowledge at the time but am keenly aware of today.

I didn't want to have Gozo Joe knocked – we had done so much to the bloke already – but experience showed me that he was the kind of man who wouldn't negotiate until you put a bullet in him. The Little Fish and I visited him in a pool room where pool was rarely played, and explained to him in a mixture of languages – I was surprised to learn the Little Fish had picked up a sprinkling of Maltish – that we were not trying to take over his rackets but trying to make life easier for him. He would no longer have to deal with the vice squad, the racing and gaming squad, the consorting squad, et cetera. He would simply make a single monthly payment to an employee of the Little Fish, who would pass it on to me to deliver to the real bosses.

I realised we were addressing an unreceptive audience when Gozo Joe pulled a sword out of his cane and slashed the Little Fish just below his left eye. As a former amateur fighter, the Little Fish was not a man to regard a physical assault personally, but nor was he one to take a blow without giving two back. He grabbed a pool cue and brought it down on Gozo Joe's head. I don't think anyone was surprised when the cue snapped but Gozo Joe was unhurt. For a moment I thought the Little Fish and Gozo Joe were going to play Errol Flynn and fence, but the Little Fish instead went for his piece. Gozo Joe got in first and skewered his hand with his sword. I didn't, as a rule, carry a weapon in those days, and I was jumped by two Malts who held me over a table and tried to split my head open with pool balls, while the Little Fish grappled unsuccessfully with Gozo Joe. We copped a flogging that day, Anthony. I couldn't see straight for six weeks, and the Little Fish had to have surgery on his hand. The next night the Malts broke into the Ligato and set fire to the recently installed kitchen, apparently believing I still owned the joint. That was the setback that induced Morrie the Magnificent and Ava the Swallower to turn their business from a restaurant into a hotel.

It's a funny thing, Anthony, but wherever there is a hole, some fucking imbecile will come along to fill it. Under the regime of the premier and the commissioner, the detectives of New South Wales had largely abandoned detecting in favour of bashing queers and fucking whores. So who should fucking well step up to fill their size-thirteen shoes but an unwashed mob of self-appointed cops from the gutter press.

I was hounded and dogged by two journalists in particular: a woman named Ham and a man called Eggs. These two went after me like greyhounds chasing an electrified hare, and with just as much fucking success. They ran themselves in circles trying to get me for this job or that. They even went after the premier – an elected official of the land – and the commissioner – an appointed official of the land. I'd've liked to see them try that in fucking Russia. They wouldn't've lasted five minutes.

Eggs and Ham – kosher and *treif* – reckoned I'd set all the club fires myself, right back to the first one at the Patton, and they were convinced they'd got me fingered as the firebug when the Little Fish sent the Maltese pool hall up in flames. This wasn't my idea – it was the Little Fish's own freelance act of revenge – but I thought, *If I burn down the old Patton building now, and collect the insurance, everyone'll think it was the Malts.*

So I sent the Little Fish to the Patton with a can of petrol and a cigarette lighter and – fuck knows how – he set fire to himself. His burning body acted as a torch that eventually sent the club up but, by that time, the jacks had arrived. Being trained detectives, they understood there was nothing suspicious about the blaze. Ham and Eggs, with no forensic expertise, came to the opposite conclusion and made it their business to hound a disabled war veteran with thirty per cent burns to one side of his body and only forty per cent feeling in his right hand. It was a moment of shame for journalists everywhere, and it was their vile slurs and groundless innuendoes which, I believe, finally pushed the Little Fish over the edge.

While Ham and Eggs were out trying to raise reported crime figures and frighten elderly people in their homes, the jacks were reassuring the general public by underreporting offences and occasionally flogging citizens who insisted a crime had been committed when obviously it hadn't, as was often the case with rapes and other so-called assaults against women.

Over in Palmer Street, Gozo Joe was not cooperating with the new order. Although he continued to pay his protection money to his traditional bagman, he refused to hand over a cent to my representative or participate in any way in the new, streamlined insurance scheme. In addition, he was flogging my boys wherever he found them, and reports of some of these attacks were polluting the press, which was putting pressure on the police to 'solve' them, even though they had no effect whatever on the average squarehead or his virginal wife. I'm a reasonable man, Anthony, and I was prepared to continue – although not accelerate – a series of tit-for-tat assaults until honour was satisfied and an uneasy peace reigned, at which point we could finish off the Malts once and for all as soon as they dropped their guard.

Fred Carol couldn't come at that. He was the shithouse rat who had covered their backs for more than ten years, but now he wanted them wiped out in an afternoon. The jacks were planning to do it themselves – just swoop on the pool hall, blow them all away and plant guns on the bodies – but I had to remind them the pool hall had burned down and nobody knew where the Maltese met any more. They could go into the brothels shooting and they might hit a sitter here and there, but most likely they would just murder a couple of molls and have the press after their blood for the sake of another headline. Besides, I said, they didn't have to knock them all. If Gozo Joe disappeared, the rest of them would cooperate themselves out of existence.

When Carol expressed doubts, I was forced to show him a print of a movie made during a certain celebrated smoko behind the Palmerstone Hotel and, on 28 May 1968, Gozo Joe Stone climbed into his silly fucking ute outside his wog mansion in Bellevue Hill, turned the ignition key and blew the shitbox to pieces. The explosion tore off his right leg. It had fuck all to do with me and even less to do with the Little Fish. His own Maltese lieutenant had given him up to Fred Carol, when he finally figured out that Gozo Joe was making all of them a target. That night, Fred Carol had the run of all the girls in the Pussycat Bordello, and enough champagne to celebrate VE Day. Because it was VE day. Victory in East fucking Sydney.

I see you are furrowing your brow in an imitation of thought, Anthony. You are attempting to wonder, *When did Mr Mendoza acquire this Pussycat Bordello, and could it be the same Pussycat Bordello I see every day from the window of my dirtbox behind the cop shop?* The answer is both yes and no. It's the same business, but it's not in the same building.

The Vietnam War, Anthony, was the war to end all wars in Kings Cross. From the moment the heroic American troops first set foot on the strip in 1967, every one of my businesses tripled in value. The marines wanted to drink all day and stoke warm pussy all night, and I was the man who could help them. It was my patriotic duty to get them drunk and fucked, so they returned to the battlefront refreshed and revitalised, ready to kill all those men, women and children who cravenly threatened the

United States from the safety of their rat-infested hamlets in the Mekong delta.

Like the Second World War, the Vietnam War was fought in many nations, on many fronts. Sydney's property developers – myself included – constituted the anticommunist front in Kings Cross, while the foul-smelling ranks of journalists, feminists, anarchists, trade unionists, whistleblowers and squatters were the local Vietcong. They might've beat us in Vietnam, but we flogged the shit out of them in East Sydney, I can tell you.

The premier, the commissioner and I were all of the opinion that nothing was too good for the brave men who were fighting to preserve our freedoms in a far-off land. If there were any remaining restrictions on businessmen operating in the Cross, they were abandoned like a stripper's knickers. And strippers were, at last, permitted to throw off their knickers and mingle with the crowd. Everywhere was open all night, everyone was for sale, and all the prices were in US dollars. There were blues around the fountain every evening as the heroes prepared for the great battle that lay ahead.

The Yanks liked a drink, but they also brought with them heroin and marijuana. These pioneering soldiers were your soul mates, Anthony. They flew in from South-East Asia with a cargo of drugs and unloaded them on the Cross. For a while they had their own gang, selling dope to the hippies in the jazz clubs: they told them it would make them play like John Coltrane. Sadly, however, most of the early dealers met their fates in Khe Sanh and Hue.

Unfortunately, the fighting couldn't go on forever. The premier retired from the government of New South Wales in January 1975, and four months later the Vietnam War ended with the victory of the Vietnamese people over their own best interests.

It's interesting to note, however, that more than four decades after the confiscation of Meyer Lansky's business interests in Cuba, there are whores on every corner of Havana. This goes to show that totalitarianism can never stamp out the human spirit, and commerce will always rescue the economy in the end.

[Ends.]

TWENTY

The biggest mistake I made while I was looking for Natural Science was taking a couple of Es from Dror. If it wasn't for that, the next few days might've turned out differently, although Siobhan was always going to find out in the end.

I started asking around for Natural Science at his gym. One thing I noticed when I was a private investigator is that some people will answer any question you put to them, just for the sake of having a conversation. A big gay bear with a beard told me he often used to train with Natural, and thought he had gone on holiday to Thailand. When I asked what had given him that idea, he said he assumed he must be on holiday because he hadn't seen him in the gym, and he'd guessed he'd gone to Thailand because that's the sort of place people go. Somebody else said Natural was in Thailand too, but their source turned out to be the bear.

Natural Science was popular among the spruikers and pimps on the strip. The bouncers said they hadn't seen him, but he had disappeared before. He had a girl in Brisbane, someone said, and another in Surfers. At the Hamilton Private Hotel, where he sometimes worked the door on weeknights, the receptionist said he thought he had gone looking for Leah. A lot of people had a thing about that girl, he told me.

There was nobody in the office at the Magic Circle Club, but a tall man with a voice full of orders walked over from the other side of the road when he saw me ringing the doorbell.

'Club's closed,' he said. 'Manager's gone on holiday.'

He had that cold anger that bikers like to pretend, as if somebody has just knocked over their Harley.

'Do you know Natural Science?' I asked him.

'Big black fella?' he asked. 'Long arms, flat nose? Sharp teeth?'

'That's him.'

'Have you tried the zoo?'

Lady Lash was being photographed by a Japanese tourist in her sex shop, posing with a blow-up doll. She said she had seen Natural last night, but it turned out that was in a dream. Luckily, however, she had psychic powers. She showed me a photograph of Natural at the Lash Christmas Party, naked except for a dog collar, and after a few moments rubbing his cock, she could see he had surrendered to the feminine side of his nature and shacked up with a leatherman at Mardi Gras. She let me take the photograph away – I cut off the head and gave her back the rest – so I at least had something to show to people.

I rang Jed, hoping Helen wouldn't answer, which she didn't.

'Do you remember the black lad who battered that bow-legged bloke from Carlisle at the Reccie, the day you got nicked for cottaging?' I asked.

'You mean the day I got arrested at the Cottage,' he said. 'For fighting. Yeah, I remember him. Called himself "Biology" or something like that.'

Jed knew somebody from Aldershot who was a mate of the Fleet boys. I rang him and he gave me a number for Natural's sister. She said he was probably diving the Great Barrier Reef, because she had seen a programme about it on TV. She asked me to tell him to call her, as she wanted to sell his CD player.

I imagined a woman the size of Natural, with skin like a seal and hips as fat as floor cushions. She said his real name was Orpheus Randall, and the easiest way to track him down was to find a white woman on her knees and look who was behind her.

I felt a fuzzy sort of responsibility for Natural because he was from Fleet, and nobody but Mendoza and I seemed to care that something so big had vanished. It was like the Coke sign had come down in the night, or somebody had run off with the fountain.

I ran into Spiegeleier drinking coffee with the last of the joy boys in Joe's Cafe on Victoria Street. I gave him Natural's picture, which he set close to his nose.

'He doesn't look Jewish,' said Spiegeleier, then began one of his lectures about what I didn't understand about the Cross.

'Kings Cross is a place people go to disappear,' he said, 'but it's also a place people disappear from. It's a vortex, a void, a vector. You see a girl on the street every day for a month, then never again. Bad things sometimes happen, for sure, but far less often than you'd think. Most of the time they wake up one morning – in a hotel room, in a hostel or on the street – and they're not driven by the rhythms any more. They clean up, they recover, they make peace with themselves and they move on. This friend of yours, maybe he was hiding from something, and maybe that thing got him but, more likely, he grew tough enough to face it. The Cross doesn't always cut you down, Tony.

It can just as easily build you up. It might crush the weak, but it makes strong men stronger.'

I waited until he had finished his speech, then asked, 'So you haven't seen him then?'

'No,' admitted Spiegeleier.

I bought a flat white, and Spiegeleier asked after Siobhan.

'You're lucky,' he said. 'You met her at the right time. Do you know the headline I'm working on? CHILD STARS BREAK HEARTS AT YESHIVA GALA.' He folded his lower lip over his chin, as if he were about to turn his face inside out. 'This isn't the life I planned, Tony. Did you hear what Siobhan said about Mike Gore? He's "still fucking half the news desk"! He'd be fifty-three, Tony. That's a year younger than me.' He patted his own cheek, swatting an imaginary mosquito. 'I haven't had a woman,' he said, 'since 1999.'

His hands circled his throat.

'It's not because Gore's good-looking,' he said. 'He's like me, as bald as a bloody dildo with a face like a basset hound. It's because he still gets the glory stories, and all the little girlies from the Home Counties come to his desk and ask for advice on how they can grow up to be an investigative reporter like him. They want him to be their mentor, Tony. Do you know who was the last journalist to want me as a mentor? You.' He pressed a dimple into his chin. 'I'm a failure, mate.'

I wished I hadn't sat down.

'I should've stood up for you,' he said, 'But look what I've done instead. You're working for *him* now, aren't you? I've sold *your* soul to the fucking devil.'

He gulped down my coffee. I looked into an empty cup.

'I didn't used to be like this,' he said. 'I used to have balls like Sherrins. They were so big I could hardly walk. I broke stories about cops on the take and politicians with their pants down. I won awards, mate. And I'm not talking about the Women's

International Zionist Organisation (NSW Auxiliary Chapter) Award for Services to the Community in the field of publicity. In which I came second, last year, to Max fucking Markson.'

I told Spiegeleier he should come out to dinner with Siobhan and I some time, but I had to get on and find Natural Science because Mendoza needed him. I decided to go door to door with the picture, starting on Kellet Street. The owner of the Continental Barber shop said he had shaved Natural Science's head, and the woman in the launderette remembered watching his washing, but not this week. I was about to ask at the New York restaurant when I noticed there was already a missing-persons notice in the window. For a moment I thought it must be for Natural Science, then I realised it was Mendoza. But it wasn't, of course. A handwritten caption under a smudged photocopy of a Polaroid of an old man read *Have you seen Maurice (M&M) Mickle? M&M has'nt been here since 20/3. BUT has'nt missed a meal at the New York in TEN years. Have called hospitals and pleas BUT nobody knows his where abouts. If you have any info, tell RITA at the till. We are all worried about you, darling xx.*'

It was like Spiegeleier said: people go missing from the Cross all the time.

I found Dror checking the security cameras outside the Pussycat Bordello. He tested them every month, usually to make sure that they weren't working, so nothing would be filmed that could be used in evidence by the police. Now he was trying to get them going, in case there was another armed attack.

'You heard from Natural Science?' I asked.

'Natural?' said Dror. 'Yeah, I got a postcard from him yesterday. He's in New Caledonia.'

'What's New Caledonia?' I asked.

'It's an island full of big boongs like him,' said Dror.

'So, what?' I asked. 'He was supposed to be bodyguarding

the old man, when he just got the idea to pack his suitcase and go to New California?'

Dror shrugged, and passed me the postcard. On the front was a picture of a pair of oiled breasts. On the back, Natural had written, *Dror, Having fun in the sun. Weather's hot, chicks are hotter. Hope you're coping without me. See you, Orpheus.*

'Why would he just run off like that?' I asked.

'How would I know?' said Dror. 'I'm not an anthropologist. Talking of which, I hear you're not a journalist.'

I smiled lopsidedly, like an idiot.

'You've got a problem with the truth, mate,' he said. 'You need some truth drug.'

And that's when he offered me the Es.

Back at my unit, Siobhan was rearranging the furniture while singing 'The Minstrel Boy'. My mum used to sing 'The Minstrel Boy'; it doesn't have to mean anything. I had no furniture left, apart from the dining table and the bed, but she had moved the bed below the window where the dining table used to be, and tucked the dining table into the corner in place of the bed. She said it would make the room seem lighter in the mornings, and the corner would be a cosier place to eat dinner. She had pushed a candle into the neck of a wine bottle and set the table for two. She must've gone out and bought a set of placemats.

'I've got pills,' I said.

She passed me a beer from the fridge, and we each put an E on our tongue and washed it down with Crown Lager.

I guess I knew what was going to happen, but ecstasy's an experience you can control. You don't say anything you don't want to say, and I needed something that would help me open up, and maybe relax Siobhan while she listened to me.

The flat smelled like a balti house. She stirred curry and rice in a shiny new pan while she told me about her day. She'd found a young police officer to help with her research into the

Cannibals. He was happy to answer her questions, off the record, as long as he could look at her tits. He said the bikers were starting to fade into a part of the old Kings Cross, like Vitto's or the New York, and pretty soon they'd get closed down, like the Rex Hotel. Their strengths were always their brotherhood, their muscle, their guns, their drug connections and their discipline. The Lebs used to have everything but the discipline. For years, they had paid off the Cannibals, used them, and watched how they worked, and now they were ready to take them over. The shooting came at a good time for the Lebs. It meant they didn't have to get rid of the old guard themselves.

Whenever Siobhan stopped talking, she sang a bit of a song about one Irish boy or another. I leaned over the stove to get a look inside the pan, and she pushed me aside. She told me she was making chicken biryani. She couldn't possibly have done that with the ingredients in my cupboard, so she must've been shopping. She dished up the curry in a bowl I didn't recognise, using a spoon I'd never seen before. She had bought me cutlery and crockery. The curry tasted good, and got better and better, even though I wasn't eating it.

'I think the E's kicked in,' I said to Siobhan.

She beamed at me.

'I think I love you,' I said.

'Everyone on eccie thinks they love everyone,' she told me. 'Eat your biryani.'

I put the spoon to my mouth, kissed the yellow rice, then put it back down on my plate.

'I've got something to tell you,' I said.

'You're doing this the wrong way around,' she said, turning her beer bottle upside down to demonstrate the idea. A dribble of beer poured onto her plate. 'First you say: "I've got something to tell you," then you say, "I think I love you." '

'No, I've got something else to tell you,' I said. 'I'm not

really a journalist. I didn't write those Billy Cobbett stories. I mean, I helped with them, but they weren't mine.'

'You mean you worked with someone else on them?' she asked, more interested in softly pricking her fingers with the teeth of her fork.

'No,' I said, 'he worked with me.'

She frowned. 'What's your point, Tony?'

'My name's not Tony.'

She sliced her chicken into small pieces.

'I think they put something in your pill that they left out of mine,' she said.

'My name's Nick,' I told her.

'Whatever,' she said. 'Shall we listen to some music?'

'I was never a writer,' I said. 'I was a soldier.'

'Ha ha,' she laughed, but not really. 'Why are you saying this, Tony? Why are you trying to spoil my dinner?'

'I love you and I've got to be honest with you,' I said.

I told her the story and, when I had finished, she smiled at me.

'Come here,' she said, 'you silly boy.'

I craned across the table to meet her kiss, and she stabbed me in the throat with her fork.

'You bastard fuck!' she screamed. 'You raped me!'

I clutched my throat and tried to keep her back with my other hand.

'You fucked me, then you told me you were a British soldier! You might as well've crept in with a mask on and pinned me to the bed, because that's no worse than what you did, you fucking baby-killing rapist bastard fuck!'

She tried to stab me again, but I caught her wrist.

'Now you're breaking my arm!' she screamed. 'You fucking monster!'

She dropped the fork. When I went to pick it up, she kicked me in the eye.

'Help!' she shouted. 'Rape!'

I reached out for her.

'Don't you fucking dare touch me, you squaddie bastard!' She caught her breath.

'You're a fucking dead man,' she said. 'Do you know who *I* am? I'm Siobhan Hughes. My uncle was Francis Hughes, the hunger striker. My baby brother Joey was shot by the Brits. By you! You and your fucking mate Jed! For what? For fucking what, Tony?'

'I didn't shoot him,' I said.

'You don't know who you shot,' she said, 'you mercenary piece of shit. Get out! Get out!'

She threw the bowl of biryani over me.

'Take your fucking things,' she said, throwing a couple of dirty shirts into a bag, 'and fuck off!'

She swung the bag at me, so it would hit me in the face.

'Out!' she cried. 'Out! Out! That's the trouble with you British bastards – you never know when to get out!'

She hit me with a plate as I backed out of the door, smeared in rice and grease and blood. I stopped in the stairwell to get my breath back. I couldn't figure out what had happened. Siobhan had kicked me out of my own flat.

TWENTY-ONE

[Aphrodite's, 2 Roslyn Street, Kings Cross. 04-04-02. 2:00 pm.]

I understand you're living with Dror.

No, I only stayed there for a couple of nights. I'm back at home now.

Really? And how is your friend, the real reporter?

She's told a bunch of local Paddies to break my legs.

They came and asked my permission.

What did you tell them?

The truth: that you're a serial conman and I'd been taken in as well.

Thanks a fucking lot.

I said you were under my protection until this job was over, but after that it was open season.

Great.

And I warned them you might have a piece, which you stole from me.

So now they'll come with guns too.

They would have anyway. They're serious people. There's a lesson for you to learn here, Anthony. Put succinctly, it is this: you are a fucking idiot, and a danger to yourself.

Isn't it time you started boring me?

If you had any sense, Anthony, you'd treasure these moments. Mark my words, you'll look back on these times and think, *Those were great days, when I learned about life from Jake Mendoza and I still had the use of my legs.*

Now, the room in which we are sitting is part of a club by the name of Aphrodite's, but it is not sited on the premises of the original Aphrodite's, although you can see the old building from the street. I know the owner of this new incarnation of the club only by association, but I accept his homage to my original name in the spirit in which it was intended: blatant fucking unimaginative bandwagon-jumping plagiarism.

Aphrodite, as you no doubt don't know, Anthony, was the Greek goddess of love. The Greeks, as you no doubt do know, are famed for their penchant for rear entry. In Aphrodite's in the early seventies there was rather more rear entry than I would perhaps have liked, and I'm still not sure how that came about. As I told you, the Little Fish dreamed of having a club of his own. I gave him Aphrodite's to run, and told him to make it profitable. If he did, I promised he would inherit it as surely as the meek would one day inherit the earth, ie, not in my fucking lifetime, nor yours either, Anthony.

People say the sixties was an era of social change, but it was really in the early seventies that civilisation went down the gurgler. For drapers and mercers it was a happy time, as men took to wearing flared, high-waisted pants, and shirts with collars like elephants' ears, magnificent garments that utilised far more fabric than was necessary to cover a body. Even ties grew two inches wider. However, the most prominent symptom of social decay was the sudden rise of man-to-man arse-fucking among the general population. Maybe it was the drugs, maybe it was the hair, or maybe it was the beards, which made some men's mouths look like cunts, but suddenly there were shit-stabbers everywhere.

They ought to put a plaque to me in Darlinghurst Road, Anthony, and sink it into the pavement, because I originated everything. One of the most successful shows at this time was a revue at the Roundabout Club called 'Girls Girls Girls'. This was a glaring misnomer if ever there was one, since there wasn't a single fucking sheila on stage. It was just a night of transvestites dancing, and it should have been called 'Dogs Dogs Dogs'. It was a big money earner for me – all the way up Roslyn Street, there used to be queues to get in – and also close to the heart of my lovely wife, whose idea it had been to reach out to various deluded imbeciles who didn't even realise they were queer, and provide them with their own scabrous cabaret.

In the days before strippers' pants came off, some of the trannies managed to squeeze their taped-up testicles into the Patton and work as exotic dancers among credulous and weak-minded drunks. One thing that has always puzzled me, Anthony – and perhaps you can enlighten me here – is why men want to fuck transvestites. A male arsehole in a skirt is still a male arsehole, and you have to take the skirt off to fuck it anyway, so what is going on in your head when you see a coconut with hairy arms and an Adam's apple dressed in his sister's flowery frock and shoes, and decide, 'My, there's an attractive sight'?

I said, what is going on in your head, Anthony?

I don't know. It's not my thing.

Not your thing, no. We all know what your thing is, don't we? Human sexuality is complex and many faceted, Anthony, and I don't care what men do with their cocks, as long as they do it in the privacy of my own clubs, and don't rub my face in it. Do you like it when they rub your face in it, Anthony?

Get fucked.

Do you know why I keep you around, Anthony? You improve my vocabulary.

So, being queer was illegal in New South Wales until 1984, and mugs who do illegal things are naturally attracted to illegal places. The queers had their hideaways, in the Rex Hotel and others, but there was nothing to stop the jacks from bursting in whenever they'd had a skinful and taking them outside for a flogging. The jacks *loved* belting the daylights out of queers. It was the main thing they used to do. I often wonder what modern police work involves now that they don't go bashing poofs. I didn't encourage queers to come to my clubs, but they knew if they did they'd be safe from the jacks. At least until closing time.

Normally, I found that once a club had attracted a certain number of queers – somewhere between twenty and thirty – the other customers either punched seven shades of shit out of them or left the place to them. When two of my establishments reached this critical mass, I passed them over to queer managers and told them to run the places to suit the clientele, but not to come crying to me if they couldn't keep the jacks on side.

The queers came to Aphrodite's, and I thought that would be the end of the place, but it seemed the rest of the customers were such pond scum they didn't feel as if they had to enforce the usual prison hierarchy of armed robbers, cats and rockspiders. At Aphrodite's, paedophiles and trannies drank with the lowest kind of crims and, of course, the most twisted and perverted of the jacks, and barely a harsh word was spoken before midnight, when the place went off like a boxing tent.

We got a lot of American soldiers in Aphrodite's, and the niggers in particular were in great demand among the faggoty contingent. They didn't do badly with the girls, either, although there was more than one marine who went back to his hotel to find his conquest had a cock. There are bodies that will never be missed, Anthony, buried in places that will never be found.

The Little Fish, to my surprise, mixed easily and well with sodomites of every persuasion, so I gave him the Roundabout Club and 'Girls Girls Girls' to look after too. Thinking back, the Little Fish always had an odd taste in women. Part of the reason we were able to stay friends for so long was that our ambitions rarely overlapped and, on those odd occasions when they did, he was able to be mature about it.

Occasionally the Little Fish and I would take our women away to Queensland for a weekend. I was usually – although not always – accompanied by Ira, while he would generally drag along some foul-mouthed whore from the depths of hell. However, on one particularly puzzling weekend in Noosa Heads, the Little Fish rented an apartment next to mine with Savannah Plains, a nice, well-mannered girl who nonetheless strongly resembled a prop forward who used to work the door of the Patton.

I didn't raise this matter with the Little Fish. I assumed he'd fallen victim to this strange contagion that had affected the entire city, and it was probably just a stage he was going through, caused by working in such close proximity with so many hideous fucking drag queens. In a way, I blamed myself.

I began subtly suggesting to the Little Fish that it might be time he found a nice girl and settled down to start a family. I actually knew of a highly skilled eastern suburbs prostitute who was about to retire, and I was able to recommend her to him through personal experience. But by this time the Little Fish was not interested in Rivka the Roarer, nor any other girl who was born a woman.

One night I was inspecting Aphrodite's with Lazarus – who, since you don't ask, is still in fucking hospital, shaking like Ira's orgasm from the fright you gave him – when my bodyguard, normally the soul of discretion, brought up the subject himself.

'When did you start arse-fucking ladyboys?' he asked the Little Fish over a bottle of the worst champagne.

Generically, men called 'Lazarus' suffer from an existential problem: in order to rise from the dead, they must first die. The Little Fish, although largely unschooled in the Christian Bible, instinctively understood this. First he grabbed the champagne magnum out of the bucket and broke it over Lazarus's head, then he thrust the jagged mouth of the bottle into his face. Lazarus picked up the table and tipped it over, and the two of them staged a magnificent fist fight. If I were a betting man – rather than a bookmaking man – I would have put my money on Lazarus, due to his extensive experience with Jeremiah Cain's World Famous Boxing Troupe. However, in this particular blue, Lazarus was unable to overcome his early disadvantage of being battered with a bottle. He wrestled well, with blood blinding his eyes, but didn't see the Little Fish's mouth coming towards him like the open jaws of a shark, to bite a chunk out of his cheek.

Lazarus was clawing at the Little Fish's eyes while the Little Fish slammed his head into the floor. He had a skull as thick as a bank-vault door, but the Little Fish possessed power in his arms and a slight advantage in size. Lazarus threw punches from his back. The Little Fish sprang upright and jumped on his head: once, twice, three times. The third jump killed him.

He came back to life, of course, although he spent three weeks in a coma. The Little Fish visited him every day in hospital, and sat by his bedside, sometimes in tears. He didn't seem to remember how the blue had begun, and believed I had deliberately stoked animosity between the two of them.

I sometimes sat with Lazarus too, and it was during these visits, listening to the Little Fish, that I realised he had no idea he was fucking a former Patton bouncer and genuinely believed his girlfriend was a woman, from the bulge in her throat to the bulge of her cock.

How were your other businesses going?

The new arrangement in the Cross was holding up well. Only a few lone psychos reckoned they could go against the premier, the commissioner, Jake Mendoza, the Little Fish and the property-development community and, when lone psychos band together, they rarely form a lasting partnership. A loose gang of lunatics had gathered around Fat Frida's Palmer Street brothel, formerly run by the Maltese – do you see what I mean about imbeciles flocking to fill a hole? – and Fat Frida got it into her best-employed-bobbing-up-and-down little head that she could frighten the Little Fish into letting her girls into Aphrodite's, using Ronnie 'Iron Fist' McQueen, the most brainless man in Sydney.

The Iron Fist approached the Little Fish outside the club, gave him Fat Frida's proposition, and was promptly put on his back by a left hook and a head butt. We often seem to return to the subject of nicknames, Anthony. The Iron Fist's was viciously literal. He was called the 'Iron Fist' because he wore a silly fucking glove made of lead, like a medieval gauntlet. You never had to guess which hand he was going to hit you with – unlike the Little Fish, who could suddenly switch from southpaw to orthodox and back.

The first time the Iron Fist came for the Little Fish, he left his hand at home. The second time, he stormed past the bouncers at Aphrodite's, his fist on one hand and a piece in the other. The Little Fish knew he was coming – *everybody* knew he was coming – so he made sure his shooters were stashed in appropriate places around the club. The Iron Fist said to the Little Fish, 'This is your last chance, cunt,' and the Little Fish reached for a Webley behind the bar and shot him twice in the back, in self-defence. Nobody in the world liked the Iron Fist, so the

Little Fish's was virtually a victimless crime. Although there were eighty-three people in Aphrodite's, including six coppers, none of them saw the shooting, because it coincided with the moment in the floor show when Tina's Talking (although now noticeably sagging) Tits turned a full circle and stood to attention to the beat of a drum. The absence of witnesses made it unclear exactly how the Iron Fist had been threatening the Little Fish with his spine and shoulders, and the Little Fish, an incapacitated war hero, was without strong memories of the incident. With no witnesses, no evidence and no aggrieved party, the charges were no-billed, and the Little Fish was left with the mistaken impression that he could neck anybody he wanted and walk away.

I let Fat Frida's dish go cold, then, six months later, I burned her whorehouse down.

I would have done more, but I was very, very tired.

Why was that?

There is one area I haven't yet said much about, Anthony, and that is my domestic life with Deborah and Ira. By this time, I had two separate families, each with one child. Deborah and my son lived in Vaucluse, Ira and my daughter in Kensington. As I have mentioned, I kept no secrets from my wife, except in cases where she didn't need to know.

In the early days of our marriage, when I wouldn't come home, I think Deborah genuinely believed I was inspecting my clubs, checking out the acts and so on – which, in a way, I was. Of course there were problems. For instance, every now and then I caught a dose. In these instances I had to go home to Deborah and admit that I was a man with a very low libido and didn't feel able to sleep with her for about a month. It was never difficult to talk my wife into a prolonged period of abstinence, so this arrangement worked for both of us. It had the added advantage that she was unsuspicious when I was away, since she knew I was incapable. During these times, I generally sought relief in the mouth of Ava the Swallow or some similar circus performer.

On the nights I was with neither Deborah nor Ira, I was sampling the full smorgasbord of international dishes that Kings Cross had come to offer. I was never a Sinatra, obsessively collecting examples of women from every race and culture on the planet, but I regularly indulged my more exotic tastes with women from Mauritius and the Cocos Islands. They're brown on the outside but pink on the inside, Anthony, as you no doubt don't know.

If Deborah suspected anything about my one-night stands, I don't think she cared, but she never came to terms with my relationship with Ira. You see, Anthony, I was in love with Ira. Not in the limp-wristed, soft-cocked, moony-eyed way you might be in love with a girl, not to the exclusion of all others or any garbage like that, but she made me smile when she came into the room, and she sucked cock like she was siphoning petrol from a puddle at the base of a cliff. Deborah was terribly jealous of 'that woman', as she called her, when she really had no reason to be. I would never have divorced Deborah. Men of my generation don't just walk away. But when Deborah heard the Little Fish and his strange partner had accompanied Ira and me on a weekend away, she banned him from the house. This was exceptionally hard on the Little Fish, who had been a regular guest at our *Shabbos* table for nearly fifteen years.

I tried to intervene on his behalf, but found myself unable to overturn Deborah's ruling. I think this, more than anything else, is what turned the Little Fish against me, his faithful friend since schooldays.

[Ends.]

TWENTY-TWO

I got a call from Jed saying he'd been asking around about Natural Science.

'Sorry, mate,' I said, 'I should've told you. It turns out he's in New Caledonia.'

'Well, I got a message he's at the tattooist's in Darlinghurst Road,' said Jed.

'That's closed up,' I said. 'It's a crime scene.'

'So don't bother looking,' said Jed. 'Pretend he's gone to Scotland instead.'

'Who left the message?' I asked.

'Fuck knows,' said Jed, 'but he mentioned your name and Mendoza's too.'

Jed said he'd meet me at the unit. It seemed dramatic, but we'd learned in the army never to enter an empty building alone. He turned up with the last flush of bruising still glowing on his cheeks, and short lines of tight stitches crossing his forehead like railways tracks. I was waiting outside with the derringer in my pocket. He wore a small backpack full of kit. He slapped me on the shoulder. I grinned at him. Oh fuck, this felt good. Back to work with the Jedi.

I was twice as alive as before he turned up. I could see and hear everything, from the street chatter of strangers to the rhythm of Jed's heartbeat. We walked down the strip like whore-hound tourists, but in our hearts we were soldiers on a mission. It was strange, really, because we never felt much like that in the army. I moved in perfect time with Jed, checking to the left and right, watching his back while he looked ahead.

The tattooist's window was boarded up, its door chained shut, the whole building sealed with tape. We checked the exit onto Kellet Street, but that was barricaded too. We'd have to get in the way the commandoes had, behind the facade and through the roof. Jed climbed first, shinning up the drainpipe and smiling like a pirate. This was better than being soldiers, this was being *kids*. I wished we had thought of a codename for the operation. I scrambled onto the roof, scraping skin off my elbows, imagining camouflage paint on my cheeks and a knife between my teeth. Jed pulled a pair of bolt cutters – bolt cutters! – from his bag, tore away the crime-scene tape, unchained the frame of the skylight and wrenched it open. Ideally we would have abseiled down on rappelling ropes, just for the buzz of it, but without the right equipment we had to dangle and jump. It was a three-metre drop onto a hard tiled floor, but I made it all right. Jed landed with a roll, just to show that he could.

We hit the ground in the waiting room, where the couches had been shredded by gunfire, and the mermaids, hearts and roses flaked, scorched and curled from the walls. Jed drew his pistol, I pointed the derringer, and together we burst into the studio, laughing.

In the middle of the room, bound to the tattooist's chair, was a black man who had once been Natural Science. Somebody had cut off his nose and his lips, and left his teeth scattered around his feet.

I patted down the body and found Natural Science's wallet, passport and keys. Jed said we should leave in case there was a bomb.

'How the fuck are we going to get back up to the skylight?' I asked.

We couldn't, of course, so we had to kick the back door in, which we might as well have done in the first place, if we were going to do it at all.

You can't cry for every casualty in a war. You have to protect yourself against grief and horror. We learned that in Kosovo, sifting through the mass graves. You have to discipline your mind so that it doesn't think about what it must've been like for that poor bastard tied to the chair and tortured. You have to look at a body and think, 'Well, that was someone once, but it isn't now,' and get on with your own life. That night, we had a drink for Natural Science. I phoned the police from a call box to tell them where to find the body, and I tried never to think about him again.

The papers needed a name for everything. They called Natural Science 'The Body in the Tattoo Shop' and later 'Orpheus of the Underworld'. The tattoo studio became 'The Ink Blot', as if the building itself were to blame for the killings. The Cannibals were victims of 'Bikie Wars'.

I was having a beer with Jed in the Southern Star when Suicide, the president of the Cannibals, appeared on Channel Nine news, wearing a collared shirt fastened up to his throat to cover the huge flaming tattoos that licked his neck. The barman turned down the jukebox and turned up the television, while Suicide read from a written statement. The point he wanted to make was that bikers weren't interested in drugs or violence, and these lunatics who were targeting them weren't interested in bikes. They were just thugs, gangsters and gutless murderers, mowing down innocent motorcycle enthusiasts going about their lawful hobby.

The ranks of the Cannibals included men with university degrees, responsible jobs and amateur boxing titles. Their name referred to their habit of cannibalising old bike parts to restore vintage choppers, which was an important part of their lifestyle. And, like the Oddfellows or the Lions Clubs, they regularly raised money for kids with cancer. They were persecuted because of the clothes they wore, and misunderstood because they had sometimes failed to explain themselves. But they were just a bunch of ordinary Aussies who wanted to be free to live the life they chose, assisting deserving charities and celebrating their larrikin brotherhood with barbies in the summer and a two-up game on Anzac Day.

After the news was a panel discussion with the Premier of New South Wales; a criminologist; and a biker expert who was wearing a black T-shirt to show off the tiny skull tattoo on his forearm. Between them, they were trying to work out what needed to be banned.

The premier, looking out with toad's eyes from behind his spectacles, wanted laws against everything: men riding motorbikes in gangs; gangs riding motorbikes wearing badges; and men wearing badges in gangs. The criminologist pointed out that there were already laws against men shooting each other, but that hadn't stopped the killings.

'Are you saying,' asked the premier, his voice trembling with his jowls, 'that you are in favour of carnage on our streets?'

The criminologist said outlaw bikers were a tiny minority of motorcycle-club members, and called themselves 'one-percenters' because the other ninety-nine per cent were law-abiding citizens. Why should the premier make thousands of ordinary motorcyclists suffer for the actions of a few hundred renegades?

The premier said it was hardly a hardship to a decent motorcyclist to refrain from riding around in armed gangs, terrorising the community.

The presenter asked if any of the panel had any idea what was behind the recent killings.

'Criminality,' said the premier.

The expert said we were witnessing a time of change in the outlaw clubs, which were traditionally based on brotherhood blah blah fuck blah, blah blah fuck. I went to the bar to get drinks for me and Jed, and when I came back the expert was still going on about the outlaw code of honour, which always seemed to me about as real as their commitment to road safety. The problem was, he said, that the old-style bikers were being usurped by criminals who were using the image and structure of biker gangs as cover for their unlawful activities. Some of these new breed of 'Nike bikies' didn't even own bikes. The premier agreed this was a new and disturbing trend.

'So what's the point of banning bikers who *do* ride bikes?' the criminologist asked him.

'Non-riding bikies will be dealt with under our proposed insignia laws,' said the premier.

'What?' asked the criminologist. 'Are you going to ban Nike?'

'No,' said the premier, imitating patience, 'we are going to ban open warfare by outlaw gangs.'

'But that's already banned,' said the criminologist. 'The bikers are the symptom, not the disease.'

'Here we go . . .' said the premier.

'This isn't about a bunch of clowns in leather jackets, breaking the speed limit,' said the criminologist, 'it's about the international drugs trade.'

'Oh, come on, Geoff,' said the expert, who agreed that a small number of bikers might be involved in drugs, but there were many others – including men he was proud to call his friends – who rode with the clubs simply for comradeship.

'If drugs were legal,' said the criminologist, 'there would be no outlaw bike gangs.'

'If drugs were legal,' said the premier, 'we would have begun the slow descent into hell.'

Unfortunately that was all they had time for that evening, although viewers were encouraged to phone a toll line and give their opinion on what people with motorbikes shouldn't be allowed to do.

On the same day as the police found 'The Body in the Tattoo Shop', a couple of garbos emptied 'The Body in the Bin' into the back of their truck, then vomited when they saw somebody in the Cross had thrown away a broken old man. It was M&M from the New York restaurant and, like all old men who die alone, it turned out he was somebody back in his day: a handy welterweight, a merchant seaman, a jazz saxophonist, a trade unionist, a kindly old fella who was everybody's friend.

I saw Siobhan's byline on a couple of the stories. She was the first writer to suggest M&M might have been killed because he looked like Mendoza, but her theory seemed ridiculous because the paper ran its favourite photograph of Mendoza – a sharp young gangster, looking out from under the fishnet legs of a stripper – next to a picture of the New York's photocopied missing-persons poster.

Siobhan actually called me to find out if I knew what had happened to Natural Science. I suggested we meet for a drink, but she said she was too busy following up leads and verifying her sources, and doing other things that I wouldn't understand because I wasn't a journalist and never had been. She asked if Mendoza had ordered Natural Science's execution as a deserter, or if I had murdered him myself because he had found out my secret.

Then she softened and said how sorry she was to hear about Natural Science, and how disgusting it was that somebody could do that to another person, and how she hoped Mendoza caught them and made them swallow their own teeth.

'Isn't that what you've got planned for me?' I asked.

She called me a fucking idiot who would believe anything about the Irish.

'Your kneecaps are safe, soldier boy,' she said. 'I know you need them for sucking off your officers.'

She asked if I'd noticed that all the out-of-town Cannibals had disappeared. She said they'd left a stack of weaponry with the Sydney chapter, but couldn't find anyone to use it on. The hit team from Ink had left the country, flying to Moscow via Bangkok and Frankfurt. They had boarded planes on separate days, travelling on passports from the Ukraine, Kazakhstan, Germany and Israel. Two of them were held by police at the airport, but they weren't carrying anything connecting them to the shootings, and they were back home before Natural Science's body turned up.

Her contact at the police station had got all this from a friend in the AFP. He was a really nice bloke. I ought to meet him. He lived quite near me, but in a much nicer flat. He had a very modern bathroom, said Siobhan, with a power shower.

Mendoza was angry and uncooperative, as he was whenever I tried to save his life. He paced around his living room, swearing and shaking, railing against the Maltese.

'Torture and murder,' he said. 'That's their hallmark. Cutting up the face: it's a traditional thing. It comes from the Knights.'

'Bullshit,' I said. 'It comes from whoever got his nose bitten off by Natural Science.'

'A nose for a nose?' said Mendoza. 'That's a theory.'

He smiled like a man with no enemies, and nothing to fear in the world.

'You're in danger here,' I told him. 'These people'll finish what they started. You should get out of the country, maybe go to Israel.'

'Really, Anthony?' he asked. 'I thought you said the hit team had gone back home to Malta.'

'To Moscow,' I said, 'for fuck's sake.'

'You don't know where they went,' said Mendoza.

'Whatever,' I said, 'but they aren't retreating, they're just rotating. There'll be another team in the country by next week. That's why you've got to leave now.'

'Who said that?' he asked. 'Siobhan the shape-shifter?'

'She's got her sources,' I told him, and he leered as if I'd said something dirty.

Mendoza sat in his favourite chair, in front of a glass cabinet filled with photographs of his wife and family. 'I'm not concerned with predictions, Anthony,' he said. 'I'm only interested in facts. I want to know what happened to the *schvartzer*: why did he go to New Caledonia, and why did he come back? I want your friend Jed to fly there and find out for me. And I want him to leave this afternoon.'

TWENTY-THREE

[Holiday Inn, Victoria Street, Potts Point. 18.04.02. 2:03 pm.]

Development, Anthony: the premier was all about development – residential development, commercial development, business development. Sydney in the early seventies was like London after the blitz. The difference was, we hadn't had a blitz, so the business community itself had to clear all the rotting old housing from the inner suburbs.

'Development': every race and creed on earth has development, except for the boongs, and look where it's got them. Sydney was crying out for development. You could hear it in the wind blowing through the paperbark trees in Victoria Street, a demand to change with the times, to show the world that Sydney was a world-class city where residents could tower above their origins, in skyscrapers to rival anything in New York, and relieve themselves in ensuite bathrooms, perhaps pausing for a douche in the bidet.

There were many visionaries who understood the need to transform the urban landscape, including my good friend

Sir Peter, who created the Monorail, a boon not only to those imbeciles who, through physical or mental incapacity, are unable to navigate the five-minute downhill walk from Town Hall to Darling Harbour, but also a gift to the entire city. Who can help but admire the way in which its futuristic lines paint smiles across the grim and tired faces of the handful of nineteenth century buildings that continue to pollute the visual landscape of our vibrant and forward-looking central business district?

The Sir Peter of Kings Cross was a German Jew named Willie Frankel. Willie knew all about development. He'd already developed his lingerie business into one of the largest in Australia, but the development that made his name, and secured his place in the history of this city, was Victoria Spires, the flower of Victoria Street.

There is something you should know about Willie: he was not a quitter. He was driven out of Berlin by the Nazis and thrown into a concentration camp, from which he escaped to Shanghai, the China of the Jews. From Shanghai he boarded a boat to Australia, where he had dreams of building an empire of underpants as large as the one his family had left behind in Frankfurt.

During the war, he was considered an enemy alien, and therefore could not join the army, as you and I did, but nonetheless served with distinction as a draper and a mercer, putting his skills to work making parachutes for troops like me.

For clerks in the Pay Corps?

For troops, Anthony, for enlisted men who were prepared to work in any suitable capacity, provided such an opening could be found.

When Willie had become Sydney's Underpants King, he felt bound to look for other opportunities to help develop his adopted homeland. Like so many visionary businessmen, he turned his eye to property. I didn't suggest he build Victoria

Spires, but I certainly supported the project, both with a generous line of credit and the loan of some of my best operators in the relocations industry.

Willie had gone through the proper channels to get approval for his development – he'd joined the Liberal Party and donated generously – and was entitled to believe he would be able to proceed.

At first there might have been a few legitimate residents of Victoria Street, battlers whose families had lived behind the railway station for generations, suffocated by the fumes and deafened by the noise, in nineteenth century squalor, with their houses falling down around their ears. These were Willie's people, he understood them. He bought their worthless homes from their landlords, allowing them to leap to the very top of the waiting list for capacious villas in Mt Druitt and elsewhere. Lying journalists, such as Ham and Eggs and Sausage and Chips and Barbecue-fucking-Sauce, have since tried to paint the so-called Battle of Victoria Street as a conflict between the left and the right, but Labor and the Liberals were united in seeing the need for urban renewal and growth. The opposition came from people who were entirely outside the political spectrum.

Once the real residents had gone, Victoria Street was a kind of terra nullius, populated by anarchist squatters with no concept of land ownership. The anarchists screamed that the police were 'fascists', but it was they who were the real Nazis, depriving a refugee of his rightful property as surely as the Gestapo did in prewar Berlin. Willie was particularly angry that the anarchists had made common cause with the feminists, who had already been responsible for the downfall of one of his businesses when Frankel's Beautiful Brassieres was forced to close due to the inexplicable outbreak of bra burning. Willie began to feel that all of feminist ideology was directed against him personally. First they burn bras, he warned, then they burn books, then they burn bodies.

Willie enlisted the aid of a prominent construction consultant who had adopted the nom de guerre Johnny Dracula, an unusual man who, in the tradition of his namesake, claimed to be a blood-drinking vampire from Transylvania. He was what is commonly described as a karate 'expert' (although I have yet to meet anybody trained in the martial arts who is not an 'expert') and a world karate champion (although I have yet to meet anybody prominent in the martial arts who was not a world champion). There is no doubt, however, that he excelled at kicking men in the balls, and if you are only good at one thing in life, it might as well be that.

He ran one of Sydney's earliest karate clubs, and many of the doormen who worked in the Cross trained with him. Interestingly, although Johnny Dracula was an active member of the Labor Party, he was not a communist. I think you'll find, Anthony, that few of the real refugees from Eastern Europe ever were. They had seen communism in action – the purges, the show trials, the indiscriminate executions – and they vowed, to a man, never to allow a repeat of that bloodthirsty chaos on the beloved soil of their adopted homeland.

Willie and Dracula went about explaining to the last residents of Victoria Street that they were blocking a great and noble enterprise, and sped them on their way by removing their windows, roofs, doors and so on.

The jacks were equally eager to see the back of these remnants from another time and pitched in whenever they could with a crowbar or an opportune arrest. Fred Carol, now invalided out of the police force, coordinated the cooperation between the forces of law and business. In response, the residents set up an illegal, antipolice vigilante patrol, which went about intimidating real workers in the Cross, such as the bouncers. The anarchists called in their friends, the Maoists. You see, in those days, Anthony, there was a trade union in Australia called the

Builders' Labourers Federation, whose task was to make sure no builders' labouring ever took place anywhere. The BLF put a so-called 'green ban' on development in Victoria Street, as if the shitty fucking workers' cottages were rare patches of rainforest.

Poor Willie had nowhere to turn. He came to me to ask for help. I had sympathy for his cause, and great admiration for his enterprise, but I was not going to get mixed up in a murder blue just because some fucking Kraut owed me a quarter of a million dollars. Also, the trouble in Victoria Street had become bad for business. It was drawing people's attention to things they didn't need to know, and undermining their faith in the very institutions that kept them safe from harm. I advised Willie to settle things quickly and quietly, but instead he gathered all the jacks together, and all Dracula's karate boys, a gang of skinheads and one fucking imbecile named Jack Brun, and flogged the whole street – the unions, the anarchists, the pensioners, everyone. Broke their fucking heads. It's not how I would have done it, but it did the job.

During this long period of wasted energy, Willie became mates with the Little Fish and was sometimes seen in Aphrodite's, chasing the easiest skirt in Kings Cross. The Little Fish had already done one job for him – a leader of the residents had been kidnapped and taught the facts of life – and I kept a close eye on their relationship, because a man can't serve two masters, and I had a feeling the Little Fish was going cold on me.

There was a moll in the Cross named Anita King, whose father owned Kings Department Store on Liverpool Street. The old man liked to boast he'd brought the first escalator to Australia, but I reckon more blokes would've been up and down on his daughter. She was a big-mouthed, bed-hopping slag who was always poking her nose where it wasn't wanted. Just your type of woman, Anthony.

She would probably have had a great future in the world of

dry-goods retailing – or, for that matter, in the Pussycat Bordello – but she chose instead to make her way through life as a professional pain in the arse. She ran a so-called newspaper that I called *No*, because all it ever wrote was 'no' to this development and 'no' to that development. Willie knew the only way he could get the green ban lifted was if he bought off the BLF. Luckily, there were realists in the union who, although they may have been commos, preferred to fight another day than fight at all. Willie dropped them a quid and they dissolved the whole NSW branch.

But Anita King started fucking some union boss – the crane drivers or something – and he took over the BLF's shitty campaign to keep Kings Cross in the nineteenth century. Willie tried to talk some sense into King, but it was her way or the highway, which was ironic, considering where she probably ended up.

Willie's new best mate, the Little Fish, had become the biggest heroin dealer in the Cross, using my club as the centre of his own operation, and cutting me in on no fucking per cent whatever. I didn't care because drugs as a business didn't interest me. I couldn't imagine there'd be much growth in a product that killed its customers, and then there was the problem with Big Stan, which I'll return to later. But the Little Fish loved drugs, because he thought they would help him escape from my influence and build his own empire of lunacy, starting with Aphrodite's.

The Little Fish told Jack Brun, who was night manager at the Roundabout Club, to bring Anita King in for a meeting. Brun made a couple of useless attempts to get her to the office – he had the idea you had to kidnap someone to transport them from Victoria Street to Darlinghurst Road – but she came off her own back when he rang to say the Little Fish wanted to buy an advert in her arse-paper for a businessman's lunch he was planning, which was a bit fucking unusual since Aphrodite's – like the Ligato – had no kitchen. Nobody has seen Anita

King from that day to this. The jacks initially pursued two lines of enquiry. Number one: they interviewed all her communist lovers, to see which one of them had knocked her, or whether it was a conspiracy between all of them. Number two: they tested the theory that she might have staged her own disappearance in order to discredit the legitimate activities of pioneering property developers. It never occurred to them that the Little Fish might have been involved, because the Little Fish was paying them for things like that not to occur to them.

But the shit-raking, smear-mongering journalists – led, as usual, by Ham and Eggs – wouldn't leave the story alone, so somebody had to cop it sweet. Jack Brun put his hand up and pleaded guilty to a charge of conspiring to kidnap the slut. The 1970s were truly a time of miracles, Anthony. The Little Fish could shoot the Iron Fist in the back in self-defence, and an imbecile like Jack Brun could conspire on his own to kidnap an heiress.

Just before the so-called 'disappearance' of Anita King, Willie paid the Little Fish a large sum of money to give his son, Felix, a start in the nightclub industry, in which he has never worked from that day to this. Up until the end of his life, Willie saw the Little Fish right for his help in getting Felix on the right track (I believe he is currently in prison in Thailand) and Jack Brun received a hefty sum, too, probably in return for some service he also supplied to Felix, such as reading him bedtime stories.

You were going to talk about Big Stan.

Ah yes, Big Stan. I had him managing the Pussycat Bordello in Darlinghurst Road, when the fucking place caught fire. As usual, the fucking journalists reckoned I was burning myself out, but why would I? The Pussycat burned down because Big Stan was an imbecile junkie who nodded off with a cigarette in his mouth and a newspaper in his hand.

He'd been on heroin ever since the GIs first brought it into the Cross, and I was the last to know. He got his supply from the Little Fish, which was another low act of treachery towards me. When Big Stan burned down my brothel, he tried to say it was the Malts, but one of his whores came to me with the truth.

I let Stan know how disappointed I was in him. Maybe I shouldn't have said anything. Perhaps I should've let him carry on setting fire to my properties. If I had, he might still be alive today. From what I understand, soon after our conversation Big Stan returned to his unit in Elizabeth Bay and shot himself in the stomach. I agree with everything that was said at the time – it was an unusual way to commit suicide – but my theory is that it was not a genuine suicide attempt but a cry for help. And anyway, who expects somebody to die after they've been shot in the stomach? It's bad luck, that's all.

After Big Stan had ruined the top floor of my building, I tried to get the whole thing knocked down, but the fucking unions green-banned the fucking facade, just to piss me off. I saw the story regurgitated in all its inaccurate detail by a Siobhan Hughes, after the tattoo studio got hit. That wasn't your doing, by any chance, was it? It wasn't the product of your original research? You didn't pass it on in exchange for the perceived promise of cunt at some unspecified future time?

I was helping another journalist.

Really? I didn't realise your profession – not, of course, that it is *your* profession – had such collegial ethics. Talking of which, the story of Anita King should have ended there, but it didn't, due once again to the stale obsessions of Ham and Eggs. Even though I had less than fuck all to do with anything that happened to that woman, she caused me ten years of trouble from beyond the grave, or under the tarmac, or wherever she might rest.

The mystery of the disappearance of Anita King may cast a shadow over his legacy, Anthony, but Sydney will not soon forget the name Willie Frankel. There is even a mural to him in Woolloomooloo, in which Willie is pictured in a heroic moment of property development, examining his plans for Victoria Spires, flanked by his faithful lieutenant, Dracula, and our good friend Jack Brun, towering over the faded faces of Anita King and a Maoist who quite probably murdered her in a crime of passion. **[Ends.]**

TWENTY-FOUR

I was lying on my bed, imagining what it might be like to have Siobhan bouncing on my lap and Leah sitting on my face, when the door opened and Helen walked in. I rolled into the quilt red-faced like a frankfurter in a hotdog.

'I *know* what you were doing,' she said.

She looked pretty. She was pretty. She had a lovely mouth.

'What the fuck are *you* doing?' I asked.

Nice legs, too.

'This is my flat,' she said.

'Oh, so you're here to pay the rent?'

She walked over to the kitchen and took a seat on the stool.

'I'd offer you a cup of tea,' I said, 'but you stole all the mugs.'

She passed me my pants and I got dressed under the quilt, like a swimmer changing on the beach.

She lit a cigarette.

'I don't smoke in the flat any more,' I told her.

'Don't you?' she said.

'No,' I said. 'You took the ashtray.'

She flicked her ash onto a dirty plate.

'Can't you buy *anything* for the house?' she asked.

'What do you care?'

'I care about you, Slick.'

'Nobody calls me "Slick" any more,' I said.

'My, your life has changed,' she said. 'Did you do a course or something?'

She kissed the air with smoke rings. Helen was the only person I knew who still blew smoke rings.

'How's Jed?' I asked.

'He's in New Caledonia,' she said, 'doing that job for your boss.'

She gazed out of the window at the Pussycat Bordello.

'Do you ever think about what it was like before we came here?' she asked. 'We were happy then. Do you know why?'

'You weren't fucking my best mate,' I said.

'No,' said Helen, 'I *was* your best mate. Then we got to Australia, and all the fun went out of our lives. I came here for a working *holiday*, Slick. I thought we'd see Ayers Rock and the Great Barrier Reef. I never realised we'd be stuck for a year in Kings Cross while you tried to change your career.'

It was nice to hear the sound of her voice. She dropped her Ts and rolled her Rs. I closed my eyes.

'I already had a career,' she said. 'I worked in banks for eleven years. It's all I've ever done since I left school, and you wanted me to come here and get a job at the NAB. What would be the point, Slick? Why wouldn't I just stay in Aldershot and look at pictures of Australia?'

I watched her lips trembling gently.

'Even when I found a nice part-time job in a sandwich shop, you were on my back all the time about earning my keep. I didn't come here to earn my keep. I wanted to live in backpackers' hostels and drink wine out of boxes. You went on at me all the time about being lazy. Who do you think did your shopping? Who do you think cleaned up after you? Who cooked your food? Who washed your clothes? You couldn't even see me, Slick, because all you could see were these bizarre fantasies of yourself.

'You've changed so much since I met you. When you first got out of the army, you just wanted to have fun. Now, all you want to do is work, but your jobs always involve some weird fucked-up lie. It was bad enough when you started pretending to be a Catholic, but a Jew . . . What were you thinking? You made me go to the synagogue, do you remember that? This is my once-in-a-lifetime holiday in Australia, and you took me out to St Mary's Cathedral and Temple Emmanuel.'

I shook my head at myself.

'I tried to support you, babe,' she said, 'because you're a lovely, lovely bloke. You're kind, you're gentle, you're good-looking, you're funny. But you know what? You're not a journalist. And you're never going to be a journalist, because you can't fucking write. It's like me trying to be a model or something.'

She had tears in her eyes.

'You could be a model,' I said.

'I'm thirty-one years old. You don't become a model at thirty-one. You become a mum. Don't you see what I'm saying?'

'You want to have kids.'

'Yeah, I want to have kids,' she said, 'but not right now, not in Australia, and not with a bloke who might wake up any morning and start acting like a Hindu or a Sikh. I want to have a holiday, then I want to settle down.'

'With Jed?'

'No, not with fucking Jed. Jed doesn't even look at me. He just closes his eyes and thinks about that little slut he met in Thailand.'

'So why did you go with him?'

'You pushed me away,' she said. 'You wanted it to happen, babe. Admit it.'

Maybe I did. I don't know. It seemed like a long time ago. Maybe I felt she was holding me back. Maybe I wanted to convince myself she was bad, so I could let her go. But maybe sea cucumbers have dance parties on the ocean floor. Who knows and who fucking cares?

'There's beer in the fridge,' I said.

'You've figured out how to use the bottle shop,' said Helen, 'but not the supermarket.'

She brought me over a bottle of Crown, opened one for herself and sat on the edge of my bed, drinking slowly.

'What are you doing here, Helen?' I asked.

'I've been waiting for you,' she said. 'When you burst into the van with that daft purple helmet on, I thought you'd come to get me.'

'But I hadn't,' I said.

'No,' said Helen. 'You'd come to kidnap Jed, hang him upside down and torture him.'

I blushed, for a number of reasons.

'Was any tiny part of that because of me?' she asked.

'No,' I answered honestly.

'Do you think you might sometimes jump to conclusions,' she asked, 'and take things a bit too far? Do you think, babe, you might be some kind of nutter?'

'It's the army,' I said. 'PTSD. I've got no impulse control.'

'Bollocks,' said Helen.

I shrugged. I mean, who could say really?

'Do you know what I've been doing all this time?' she asked.

'Fucking Jed,' I said.

'I've been watching over you,' said Helen, 'like a guardian angel. Jed was watching Mendoza, but I was watching you. And you need a guardian angel, babe, because somebody's trying to kill you.'

'Me?' I said. 'Why would anyone want to kill me?'

'I don't know, babe,' said Helen, squeezing my hand, 'but he's already tried twice and, when I came in he was waiting outside.'

We walked together slowly down the stairs. Helen had noticed the guy about a couple of months ago. Wherever I was, he went too. Jed thought it was a coincidence, but a coincidence happens twice, not every day. The first time he'd come to kill me, I was sitting outside La Fontaine, and he'd jogged past wearing a tracksuit. Once he'd made sure who I was, he came back in a T-shirt and board shorts, with a pistol stuck in the small of his back. Jed didn't want to give away their position, but Helen climbed out of the van, doubled backed one block, walked up to him and asked if he wanted a girl. He said he didn't, and tried to walk through her, but she blocked him and asked whether she wasn't good enough for him. He said it was not that, it was just a bit early in the morning. She asked if he liked boys and he told her to get out of his way. When she wouldn't, he reached for her shoulder and almost pushed her. Jed jumped out of the driver's seat and yelled what the fuck did he think he was doing. He shouted they were both mad, and jogged back the way he'd come.

The second time, Jed had left Helen in the van, watching the window, while Mendoza and I talked in a private room at the Bellisimo. My stalker had followed me up the street, waited until I was inside, then returned clutching a man-bag. Helen tried to call me but my phone was turned off, so she stopped him again and asked if he was still too cheap to help out a working girl. He told her to fuck off or he would kill her. She asked how he would do that. He said he had a gun. Helen screamed, 'He wants to shoot me, and I'm carrying his baby!' and the bouncers and spruikers stirred in the doorways, and the assassin spat at her and ran.

I was holding the derringer in my hand as I opened the door into the street. I pushed Helen back against the wall and darted out into the patio, where Dror was standing, smoking a cigarette. He looked down, surprised, at my gun.

There was a loud pop. Dror dived behind the recycling bins. The bullet hit a drainpipe about a metre to my left. Amateurs. I thought about rolling, just to impress Dror, but I decided to zigzag instead. I caught up with the shooter in two zags. The recoil had made him drop the gun and he was scrambling to pick it out of a flowerbed.

I kicked him in the face. I recognised him, but I couldn't remember why. He called me a bastard and lashed out without looking. I caught his arm, hauled him upright and threw him against the wall of the building. Dror was on him, with a pistol stuck in his temples. I jammed my derringer under his chin. Blood bubbled from his nose.

'Do you know this bloke?' asked Dror, shaking the prisoner.

I looked closer. Oh no.

'Jesus,' I said, 'he's some kid I beat up at the Hamilton Hotel.' The boy burbled blood.

'What're you doing here, anyway?' I asked Dror.

'I just came around to see if you fancied a drink,' he said. 'I thought maybe we could go out and get into some trouble.'

An hour later, Dror had taken the boy away and I was lying in bed with Helen, kissing her neck as she stroked my hair. My clothes made a mound at the bottom of the bed, hers were folded over the back of a chair. It was good to smell her again, a perfume I had bought. I ran my hands down her thighs. She slid her tongue into my ear. I pulled her against me and felt as if I had found a missing part.

'Go gently,' she whispered, 'go slowly.'

TWENTY-FIVE

[Holiday Inn, Victoria Street, Potts Point. 20.04.02. 2:04 pm.]

A man might have felt entitled to believe that once Anita King was dead, she would stop fucking around with his business, but the people's collective of ratbag communist anarchist reporters, editors and commissars wouldn't accept that the story was over and it was time they buried their suspicions about Willie and the Little Fish and got on with fabricating lies about the government. Ham and Eggs kept on trying to link me with the King case, because if Jake Mendoza was involved, that would explain everything. No wonder she fucking disappeared if I had anything to do with her. People I know disappear all the time, don't they? Name me one, Anthony. Name me just one.

The business community had a meeting and decided it was time to tip Ham and Eggs out of the frying pan and into the fire. Now, I'll tell you a secret, Anthony: I always had a soft spot for Eggs. He amused me because, unlike virtually anyone else I have ever met, he was in no need of a nickname. He had a bald, bullet-shaped head and a fat, round stomach. He actually looked like eggs. Before I let the others set the gunnies on him, I offered him the chance to do business with us, but he spat in my face and left me with no choice but to allow events to take their course. Eggs took a little beating and lost interest in the case. Ham lingered on, like the rancid smell of swine. No one was game to bash her in case she became 'another Anita King', but the jacks took her in for questioning and confiscated all her notes.

Did that warn her off?

No, she wrote a fucking story about it. But what can you do? You can't kill all the journalists, or there'd be nobody to report the football scores.

What happened to the Little Fish?

He was flush with Willie's cash and came to me with an offer to buy Aphrodite's. It was a good price and I would have sold, except I knew that would just be the start. He would set himself up in competition with me, and he would bury me, since he had the additional income stream of heroin sales to prop up his clubs. I offered him a partnership, on very favourable terms, but he turned me down. The problem with people in this business, Anthony, is they always want everything. I knew what was going through the Little Fish's head. He'd knocked the Iron Fist and he'd knocked Anita King, and never even had to face a beak. He was a fucking koala, a protected species. He had a green light from the jacks – *my* green light, by the way – and a reputation as the hardest man in the Cross. Why shouldn't he just knock me, his best mate and lifelong benefactor, for the sake of a fucking scumhole of a strip club? Then he and his hermaphrodite coconut could be the king and queen of the Cross, and rule over every gibbering imbecile junkie from the Coke sign to the fountain.

He didn't have the balls to neck me himself, so he put the word out that he needed a gunnie. I sent one of my new boys to pose as a contract killer from Perth. The Little Fish offered him the price of a new Roller – my life for a fucking car – to shoot me in one of the apartments I had stashed around town in case I needed a room to take a girl, and my wife and mistress were not feeling their usual understanding, angelic selves.

His plan – if I can dignify his drooling imbecility with that word – was to kidnap a stripper I was seeing at the time (Bernadette Taylor – fake tits, real arse). He was going to have my boy put on Bernie's stage wig and cocktail dress, ring my doorbell, and shoot me in my doorway before I saw through his kindergarten disguise. No doubt when the assassin reported back to him with shaved legs and a stuffed bra, the Little Fish hoped to bend him over and bugger him.

His scheme's success – or lack of it – rested on the assumption that everyone was like him and believed the difference between men and women was purely sartorial. I think the part that made me the most angry, besides the insulting price of the contract and the low treachery of that mongrel dog, was the fact that, if he'd succeeded, I would have always been remembered as having been knocked by a fucking drag queen. It would have overshadowed all my achievements in the various branches of the entertainment and gaming industries, and my pioneering work for the causes of racial equality and the social acceptance of midgets.

While he was waiting for some suicidal imbecile to take up his offer to murder me (my boy declined due to other commitments), the Little Fish expanded security around Aphrodite's. He fired every bouncer he thought might have had any loyalty to me and replaced them with shit-thick coconuts who were all muscle and no heart. When I went to the club to make my weekly collection, they told me the place was under new management, and barred my way in.

I took all the Little Fish's sacked workers back into my

organisation and doubled the number of men on my doors. They started selling heroin, but I let it go. My girls were happy to have a safe source of supply close by, and I noticed that when they were on the gear they were more susceptible to imaginative suggestions about how they might spend their working lives. This was when the midget shows really took off and, for a brief period, I was able to incorporate a German shepherd into some of the early morning performances. I named it 'McCoy' because (a) it was a mad dog; and (b) if he'd been around, McCoy would have married it to save it from a life of exploitation. McCoy the dog became a star of both stage and screen, appearing in classic loop movies such as 'A Girl's Best Friend' (in which he was billed as 'Diamond') and 'The Dog's Breakfast'. These productions – my first professional work in the film industry, with paid actors and a skilled crew – were internationally successful, although it proved difficult to collect any royalties from overseas sales due to the distribution arm being the fucking Mafia. McCoy died of canine transmissible venereal tumour, a disease that showed alarming signs of spreading through my workforce, and I abandoned my cinematic ambitions in favour of clawing back my clubs. First, I went for the Roundabout Club.

I could have used various former and serving officers of the New South Wales police force to help recover what was mine, but many of them were still under unwarranted scrutiny from the sanctimonious, self-appointed jacks and beaks of the journalistic so-called profession, for their role in routing the various communes and soviets that had poisoned the air in Victoria Street. Instead, I turned to an old friend, a fellow club-owner and prominent member of Melbourne's Sicilian community, who offered me the loan of certain of his specialists who had gained important professional experience in Palermo and Messina.

They turned up at the Roundabout Club an hour before closing and made a big thing about negotiating a group discount with the coconuts. They were supposed to be tourists from Italy, out on the razz, who didn't realise the floor show was over and all they would get for the price of their entry was the right to pay five bucks for a glass of cheap spirits poured from expensive bottles and a chance to press up against the hairless arsehole of a cuntless chorus girl in the bar.

Once they were in, the wops started to make a noise about being ripped off, and the coconuts mobbed up like a rugby team to put them in their place. Then the toys came out and it was on for one and all. The coconuts called for help from further up the evolutionary scale, but their reinforcements never arrived, because my boys caught them at the corner with cricket bats and fence posts.

When we'd dealt with those bastards, we swarmed down to Aphrodite's – and I'm not using the royal 'we' (although, as King of the Cross, I would arguably be entitled to do so), I was actually there, leading my troops into battle – where the Little Fish made his last stand with a few men he thought were good but turned to be as weak as coconut milk when the shit hit the fan. I even took down one of them myself, albeit with a gunnie at either side of me and a wrestler at my back. I should have knocked the Little Fish then and there, but it was like a fucking mardi gras on the strip, with all these drag queens and hoons chasing after us and screaming, and tourists taking pictures and jacks looking so far the other way that their heads almost twisted off their necks. The Little Fish lost two teeth from the unimpressive collection he'd managed to salvage from the boxing ring and the war, and no doubt the extra space made it easier for him to fill his mouth with big brown cock. All in all, it was a very successful evening. I'm not a man who enjoys violence, Anthony, unless it's directed at my enemies.

The next morning the Little Fish vanished, and didn't turn up again until the pointless inquest into Anita King, who was as dead and disappeared at the end of the proceedings as she was at the beginning. You might have thought, Anthony, that the coroner's court would be concerned to discover how the Little Fish had knocked her and where he'd buried the body, but this would display a basic misunderstanding of the motivations of the legal establishment in New South Wales, which were (a) the destruction of the reputation of Jake Mendoza; and (b) see (a) above.

The Little Fish, under the protection of so-called 'honest' jacks – ie, they were in the pay of a different set of crims – took the stand in a suit he must have stripped from the body of Al Capone, and played the big-time gangster to an audience of gullible squareheads and vampire journalists. He said he didn't know what had happened to Anita King after she left Aphrodite's but, sad to say, the club that he happened to manage was, through no fault of his own, a den of sin and debauchery, where he was forced to keep two sets of books, one for the taxman and one for Mr Big. He named names – mostly mine, but also those of a few jacks he had a grudge against, and a couple of businessmen he'd met in his brain-fucked, arse-struck imagination. He told the court I bribed and blackmailed everyone, corrupted the course of politics, brought rain to family picnics on sunny afternoons in November, and made matzos out of the blood of Christian children. On the rare occasion when he was asked about the heiress, he repeated the legally proven theory that her departure was the result of Jack Brun's conspiracy of one.

When the inquest was over, and a cretinous, unapologetic, we've-wasted-everybody's-time open verdict reached, the Little Fish, like some demented cabaret artist with no fans and no gigs (I'm thinking here of Arnold Zwaybil) embarked on a tour of royal commissions, crooning his crowd-pleasing repertoire of lies.

What happened to the Little Fish's business interests?

Christ, Anthony, for the first time in your life you've hit the nail on the fucking head. I didn't even realise you were carrying a hammer. There was only one outcome of any historical significance to all these play-acting commissions and kangaroo courts: the Little Fish resigned from the heroin business, leaving the field open to the organised imbecile community in the shape of a succession of biker gangs up to and including the Cannibals MC.

In the light of all the unwelcome publicity, I also withdrew from formal involvement in all my remaining operations, with the exception of the training and recruitment of showgirls, strippers and whores. I became, if you like, a human resources manager, in a vertically integrated, people-centred organisation whose core strength was the quality of its staff.

Sad to say, in the years that followed I became distant from Ira, as she grew grey hair and saggy tits and began to affect a certain unattractive cynicism about the way her life had turned out (ie, exactly how she had wanted it). She pressured me to divorce my wife and leave my lovers, but didn't realise that the only leverage she had ever possessed had vanished with the years.

I left her with a heavy heart and a heavier ballsack, which I lightened in the company of my Perth mistress, Amy Monk, who I imported from West Australia for that purpose. My little Sharon, tragically, felt that I had abandoned her, and this was the start of a long and wretched estrangement between loving father and beloved daughter, which concluded with her declaration, at the age of eighteen, that she wouldn't join the family business as an office manager but pursue instead a so-called career as a blood-sucking, dustbin-diving, scandal-mongering journalist. Even so, I still loved her, as she had brought light to my life and laughter to my days. I was there the evening she graduated from university, in her cap and gown, clutching a certificate that gave her a licence to peddle half-truths and exaggerations and tip shit over the good names of progressive businessmen and far-sighted entrepreneurs.

In the 1980s, Anthony, the winds of change farted on me. As restrictions were gradually relaxed on drinking, gambling, prostitution and pornography, most of my activities became legal and accepted, although I personally gained precious little acceptance, let alone acclaim, for my trailblazing vision. With legality came a sharp drop in profits, since we were no longer able to charge a premium for services that any semi-squarehead could provide. Many businesses no longer required protection from the police, who could no longer threaten credibly to raid them because – all of a sudden – they weren't doing anything wrong. My role as an intermediary diminished then finally disappeared.

The premier had long since lost his position, but the new Labor Party administration initially proved to be as sympathetic as its Liberal predecessors to the spirit that made Australia great. The people had chosen and, although initially I disagreed strongly with their choice, I saw it as my democratic duty to bow to their will and extend my program of political donations to include the newly elected government. In a departure from usual practice, however, I didn't withdraw my patronage from the democratic opposition, and thereby rescued them from falling into the trap of opposition-for-its-own-sake. In this way, Anthony, the property development and leisure industries of New South Wales have become the backbone of the democratic process in our state. A seat on the local council was traditionally a thankless and unpaid sinecure. Without our financial injections, only the very rich could afford to waste their and everybody else's time formulating imbecilic objections to clause 7B of subsection 5 of the 1978 amendment to the planning act of 1954, about which they knew two-fifths of fuck all. Political contributions from the business world have enabled even the humblest single-issue imbecile to afford to give a portion of his time to the public service, and walk away heavily rewarded at the end of a long hard lunch.

However, the governments that followed proved more difficult to deal with. The principle of practical expedience gave way to backward-looking notions of accountability, eventually leading to the creation of the vile Independent Commission Against Corruption, which – ironically but predictably – proved itself to be corrupt. It was staffed by fucking jacks, for Christ's sake. What did they expect?

I dabbled in a number of so-called respectable businesses, all of which worked on exactly the same principles as my previously unrespectable businesses. I met plenty of bigger crooks than ever found their way to jail, and some of them even had the fucking indecency to rob me. I had properties in Perth, Adelaide, Geelong, Melbourne, the Gold Coast, Goulburn and Sydney. I made a comeback in the music industry, managing artists who sang about as well as McCoy the German shepherd and fucked just as indiscriminately.

I dissolved my partnership with Izzy Berger when it turned out he'd been cutting me out of music-publishing deals and, one sad morning in spring, he found himself lying in an alleyway outside his office with a bass guitar broken over his head and a vinyl sandwich jammed in his mouth.

I made investments, and some of them failed. I took bad advice – sometimes badly motivated – and began to doubt my ability to read squareheads after having spent so much time in the informal sector. I started to feel old. I joined a gym, where I spent hours staring at twenty-three-year-old office workers in Lycra shorts, and imagining what was sweating inside them, and it made me feel older still. But I was a strong man, Anthony, and strong men don't bow down to anyone or anything – not even age and time. I had become a distant figure, but I was known and respected in every cafe and club. People still came to me for favours, and I never had to buy a meal or a drink. I dyed my disappearing hair, used volumising shampoo, wore hats in all weather and became wary of looking in the mirror, because it was always my father's face that stared back, with all its malice and venality. But I was not him and I never would be. He was the frightened peddler son of peasants, and I was still Jake Mendoza, the King of the Cross.

[Ends.]

TWENTY-SIX

Jed stepped off the plane from Nouméa with his Oakleys wrapped around his head like an Alice band. He was wearing a Hawaiian shirt and Billabong shorts, and carrying a swollen bag of duty-free booze. I met him in the arrivals lounge and said, 'Return of the Jedi,' just like always.

I drove him back into the city while he told me the story that I'd already heard, in part, over the phone. He'd arrived in New Caledonia with the idea that he had to hire someone who was bilingual in English and Caledonian. He'd been surprised to find the locals spoke French, but it turned out he didn't need any language skills anyway. When he showed them a picture of a six-foot-six black man with a gold tooth, anyone who had seen Natural Science – which was almost everyone – nodded and smiled. He stood out in New Caledonia as much as in Kings Cross, because it turned out the local aborigines were a dark mustard colour rather than tyre-black.

A Frenchman in a cafe told Jed he had seen Natural Science with an Arab, so Jed – who had taken a cultural awareness course in the army – went straight to a kebab shop. The Syrian behind the counter said the Arab was a Lebanese businessman from Sydney, and Jed bought a Syrian pizza. ('Fucking rubbish, mate. No cheese.')

Nouméa was so small that Jed figured if he sat at a pavement table for long enough, everyone in town would walk past, but he got distracted by French women wrapped up like Christmas presents and forgot to look out for Arabs. At a coffee shop near the kebab house, he learned the businessman was a nightclub owner, which gave Jed the excuse to visit all the city's nightclubs in case the man had come out on a study tour. Jed eventually found a girl who had followed Natural Science back to his hotel. She was very small, apart from her tits. She said the businessman's name was Mahmoud and he was the owner of Magic Circle. She'd had a drink with Mahmoud in the hotel bar and he had offered her a job as a hostess. Natural Science hadn't said what he was doing on the island, but she had the feeling he might be acting as Mahmoud's minder.

Jed took the name of the hotel then tried to chat up the girl, but after listening to his army stories for half an hour, she refused to speak to him in any language but French.

The next day he exercised his peculiar talent to find Aldershot wherever he went, and ended up drinking vodka for breakfast with two legionnaires in the worst bar in Nouméa. One of them was a Geordie and the other from Moscow, so they were both foreign to Jed, but at least he could understand when the Russian spoke English. They remembered Natural Science, who had turned up at the same ocean-front bloodhouse. The Geordie had wanted to twist a broken glass into his white eyes for looking like he thought he was hard.

When the bar closed, Jed went back to their hotel room to help them clear out the mini-bar. They showed him a couple of pistols they had bought from local French soldiers, fired a half-a-dozen shots out of their seventh-floor window, and took the back legs off a dog.

Jed had many rare qualities, such as the ability to eat a balti chicken while standing on his head, but his only useful skill was that he could get as drunk as a legionnaire on leave but never forget his mission. They had all been going for eleven hours when the Geordie passed out while arm-wrestling the Russian, who fell asleep trying to help Jed learn the words to 'Le Boudin' (Jed, in exchange, taught the Russian 'Agadoo').

Jed stole a room key and a gun, and staggered off to Mahmoud's hotel near Anse Vata beach, trying to sober himself up by taking deep breaths. He recognised the solid, bullet-headed man in the hotel restaurant and realised he had seen him around the Cross. He was dressed in a black T-shirt and a black suit that Jed called Zegna, but Jed wouldn't know Zegna from Lowes. Jed bought a black coffee and watched Mahmoud eat steak washed down with burgundy. When he had finished his dinner, Jed followed him into the elevator and up to his room. As Mahmoud opened his door with his key pass, Jed jabbed the barrel of his pistol into his back. Mahmoud smashed him in the face with an elbow. Jed reeled, Mahmoud turned around and kicked him in the balls. At this point, two things happened: Jed realised how drunk he had been, and Jed sobered up. But by this time Mahmoud was holding Jed's pistol in one hand and dragging Jed into his room with the other, while kicking him in the back of the neck.

Mahmoud shouted at Jed in French, which was like yelling in Latin at a cat, but when he shoved Jed onto his desk chair and pressed the pistol to his cheek, Jed was able to read his body language.

'My name's Jed,' he said. 'I'm a mate of Natural Science.'

Mahmoud hit him on the head with the handle of his gun.

This was the direct opposite of what Jed had hoped would happen. He had imagined Mahmoud sitting on a chair while Jed hit him on the head.

I was laughing so hard that I couldn't breathe. I had missed hearing Jed's stories, which always went pretty much the same way: Jed makes plan, Jed fucks up plan, Jed takes a kicking.

'Where is Natural Science?' asked Mahmoud, stamping on Jed's feet.

'He's dead,' said Jed.

Mahmoud poked Jed in the neck with the gun, and that was the point when Jed realised it wasn't loaded, since the legionnaires had wasted all their ammo on the dog. So Jed did a thing I had seen him do once before: he threw himself and his chair backwards onto the floor and kicked out like a donkey at his opponent's knees.

They had a bit of a tussle, but Jed knew he was going to win because Mahmoud thought the important thing was to keep hold of the gun, whereas Jed realised it didn't matter who had the gun. They grunted and pushed and twisted and punched, but Mahmoud could only use one hand whereas Jed had two. Jed eventually subdued him with the 'Jedi Death Grip', a move that was feared throughout our old regiment, particularly by men waiting in line for the showers with only a towel for protection.

Jed wrestled back the empty gun and pointed it at Mahmoud, and explained they both wanted the answer to the same question: what had happened to Natural Science. Mahmoud quickly became calm and tried to talk himself into a smaller target. He said he was just a nobody who ran an unimportant club that was owned by men from the same village as his father. He saw Natural Science as both a colleague and a friend, and when the chance came to save his life, he was glad to be able to help.

Mahmoud, like many others in the Cross, had become aware of a small Russian presence, whose intentions were unclear. The Russians had come to the Lebs and told them that Natural Science had disrespected one of their people by eating his nose, and they were going to knock him on the door of Mahmoud's club. The Lebs knew they stood to inherit Natural once Mendoza was out of the way, and Natural was an asset to any security team, because he was not mad, weak or stupid, so they tried to bargain down the Russians and asked if they would let Natural Science live if they got him out of the country. The Russians agreed to grant him safe passage if he left immediately, and provided the Lebs did something for them in exchange. The Russians needed a bloke to go to New Caledonia for some sort of meet.

Mahmoud was the Lebs' shitman, so they told him to close his club and sort things out. They suggested he buy Natural a ticket to Bangkok and send him to party with a bunch of Arabs and their whores in Pattaya for a month, until the Russians completed their business and went home. They also gave him the New Caledonia job.

Mahmoud didn't want to go to Nouméa alone, especially when the big Lebs were so sketchy about what the Russians wanted him to do. He worried that his bosses might have promised his club to the Russians, and he was going to get knocked on the beach and fed to the sharks. He decided to take Natural Science with him as a bodyguard and leave him there for a while once his mission was over.

When Mahmoud got to Natural outside Ava's, where Mendoza was telling me the bullshit story about Maltese bikers, he had the air tickets in his hand and a big advance to pay for his services, but Natural refused to leave the door until Dror came along and told him to disappear. Dror said he would personally look after Mendoza and explain to him what had happened. There was no need for Natural Science to contact Mendoza and, if he did, it might put them both in danger. Mahmoud and Natural Science flew out that evening and partied in Nouméa for a couple of nights, waiting for instructions that never came.

After a few days Mahmoud received an angry phone-call from one of the boss Lebs, who wanted to know what the fuck Natural Science was doing in New Caledonia. The big Leb said the Russians' mission couldn't possibly go ahead with Natural Science on the island, and Mahmoud should send him somewhere else immediately. He suggested Tahiti.

But Natural Science was bored. He missed the girls from the Magic Circle, didn't like the French, and believed people would think he was a coward for running away, so he took the next plane back to Sydney, and that was the last Mahmoud had heard of him.

Jed told him how we'd had a tip-off and found Natural's body, and Mahmoud broke down in tears. They hugged like brothers and apologised for trying to kill each other, then went back to the bar to drink to Natural Science's memory.

The next morning Jed returned to the legionnaires' hotel to give them back their gun. They were both still asleep, so they never knew it had gone. He woke them for breakfast, and they all went back to the bar for two days. Jed became their blood brother and an honorary member of the Foreign Legion, C18 and something called the Solntsevskaya bratva. On the fourth day the legionnaires realised their leave passes had nearly expired, leaving them only a short time to desert the Legion. It was a secret, said the Russian, but he would tell Jed: they had been offered jobs in Australia, working for a friend of his brother. The plan was there should be four of them, but the other two were stuck in a Legion prison. The Geordie and the Russian were supposed to pick up clean passports in Nouméa, but they had failed to meet their contact because they were always pissed.

When the Russian mentioned the name of their contact's hotel, Jed realised they were supposed to meet Mahmoud. When he named his brother's friend, he realised they were working for Dror.

So Jed came home.

'And here I am,' he said.

I asked Jed if he fancied a drink before he went back to his house. He said he fancied a drink before he woke up. I took him to the Hollywood Hotel, a pub in Surry Hills which was as similar to a Hollywood hotel as the New York restaurant was to a New York restaurant.

'Look,' I said, 'I've got something to tell you, mate. Helen's moved back in with me.'

'Thank Christ for that,' said Jed.

We knocked glasses.

'Cheers.'

I made an appointment to meet Mendoza outside of our regular schedule. These days it was Dror who answered his phone and, unlike Lazarus, he said things like, 'Mr Mendoza's office, how can I help you?'

Mendoza said he had a busy day – although, from what I could tell, he didn't actually do anything – and could only see me over dinner.

'I hear you've got your woman back,' he said. 'That's good news, Anthony. You were never going to get another one.'

I said nothing, just breathed heavily, like those obscene phone callers you don't hear much about any more.

Mendoza suggested a table at a trattoria in Palmer Street, near the brothel he'd torched in 1972. He reserved a private room, where the walls were lined with cellared wines. The setting was decorated with flowers and candles and, when Helen arrived, he kissed her hand.

'Lovely to meet you,' he said. 'You look beautiful.'

The table was set for four, but the seat next to Mendoza was empty.

The sommelier asked if we had a preference for red or white wine. Mendoza ordered a magnum of Moet and a bottle of Grange 'to celebrate the rekindling of love's eternal flame'. The reflection of the lighted candle flickered in his eyes and made him look like the devil in hell.

'Nicholas tells me you've been pursuing other interests,' said Mendoza.

'Yes,' said Helen, 'I've been fucking our best friend.'

That got the bastard. He had nowhere to go. I thought he'd probably planned his evening's conversation around abusing her but, as usual, I had underestimated his genius for malice.

'And I've been watching you,' said Helen. 'That's been my job.'

'Were you able to combine business with pleasure?' asked Mendoza as the waiter lingered to read out the specials.

'It was always a pleasure,' said Helen. 'You're a very interesting man.'

Oh, she was good. She brought in her shoulders slightly, to give him a better look at her breasts.

'I have only ever seen you carrying things and running away,' said Mendoza. 'First it was a television, then it was your clothes.'

'I've only seen you take women to dinner,' she said. 'I've never seen you take them home.'

'I thought you might be a burglar,' said Mendoza.

'I thought you might be impotent,' said Helen.

'Can I interest you in the specials?' asked the waiter.

'Not yet,' said Mendoza. 'We're waiting for one more.'

I didn't want to talk in front of a stranger, so I tried to get business over with while there was just the three of us.

'Look, Jake,' I said, 'there are no Maltese.'

'No,' he said, 'and the Holocaust was just a myth concocted by the Jews to win the sympathy of the world. That is why we are looked upon so sympathetically today.'

'For God's sake –'

'If there are no Maltese, Slickolas, who the fuck do you think lives in Malta?'

'Okay,' I said, 'I didn't use the right words, and you – quite rightly – tried to show me up in front of my girlfriend for trying to save your life. Why don't we just eat dinner while you keep a lookout for the Maltese, then the Russians'll come in and kill you and we'll all be happy.'

'Russians,' said Mendoza, shaking his head.

'Yes, fucking Russians,' I said. 'Who else do you think has the kit and the training?'

'You don't need to be Spetsnaz to take on the Cannibals,' said Mendoza.

'The Russians paid us to watch you,' said Helen.

'So?' said Mendoza. 'They must've had thousands of opportunities to kill me.'

'They weren't ready,' I said.

'How the fuck would you know?' asked Mendoza.

'It's obvious. They don't want to take on everyone at once. They had to finish off the bikers before they came for you. As soon as they did: bang bang.' (I felt stupid for having said 'bang bang', but I didn't let it derail my train of thought.)

'Also, they needed time to get to know your organisation, to understand what they were taking over. This is all new to them.'

'You don't know what's new to Russians,' said Mendoza. 'You don't know anything. You're not Russian. You're not even Jewish.'

'It's the way I would've done it,' I said.

'Then certainly the most successful criminal organisation of our time would do things in exactly the same way as you because you, after all, are something of gangster yourself, having been discharged from the military for selling ecstasy.'

'You know what else I'd do?' I asked.

'You would charge at them, hurl your gun in the air, then roll under a car.'

'I'd look for someone in your organisation to turn,' I said.

'That would be you,' said Mendoza.

'That would be someone who spoke Russian,' I said, 'and knew you were going to be at the motel. It would be the person who let Natural Science go to Nouméa, who got a postcard from him and gave him up, and who invented the fucking ludicrous theory that you were being stalked by Malts.'

Mendoza smiled.

'My date should be along at any minute,' he said. 'Ah, here she is.'

The waiter pulled out the empty chair for a woman to sit down. I recognised her perfume before I looked up.

Mendoza introduced her to Helen.

'Delighted to meet you,' said Siobhan.

'Were you fucking her?' asked Helen as we walked home through east Sydney, past men with mohawks and moustaches eating small meals off big plates.

'What did you think of Mendoza?' I asked her.

A beautiful woman in a low-cut dress walked out of a bar and onto the pavement, and I didn't even look at her.

'He's exactly what I thought he'd be,' she said. 'Evil, funny, sexy . . .'

She smiled, as if she was enjoying thinking about him.

'Sexy?' I said.

'Yeah, he's got something, you know.' She ran a finger along her lower lip. 'Some kind of older man charm.'

'You're sick,' I said.

'How many other women have you been with while I was away?'

'Thousands,' I said.

She dropped my hand.

We went back to the unit and made love. I closed my eyes and pretended she was Siobhan. She closed hers and pretended

I was Jed. Or Mendoza. I kissed her all over her face and neck. She drew her fingernails down my shoulders and cut tracks into my back.

'I love you,' I said.

'No, you love *this*,' she said.

'But that's a part of you,' I said.

'Not *that*,' she said. '*This!*'

When it was over, I didn't want to let her out of my arms. She fell asleep cuddling me, her blonde hair flared out over the white pillowcase. I wondered why Mendoza wouldn't believe Dror had given him up. We had to confront the guy, maybe hang him upside down for a bit. He was obviously going to set Mendoza up for another hit once the legionnaires arrived.

Helen moaned in her sleep. I slipped out from under the quilt and sat at the table to smoke a joint, staring out of the window at the Pussycat Bordello. There were people drinking in the street and laughing. I could hear music, shouting and a glass shattering. I felt in the middle of it all and outside it, looking down on Mendoza's kingdom of the night. He'd made this place, with all its terrors and disappointments, all its trash and hope and mechanical sex, and it was about to be taken from him.

I squashed the joint and stumbled back to bed. Helen rolled against my chest, tucking her head beneath my chin. I dreamed of flying over the city, as someone shot out the lights, one by one.

TWENTY-SEVEN

[Seaview House, Greenknowe Avenue, Potts Point. 30-04-02. 2:11 pm.]

I gave my children everything and they blamed me for everything. When Daniel came back from France, he asked me for a fire engine, and I organised the delivery of a decommissioned tanker from the City of Sydney Fire Station. For two years Lazarus used it to drive him to school and, if there was traffic, they had permission from the fire commissioner to turn on the siren. Twice they were flagged down by residents whose homes were in flames but, despite my son's pleas, the vehicle travelled empty. He was a good-hearted lad, who yearned to pump water where his father would have poured petrol – because a half-burned-down building is no fucking use to anyone. You end up with a dog's breakfast like the top floor of the tattooist *alav hashalom*.

Daniel was very much his mother's son and shared both her morbid obsession with my private life and, later, her love for the imbecilic pastime of machine gambling. He had his bar mitzvah at the Great Synagogue, but became a man one year later between the legs of a woman known – for reasons that now escape me – as 'the Performing Seal'.

It was a great relief to me when the Seal reported back that my son had acquitted himself with enthusiasm. After all, he'd repeatedly told me he hoped to become an 'actor', which, as we all know, is a contraction of 'arse-fucker'. Daniel was uncharacteristically cheerful for weeks afterwards and didn't return to his miserable, effeminate self until he found out from McCoy that I had paid the Seal to unburden him of his load. In later years he came to hold this against me, along with a thousand other fucking things you would have thought he would be grateful for.

Daniel became a leading light in the Moriah College dramatic society, and I did my best to help him make his way in his chosen profession. Did I fuck. I told him to get a proper job. He wanted to go to university, but you don't learn anything at university except communism and faggotry, so I made sure he left school at seventeen and started work in the family business. I apprenticed him to McCoy, who was a weak influence on his mind and taught him to fall in love with every big-titted stripper I shoved his way to distract him from his imbecilic ambitions.

If you don't want your son to tread the boards, Anthony, don't give him a job in a fucking nightclub. I think of myself as a clever man, but perhaps I have an exaggerated idea of my own intellect because I surround myself with imbeciles. I never guessed that Daniel would start his career as a warm-up act for the strippers. He got away with it for years, until one night I made an early inspection of Aphrodite's, in time to catch him being booed off stage. He was about as funny as a curtain – as this curtain in this room. And this curtain is not funny at all, unless you are an imbecile. Are you laughing at the curtain, Anthony? Even worse, Daniel was working a double act with Big Stan's imbecile son, who was Daniel's straight man, if that were possible. It was pathetic. When Daniel came off stage, I congratulated him on his performance and invited him up to my office. I think he thought I was going to shoot him. I told him I was sorry I had overlooked his hard work and talent all these years, and I had finally decided to promote him to head of my overseas arm, which I had just fucking invented on the spot.

The next day I gave business-class tickets to Las Vegas to Daniel and his wife.

In Nevada I asked Daniel to investigate various impossible possibilities which, I calculated, would consume his inconsiderable energies for about three months, while I figured out how to stop him sinking the family name in shit. Meanwhile, I suggested, my grandson Martin could stay with Deborah and me, since there was no point in uprooting the poor child for such a short period, and bearing in mind that Daniel had never fucking shut up about being left in France about a hundred years before.

I have another hint for you, Anthony, which might save you from disappointment should you ever find yourself trying to prevent your child from making an imbecile of himself as a stand-up comic: don't deport him to the cabaret capital of the world. I had people watching Daniel, and they soon reported that he was getting gigs in shitty titty clubs as 'the most famous comic in Australia', and nobody in Vegas knew any different. He had worked up a new act, around the persona of a nice Jewish boy who grows up in a Mafia family (when other kids got horses, he got a horse's head et cetera et cetera – no fucking mention of the fire engine). It was obviously too late to save Daniel from himself, so I left him in Vegas to make a deal to ship the Luxor Hotel to Kings Cross.

The only good thing to come out of all this bullshit was that I was able to bring up my grandson in the way I should have raised Daniel, and finally ensure there would be a real man to succeed me as the head of this family.

How did you fall out with Sharon?

What you will learn, Anthony, if you ever have children, is they will always side with their mother. This is because their mother's life often seems less complicated than their father's, and also because their mother has more time and inclination to explain herself to them.

Sharon's mother Ira was the love of my life, but that does not mean she was the only woman in my life. From an early age Sharon was aware that Daddy – as she called me – shared another house with another family. When a child is very young, she accepts that, and believes every daddy serves two mummies. If only grown women were as understanding as little girls, the world would be a happier place, with love spread more evenly around, and more marriages would last as long as mine: forty-nine years to the same woman.

As Sharon grew older, she came to question why I was not around at so-called 'crucial moments' in her life, which invariably occurred on a Tuesday or Friday night. (Strangely, according to my son, all his milestones took place on a Thursday or Saturday.) I tried to compensate for my absences by buying her first a pony and then a Mini Cooper, but my children have no memory for gifts and total recall of slights. Sharon complained that I was not there when the horse fell sick, or the car broke down, or she suffered from some other unavoidable fucking misfortune that an omnipresent father – God, for instance – might somehow have prevented.

Of course, the day came when Sharon became interested in boys. If it were left up to me, she would have stayed clean until she either left home or turned twenty-one, but in response to her mother's pressure I allowed her to go out whoring so long as she was accompanied by a chaperone. The gunnie would drive her to her date and, if the whole thing were visible through a window – if she was going to a cafe for coffee, for example – he would wait outside, then chauffeur her home at an appropriate time. If her liaison took place in a cinema, or the home of a friend, he would join Sharon inside and keep watch on her as unobtrusively as possible, without spoiling her evening. Needless to say, I did this for her own protection and, needless to say, I never got any fucking thanks.

At the age of eighteen Sharon decided she was old enough to go out on her own, but she knew nothing about the real world, or all the terrible things that can happen to a girl if she falls in with the wrong sort of people – ie, men. Reluctantly, I let her have her 'freedom', but I always had somebody following her. At first it was one of my own people, but she knew them all and figured out how to give them the slip, so I hired a firm of private investigators to do the job.

Their reports were disturbing. Although she didn't dare stay away when I was at home on a Saturday, she took to spending Friday nights with a bespectacled, dope-smoking communist. The PIs bugged the bedroom in his mouldy fucking squat, with instructions to break in if things between them went too far. Luckily, Shy Guevara turned out to be a dud, a fizzer, a soft cock who couldn't get it up, so they spent most of their time together listening to records and talking about politics, which neither of them had the first fucking idea about. When it turned out she couldn't cure him of his faggotry, Sharon moved on to the next man. I had mixed feelings about Shy. I was almost grateful to the little scumbag for not moving in on my daughter's cherry, but on the other hand I felt he'd insulted her with his inability to give her what she thought she wanted. Eventually I had him bashed, but not too badly.

Boyfriend number two was another student. He seemed respectful enough at first, but I looked into his background and found that he'd got a girl pregnant the year before, so I had him thrown out of a window. Then, against my express wishes,

Sharon went on holiday with her girlfriends to Fiji. Obviously my worst fear was she would be split open by some huge fucking coconut, but it turned out she lost it to a skinny white backpacker in a hammock between two trees. She came home with a smile like a Lotto winner. I had the boy tracked back to Brisbane, where he fell victim to an unforeseeable road accident caused by his inability to run fast enough to get away from the car.

After that, I more or less gave up. If Sharon, however misguidedly, wanted a sexual relationship, there was nothing I could do about it, but I was determined she wouldn't be exploited or preyed upon by the pond scum that use women and destroy them.

Oh, come on . . .

You think I'm a hypocrite, Anthony, because I would kill any man who tried to treat my daughter the way I have treated women, but you are the only fucking hypocrite in this airless room, because I tell you this: it's every man's responsibility to take charge of his own destiny. If they want to kill me, these raging imbeciles who believe I stripped their daughters of their honour when I stripped them of their clothes and coaxed them onto their knees, they can come after me. I won't call the fucking jacks. I can give it and I can take it, Anthony. That is the true mark of a man.

You think I don't know the difference between right and wrong, but if morality boils down to 'do as you would be done by', how should we deal with Germans? And I'm not even talking about the war: there are some Germans who are happy to be pissed and shat on; and, only recently, one German consented to being eaten by another German. Does that mean we should eat Germans?

So how come Sharon doesn't speak to you now?

She graduated from university with her degree in dustbin diving and got a job with a bottom-feeding, free-sheet of the type that might even have employed you, Anthony, until you turned in your first comically execrable story.

As a junior she was given the lowliest tasks, such as compiling the local-history page. As my daughter, she was determined to do the best job she could, even though nobody gave a shit. The editor told her to concentrate on historical mysteries and I'll give you one fucking guess what topic she picked – not Bogle-Chandler, not the shark-arm murders and not the Murrumbidgee River bunyip. Sharon chose the disappearance of Anita fucking King. For fuck's sake, we've had a fucking *prime minister* disappear in Australia. What is it about Anita King?

Sharon was sharing a house with a bunch of hippie drop-out drugged-up free-loving anarchist atheist scum, but she still came home for dinner with her daddy every Saturday night. Typically, we talked about affairs of the day and whether Sharon's talents might not better be employed in the public-relations industry. On this particular evening she asked me if I had ever met Anita King. I said no, because I hadn't. Then she asked if Uncle Morrie – which was her name for the Little Fish – knew that dead, bed-hopping slapper. I said I believed he may have had some business dealings with her, but nothing important. Then she asked if I knew who had killed Anita King, and I said, 'Is this a dinner-table conversation, Sharon, or are you fucking interviewing me? Because, if you are, you can get out of my house right now, because I don't allow journalists in my home, and you can be a journalist or you can be my daughter, but you can't be both.' Then she asked me if *I* had necked Anita King myself. Can you imagine that, Anthony? She asked her own father if he was a killer.

But you are a killer.

And who are you? Fucking Perry Mason? I'll bet you've knocked more blokes than I have.

So what happened then between you and Sharon?
What didn't happen? I said she was as bad as the jacks. She said most people wouldn't take that as an insult because in ordinary families it was the police who were held up as role models, rather than gangster hoons who ran strip clubs and slept with a loaded gun under their pillow. (She was already prone to journalists' exaggeration. Yes, I had a shooter in the house, but I stored it in the bedside cabinet. If I'd kept it under the pillow, I would have blown my own ear off.) I said, 'How dare you call me a hoon?' She asked me what I would call it. I said I was a protector.

She said she had learned about me in her university lectures, and she felt ashamed to be my daughter, and the only thing she could do about it was try to make up for some of the terrible things I'd done, and she was going to start by putting that poor woman to rest.

For fuck's sake! It wasn't me that had the bitch knocked! Why wasn't she running up to Willie Frankel's place on a Saturday night and disturbing his dinner and asking him who paid to put Anita King under the tarmac?

So she threw her napkin in my face, got into the car that I had bought her and drove to Bellevue Hill. She got herself invited in to Willie's house because she was my daughter, and that still meant something in those days, and she threw her tape recorder on the table and said, 'Uncle Willie, tell me the truth: were you behind the disappearance of Anita King?'

I sent Lazarus to fetch her, and she tried to knee him in the balls, but he managed to bundle her into her own car and drove it back home just like he used to do when she was seventeen years old. She said she hated him, and he was a bastard, and it was probably him who'd knocked Anita, because he had no morals, he only did whatever I told him, and I had no morals, I only did whatever I could get away with, and we were both fascists.

When Lazarus brought her back into the living room, she was so hysterical he had to tie her to a chair. 'What're you going to do now, Daddy?' she screamed. 'Slit my throat and chop me up and feed my body into a garbage-disposal unit?'

Do you know how many times I've heard this shit, Anthony? Can you imagine how boring it is for me?

She calmed down a bit, so Lazarus untied her. Then she said she had been kidnapped – just like Anita (they were on first-name terms now) and probably by the same people – and falsely imprisoned, and she was going to the jacks, and if the jacks wouldn't help her, she would go to the press – which was a joke, because she was the fucking press.

Her mother started howling like a car alarm and begged her to let it drop, and I said I was sorry for what she had made me do to her and asked if there was anything I could buy her to make up for it, but that just set her off again.

'You can't buy me!' she screamed.

I didn't want to fucking buy her. I already owned her. I wanted to buy her a new bag, or something.

She left in tears, saying she never wanted to see me again, but she has been stalking me ever since. If ever there is a pack of journalists outside one of my clubs, I know exactly who will be at the front, waving her microphone like fucking bolas, as if she could throw it and cut me down. Whenever they need a head to talk about things that are best forgotten in the Cross, my own lovely daughter opens her gorgeous mouth – full of pretty white teeth that I bought for her – and spews vomit over the good name of her father, who once loved her with all his soul, and whose heart almost burst with pride on the day she first called him 'Daddy' . . .

Jake, are you all right?

[Ends.]

TWENTY-EIGHT

I refused to sit in on sessions with Mendoza if Dror was guarding the door, so Mendoza sent him off to Granville to find some Mutineers. I sat at home with the old man, both of us tooled up, while he knotted all the loose ends of his life. I was fairly sure he wasn't fucking Siobhan – just because she'd sleep with a fifty year old didn't mean she'd go with an eighty year old – but if he was I couldn't complain: I had my girl back. I missed Siobhan, though. I missed her talk and her smile. And her tits.

Mendoza was stuck on the idea of Victoria Street. If it hadn't been for Anita King deliberately getting herself murdered to stir up publicity for her gutter newspaper, Mendoza's reign might have lasted another ten years.

'And look what happens when I loosen my grip,' he said. 'Chaos, fighting in the streets, heritage buildings wrecked . . . Can anyone truly say the Cross was not a safer place in the days of Jake Mendoza?'

I listened to this kind of thing for hours and didn't even bother to turn on the recorder. I figured he was talking to himself anyway. Then one day, when I said, 'Come on, Jake, you were a gang boss, not a fucking pastor,' he said, 'I was a pastor to my flock, Anthony,' and I suddenly realised he cared about what I thought of him.

'You're the only one who knows the whole story,' he said. 'Do you understand?'

'What's there to understand?' I asked. 'Like you said at the start, it's not rocket science.'

'Not rocket science, no,' said Mendoza, 'but it is progress.'

He thumped down his coffee and stood up. 'We're going to Victoria Street,' he said.

He walked more hesitantly than before, and fewer faces seemed to recognise him on the street. People in the Cross were less willing to meet each other's eyes since the killings. They were in more of hurry to get to where they were going. Only Mendoza lingered and remembered.

We stood outside Victoria Spires, an ordinary apartment block in a street of terraced houses. 'This is it,' said Mendoza. 'This was the dream. In Willie's eyes, it would have been four times this size – forty storeys high – and flanked by a similar building on either side. New York had is twin towers, but Kings Cross would have had three. Do you see, Anthony? Do you see?

'Victoria Spires was the first high-cost housing for decent people on Victoria Street. As it rose, it dragged up the entire area. Thirty years ago this was a slum. Now it's the heart of the new Potts Point. Financial planners live here, Anthony! Estate agents! Bankers! Bond traders! Advertising executives! In 1975 there was Ham and Eggs, squatters, drunkards and Anita fucking King.

'Look at this street! The comfortable homes! The beautiful trees! None of this would've been here without Willie and me.' He paused. 'Actually, the trees possibly grew before Victoria Spires,' he admitted. 'And there might've been more of them.'

He started to shiver, although it wasn't a cold day.

'You can't stand in the way of something like this, Anthony,' he said. 'You can't hold back humanity. But that's what government tries to do. Do you know why squareheads love gangsters? Because we give them what they want. We gave them booze. We gave them sex. Now we give them drugs. And as sure as it's legal today to serve beer after 6 pm, to sell your body to a stranger, or for a man to engage in a vile parody of coitus with another man, you, Anthony, are going to live to see the day when you can buy your cocaine from a pharmacist – just as you could anywhere in Australia before 1925. I'm not saying the country will be a better or a worse place for it, only that it is inevitable.'

He held his fists clenched and quivering at his thighs, determined to make me understand his point.

'History was on my side. I reached out to embrace the future while others clung to the past. Of course, all the fighting and the fires were pointless, but if they hadn't happened, everything good would still be illegal, and Australians would be unable to enjoy many of the freedoms we take for granted today, such as strippers without pasties, and twenty-four-hour drinking.'

'But what's that got to do with Anita King?' I asked.

'Jesus, Anthony,' he sighed. 'Haven't you listened to a single fucking word I've said?'

I phoned Spiegeleier at his office and the girl who had taken my job told me he was in Joe's Cafe. He stood outside, a cigarette stuffed too deeply into his mouth, his feet tapping the pavement while his fingers played on his thighs. I coaxed him back inside, although his feet seemed to be trying to shuffle out again.

I wanted to ask him about Victoria Street.

'Was I there?' asked Spiegeleier. 'I don't know. I was a different person then.'

'What were you like?' I asked.

'I believed my own bullshit,' he said. 'I thought that I was brave, because I'd stand in front of police horses at demonstrations and run towards the fighting. That's not brave. It's knowing you're a journo and nobody wants to bash you. I was brave like cops are brave. A cop in uniform can knock out a man who wouldn't even blink if he was punched by a police officer in civilian clothes. Sometimes your profession gives you the edge.'

He took hold of a spoon and thwacked it against the table.

'When they came for Anita King, it showed that even journos weren't safe,' he said. 'Even heiresses weren't safe. They were going to do whatever they wanted, to wreck the city and murder the residents, and nobody could stop them because they had paid everybody off. It's funny, the squatters called themselves anarchists but the developers were the real anarchists. They didn't believe in rules. They made their own laws. And they were going to get away with it.'

He slit a packet of sugar and poured the powder into an empty coffee cup.

'But I didn't understand that at first,' he said. 'I thought, *Those bastards have crossed the line. They killed a journo. Now the rest of us'll make them pay*. I got all the usual phone calls in the middle of night, from men who'd hang up or say one word, like 'dog' or 'dead', but I'd been taking those calls for five years and if they could scare me like that I would've just left the phone off the hook.

'I snooped around the Cross, but I did it in plain sight, walking the strip with my notebook, interviewing anyone who would talk. I didn't find much out, but the fact I was still asking questions disturbed the people who wanted to pretend there was no story because there was no body.'

He took off his spectacles and looked through the lenses backwards.

'I got called in to see Mendoza,' he said, 'sitting on his throne in his office. He was an impressive-looking man in those days. He was never big, but somehow he stood taller than everyone around him. He said, "I'm sorry to hear you journalists believe you've had a death in the family. I'd like to make a donation to the memorial fund." And he offered me five hundred dollars to fuck off back to London.

'I said I was staying until I found out who had killed Anita King. He told me ninety per cent of murders were domestic, and if she was dead – which he didn't believe she was – she had probably been knocked by the leader of the crane-drivers union or the BLF official she had been fucking while he was out stopping his members from driving cranes.'

He bit his own shirt collar.

'Mendoza sent for me again. He said he wanted to do an interview, but it would be off the record. I came in with a set of questions, but it turned out he was going to interview me. He asked, "Why are you doing this to Willie Frankel? You're both Jewish." That surprised me, because I didn't think of myself as Jewish in those days, I thought I was a socialist. Judaism was just an accident of birth. Socialism was what I'd chosen for myself, just as Frankel had chosen capitalism and murder.

'Mendoza asked me what I thought the goyim would think of the Jewish people if I kept on printing gossip and speculation about Willie, who, like my own father, was a refugee from Nazi persecution, and had come to Australia only to be persecuted again by the press.'

Spiegeleier spat out his shirt collar but started to undo the buttons around his belly.

'Mendoza told me that some questions don't have answers, such as what became of the dinosaurs and why are they not mentioned in the Bible. He told me journalists shouldn't try to play God and insert a brontosaurus into the Garden of Eden, because even if that were more historically accurate, it would bring us no closer to understanding the miracle of creation. He said he respected my perseverance and offered me a job as the chief publicist of his music business, with special responsibility for an act he called the "Eastern Suburbs Frank Sinatra". I said I'd think about it, but I couldn't see there was much room to improve on the New Jersey Frank Sinatra. He said, "Imagine if Frank were Jewish."

'When I finally got out of his office, a man in the street punched me three times in the face, breaking first my glasses, then my nose. I lined up at the emergency ward at St Vinnie's, thinking, *I've got the bastards*. Do you see? I still wasn't scared.'

Alarmingly Spiegeleier took off one shoe.

'I worked with a photographer, Jack, who was as brave as a lion, or at least that's what we told each other. He thought ex-cops were behind Anita's disappearance, whereas I believed it was the psychotic Scotsman who – for whatever fucked-up reasons of his own – Mendoza has recently started referring to as "the Little Fish". But in the end it didn't really matter whose hand had held the pickaxe handle: it was the climate of corruption that Mendoza had created that made her murder possible. Willie Frankel was just a weak and stupid opportunist who took advantage of that.

'So there I am walking down the strip with Jack, with a big white bandage across my nose just to ensure anyone could recognise me, and we're suspecting everyone and everything, and linking the cops to the crims and pollies to the pros, and we're thinking the worst thing the thugs are prepared to do is to hit us in the schnozzle, and that's just an occupational hazard for hardened street fighters like us, when suddenly everything goes black and I'm choking and I'm falling, and I can hear Jack's muffled shouting as we're lifted off the pavement and thrown into the back of a car. There's a bag over my head and they smash our skulls together, for a joke, and rebreak my nose. Then they tie my hands behind my back and the joke is one of them hits me in one place – like, say, my chin – while the other kicks me somewhere else – for example, my shin – so I never know how or where they're going to hurt me next. It was terrifying. I was helpless, with a mouth full of blood, and I didn't know who they were or where they were taking us or if anybody had told them when to stop. The only good thing I could think of was if they were going to kill us we'd be dead by now, but I knew even that wasn't true because sometimes it takes a long time to kill somebody, especially if you haven't got guns, and sometimes they want to do it slowly to make an example of you, and sometimes you just die because a beating gets out of hand, and Anita might have been killed while she struggled against being kidnapped, so what the fuck did I know about whether we'd be dead by now? If anything, they probably weren't going to kill us in a car – they were going to take us somewhere and do it there. They pummelled my groin and I pissed myself, and I heard them laugh because Jack had done the same thing.

'They drove us around in circles for a while, and I thought that was a good sign, because they didn't want us to know where they were taking us, which meant they were going to let us go. The driver braked hard, so my face slammed into the seat in front, and they dragged us out of the car, pushed us through a door and threw us down some steps. While I was on the ground, they kicked me in the stomach and the face and I felt the life start to seep out of me, in the blood and the piss and the tears. I remember thinking, *I wish I'd've had more women. Preferably at the same time.* I made a joke to myself while I was dying, and for years I tried to take comfort from that, to convince myself that they hadn't broken my spirit, but they had.

'I said, "Please, please don't. Please let me go." Not even us, mate. Just "me". And a voice said. "You wanted to know what happened to Anita King. How much more do you want to know?" And I said, "Nothing." They said, "There'll be no more fucking questions, then, cuntly?" And I said, "No. It's over."

'After that, they beat us up a bit more, just for the fun of it. Their last kick burst my eardrum, and I haven't been able to hear properly since. Then they pulled us up the stairs and untied our hands. They marched us out of the building and shoved our faces against a brick wall while they took the hoods off our heads. I heard a pistol click, and they told us to look straight ahead for five minutes, and if we turned away from the wall, we were dead.

'Jack collapsed, but I counted to five hundred before I bent down to help him. I didn't have far to carry him to the hospital. They'd left us outside the back door of Kings Cross police station, and I could see my blood smeared on the door handle.'

He took a sip of his coffee and dribbled it down his open shirt onto his chest.

'I resigned my job that day,' he said. 'I didn't have the stomach to be a journo, if that was what it involved. I went drinking for five years. I was in the Matthew Talbot, sitting in my own soiled pants, when a volunteer found out I was Jewish and sent around someone from a Jewish care organisation to pick me up. They dried me out and put me back together but, even when I was whole again, I had all these tics, like I can't stop raising my glasses or pulling on my nose or stroking my head or pursing my lips, and I'm still not continent, Tony. I have to wear a nappy.'

'My name's Nick,' I said.

'Yeah, so I heard,' said Spiegeleier. 'My name's Daniel Eggs.'

He said he had been born Spiegeleier but had anglicised his name – which means 'fried eggs' in German – when he turned eighteen. He wanted to distance himself from his Jewishness, and he thought eggs would make a better by-line. When he recovered from his sickness, he reclaimed his name and briefly joined the Hasidim, waddling up and down Bondi Road in a loose black suit and a Borsellino hat. It wasn't until the nineties that he felt strong enough to go back to journalism. He started on the *Jewish Times* as a junior reporter, at forty-five years old, but quickly became the editor. It was a political position, he said. It was about pleasing all of the community all of the time. But the stories were simple and colourful and sometimes life-affirming, and the phone never rang in the middle of the night, and nobody had ever tried to warn him off a story until I stepped into his office and brought all the helplessness and terror back into his life.

'You want to know the truth?' he asked. 'There was no phone call from my publisher. Mendoza has no influence left in the business world. *I* fired you, Nick, because I knew you were trouble. I'm sorry.'

TWENTY-NINE

[Seaview House, Greenknowe Avenue, Potts Point. 01-05-02. 2:34 pm.]

They had needed the Little Fish to bring me down, but they'd no-billed a shitload of drug dealing and at least one murder blue, just to ruin an elderly returned serviceman. Everyone reckoned he was being groomed to fit up another poor mongrel on the National Canine Authority's shitlist.

Rumours spread like canine transmissible venereal tumour that the next target of the Little Fish's denunciations would be a cop. The most likely candidate was Fred Carol because (a) he was the most evil cunt of them all; and (b) he was the only one left who could take a fall for all the dead blokes who couldn't tell tales, like the premier and the police commissioner.

Fred Carol heard – because he had told it to himself – a rumour that the Little Fish was abusing prescription drugs and contemplating suicide. He tried to get permission from his handlers to visit his old mate at the dog pound and cheer him up with reminiscences of happier times when they both ran through the Cross, bashing and knocking blokes whenever they pleased.

The Little Fish was not keen to see Carol but, in his isolation in the isle of dogs, he found himself missing the sweet smell of she-male arsehole, so he sent word that he would like a visit from Savannah Plains.

Bear this fact in mind, Anthony, should you ever be tempted to post your desperate cock into the nameless slot of a transgender abomination: a man with a trannie does not have a girlfriend, he has a lieutenant he can fuck. And a lieutenant can be turned like the pages of a book.

When Fred Carol heard through bent cops in the NCA that Savannah Plains had been to see the Little Fish, he went to find he/she/it in the Bottoms Up Bar of the Rex Hotel. In the old days he only used to go there when he fancied handing out a bashing, but he'd mellowed with age and, I believe, sometimes took it up the Patton himself. He bought Savannah Plains a Pimm's and lemonade and said he personally had organised a whip-round among various identities in the Cross, and we had come up with the money to pay for his/her/its operation, so it could become whichever thing it was that it wasn't to begin with.

In exchange, we just needed the Little Fish's address. Savannah Plains had already moved on from the Little Fish to Johnny Johnny, a plastic gangster who was unhappy that Savannah had favoured the Little Fish with a conjugal visit. He persuaded Savannah that our deal was a good one, and once he-she-it had her cock put on or cut off, and her tits strapped down or pumped up, the two of them would live together as man and man, or wife and wife, or whatfuckingever.

That was good enough for Savannah Plains, who told Carol that the dog show was held at a kennel club in Victoria, in a motel on the highway between Warrnambool and Geelong. Fred Carol filled a bag with the prescription drugs he'd heard the Little Fish was abusing, picked up two of my boys and a bag of my money, and set off on a road trip that eventually led to the Little Fish's well-documented suicide.

That was the last of the funerals until McCoy. I buried everyone in the 1980s, even my dear fucking father, who lived to the vile old age of ninety-four, just to piss everyone off.

Abie the fighter, the one who should have been the gangster, became a hotelier, but retired early and spent the last twenty years of his life looking after *tate*. The old man wouldn't speak to me after the first royal commission, and he never reconciled with Saul after he married the *shiksa*. Saul died in an accident – an accidental one, not the other kind – without ever seeing him again. My mother passed away one winter when I was in the Philippines, so there was only Abie left for him.

One morning Abie called and said he thought *tate* was about to shuffle off, and if I had anything to say I should come and say it, because *tate* didn't have the strength to push me away. Also, he thought that *tate* had something he wanted to let me know, but he was too proud to send for me after all these years.

Fuck him, I thought. Let him die with his pride. I didn't need his apology. It was too late.

But then I thought, maybe there was a reason for what he did to me. If I knew, perhaps I would come to understand myself. So I went to visit him, in a Catholic hospice where he lay in bed surrounded by Poles. He looked like a shrunken angel, shrouded in a cancerous glow. When he saw me, he smiled, and some of the pain fell from his face.

'*Mayn zun*,' he said, 'you came at last. I'm so sorry, *mayn zun*.' Fat tears swelled in his *malekh* eyes. 'I have always loved you,' he said. 'Come closer to me, Saul.'

'It's not Saul,' I told him gently, 'it's Jacob.'

'What the fuck are you doing here?' he asked. 'Why aren't you in jail?'

I sat by his bedside and tried to take his hand, but he pulled it away.

'Tell me, *tate*,' I said, 'why do you hate me?'

'Don't call me *tate*,' he said.

Then my father told me a story. It was the only story he ever told me. It should have been something special.

'We come from Tetiev,' he said, 'a *shtetl* that is now a part of the Ukraine, a country bathed in Jewish blood. In Tetiev there were many pogroms in which the peasants rose up against the Jews. Before the revolution they called us capitalists; after the revolution they called us communists. At the bottom of it all they wanted to be left alone to live like pigs, but they could sense the world was changing – like rabbits, they felt it in the ground – and they blamed the Jews.

'They came for us sometimes in small gangs, often in big mobs. They came with torches and pitchforks, the weapons of peasants. They came with scimitars and guns. It was like a party for them. They sang and they danced and they drank, like your goyim in Kings Cross, and they burned the synagogue with the Jews trapped inside, and they burned our homes with our children in their beds.

'For some of them, there was no hatred. They simply saw the chance to steal from the Jews and rape our women. The peasants loved to rape. It was their holiday treat: a clean woman, without rabbit diseases; a woman who wore underwear.

'I was a famous wrestler, a leader of our community. I organised a self-defence group, and we armed against the peasants. They said we were in league with the Bolsheviks. I didn't know the Bolsheviks, but I prayed they would come. With each pogrom, our numbers grew smaller. I chose as my lieutenant a war veteran named Bickoff, who had lost everything, and we organised the others like soldiers, although in truth they were pedlars and bakers, butchers and woodsmen, tinkers and fools.

'When the White Army and the renegade militia swept through Tetiev, there was fighting through the night. Some died, some survived. In the end, it made little difference. The things we had seen had killed us all. We lived on only for our children. I hid your brothers in a hole beneath the kitchen floor.

'Word came that the Red Army was close by. I sent my lieutenant to meet their commander. He said the Bolsheviks would save us, but only if we first laid down our weapons. Theirs were to be the only guns in Tetiev. I sent our weapons out with Bickoff in a cart. I never saw him again. He sold them, he sold us.

'The peasants came for us that evening and they attacked my home first. I fought them for hours, but they dragged me out into the street, tied me to a pole, stripped your mother and forced me to watch them violate her, time and again. They made her eat pork while they destroyed her. They made her drink vodka and swear in their language. They made her plead for them to continue. They forced my brother to violate her, then they took an axe to his head.

'While they tortured us, other Jews rode to the forests where the Red Army was camped. You see, the peasants only wanted the leaders like me, the families who had stood up to them. If you slinked and hid, if you cowered and begged, they let you live, as an example of what the Jews were. If I were a smaller man, or a meeker man, my brother would have survived to see Australia with me, and my wife would have been able to smile and make light of life.

'Our neighbours begged them to come into Tetiev and save us, but the Bolsheviks weren't interested in dying for the Jews. It was only when they pledged the commander a ransom, money to buy the Reds guns and vodka, that they set off slowly for the *shtetl.* The peasants fled when the Red Army arrived. The Russians restored order but said there were to be no retaliations.

'Some time later the Jews were freed to go. We put all we

had left in the back of a cart and walked west to Poland, then on – we thought – to America. The peasants came out into the streets to watch us leave. As your mother passed them, they chanted the number of men who had violated her. They threw stones and their children ran beside me, kicked me and stole my cap.

'Nine months after the pogrom, you were born, Jacob. Your mother wanted to spear you in the womb, but I couldn't allow that. You might be the son of Ukrainian pigs, but you might also be my brother's son, my nephew. As you grew up, and you drank and stole and fought like the goyim, it became clear you were the child of savages. Each time I saw you I remembered Tetiev, and I felt such terrible pain in my heart, such violent anger in my breast, such hatred for you, and I know your mother felt the same. When we wrestled I hoped to strangle you, or break your neck, but you grew up strong, Jacob. You are a tough man, like a peasant and, like a peasant, you chose to live with pigs.

'Leave me now,' said my father. 'If I have wronged you, I ask you to forgive me. If you are my brother's son, I ask you to understand me.'

I took the arm of a nun and I left him in his bed embalmed in self-pity. There was a hotel close to the hospice and I stopped by for a drink. I ordered a vodka – I never drink vodka – and I tried to put words to how I was feeling. Nothing. I felt nothing. When I'd had time to consider all that my father had said, I realised he had set me free. I'm the son of my mother's rapist and my uncle's murderer. How could I expect to be any better than I am?

And that was the year you were put away?

Yeah, that's right: the year of shit.

In the end, despite all the smears and insinnuendo, the only thing they could get me for was tax evasion. 'Tax evasion': what a fucking joke. I'd been paying taxes to the jacks all my working life.

You look around Kings Cross, Anthony, and you tell me where my taxes go. You show me what the government is doing for the heroin addicts, the homeless, the street kids or the boongs? Where is the affordable housing? Where are the social services? All I see is misery and pain. I was charged with tax evasion, but I was tried for all the suffering on the strip: the drug dealing, the suicides, the runaway children and all the bodies in every gang war. After six weeks I was found guilty of being Jake Mendoza, the King of the Cross.

I did seventeen months inside – nearly a year and half in a green fucking T-shirt – and every moment was wasted. The Bay was run by the usual alliance of bent screws and imbeciles, and for about five minutes they shit themselves that I might try to take over their weak fucking rackets. They thought that Jake Mendoza – a millionaire fifty times over, the man who brought Frank Sinatra to Sydney and invented striptease – might try to muscle in on their homebrewing scam, or have my lover smuggle drugs into prison in her *tokhes*.

I told them they could do whatever they wanted. I couldn't give a fuck who was the hardest man in A Wing, or whatever fucking wing it was. I had bodyguards to make sure no one ever gave me any trouble but, truth be told, most of the crims in the Bay didn't care about an old man either. It was in prison, Anthony, that I realised my time had passed.

Many people came to visit me, including a rabbi. He was the *rov* charged with visiting all the Jewish prisoners in Sydney, and since I was all the Jewish prisoners in Sydney, we spent a lot of time together, developing his understanding of certain card games. The rabbi sent Henry Aaron, the treasurer of the Great Synagogue, to see me and we became firm friends, based on a mutual interest in my money. It was Aaron who eventually talked me out of five million dollars for his fucking steeples, although I made him wait thirteen years for it.

Deborah and Martin visited me every week, as did Ira, although on different days. Daniel bumbled in from Vegas and bored me with his egotistical babble. Sharon came only once, and my heart sang when I saw her beautiful brown hair and her black, shining eyes. She sat across a table from me and opened up a notebook. There had been a new development in the Anita King case. After a decade and a half of amnesia, Savannah Plains had remembered that the Little Fish had knocked the bitch after all. My daughter wanted to know if I had any comment to make.

That night I took down her photo from the wall of my cell.

I did what I could to help the time pass. At Christmas, I organised a special show featuring Angelica Angel and the classic cast of 'Girls Girls Girls'. On my birthday I ordered a Chinese meal for everyone in the wing. The radio announcers raged against me. How dare prisoners look at men wearing dresses, or eat egg-fried rice, when it had been proven in court that they had dodged their obligations to the ATO?

I had an almost spiritual experience in the Bay, Anthony. I realised that, while the body can be confined within four walls, so can the soul. A man cannot soar free of his surroundings. He is the physical embodiment of his ideas, nothing more or less. When you are in prison, you are in prison totally, and anyone who says different is a fucking imbecile. Without the company of women, you might as well be dead.

So many people died while I was inside, including Willie Frankel and both Abie and my sister Dora. I was given leave to attend their funerals, and it was almost more than my heart could stand. I had buried my enemies, my friends and now my family. It seemed as though there would never be an end to my loss. When I got out, ready to begin my life again, I buried my fucking wife. We were going to cruise around the world, Anthony. I was going to make everything up to her. She could sit on the *QEII* playing poker machines all day, and in the evenings we would dance to the piano man in the Chart Room. We would be together every night of the week, even Thursday and Saturday. But she died, Anthony. She went to join the others, and left me alone with my grandson and the ghosts.

The premier's wife died, too, and she willed all the money I had collected for him to the RSfuckingPCA. The funny thing was, Gozo Joe did the same thing. You explain to me what that means, Anthony. You tell me what it says about people.

It's all over now, Jake. You don't have to think about it any more.

I see the dead every day in Kings Cross, Anthony, at the places they used to eat and drink and dance and fuck. I pass Big Stan in the mornings as he hoses down the pavement in front of the Pussycat. I tap my hat, but he looks through me, as if *I* were the phantom. I shout to McCoy as he scampers like a puppy dog after a hard-faced Asian whore, but he never turns around. Gozo Joe Stone stands on one leg outside the cafe that used to be Sweethearts, drinking Turkish coffee and smoking Sobranie Cocktails. The Little Fish calls me into Aphrodite's, but when I go to follow him he disappears. Willie Frankel, standing in the shade of a gum tree on Victoria Street, beckons me to look once again at his wonderful plans. At home Deborah haunts every room, and Abie sits by my side at the dinner table on a Friday night. I cut him a slice of challah. He says the blessing as she lights the candles.

But do you know what is the worst? The most terrible thing in my whole fucking life? Sometimes I walk past a builders' skip and I see a piece of wood or metal, and from the corner of my eye it looks like a leg or an arm. I hear a cat mewing, or a baby crying, and I think there is something small and helpless trapped in there, so I run to rescue it, but when I peer over the lip of the skip, there is nothing there. Sometimes, if I'm careless, I walk over newly laid bitumen, and as the ground softens under my shoes I think I feel fists pounding under the pavement and, buried deep underground, I make out the muffled voice of Anita King, pleading for her life.

Of course I killed her, Anthony. We all did.

THIRTY

We invited Jed around to dinner, but at first he didn't call us back. I thought he must be sulking and not want to see us together, but he turned out to be in hiding. When he finally turned up at the unit, he was carrying a kitbag stuffed with clothes.

Helen cooked him steak and chips. It irritated me that she knew he liked it medium rare. As we started on the beers, Jed said, 'I've been talking to the Russians. They want everything. All the drugs, all the clubs, all the whores, everything. They came here looking for a partner. They watched everyone. They had people following the Lebs and the Cannibals, just like they had us shadowing Mendoza. They chose Mendoza because they thought he was the most reliable operator, but he told Natural Science to bite off their bloke's nose. Now they've got the bikers out of the way and done a deal with the Lebs, they'll be coming for Mendoza again.

'They offered me a job,' said Jed, 'but I'm leaving. I've had enough of this fucking country. I want to get out of here before the legionnaires turn up.'

'Yeah,' said Helen, 'let's all go home.'

We each opened a fresh beer.

'How are you two getting on anyway?' he asked.

'Good, yeah,' I said. 'Everything's fine.'

'I suppose you'll get married now,' he said. 'It usually takes something like this.'

Jed looked glum.

'Are we still best mates, Slick?' he asked. 'I didn't want to do it, honestly. She threw herself at me.'

'Fuck off,' said Helen.

'Yeah,' I said, grabbing his hand. 'Still best mates.'

'How about a threesome then?' asked Jed.

The handshake became an arm wrestle, then slap-boxing, then a hug.

We played music – since Helen had brought back the CD player – and smoked a bit of dope. Jed had a flight out the next day and asked to stay in the unit for the night. I told him he was sleeping on the couch, but we stayed up all night talking. He said Australia was the same as England. Helen said that was because we had made it that way. Anywhere was going to be the same if we just did the same things with the same people. We should have bought a Kombi van, she said, and crossed the Nullarbor.

'Bollocks,' said Jed. 'It's too hot here, and I miss Aldershot.'

Helen said she missed Aldershot too. She wanted to talk to her friends, and cuddle her mum. I didn't say anything because I didn't miss anything. England was okay, but Australia was where I was going to be a writer.

'What will you do back home?' I asked Jed.

'I thought I might become a great painter,' he said.

'Fuck you,' I said.

'No,' he said, 'I think I'll go back to selling drugs. It's what I'm good at.'

'You weren't that good at it,' I said. 'You got us both caught.'

We had been through a lot together since the *Aldershot News*, Jed and me. We talked about when we were couriers, and how everyone used to hate us, but we were fitter than when we were in the army. They were shit days, but we remembered them as if they were fun. We worked with some good people – Homeless Paul, House Paul and Two-Tone Richard – and loads of idiots. Friday afternoon drinks were okay, but I never thought I would be talking about them twelve years later. Three of the kids we used to ride with died delivering documents. We only lost two men in Northern Ireland. It was more dangerous to be a cycle courier than a soldier.

Northern Ireland: that was another big time. We shouldn't have been there, ever. If I'd been born Irish I would have joined the IRA. Sometimes I think that is what growing up is: doing the wrong thing, then coming to terms with it.

Helen started to cry, but we said it was okay. We were all right with everything. When we had signed up to be soldiers, we were old enough to know we might have to fight.

'We've done some things, eh, Slick?' said Jed, with a grin.

Oh, fuck me, we had done some things. Twice, I had thought Jed was dead. Once he got stabbed in a bar fight and there was so much blood on the floor I couldn't believe there was any left in his body. That's when I got my forearm slit open, holding it between Jed's face and the nutter with the dagger. Another time, he took so many drugs that he went into a coma, and I had to take him to hospital and sit with him for two days until he opened his eyes.

'Yeah,' he said, 'and you fucked the nurse, too.'

I didn't, I just told him I did.

'I didn't want you to feel bad for ruining my weekend,' I said.

Helen said we were lucky to have each other, and she felt

sorry that she had come between us. She kissed me on the lips, then Jed on the cheek. She put her arms around both of us, and I knew what was going on in his head and I said, 'Try it and I'll fucking kill you.'

We played some old-school hip-hop and Jed did a kind of dance.

'You are the worst dancer in the whole fucking world,' I told him.

'I can't believe you hung me upside down,' he said. 'I thought you were gonna bugger me.'

'In your dreams, mate.'

'We're like brothers,' said Jed. 'There's nothing in the world we haven't done.'

'Except that,' I said.

Jed rolled a joint and Helen rolled a joint and I rolled a joint all at the same time, so we ended smoking one joint each.

I woke up to the intercom buzzing over and over again. I was in bed with Jed and, disgustingly, he had a hard-on. Helen was asleep on the couch. I stepped over bottles and cans and plates full of cigarette butts and roaches, while the two of them tried to bury their heads in their pillows.

Dror was at the door, with the kid who had been trying to shoot me. Shit. I had forgotten I had arranged that.

'Meet us at La Fontaine in half an hour,' said Dror.

I was still drunk and stoned. We couldn't have been asleep for more than a couple of hours. I emptied Jed's pockets until I found his stash, and racked up three lines of coke on Helen's compact.

'You've got to get up,' I said to Jed. 'You've got a plane to catch.'

I snorted my line and brought Jed's over to him in bed.

'Breakfast,' I said.

Helen, her eyes still closed, stumbled to the shower. Jed tried to follow her.

'No,' I said.

I snorted Helen's line too.

'What the fuck are you doing meeting Dror?' said Jed. 'He's the dog, mate. Mendoza should've killed him.'

'I've just got to sort this thing out,' I said. 'Then I'm gonna sort him out.'

Helen stayed in the unit while Jed and I went to La Fontaine. Jed was hungry, and had another two hours before he had to set off for the airport. We staggered outside, unshaven, and were ambushed by the sun.

Dror was waiting for us with Jordan, the boy from the rugby team, the one I had beaten up in the toilets at the Hamilton.

'Look,' I said, 'I'm sorry for what I did to you, Jordan, but you've got to stop trying to kill me.'

'Fuck you,' he said.

'No, not fuck me,' I said. 'Listen to me.'

'He wants money for his teeth,' said Dror. 'He says you knocked out three of his teeth.'

'How much are teeth?' I asked.

The kid wanted four thousand dollars. I had about fifty bucks.

'Jake has agreed to advance you the money on top of your regular fee,' said Dror, 'but you've got to show him some of your new pages: the ones you think are "better".'

He said it exactly as Mendoza would have said it.

'Fine,' I said. 'Is that it?'

'He wants you to apologise . . .' said Dror.

'I'm really sorry, Jordan,' I said.

'. . . and for you to explain, why him?'

'Because he grabbed the barmaid's tits,' I said.

'You're fucking kidding me!' cried the kid. 'She dared me to do it!'

'Okay, Jordan,' I said, 'now I'm really, really sorry.' I looked at Dror. 'I liked the girl, I thought he was taking liberties with her. I'll buy him his teeth. Is there anything else?'

'Yeah, he says he's sorry for stealing your scooter but you deserved it, and he wants you to take him on in a fair fight,' said Dror. 'No king hits and no guns.'

'Look, this is stupid,' I said. 'He's miles out of his depth.'

'He doesn't think so,' said Dror.

The kid lunged across the table and tried to hit me. I slipped the punch but I moved too far and fell off my chair. The kid jumped on me.

Somebody yelled, 'Hey you!'

I looked up as I pushed the kid off and saw a passenger on a Harley pointing a pistol at Dror. Just before the gun fired, Dror threw himself on the pavement. The bullets hit Jed, in the neck and the chest and the mouth.

I thought I heard the rider or the gunman shout 'Jed!', but his accent was thick and his engine was loud and I was shouting 'Jed!' myself, over and over again.

THIRTY-ONE

Dror was rolling away, struggling to pull out his pistol as he tumbled towards the cafe. I picked up the table and charged at the shooter, trying to knock him off his bike. I heard a scream. I thought it was Jed, which would mean he was still alive, but it was me. The motorcyclist pulled away, and I landed on my face on the table in the road. Jordan ran after him, pelting him with ashtrays and cups.

I thought the police would come racing out of the station behind us, but they arrived in cars from the top end of Darlinghurst Road. Dror and Jordan disappeared into doors opened by unseen hands. A security guard tried to drag me after them, but I had covered Jed's body with my own, as if I could shield him from what had already happened.

I let the cops take me to the station. By the time Mendoza's lawyer turned up, I had already made a statement. I had no idea why we were targeted. It must have been a case of mistaken identity. The sergeant wondered why I should be shot at twice in two months. I said he should find the blokes who were doing the shooting and ask them. They wanted to hold me, but it isn't illegal to witness your best mate's murder, so they had to let me go.

Back at the unit, I cried with Helen. As we cried we cleaned up the unit, except for Jed's things, which Helen left where they were, on the floor, on the table and on the bed. I cried with my head in my hands and my head out of the window and my head tucked into my knees. Helen stroked my hair and waited her turn, then she cried in the bathroom while I hugged her from behind.

I rang Jed's mum. She said, 'Nick! It's lovely to hear from you!'

I couldn't even tell her, couldn't speak. I had to put Helen on the phone.

When Helen had given her the news, Jed's mum asked to speak to me. I held the phone away from my face but I heard her ask, 'Are you all right, Slick?'

'My boy,' I said. 'My boy. My brother. My boy.'

Helen arranged the flights. We flew home together, with Jed's coffin in the hold. I was glad that Helen had slept with him, because it meant he'd been sleeping with a good person and she could understand something about the way I was feeling. When we were soldiers, we had talked a lot about how we would like our funerals. Jed wanted 'Dead Homiez' by Ice Cube at the service, and for everyone to hold up a can of beer to him in the chapel. He wanted me to speak and to name all the people he'd loved. He'd made the list in Belfast and I had carried it around in my wallet ever since, just as he'd carried mine.

The boys from the regiment were all back from Kosovo. Rocky and Gooner were waiting for us at Heathrow. Helen and I were both so drunk we could hardly stand. Gooner found a luggage trolley and wheeled Helen to his car. I walked with my arm around Rocky's shoulder, bawling 'Agadoo' in his ear, because that was the last song I had heard Jed singing.

'We ain't gonna forget this,' said Rocky. 'We won't fucking let this one go.'

We arrived early in the morning, so the traffic was clear on the road to Aldershot. We passed council estates and green fields, allotments and pubs, and I knew I was home. My mum was waiting on the doorstep of our house. She hugged me and my dad shook my hand. I carried Helen to bed and got stuck into the whisky with Dad. He said he had seen too many friends die, but the only thing you could do was move on. Wars end, he said, and, whatever this one had been about, I had to realise it was over.

We were both too drunk to drive, so we sent a taxi to pick up Jed's mum, who was wearing a flowery dress like my mum. When they stood together, they looked like a pair of curtains. She wanted to know everything about Jed's life in Australia, and nothing about his death. I told her he'd had a great time and lived in a part of the world he thought he'd only ever see on TV.

The women drank tea while the men gulped Scotch, and I got teary again while I described a life for Jed that I had pulled out of the air. He was young and fit and excited and in love. Every day was full of wonder. He never got used to the sight of kangaroos and koalas, and he never regretted his decision to go.

His mum wanted the funeral arranged quickly. At the chapel in the crematorium, on a storm-black afternoon, his father sat apart from the family and listened to the words that would have to keep him for the rest of his life.

Jed had asked that nobody turn up in uniform – when he got kicked out of the army he finished with that shit – but all the pallbearers were from the regiment, including Rocky and Gooner, who had helped carry Bob Edmonds to his grave. They laid his coffin by the pulpit – my friend was in there, my fucking best mate was locked in that box – while the vicar talked about the God who was a comfort to Jed's mum.

I spoke after the minister. I described the way Jed had died as an accident, and told other kind lies. His brother projected pictures of Jed onto a screen behind me: riding a tricycle then a bicycle then a motorbike. There were loads of photographs he had sent home from the army, of the two of us posing with mortars and rifles, climbing tanks and bunkers, drinking in the NAAFI and swimming in the sea. There were so many pictures of me that it felt like I had died too. Jed was smiling, always smiling, as if everything was one big fucking joke – which was more or less the way he felt about it – or he was stoned all the time – which he more or less was.

I remembered what was written on the Jewish War Memorial – *Your youngest and strongest shall die by the sword* – and I couldn't get it out of my mind: those words, and Aga-fucking-doo.

I told the funny stories that Jed and I had rehearsed on his last night in Australia, about Homeless Paul and House Paul, and brakes that failed and drivers who swerved to try to knock us off our bikes. I didn't say much about Belfast, but we had some great times, even over there.

While I was speaking, I realised what it must be like for Mendoza. These stories used to belong to me and Jed. Now that they were only mine, it felt like they might never have happened.

Jed's mum held the wake at her house. Helen helped with the catering. Army boys stood at one side of the room, family and school friends at the other. His father smoked alone in the garden. Three of Jed's ex-girlfriends turned up, including the woman he should have married. She hugged me long and hard, as if she were trying to feel him on me.

'He carried you with him,' I told her, although I knew he didn't. Jed never looked back, not even to see if there were people coming after him.

The boys from the regiment went out together afterwards. We hit a few of the pubs in Aldershot and started a fight in the

South Western in his memory. We finished up in a terrible club and somebody asked the DJ to play 'I'll Be Missing You', the song for Biggie Smalls. We chanted the chorus like a football crowd. I cried again, and nearly picked up a girl. When we left, the DJ thanked us for not smashing the place up.

The next morning Helen helped Jed's mum clean the house. They had already started when I got in. I slept all day and woke when Helen crawled into bed beside me. I got up and walked the streets, lingering around the pubs at closing time, looking for a fight.

Helen cooked bacon and eggs, which is what Jed had been waiting for when he was shot outside the cafe. She said she was glad to be home. Australia was all right, but this was where we belonged. I agreed.

'When I get back,' I said, 'we'll buy a house here.'

'Babe,' said Helen, 'we're already back.'

Rocky and Gooner turned up to drive me back to Heathrow.

'What are you *doing*?' screamed Helen.

She wouldn't kiss me, wouldn't even speak to me.

On the short drive west, raindrops cracked like bullets on the windscreen, and we sang Irish rebel songs – 'The Croppy Boy' and 'The Minstrel Boy' – for a laugh.

I drank for the entire twenty-three hour flight.

Mendoza met me at Sydney Airport. He shook my hand and said, 'I wish you long life.'

THIRTY-TWO

The man who answered the phone gave the name of a panel-beating shop. He seemed angry that I had called. He roared down the phone, as if his problems were my fault.

'Look, mate –' I said.

'Don't fucking call me "mate", scumbag,' he shouted. 'I'm not your fucking mate.'

But he agreed to take me to Suicide.

I still had the purple scooter under tarpaulin in the street. In fact, since Jordan had returned the one he'd stolen, I had two of them. I could've started my own home-delivery service, except I'd taken off the pizza signs. I started up the first scooter. I knew the bike was going to cause trouble, but I thought fuck them if they can't take a joke.

I weaved and wound my way to Chippendale, to an industrial park crammed with tow-truck depots and smash-repair shops, where a dozen Harleys lined up outside a windowless yellow wall. I carefully parked my Vespa between the ape hangers of a Night Train and the flat bars of a Fatboy, and walked up to the heavy door. A security camera swivelled towards me as I pressed the buzzer.

The door opened on a chain and an angry bald man holding a torch like a truncheon looked at me, then looked at my scooter.

'You are fucking kidding me,' he said. 'How dare you fucking – this is our fucking –'

His chin shook.

'It's just a bike,' I said.

He pushed me inside the clubhouse and marched me to the bar, where the colours of patched-over clubs hung upside down like bats. On a stool sat Suicide, an old man wearing heavy gold jewellery around his neck and wrists and sipping Jim Beam and Coke.

'You wouldn't believe this cunt,' said the bald man.

Suicide smiled, showing two gold teeth.

'Drink?' he asked.

The barman was a young Cannibals prospect. There was a television groaning in the corner and a handwritten price list on the wall.

'Don't worry,' said Suicide, 'no charge.'

A flaming red swastika flag hung over one wall.

'Bother you?' asked Suicide.

'It's just a flag,' I said.

'Hitler was a strong leader,' said Suicide. 'I admire strong leaders. Mendoza was a strong leader. That's why I'm talking to you. What's your name? Hymie?'

'Nick,' I said.

'My name's Genocide,' he said. 'Sorry, Suicide.'

Suicide had a head like a block of wood, with a jawbone that had been finished off with a plane. It looked as though it would hurt to punch him, and knuckles would shatter on his chin.

'You cold, Hymie?' he asked. 'Want me to turn on the gas?'

I told him I was fine. When he stood up to silence the television, I realised he was almost as tall as Giant, whose photograph sat behind a burning candle on a ledge behind the bar.

'You were there,' said Suicide.

'Yeah, I was. He was a brave man.'

'Some people are pissed at you, Hymie,' said Suicide. 'Reckon this was your fault.'

'Mine?' I asked.

'Collectively,' said Suicide. 'Reckon we've been caught in a war over the holy land. Doesn't matter to us who runs Jerusalem, but we're the only ones dying. Explain that to me, Hymie. Conspiracy, maybe?'

He pointed to a photograph of Rabbit and Devil.

'Lost three brothers,' he said.

'I lost one,' I said.

'Yeah, I heard that,' said Suicide. 'Heard a lot about you. Supposed to be a soldier, kicking up shit in the Cross, starting blues over fuck all. I was in the army, Hymie. A real army.'

There were pictures of Rabbit, Devil and Giant collaged on the walls and doors, riding their choppers, hugging biker girls, spraying beer on camera lenses. An arch of gothic lettering read *CFFC*.

'Cannibals Forever,' said Suicide. 'Forever Cannibals. My problem: what were you doing buying a T-shirt from Ink in the middle of the fucking night, when you live around the corner?'

'I didn't want my girlfriend to see me,' I said.

'But she'd gone.'

'I didn't know that,' I said.

'Take your T-shirts, did she? Cut them up? Psycho bitch.'

'No, she didn't.'

'My problem: security pictures of you walking down the street, no shirt, doing recon on Ink. Ex-soldier, looking for holes in our defences. Then a cunt with no shirt kicks over our hogs, steals our shotties, murders our brothers. Coincidence? New gang with no shirts?

'We get the word that somebody's coming after us, but not

who or why. We try to find out – established channels – get back some drivel fucking bullshit about Mutineers repatching GraveDiggers. Everyone on the lookout for unpatched Mutineers, when shirtless Yids've been casing us for weeks.

'And GraveDiggers're not even a real fucking MC. Some weak dog lifted the name from a fucking seventies movie. Mutineers don't give two fucks about the Cross, and Charlie Adami fought in fucking Vietnam with me, so he's not going to fight me in Darlinghurst Road, is he?

'My theory: Mendoza growing old, dribbling in his dinner, pissing his pants, can't even get it up to rape the waitress. You – some sort of lost son, distant cousin, family hard man, Yiddisher Rambo – come out from your Jew-hole in Golders Green to take over the family business. First thing you see: biker goyim in the drugs trade. Should be one of your rackets, but Mendoza's too slow to move. Can't take on the clubs yourself, but think you can turn us against each other – thick-as-shit bikers, what would we know? Attack us outside Ink, try to make us think it's the Mutineers, hope we'll wipe each other out, and Jews can step in over the bodies. Doesn't all go your way. Your offsider – watch your back, Hymie, they'll knife it every time – runs off with your goyish vagina, so you've got nothing to fuck. Then somebody has him knocked. My heart says you, but my head says these Russian cunts I've heard so much about but never seen since they come bursting out of a window behind me. So must be at least two factions in the Jew War, tribe of Fagin versus tribe of Shylock. Well, the Cannibals are going to step out of this, let you kill yourselves. We'll ride up to Queensland. Why? I'll give you six million reasons, although a more realistic figure might be four million, one and half million, or even none at fucking all because, if you look at it demographically, there are just as many reasons now as there were in 1939 – so what does that tell you, eh?'

'I don't know what you're talking about,' I said.

Suicide shook his head and laughed.

'Why are you here, Hymie?' he asked. 'What do you people want?'

'I heard you took a shipment of kit from interstate,' I said. 'I'll give you a very good price for anything I can use.'

'*Gelt*, *gelt*,' said Suicide, rubbing together his fingers and thumbs. 'I might've known it'd be about *gelt*.'

The bald man came to march me away, and muttered and swore as he pushed me to the door. When I stepped out of the Cannibals' bunker and into the late-afternoon light, I was surprised to see my scooter was still there. There was an odd smell around it, though. At first I thought I must have ridden through something, then I noticed the pannier had been jemmied.

I lifted the lid, and inside lay a fat brown turd.

THIRTY-THREE

Mendoza and I met daily, in one of half-a-dozen units around the city, which he used to keep for his liaisons with showgirls, or offer to cops and politicians. We talked about his children, or I told him stories about Jed. We were marking time but enjoying each other's company. The book was coming along well – I felt I had finally found my voice – but Mendoza was taking a long time to read my chapters. He'd begun falling asleep in the afternoon, and sometimes when he woke up he thought it was 1974, or 1956. We never got together at the same apartment twice, until Mendoza suggested we meet at the Centennial Park unit for the second day in a row.

'It doesn't matter,' he said. 'After today, everything will be taken care of. I will not have to watch my movements again.'

I thought I understood what he meant. I ran a finger over my tattoo, snorted coke from a CD case, grabbed my Heckler & Koch from the bedside drawer and jammed it in the small of my back. I dropped a Browning Hi-Power into my shoulder holster, strapped a diver's knife to my ankle, and padded three hand grenades into my pack, along with a 40 mm grenade launcher, and a stripped-down M4A5 rifle. When I had put in my order for weapons with Suicide, he'd thought I was arming a team.

I was dressed like a traveller, in fisherman's pants, a Singha T-shirt and sun hat, so as not to look conspicuous carrying such a large pack. I jogged up to Centennial Park, humming 'I'll Be Missing You' like the rumble of an engine, burning energy to kill the excitement. This was the last thing I was ever going to do for Jed, my brother, my bright, shining friend. This was the end of everything.

The entrance to the apartment block was jammed open with a pile of shrink-wrapped Yellow Pages. The door to the unit was unlocked too. I opened it slowly and, as I did, a cosh came crashing down on the back of my head. It was Mendoza, hitting me with the new chapters of my manuscript rolled up like a club.

'You are the worst writer in the whole fucking world!' he yelled.

I rubbed my neck.

'I told you to write more like you speak,' he said, 'but the word "fucking" is not an adjective in written English. You can't use it to qualify a noun. You say, "The Little Fish was a fucking hard man." What you mean is, "The Little Fish was a very hard man." Except of course, you don't even say that. What you have actually written here, Anthony, which I have managed to interpret based on what I consider to be the most likely meaning, is "The Little Fish was fucking a hard man." I would quite understand this if you were referring to his gaping-arsed drag queen, but you are in fact describing him in relation to Gozo Joe Stone, the biggest cocksman in the southern Mediterranean hemisphere.

'Do you even read through these pages once you print them out? No, don't tell me, because I know the fucking answer. It's written here, between the lines, like the only other parts of your manuscript that make any sense. I see you have followed my suggestion and employed a spelling-check programme, but you have accepted each of its judgments as if it were Sir Garfield fucking Barwick.

'It's bad enough that you misspell my name – in my own fucking biography, my testament, my memorial – as "Mindozer", but halfway through you allow your computer to style me as "monomer", then "misnomer", then fucking "misdoer"! Tell me, please, that you're trying to be fucking funny.'

'They're just little things, though,' I said, 'aren't they, Jake?'

'I don't have time to talk to you about the big things, Nick. It would literally take me the rest of my life. Come here.'

I stepped towards him. He took hold of me and hugged me, then stood facing me, with his hands resting on my elbows, bowing his head into my chest.

'The Russians called,' he said. 'They made a final offer on the strip clubs and the brothels and the sex shops and the hotels.'

'What did they offer?' I asked.

'One dollar. It's what passes for a joke in the famously humorous Russian mafia. They pretend to negotiate while they change over their hit teams.'

'So you *do* know it's the Russians?' I said.

'Of course it's the Russians,' said Mendoza. 'They sent a Russian to do a deal with me. I had Natural Science bite off his Russian nose.' Mendoza chomped his dentures, like a shark taking a bite out of a surfer, then wiped his mouth with the back of his hand.

'I'm ready to do what needs to be done, Jake,' I told him.

'And what do you think needs to be done?' he asked me.

'When they come for you, we'll get them first.'

'There is no "we", Anthony,' said Mendoza. 'You're fired.'

He picked up a Samsonite briefcase from the floor and opened it on the table.

'There's a hundred grand in there,' he told me. 'Spend it on wine, women and song, but be sure to allocate the smallest portion to song. Never manage a recording artist, Anthony. You'll get no thanks from anyone.'

I looked at the money, laid out like loaves in a baker's oven. Strapped to the lid of the briefcase was a manila envelope.

'Inside is the video of you and Leah,' said Mendoza, 'and also the micro-cassettes containing the recordings of our interviews. There are no copies of the film or the tapes in existence.'

'We're not beaten, Jake,' I told him. 'Look what I've got in here.'

It was my turn to open my bag.

'Jesus fuck!' said Mendoza.

I put the grenade launcher aside, dropped both pistols on the table and began assembling the assault rifle.

'Take the nine mil,' I said. 'It's yours anyway.'

Mendoza weighed his pistol in his hand and smiled.

'I'm eighty-one years old, Anthony,' he said. 'And you expect me to kill someone? I would be taking from them more than they could ever take from me.'

'Look,' I said, 'I don't expect you to kill anyone or not kill anyone, but I don't expect you to die like a dog when you could live like a man. How many people will they send after you, Jake? Two? Three? We could hold off the fucking SAS with what we've got here.'

'But for how long, Anthony?'

'I don't know. An hour. Ninety minutes, maybe.'

'No,' he said. 'In the long term. In the future.'

'You mean: can we beat the Russian mafia?' I said. 'I've been thinking about this.'

'Fucking God preserve us,' said Mendoza.

'Obviously we don't have the resources to take them on globally,' I said.

' "Obviously",' said Mendoza.

'But I really believe we could drive them back to Moscow.'

'Listen to Napoleon,' said Mendoza.

'You'd rather listen to that cunt Dror,' I said.

'Dror has been working for the Russians for seven months,' said Mendoza. 'If I listen to him, I learn what they want me to think, and I know to do the opposite. But the day Dror turned dog, I knew it was over for me. I started to put my affairs in order. I began the preparations for my book, and I waited for the writer to arrive.'

'So you always knew it was Dror?'

'Life is like the Malts, Nick. It throws the same shit at you every time. It's always the lieutenant. They are never satisfied. They can never wait.'

'I'm gonna fucking get Dror,' I said.

' "Get Dror",' repeated Mendoza. 'You have nothing to "get Dror" for. He didn't deliberately target your friend; he didn't even know he'd be there. Dror knew I was suspicious of him, so he organised an attempt on his own life to throw me off. Fucking idiot.' Mendoza laughed. 'It's what they always do.'

I said I wanted revenge. He said that Dror had started off as a good man, and so his own treachery would destroy him.

'Betrayal gnaws on the intestines,' said Mendoza, 'makes offal of your kidneys, takes bites from your heart. He will be at the funeral, pretending to grieve, knowing he is lower than the lowest mongrel dog. I know what I'm talking about, Nick. I was there when they buried the Little Fish, gripping limp hands and wishing them all long life, handing out money to the caterers and that fucking drag queen. There are better ways to settle these things when you are dealing with friends, but at the time you are too caught up in the logic of the situation to realise there is a path between kill or be killed, to remember that we write our own rules. This comes to us with age and, when it does, we know it's over. It will catch up with Dror in the end.'

I shook my head.

'Will you be coming to my funeral, do you think, Nick?' he asked.

'There needn't be a funeral,' I said.

'Oh, there has to be a funeral,' said Mendoza. 'It might as well be mine. My wife is dead. My mistress doesn't love me. My daughter doesn't speak to me. Lazarus, they tell me, is unlikely to come out of hospital. As for my son . . . pah! All I had left of my life was my story, and now it's told. I've written my own eulogy, Slick. I'm ready to die.'

He rubbed his hands together.

'Tell me you will come,' he said.

'I'll come,' I promised.

'Make a friend of Dror,' said Mendoza. 'Help him with his grieving. Tell him you know how it feels to lose a man you love. Tell him how highly I thought of him, how warmly I spoke of him, how I thought of him as my son.'

'I'll do that,' I said.

'That will be our revenge on the mongrel dog maggot cunt.'

Mendoza poured me a whisky from a cut-glass decanter.

'The famous Russians!' snorted Mendoza. 'Do you know why I set Natural Science on their messenger like a dog? So it would end like this.'

I asked if he was sure that they would come for him today.

'I had until midday to accept their offer,' he said. 'My deadline has expired.'

His mobile phone beeped. He glanced at the screen.

'A text message,' he said. 'Dror is worried about me. He wants to know where I am.'

Laboriously he stabbed each small key with his right index finger, tapping his address into the phone.

'There,' he said, and sat back and lit a cigar.

'I'm an abomination,' he said, 'a monster who should never have been born. We kill our own, Nick, that is the law of history.

But there are no Jews left here to knock me. I pass on my legacy to the Solntsevskaya bratva, as Phil Jeffs left his to me.

'Write my story, Nick,' he said. 'But write it so my grandchildren don't have to believe it was me. Change the small details: my name, the date of my birth, the suburb where I was born, the names of my clubs . . .'

He looked at me and through me.

'Give the story a point,' he said. 'Give me some motivation other than the love of money and the pursuit of cunt. And have me die younger, and braver. And do something about that mad fucking jock, will you? But before you start,' he said, 'get somebody to help you, someone who knows how to write.' He coughed. 'You fucking imbecile.'

We sat in silence, listening to the sounds of the road. When Mendoza heard a car pull up outside the apartment, he raised an eyebrow. He drew back his curtains and looked down. I lifted my rifle to my shoulder, Mendoza shook his head. I smiled and shrugged, put down the gun and poured another whisky.

Mendoza left the apartment with his Webley in his hand. I knew he was not going to use it. He just wanted to make sure the Russians shot him.

THIRTY-FOUR

I rang Helen to tell her I wouldn't be home for a while. She said thank you, fuck you, and have a nice life. I opened the window to let fresh air into the flat. I smelled restaurant grease and burger waste, exhaust fumes and beer. I shaved and stretched, lingered in the hot shower, and splashed myself with aftershave that Jed had left behind. Suddenly I could only smell the life of my dead friend. I had to sit down, breathe deeply and slowly, and remember he was gone.

I would never see the Jedi again, put up with his mad driving or listen to his stupid stories. Nobody was ever going to phone me at three o'clock in the morning and tell me he'd just fucked a girl until she squirted. Nobody was ever going to back me up and let me down like he did.

Jed was not a killer, not the way I was. He was not even a soldier, really. He hadn't been brought up to do what we did. He was just a big, lovely Aldershot boy with a smile that could draw your pants to your ankles, bend you over a coffee table and part your legs like an alcopop. I smiled, shook my head and raised a mug of tea to Jed in heaven.

I had bought a black shirt to wear under my black suit, and hid my eyes under a pair of Ray Ban Aviators. I polished my black boots like a wingnut and trimmed my black stubble for the second time that morning. I sat at the kitchen table, reading a book about the pogroms in Russia, until the car arrived. I didn't recognise any of the old men inside. We were silent as we drove in convoy through Oxford Street to Woollahra's Chevra Kadisha.

Reporters and TV crews were kept out of the chapel by a team of Maori bouncers wearing black yarmulkes and led by Lazarus, who stood unsteady but proud. We shook hands at the door, and it felt as if I were holding him upright. By his side was the boy Jordan. He took everything personally and now felt that his enemy was whoever had shot at us, and wanted to kill them like he had hoped to kill me. We needed men like him in the organisation, I decided.

I recognised a couple of faces in the media pen from the evening news, and one from Mendoza's photographs. Sharon Stevens had chosen to stay outside with the press, rather than go in with the family. Mendoza was right. His daughter had beautiful hair.

'Sir!' she called as I walked past. 'May I ask who you are, sir?'

I followed Lady Lash into the redbrick chapel, where she turned to the right, to sit with the women. The men gathered on the left. At the front, below the lectern, stood Daniel Mendoza, whose face was his father's twisted in a bench vice, and without the laugh lines, the lie lines and the cold, amused eyes. His younger children surrounded him like bodyguards. His thin wife looked distant and pained, as if she had heard too many jokes delivered badly and the effort of smiling had palsied her face.

'You must be Nick,' said Daniel, holding out his hand. 'My father told me all about you. He said you know all the family secrets, and where the bodies are buried.' He grinned, as if this was just an expression, and his family secrets didn't actually involve buried bodies.

Daniel had lost his accent in the Pacific Ocean, and sounded like an American with a cold. He wore a dark, tailored suit, a cream shirt and black tie, with Donald Duck socks. His breast pocket was torn, hanging down like a dog's tongue, to show that something had been torn out of his life.

'As my father's lifetime right-hand man and only legitimate heir, I'd normally have to stay in Sydney and help you finish your book,' said Daniel, 'but, as you know, I'm based in Vegas, and I'm on the verge – the absolute edge – of making one of Dad's greatest dreams come true. It looks like I've finally got the casino licence for Christmas Island, and we're going to ship the Luxor Hotel there. It'll be incredible – beyond anything Dad could've imagined – the only pyramid in the Indian Ocean. In 25,000 years archaeologists will ask, "What kind of civilisation could have built this structure? Were they, in some distant way, related to the pharaohs of Egypt?"

'A casino isn't just a centre for gaming, either,' said Daniel. 'It's a destination in itself. We'll put on all kinds of international acts: singers, dancers, stand-up comedians . . .'

As Daniel's hands painted his casino in the air, the mourners queued for their seats at his father's funeral.

'Look at them,' said Daniel. 'Who are these people? Fucking low-lifes, the lot of them. My father knew premiers and police commissioners. He was a friend of Frank Sinatra. He promoted Digger Ronnie Blake and Lucky Jack Gold. Where are they today, Nick? And, for that matter, where is Arnold Zwaybil?'

A small, wiry man, dressed in a leather coat and pork-pie hat, squeezed between larger bodies than his to make his way to the front.

'My God,' said Daniel, 'it's Izzy Berger.'

Berger grasped Daniel's hand and wished him long life.

'The entertainment industry has lost an icon,' said Berger, 'and I have lost a dear friend.'

Beneath the brow of Berger's hat, I could make out a deep dent in his forehead.

'He was a man of vision,' said Berger, 'and also a vision of man.'

A solid, black-haired guy approached Daniel, but stopped a little way off. He had thick thatched eyebrows and an urchin's sad smile. When Berger saw Jack Brun, and went to chase him for a fifty-dollar debt, the man stepped forward and hesitantly held out a tattooed hand.

'I didn't know your father,' he said to Daniel, 'but my own father held him in high regard. When I was young he used to tell me stories about him. He called him a great man. Whatever people say, you should be proud that he was your dad, as I am proud that my father is mine.'

'Who's your dad?' asked Daniel. 'Do I know him?'

The black-haired guy leaned in to Daniel and whispered. Daniel nodded and patted him on the shoulder. As he walked to the back of the chapel and took a seat alone, Daniel asked me, 'Who the living fuck is Gozo Joe Stone?'

A soft, chubby hand gripped my sleeve. Spiegeleier was tugging at my arm.

'I thought the press were supposed to stay outside,' I said.

'Mendoza asked me to speak to you,' said Spiegeleier. 'He wants me to give you your job back.'

'He's dead, Dan,' I said. 'He doesn't "want" anything.'

'He thinks you need some writing practice,' said Spiegeleier. 'He left me a year's wages to pay you, as long as I get someone else to write his obituary.'

'Do you think I'll ever make it as a journalist?' I asked.

'No,' said Spiegeleier.

An old woman with a sharp nose and high cheekbones, and a narrow tear across the front of her blouse, walked down the aisle in small steps, like a hesitant bride.

'Fucking Ira,' whispered Daniel, 'the bitch with no shame.'

She looked nervous and sad. She reached out for Daniel's arm. He leaned away, as if she were a monster. I touched her on the lightly on the shoulder, to comfort her.

'Keep your hands to yourself, fuck-face,' she hissed.

Martin, the grandson, stood apart from the rest of his family, but greeted more mourners than Daniel, and spoke briefly with all of them. When Ira approached him, he waved her away. She dropped her eyes. He hugged and kissed a woman who looked like Mendoza in drag, who I guessed must be Hannah, the surviving sister. Slow Eddie Finkel whispered to him in Yiddish.

Siobhan walked down the aisle, beautiful and veiled, and stood talking with Leila from Le Fontaine. It looked as if she had draped her face in fancy lingerie. I wanted to tear it off and eat her.

When the room was full, the rabbi began to speak, and he had a voice like a soul singer, which made everything he said sound true.

'Jacob Mendoza was a good man,' he began. 'That's why there are so many good people here to mourn him. He was a family man who will be deeply missed by his loving son, Daniel, and daughter, Sharon.'

Daniel scowled at the mention of his half-sister.

'His wife, Deborah, a woman of valour, passed away, leaving him lonely but not alone.'

The rabbi looked down at Ira, who had taken a seat next to Daniel. Daniel moved aside and Ira spread her dancer's legs to fill the space.

'He had many friends and companions,' said the rabbi.

Daniel dropped his face into his hands.

'I knew Jacob well,' said the rabbi, 'through his generous responses to every community appeal. If a Jew was in need, he was there for them, and he never expected anything in return. One of his last and most wonderful mitzvoth was to present this synagogue with a gift of five million dollars to carry out much-needed renovations. He would no more see his *shul* suffer than he would pass a beggar in the street without giving *tzedakah*.

'Jacob was an Australian icon, a man whose title was so well known it appeared in crossword puzzles. During the war against the Nazis, he served his country on both land and sea, and didn't rest until the Axis powers were routed and he could trade in his proud uniform for a suit he'd cut with his own hands. He was an unapologetic patriot, a proud Australian. In the post-war years, his name became a byword for entertainment in this city. He named his famous Patton Club after the great American general who was his wartime hero and under whose command, it was sometimes whispered, he'd served in Sicily, where Jacob acquired his love of Sicilian traditions such as honesty, loyalty and discretion.

'The Patton Club was a place where lawyers, judges and policemen had the opportunity to dine in the company of the foremost entertainers of their day. Jacob loved to drink champagne and laugh. He once said he would never rest until he put a smile on the face of every man in Sydney. Well, Jacob, you can rest now. Your work is done.'

The rabbi's words rose above the click of heavy heels marching in time, like drum sticks bouncing off the rim of a drum. I looked up to see two towering drag queens, each wearing butterfly sunglasses and a short black dress, strut to the front of the mourners.

'Oh no,' said Daniel. 'What a fucking travesty. What a fucking farce.'

The trannies tried to take the space between Daniel and Ira, but Daniel suddenly shifted down the pew, forcing them into a corner.

They sat in front of me, their hats blocking my view of the rabbi. I guessed they were Savannah Plains and Angelica Angel. They arrived with Cecilia Preciosa Bong Bong McCoy, but I think that was a coincidence.

'Jacob was a mensch,' said the rabbi, 'a Mr Big in every sense of the word. He towered over this city like a statue of liberty. And, truly, liberty was his credo. His lasting legacy will be his lifelong struggle for the rights of the individual to live free from excessive regulation. He championed socially progressive causes, such as the liberalisation of laws regarding the service of alcohol, the emancipation of sexual and other minorities, and the social integration of negroes and midgets.'

Suddenly Angelica Angel screamed. She pointed to Daniel and Ira, and the clothes they had torn for their mourning, and slammed the heel of her hand into her head. Then she grabbed her dress and ripped it from the breast to the waist, exposing a narrow nipple sitting hard on a tightly drawn breast.

Two Maoris hurried to the front and dragged her away.

'Jacob was admired and respected by all who really knew him,' said the rabbi. 'Of course he had his critics, of course he made his mistakes, but this city, even this country, would have been a different place had he never lived. Jake Mendoza did what he had to do, he did what others feared to do, but most of all, to paraphrase his great friend Frank Sinatra: he did it his way.'

The old men didn't make the journey from the *chevra kadisha* to the burial ground. When my car left for the cemetery, I shared the backseat with Spiegeleier and Siobhan, and felt her thigh rest reluctantly against mine.

'Will you help me with the book?' I asked her.

'Not in a million fucking years,' she said.

I felt as though I had seen enough of graveyards and graves, dark suits and sunglasses, and the wind always blowing. It had been a year full of loss, and it had left an empty space in my heart. I didn't think a book could fill a hole that had been made by bullets. Perhaps it was time to stop pretending to be the man I wanted to be and start being who I was.

Henry Aaron, the synagogue treasurer, led the pallbearers to the grave, where the mourners passed the shovel from the male relatives to Spiegeleier, then down to me. As I tossed my load of dirt onto the coffin, I found a tear in my eye. Mendoza was the worst person I had ever met, but he made me laugh. Fuck his book, though. I wasn't staying in Sydney for Mendoza. I was back here for Jed. This time, we'd agreed in Aldershot, the boys were going to get payback. This time we were going to kill the guilty men. I'd sort out the Russian and the Geordie on the bike, but the way I saw it, Jed was murdered by the spy who arranged the shooting, and that traitor was going to hell the moment he dropped his guard.

Stopcocks rose like question marks between the rows of graves. The mourners washed their hands and left them hanging in the air to dry. Dror was weeping by the graveside, in a beautiful Giorgio Armani suit. I told him how much Mendoza had valued him, how the old man spoke of him as the son he had always wanted, as opposed to the son he actually had. Dror said he owed Mendoza everything.

'As the new boss,' he said, 'my first task is to end this war. I know it sounds cold, but I've already opened channels of communication. We can't have the bastards going after Daniel or Sharon.'

'It's what the old man would have wanted,' I agreed.

'I think I can negotiate favourable terms with them,' said

Dror. 'It doesn't hurt that I'm Russian too. We might be able to keep enough of the businesses to leave something for the kids.'

He tried to light a cigarette with shaking fingers. I offered him the flame of my lighter, and a firm, steady hand.

'You'll be looking for a lieutenant now,' I said.

Dror sucked on his cigarette.

'I can't think of any man I trust more than you, Slick,' he said.

We hugged and shook hands.

'I wish you long life,' I said to Dror.

– Nicholas Anthony and Siobhan Hughes, Kings Cross, Sydney, June 2009

ACKNOWLEDGMENTS

Thanks to Claire Waddell, Mark Abernethy, Alison Tait and Andrew Rule.

King of the Cross owes debts to a number of 'true-crime' books of varying veracity, but particularly to Tony Reeves's *Mr Sin* and Larry Writer's exhaustively researched *Razor*.

ALSO AVAILABLE FROM PAN MACMILLAN

Strange Country
Mark Dapin

As anyone who's ever read Mark Dapin in *Good Weekend* magazine knows, he's one of our funniest, most acute observers of Australian life. In *Strange Country*, he takes us on a journey through a very different Australia – a country that's eccentric, puzzling, big-hearted, small-minded, nostalgic and sometimes just plain mad. From camel wars to the last travelling boxing tent to women who talk to angels and the annual Parkes' Elvis Festival, his writing illuminates the stranger side of Australian life in a travel book like no other.

'This may be your perfect Christmas gift.'
THE AGE

'this is no ordinary travel book . . . Dapin grasps the stranger aspects of Australian life with insight and humour.'
COURIER MAIL

'Funny and insightful.'
AUSTRALIAN WOMEN'S WEEKLY

'This gritty travelogue by one of our nation's funniest writers is packed with riveting characters. If you like Bill Bryson's work, then this will hit the spot.'
MADISON